D0174891

THE SUCCESSOR

BALLANTINE BOOKS

NEW YORK

THE
SUCCESSOR

A NOVEL

STEPHEN
FREY

Published in the United States by Ballantine Books, an imprint of The Random House Publishing Group, a division of Random House, Inc., New York.

BALLANTINE and colophon are registered trademarks of Random House, Inc.

ISBN 978-0-345-48062-0

LIBRARY OF CONGRESS CATALOGING-IN-PUBLICATION DATA
Frey, Stephen W.
   The successor : a novel / Stephen Frey.
     p.   cm.
   ISBN-13: 978-0-345-48062-0 (acid-free paper)
   1. Corporate culture—Fiction.   2. International business enterprises—Fiction.
3. Investment bankers—Fiction.   I. Title.

PS3556.R4477S83 2007
813'.54—dc22

                                              2006047908

Printed in the United States of America on acid-free paper

www.ballantinebooks.com

9 8 7 6 5 4 3 2 1

FIRST EDITION

For my wife, Diana
You make every day so special.
And for our daughters, Ashley,
Christina, Courtney, and Elly

ACKNOWLEDGMENTS

Special thanks to Cynthia Manson, my agent; and Mark Tavani, my editor.

Thanks also to Gina Centrello, Matt Malone, Kevin "Big Sky" Erdman, Jim and Anmarie Galowski, Dr. Teo Forcht Dagi, Stephen Watson, Chris Tesoriero, Andy Brusman, Gerry Barton, Baron Stewart, Jack Wallace, Gordon Eadon, Marvin Bush, Bart Begley, Barbara Fertig, Bob Wieczorek, Scott Andrews, Jeff, Jamie and Catherine Faville, John Piazza, Chris Andrews, Bob Carpenter, Pat and Terry Lynch, and Mike Pocalyko.

PROLOGUE

January

DR. NELSON PADILLA was a gifted surgeon, an *especialista de 2ndo grado* after operating for almost twenty years and publishing several highly acclaimed research works. Works that had won him awards in Cuba and Toronto, where he'd attended medical school long ago as a younger man, determined to honor his dead father's wish for him to change the world. As such an accomplished doctor, it was unusual for him to be on duty during the Saturday graveyard shift in the emergency room of Hermanos Ameijeiras Hospital in downtown Havana like some wet-behind-the-ears intern. But that was Cuba—a land rife with conflicts and inconsistencies.

Padilla had gotten a frantic call yesterday at home around noon from one of the hospital's senior administrators. With only a few hours' notice, the Party had ordered the hospital to send a large medical brigade to Venezuela. Unfortunately, the one due back from El Salvador today had been delayed because of terrible weather in the hills where they were serving. Which meant the hospital was dangerously short on surgeons and Padilla was needed to oversee the ER from eight o'clock Saturday evening until six Sunday morning. His wife and children had begged him not to go in because they knew how exhausted he would be when he got home, but he always felt a duty to serve, to do whatever he could to help those in need. But for him, it was the individual—not the Party.

He'd already saved the lives tonight of two small children—a seven-year-old boy and his five-year-old sister—who'd been thrown from a pickup truck in a terrible accident on the east side of Havana. Their survival warmed his heart and made the long hours away from his family worth it.

Unfortunately, he hadn't been able to save their mother, who lay before him on the operating table. A pretty young woman who'd been crushed between the steering wheel and the bench seat of the pickup for fifteen minutes before the emergency people could pry her out. Still, he might have saved her if he'd been able to operate as soon as she'd been admitted. But he'd taken the children first as they were critical, too. There hadn't been anyone else on duty with the skill to save their mother.

Padilla pulled down his mask, then slowly peeled off his bloody surgical gloves and tossed them toward a trash can along the wall. This was the insidious part of the job—having to play God. He loved doing God's work, but he didn't want to have to make the decisions, too.

"She's gone from this world," he said softly to the resident and nurse who'd assisted him on all three operations. He didn't use the word *dead* because he believed in heaven. "There's nothing more we can do."

With that, Padilla headed out of the OR, once again concerned for the children, wanting to make sure their recovery was going well. As he moved into the taupe-tiled corridor, he spotted a nurse rushing toward him.

"Doctor. *Doctor!*"

"What now?" he muttered to himself, suddenly feeling the strain of three straight life-and-death surgeries. "Calm down," he said to the distraught woman when she reached him. "I'll take care of it. Just lead me to the patient."

"It's not a patient, it's a man on the phone," she cried, pointing back toward the front desk. "He said he needed to speak to you immediately. I told him you were in surgery, but he didn't care. He said if I didn't get you right away, I'd pay for it." She brought her hands to her face, eyes wide with terror. "He knows where my husband works. He knows the names of my children."

Padilla put his hand on her arm and squeezed reassuringly. "Everything will be all right. Which phone is this man on?" He trotted after her down the corridor to an office behind the front desk.

The nurse grabbed the receiver off a blotter with both hands and thrust it out toward Padilla, as if she were holding a live grenade.

He took it from her gently, one hand covering the mouthpiece, then gestured for her to leave the room. When she was gone, he answered, "Hello. This is Dr. Padilla."

"I have an emergency at my home," the man on the other end of the line said gruffly. "One of my children is very sick. I need you here now. There is a jeep waiting for you outside the emergency room entrance."

Padilla gritted his teeth. He understood a parent's panic, but there was no reason for this. "Look here. First of all, you don't threaten my nurses like that. *Ever.* Second of all, you don't—"

"Dr. Padilla," the man interrupted, his voice turning as smooth as the side of a shiny knife blade. "The jeep waiting for you outside is being driven by one of my first lieutenants. If he doesn't call me within five minutes to tell me that you are with him, I will have your wife killed. Do you understand?"

"Listen, you son of a—"

"Your wife is forty-three and has a small mole on the left side of her neck. Her name is Rose. She's quite pretty."

AS THE FIRST LIEUTENANT steered the loud jeep back toward the hospital two hours later, Padilla realized that his father's wish for him to change the world might actually come true. But he'd never anticipated he might have to risk his life to do it.

PART
ONE

1

March

CHRISTIAN GILLETTE reached into his suit jacket and pulled out his favorite pen—a fifty-cent Paper Mate you could pick up at any drugstore in Manhattan. White plastic with a light blue cap and black lettering down the side. He'd been using these for twenty years, ever since Stanford Business School. He liked the way the ink flowed evenly and smoothly all the time, and when he found something reliable, he stuck with it. From pens to people.

One of the army of attorneys on the other side of the long conference-room table snickered. "We had special ones made for the occasion," the young man explained quickly when his white-haired senior partner gave him a mortified look from the far end of the table. "As mementos." He pointed at a cardboard box in front of him. "Nice Cross pens." He was younger than everyone else in the room by nearly a decade, a bottom-rung associate less than a year out of Columbia Law School who'd been working on this transaction for nine months, basically since he joined the firm. That was how long it had taken to get all the government approvals from both the U.S. and Canadian governments so they could close the transaction. "They've got the deal parties inscribed on them in gold letters," he added, babbling at this point. "ExxonMobil acquires Laurel Energy. The date, too. They're way cool."

Christian watched the associate turn beet red. *Way cool* had sounded *way wrong* in this staid fifty-seventh-floor conference room overlooking a darkened Wall Street. The senior partner looked as if he were about to explode, too.

"I'm sorry . . . I just meant that . . ." The associate swallowed the rest of his sentence, realizing that the hole he'd dug would only get deeper the longer he went on, no matter what he said. The experience of being involved in such a huge deal at this tender a career age had gone from euphoric to nightmarish in a heartbeat, and he was seeing his short stint at the firm going up in flames over ink dispensers. "I just wanted you to have a nice pen for the occasion, Mr. Gillette. For all of you to have a nice pen," he mumbled, gesturing around the table, unable to stop himself from talking. "Sorry if I—"

"Enough," the senior partner broke in. "Good God, where do we get these young people—"

"I appreciate you doing that," Christian spoke up. The kid had probably done more work than all the other lawyers on the other side of the table put together, but they still wanted to charge Exxon $20 million. Incredible, he thought to himself. Even more incredible, Exxon would pay it. "Can I have one now?"

"Sure." The kid reached into the cardboard box and pulled out a smaller one from inside, then rose from his seat and brought it to Christian. "Here you go, sir."

Christian winced. He hated it when people called him sir, made him feel like somebody's grandfather. And he wasn't that old, just forty-three. But the kid was only being respectful, he knew. "Nice," he said, taking the pen out and admiring it. "Thanks."

"We'll have tombstones made up, too, of course," the senior partner added in an official voice, making it sound as if the pens were cheap trinkets compared to the tombstones.

Christian gazed silently at the older man for a few moments, then looked up at the kid, who was still standing beside his chair. "I understand you're the one who finally got the DOJ and the Department of Energy off their asses. Probably would have been another nine months if you hadn't. Nice job." Christian smiled. "You and I ought to have lunch sometime."

"Sure," the kid agreed, realizing that in a flash he'd just regained all of his credibility—and more. Christian Gillette was a legend on Wall

Street—the chairman of Everest Capital, one of the most powerful private-equity buyout firms in the world. Their bond had been nothing but a quick burst, but it had been real and now he was protected. "That would be great."

"Good." Christian always checked on who'd done the real work. He'd been low man on the deal totem pole a long time ago, and he knew a lot of times that was where things really happened. "Call my assistant Debbie next week and set it up." Despite the senior partner's condescending attitude, Christian knew the kid was good. He'd asked around. "I'll let her know you're calling. Who knows? Maybe you'll come work for me someday." That got a chuckle from around the table, but Christian gave the kid a nod to let him know he wasn't kidding. He leaned forward over the table. "We ready?" he asked impatiently, tapping his watch. "It's getting late."

The senior partner motioned to the young associate, who trotted to a cart sitting at the far end of the room. On the cart were ten two-inch-thick purchase agreements detailing the terms and conditions covering ExxonMobil's $4.8 billion purchase of Laurel Energy from Everest Capital. Several years ago Christian had bought Laurel—a Canadian exploration and production company—for $300 million. Soon after buying it, his company engineers discovered a major new oil field on several option properties Laurel controlled, making the company worth multiples of what he'd paid. Now he was about to make $4.5 billion on the sale.

When the associate had finished piling the books up in two neat stacks of five, Christian's attorney reached for the top one on the closest stack and opened it to a page near the back. To a page with a long black line above Christian's name, which was typed in big bold letters. "ExxonMobil's already signed everything, Christian," she explained. "It's up to you now."

"You satisfied?" he asked her. Mountains of documents supported the purchase agreements—$25 million worth because her firm was charging him another $5 million—but this was the only page requiring his signature. "Everything okay?"

"Yes."

Christian rotated the bottom of the Cross pen half a turn so the tip extended, then stroked his signature across the black line. Nine more times and the deal was done.

He grinned as he finished the last signature in the last book. He'd sold lots of companies in the last ten years. To big conglomerates like ExxonMobil as well as to the public. The thrill of making a nice profit was nothing new—but he'd never made $4.5 billion on a single transaction. This was like hitting Lotto.

The most amazing thing about it all was that Everest got to keep 20 percent of that profit—$900 million. It was the contractual arrangement he had with his investors—20 percent of anything he earned he kept. He was going to make a lot of people at Everest Capital very happy with all that money. From the senior-level managing partners who reported directly to him, all the way down to the receptionists. And the older he got, the more important making people happy was becoming.

He glanced at his watch—almost nine o'clock. It had been a long day, but it was still going to be another fifteen minutes before they wrapped up everything and he could get out of here. He wanted to get home in time to watch the Oscars, but that was looking more and more as if it wasn't going to happen. He had to return that important call as soon as he was done here. There was no telling how long that call would take.

MELISSA HART had been waiting what seemed like an eternity for tonight, for what she'd do *if* she won. Now her doubt was gone. She *would* win. But that wasn't where it ended, not by a long shot.

Winning was predestined. Her psychic had seen the victory play out perfectly during their half-hour session yesterday afternoon. The dramatic buildup, the announcement, the thunderous applause. The real question now was, Would she follow through? The question bothered Melissa deeply because her psychic had seen everything up through the applause—but nothing after. Her connection to the future had evaporated at that point.

The sequence had come to Melissa in a dream eight years ago, on the night of her fourteenth birthday—a few hours after her mother had succumbed to a long and agonizing battle against breast cancer. It had come to Melissa after her eyes had finally fallen shut from the anguish of a steady stream of tears and exhaustion brought on by being awake for seventy-two hours straight while her mother died.

Melissa had been bedside constantly during those three days as her mother drifted in and out, slowly fading away. In the final few moments there had been a look of utter despair in the sunken eyes, a desperate squeeze of the cold fingers, and one last shallow gasp. For a long time those images had remained vivid, shredding Melissa's heart constantly, as though her mother had died yesterday every day.

The dream had recurred several nights a week since her mother's death—until Melissa had received word from her agent last month that she had, in fact, been nominated. Then the dream had ceased and she'd slept soundly every night since. Even the images of her mother's last few moments seemed not so clear anymore.

The limousine's bar was stocked full and Melissa had taken advantage of it on the ride over to Hollywood from her two-bedroom apartment in Santa Monica. She'd downed three glasses of champagne in less than thirty minutes to give herself those last few ounces of courage. The Dom had tasted delicious and boosted her confidence, but she wondered if it would last.

When she entered the auditorium of the Kodak Theatre she was glad she'd reached for the liquid crutch. The place was intimidating even to someone who'd been trained from childhood to be comfortable in front of large audiences. It was already packed as she made her way down the aisle to her seat in the second row. Thirty-three hundred people plus seat fillers in their tuxes and long dresses standing along the walls. An eerily intimate venue for such a grand event—which only made it scarier.

Melissa wouldn't have to wait long for everything to play out. Wouldn't have to wait during the endless parade of minor Oscars that bored the audience and viewers around the world for hours to find out if her psychic truly had the power. The award she'd been nominated for would be the first presented of the evening. Best Actress in a Supporting Role for her portrayal of the sister of a borderline mentally retarded man accused of a murder he didn't commit. She was up against some tough competition—a couple of the other nominees were Hollywood legends who'd never won an Oscar—and she was young, just twenty-two.

Under normal circumstances winning would have been an unlikely scenario for Melissa this year. But her father was Richard Hart—aka Richard the Lionhearted in Hollywood—and many members of the Academy owed their careers to him. As the trade papers reported when they ranked the industry's A-list producers and her father didn't appear, it was because Richard Hart was a professional and the rest were mere amateurs by comparison. He was *the* man in Tinseltown. By giving his daughter the Oscar the Academy members would be kissing his ring, ensuring their continued success in the movie industry as long as he remained powerful.

Over the years, a few irreverent actors and studio executives had thumbed their noses at the Lionhearted, thinking they could do it without him. They all now wished they'd paid their respects. They'd been relegated to B movies or fired—no exceptions. The Lionhearted was as vindictive as he was powerful. But her father had never dealt with such a young Oscar winner before, Melissa kept telling herself. Not one who was his own flesh and blood, either.

She leaned forward in her seat and glanced to the left, searching for him. She spotted him in the middle of the first row, giving the people on either side of him that disinterested half-smile she'd seen so many times as a child when she'd tried to get his attention. Tomorrow morning he was off to Washington, he'd told her last night over the phone. In a jet President Jesse Wood was sending especially for him, he'd bragged. Richard Hart was Hollywood's most dominant figure—and a rising star in Washington.

Melissa leaned back when her father started looking around. She didn't want to lock eyes with him yet, not until she had that Oscar in hand. She glanced down and smoothed her backless, red satin dress, then tilted her chin up and shook her long blond hair so it cascaded down her shoulders. She caught a handsome young seat filler gazing at her—the way she constantly caught many men staring—and she smiled at him. She was pretty and she knew it. And she didn't mind using what she had to get what she wanted.

Finally the lights dimmed, the hum of conversation died away, the cameras came on and the show began. Seven short minutes later and it was time for Best Supporting Actress. She smiled for the camera when her name was announced third, then glanced down at her thank-you list one more time. The auditorium went silent after the presenter read the fifth and last nominee, and the scribbled names on the creased paper in Melissa's lap blurred before her eyes against the red satin. The only sounds in the theater were the ripping of the envelope and the presenter's anxious laughter as she had to try a second time to pull the envelope apart so she could read the winner's name.

Then Melissa heard her name, as she knew she would, and for several minutes the world was nothing but loud music, deafening applause, smiling faces, hands touching her back and shoulders, and the sensation of floating up the stairs onto the stage. Finally, the crowd quieted and re-took their seats as she held the Oscar up—cold and slightly damp with condensation from the air-conditioning. She gazed at it for a few sec-onds, then put it down, still careful not to catch her father's eye. He knew her face like the script of one of his big-budget movies. If she made the mistake of glancing his way, even for a moment, he might under-stand and be able to stop her. He was that powerful.

"I . . . I'm just overwhelmed," she began softly, trying to remember all the people she'd planned to thank. But the names wouldn't come and suddenly she couldn't focus on anything except what she wanted to do, what she *had* to do. As she gazed out at the thousands of expectant faces, she asked herself once more if she was really ready to do this. It was such a risk. The answer from inside was still a resolute yes.

She touched the statuette gently, then deliberately brought her gaze to her father. He was smiling proudly behind that gray beard, beneath those piercing eyes. She pointed at him and smiled back. "My father, Richard, is sitting down there in the front row."

There was a smattering of applause from those around him who hoped he might notice.

"I'm sure he's expecting me to thank him for this." She held the Oscar up again, already sensing a sudden unease racing around the audi-torium. "Probably expects to be first on my list."

People were shifting in their seats and glancing at each other with raised eyebrows.

"But I'm not going to."

Her smile transformed into an expression of steely determination. Thirty-three hundred people and it was as if the ceremony had suddenly been transported to the surface of the moon. There was no sound at all inside the huge theater. This was going to be one of those moments that would go down in Hollywood history, she realized, blood pounding in her brain. The clip would be played over and over. Not just tomorrow, but down through the years.

"In fact, I'm going to tell him in front of the whole world what a piece of garbage he is for leaving my mother and me eight and a half years ago." Her voice rose as she sensed the shock wave burst through the audience, heard the collective gasp, watched hands cover mouths, saw her father's face twist in rage. *"Right after my mother got sick!"* she shouted over the growing noise. *"Just so he could move in with another woman. Just so he could—"*

Like a peal of thunder, the orchestra cracked the room in two, breaking into a deafening fast number and drowning Melissa out. She smiled triumphantly down at her father despite being cut off. He was beside himself, standing now, waving his arms wildly, pointing at her and yelling something she couldn't hear over the music even though they were less than thirty feet apart. He'd try to screw her career now, no doubt, but what was he going to do? She was an Oscar winner, one of the youngest of all time, one of Hollywood's hottest properties. She was untouchable.

The woman in the long black dress who'd handed Melissa the Oscar when she'd first come onstage grabbed her arm and began tugging her to the right. Melissa resisted at first, then relented. She'd done what she'd come to do, said what she'd come to say. It was over. She raised the Oscar above her head one last time, waved to the crowd, and trotted offstage. The vision had been fulfilled. Her mother could rest in peace.

2

YEARS AGO, before the Revolution, when Gustavo Cruz was a young boy, his grandfather and four brothers had owned this sprawling cattle ranch—one of the largest in Cuba. Owned it outright. Then Castro had seized power—and with it their ranch. Since then the Cruz family had been just a tenant on land that had rightfully been theirs for centuries. Of course, before that his forefathers had slaughtered the native Taino Indians almost into extinction, Cruz reminded himself as he moved through the darkness toward the run-down wooden barn. Maybe they'd lost everything to karma.

The choice in 1958—when the Revolution kicked into overdrive— had been clear. Flee with nothing and probably get caught as they tried to make it out of Cuba to Miami, or stay behind and work within the new system. Cruz's grandfather had stayed, hoping that the new Communist regime's power wouldn't last long, but his four brothers had decided to run. They'd all been caught a hundred yards off a beach near Cárdenas in a small rowboat with three other refugees. None of them had ever been heard from again. There were rumors that one of them had been seen in Quivican Prison a few years ago, a broken old man. But Cruz assumed the rumors were false. Started by someone inside the Party—probably inside the Ministry of Agriculture—who hated them and wanted to torture them with a shred of hope that a long-lost family member might still be alive.

Since the collapse of the Soviet Union and the loss of billions in agricultural subsidies to Cuba, Cruz had been forced to sell an increasing amount of the milk his cows produced on the dollar-based black market—close to 40 percent now to make ends meet. To make the numbers work, he had to forge his production files to match the decreasing sales to the state. He was reporting output far below actual and reporting fewer cattle on the ranch than there actually were. It was a dangerous way to operate—he could be thrown into prison for a long time if one of the Agricultural Ministry inspectors showed up to check his figures and found out what he was doing—but there was no choice. Cruz had five children and eleven grandchildren, so there were many mouths to feed. And he paid his monthly bribe to the local counterintelligence officer, who in return made certain the inspector from the Ag Ministry never came around.

Cruz stroked the cow's bony, black-and-white head for a few moments as the old girl stood in her stall lowing to her stablemates and chewing her cud. He liked it here in the barn. The pungent odor of manure mixing with damp dirt was a smell most men disdained, but he loved. It took him back to days with his father—delivering a calf, mucking out stalls, milking the herd. And there was a good feeling about being involved with something so basic as milk production—something everyone on this beautiful island needed. He mumbled a few words in Spanish to the old cow before reluctantly leading her from the stall and out of the barn. She was a friend, an old friend. She'd been on the ranch for a long time, but she wasn't producing milk anymore. The family needed food, and unfortunately there wasn't enough money to keep pets around. Life was harsh on the ranch. Life was harsh everywhere on the island.

Cruz unlocked the rusty chain of the paddock gate, pushed it back, then headed for the long, potholed driveway that ended at a narrow country lane. At this time of night, the traffic on the lane should be mostly trucks—one of which would hit the cow on the dark, twisting road if he placed her in just the right spot. It would have been much easier—and humane—to put a bullet through her head, but that would have been a high crime in Cuba—tantamount to treason. If someone in the Party discovered the unusually large amount of beef stuffed into his freezer, he might be hauled off to jail for months, maybe years.

But if she was killed in an accident, even the police would have to admit that it would be stupid to waste the meat. He'd grease their palms with the $10 bill that was in his pocket—comparable to several hundred dollars in the United States—so they wouldn't take her. Then he and his boys would hoist her carcass onto the old horse-drawn wagon as soon as the cops left and carve her up in the morning. He hated doing it this way because the old girl might suffer with broken legs for an hour or so until the police arrived and gave him permission to shoot her. But he had no choice.

He clucked to her, urging her ahead as they both limped along. He'd pulled ligaments in his knee last week falling from a horse spooked by a snake in a back pasture. She was just lame from age. She lowed in protest and shook her head against the frayed hemp rope, but slowly they made their way toward the lane.

When they reached it, Cruz turned left. The cow's hooves made loud, clicking sounds on the pavement and mixed with the din of the frog and insect calls from above. He gazed up into the low-hanging branches as they moved toward the sharp S-turn a hundred yards away. It was eerie under the leafy canopy, and his vivid imagination made him see odd and frightening figures lurking above him. He took a deep breath. The sweet scents of wildflowers calmed him. It was just that he hated killing anything. That was the problem.

At the top of the curve, Cruz led the cow into the center of the road, untied the rope from around her neck, and nuzzled her soft face. Odd thing about these cows: If they were in an unfamiliar place, they wouldn't move. She'd stand right here for hours waiting for him to come back.

He winced and kissed her nose once more when he heard the whine of a far-off motor, then stole into the bushes. He couldn't bear to watch.

STEVEN SANCHEZ had worked for many people during his career. He'd played both sides of the mercenary fence and played them well. Proof being, he was still alive. Still had a wife and two children in Paris. He didn't see them much, and when he did, he was careful about it. But they'd never been harmed, never even been threatened. The key to this business: Check your ego at the door and stay focused on the overall objective—taking down the target. Many of his counterparts had bragged about how good they were, about the amazing jobs they'd pulled off over the years. Many of them were dead.

"Under the radar." That was the mantra, he thought, gazing down at the bright lights of the city from seat 21F of the Boeing 737 as it straightened out of a sweeping left turn on final approach. His mentor had taught him that many years ago during his first job in Iran. Appear nonthreatening, even weak at times. But not too weak, because that could also create attention. Try to be someone who slipped by unnoticed, or barely noticed. Then you'd be successful. Successful being defined in this business as staying alive, because making money would never be an issue. If you were willing to do the work, people would pay you and they'd pay you well. The issue was mortality.

Sanchez cinched his seat belt tighter when the landing gear dropped, rocking the plane. He took a deep breath. He hated flying, and the older he got, the more it bothered him. He hated it even more at night, which he couldn't figure out.

"Hey, you never told me your name."

Sanchez glanced over at the young man in the middle seat, who'd nudged his elbow. A loud, twentysomething white kid from Manhattan who'd made it clear before they'd even pushed back from the gate at La Guardia that the only reason he wasn't in first class was that he'd wrongly been bumped and that somebody was going to be fired for it. Sanchez had seen the confrontation at check-in—everybody waiting to get on the plane had. The kid had whined and yelled and demanded to know the names of the employees behind the counter. Then bragged all the way down from New York about how rich his family was.

"Emilio," Sanchez answered with a forced smile, giving his favorite alias. It would be fun to kill the kid. That would violate the "under the radar" mantra, but you couldn't be a robot. Plus, it would be good practice. He hadn't killed anyone in a year. As in any occupation, practice was a necessity in this business, even for a veteran. "My name is Emilio."

"Uh-huh. Well, look, Amilio, I know you people think you have it hard, but it's like I said. This is the greatest country in the world. You're older so it might be tough for you to make anything of yourself at this point. But you said you had a son, right? He can do something with his life. He can make some money." The kid wagged his finger, as though he were teaching a class. "Now you gotta start with school and you gotta be willing to work hard. A lot of people who come here are lazy and think everything ought to be given to them, but that won't work. You gotta fight for what you get."

Sanchez glanced at the kid's gaudy Rolex, then his smug smile. One slash to the neck with a sharp blade. How fun would that be?

"You tell your boy that," the kid went on. "You tell him what I said. Best piece of advice he'll ever get."

The kid's voice faded as the plane's tires skidded on the runway and the pilot reversed the thrust of the jet engines. When Sanchez put his hand against the seatback to brace himself, he spotted a photo on the page of the open *Forbes* magazine lying on the kid's lap. Sanchez had a photograph of that same person tucked into his bag that was stowed in the overhead compartment. A photograph of the target: Christian Gillette.

MELISSA SAT DRINKING champagne in a circular booth at Elaine's— a new Hollywood hot spot modeled after the actor hangout on Manhattan's Upper East Side. Around her were four girlfriends, all early twenties, all pretty like her. Two of them were established, already regular characters on nighttime TV dramas. The other two were still trying to break into the business. But they were all enjoying themselves tonight, all envying the Oscar sitting in the middle of the table.

One of the girls raised her glass giddily. "Here's to Melissa. Here's to—"

"Oh, stop it," the girl next to her interrupted. "Don't be so obvious."

"What are you talking about?"

"This is the third toast you've made to Melissa in the last ten minutes. Give it a rest."

Melissa laughed. "It's the coke." The girl who'd made the toast had already done way more than her share of white powder. "Waiter!" Melissa shouted over the noise of the club, spotting a young man in a white dinner jacket and black bow tie passing by. "We need two more." She pointed at one of the empty champagne bottles sitting on the table.

The man glanced at the Oscar, then changed directions and hurried toward the bar, preempting the dinner order he'd been about to place.

Melissa smiled triumphantly, just as she had at her father from the stage of the Kodak Theatre. Aware that the waiter had put others on the back burner to satisfy her first.

"That took a lot of guts," the girl sitting to Melissa's left said, finishing what was left in her glass. "Standing up to your father like that on national television? Saying those things you said?"

Melissa waved dismissively. "He deserved it."

"Oh, yeah, sure he did. But he's a pretty important man out here, you know. Aren't you worried about what he'll do to you?"

"Like what?" she asked, nodding at the Oscar. "I mean, I'm pretty bulletproof at this point."

The girl followed Melissa's nod and gazed at it longingly. "I guess you're right. I mean, now that I think about it, what could he—" She stopped suddenly, eyes widening. "Oh, Jesus," she whispered.

Melissa glanced to the left and almost dropped her glass of champagne. Her father was standing in front of the table.

"Hello, Mel," Richard Hart said calmly, using the nickname he'd given her when she was a baby. "Having fun?"

Melissa stared up at him, aware that the loud hum of conversation in the club had suddenly evaporated. Aware that everyone had stopped to stare, including the waiters. It was exactly like what had happened at the Kodak Theatre. "As a matter of fact, I am," she answered with a smooth smile, regaining her composure. "Time of my life."

Hart glanced at each of the young women in turn, making certain they knew that he knew who they were. "Isn't there something you want to say, Mel?" he asked as his gaze finally made it back to her.

"I already said what I had to say in front of the cameras."

"I'll give you one more chance, sweetheart," he said, his voice growing stronger. "And that'll be it."

"Chance to *what*?" she snapped.

"Apologize."

Melissa gazed at him for a few moments, then slowly rose to her feet. "I'll *never* apologize to you," she hissed, pointing at the door. "Now, get out of here. *I mean it!*" she yelled when he didn't move right away. *"Get out!"*

For a few moments he hesitated, giving each of the young women one more look. Then he nodded politely and headed toward the door.

When he was gone, Melissa eased slowly back onto the booth seat, trembling with rage. Then she grabbed the first full champagne glass she could reach and downed it. "See," she said when the glass was empty. "He's not as tough as he thinks he is."

"Neither are you," one of the other girls murmured.

3

PADILLA WAS EXHAUSTED. His day had started at six this morning with a difficult surgery. The removal of a stomach tumor from an elderly patient who had lapsed into cardiac arrest halfway through the touchy four-hour procedure. Fortunately, Padilla had been able to resuscitate the man despite the antiquated OR equipment and a sudden blackout the hospital had experienced a few moments after the man went flatline. It was a standard blackout, the kind that happened all the time. The kind Cubans simply dealt with as they dealt with any other daily nuisance because blackouts were as constant a part of life as night and day, as eating and breathing. Unfortunately, the blackout had occurred at a critical time during the procedure, and it had taken the hospital's backup generator five minutes to kick in. As a result, Padilla had been unable to get all the cancer out. He'd have to go back in as soon as the man's body could handle it. A couple of weeks probably.

After the surgery he'd grabbed a quick bite, then been off to his daily rounds and meetings with two other patients he'd operate on later in the week. At five o'clock he'd left the hospital, climbed into his 1956, pastel pink Chrysler Windsor Newport, and headed to José Martí Airport outside Havana to pick up his first fare of the evening. Which had turned out to be a young couple from London. They were honeymooners and they'd kissed and cooed in the backseat of the Chrysler during the entire forty-minute ride. He'd summoned every ounce of willpower he could find not to sneak a few glances in his rearview mirror—but the blonde was pretty and wearing a low-cut top—and he'd found himself stealing peeks several times. Found himself embarrassed at one point when he realized she was staring straight back at him while her new husband nuzzled her neck. Padilla loved Rose and their three children dearly, but he was forty-five, and more and more, he was suffering midlife yearnings he wished he wouldn't.

The young husband had handed Padilla five euros after they'd pulled up in front of the Hotel Nacional. It was a fare any London cabbie would have spit on after such a long ride, but for Padilla—once he'd netted out fuel costs—it came to about 10 percent of his monthly state-issued surgeon's salary. Such irony all around him, he'd thought, shaking his head ruefully as he'd waved good-bye to the couple after getting their luggage out of the trunk. The Nacional was one of the most ornate hotels in the world, yet all around it was awful poverty. The island had one of the highest literacy rates in all of Central or South America, yet there were few books to be had and there was only one daily newspaper. And doctors made more money to taxi people in Cuba than to heal them.

In all, Padilla had made the equivalent of twenty U.S. dollars today—a good day, made especially good because one of his fares had given him a $2 bill, which was highly prized by islanders—worth well more than two $1 bills. Now it was eleven o'clock and he was finally headed home, barely able to keep his eyes pried open as he sped along the narrow country lane. He had another operation scheduled for early tomorrow morning—a basic tonsillectomy and this time the patient was healthy—but he wanted to catch at least a few hours of sleep. He owed the young boy and his parents that because even a simple procedure could go terribly wrong if you weren't careful.

He owed his own three children, too, but he was seeing less and less of them these days. He'd started out doing the cab thing one evening a week just to earn a little extra cash. Now it was up to four times a week, sometimes even five. Life was expensive with three kids, and the money was too good to pass up. It was like a drug, and he hated the intensifying addiction. But there was nothing he could do about it—at least, not in the short term. Fortunately, he had a long-term solution. *Unfortunately,* there were life-and-death risks involved with turning the goals of that long-term plan into a reality.

His last fare of the night had been a senior member of the Partido Comunisto Cubano—the Communist Party of Cuba. Or in Cuba, simply, the Party. The people who ruled this island. The man had claimed to be an executive of the national oil company on his way back from a business trip to Europe, but Padilla knew better. He recognized the man from a picture in a leaflet he'd seen a few weeks ago. A leaflet produced by the Party's propaganda machine praising the great economic strides of the last six months—which was all crap. Things had gotten *worse* in the last six months. Much worse—and everyone knew it—thanks in no small part to Hurricane Rhonda, which had slammed into the island head-on from the south last fall and destroyed 30 percent of the sugarcane crop.

The man might actually have been a senior official of the national oil company, but he was definitely part of the Communist machine, too. A member of the Party. Only senior Party members had country villas like the one he'd just left. Only senior Party members had satellite phones—Cuba had cell phone service but generally it was available only in the larger cities. And only senior Party members would make sure to tell you what they did so you wouldn't think they were deeply immersed in the Party. It was a classic disinformation technique. Padilla knew that because he'd surreptitiously been studying the Party diligently over the last few months. All pieces of that long-term plan aimed at getting him off the taxi habit. More important, making Cuba a better place for his children and making his father's wish come true.

During the hour drive from the airport Padilla had acted as if he weren't listening to the man's phone conversation, as if he were just staring out at the dark countryside, but he'd overheard every word. The coded back-and-forth had been astonishing, seeming to indicate that someone important was either dead or at the doorstep. El Jefe? Padilla wondered. Rumors that the supreme leader was ailing had spread like wildfire through the tiny nation a month ago. Then, as if on cue, the old man had delivered one of his classic speeches, spewing fire and brimstone at the United States and its allies. Undoubtedly aware of the rumors thanks to the horde of DGSE officers—domestic spies—constantly mingling in the everyday lives of the 11 million residents.

Padilla had refused the healthy tip the executive offered as they pulled up in front of his beautifully maintained home. The tip could easily have been a Trojan horse. If Padilla had accepted it, he might have been hauled off to jail because it was illegal to accept anything over the fare, especially as an unlicensed gypsy. It was unlikely he'd get in real trouble because he was a doctor—and a good one—and the Party wanted Cuba to maintain its solid reputations for literacy and medical proficiency—despite that the reality was very different. However, confinement was still possible—perhaps just a week's stay in a local lockup as a warning—but clearly not worth the risk of accepting a small tip. So he'd simply smiled, shook his head, and left, content with the fare and that he was finally headed home.

Padilla fought the urge to let his eyelids close as he raced home through the night. He rolled the window down and held his head outside as he drove, pinched his thigh, rubbed his gums—all in an effort to stay awake. Just as he was about to lose the battle, he sped through a tight S-turn and a hulking form appeared out of the gloom in front of the Chrysler's high beams like a specter, directly in the middle of the road. For a moment he didn't recognize the shape. Then he knew: a cow.

He shouted, hit the brakes, and wrenched the steering wheel hard left, but the right fender took out the cow's two front legs. The animal's head smashed against the hood with a sickening thud, spraying blood across the windshield, and then he was flying into a three-foot ditch carved out of the ground by the tropical squalls that soaked the island almost every afternoon in the summer. The left front fender hit the far side of the gully and ground into the soft soil with a terrible grinding noise. The crumpled car came to an abrupt halt on its side.

For a few moments Padilla lay against the door thanking God he'd buckled his seat belt—he rarely did—slowly coming back to full consciousness. Coming to his senses, to the smell of burning rubber and oil. To the sounds of the engine revving and the crippled cow bellowing pitifully as it thrashed about in the ditch on the other side of the road. Padilla's left temple had struck the door window, and he was vaguely aware of a throbbing pain in his head and drops of blood trickling down his face.

The passenger door wrenched open.

"You all right?" a stranger shouted, reaching across the seat and shaking him. *"Hey, you all right?"*

Padilla grimaced and held up his hands. "Yes," he groaned, signaling for the man to stop shaking him, "I'm all right."

"The cow, she got out of the pasture. Must have found a hole in the fence somewhere." The stranger was speaking fast. "I'm sorry about your car. It's taken a bit of a hit, I'm afraid."

As had his second career, Padilla thought to himself, turning off the engine and climbing across the seat, his head pounding.

"I'm Gustavo Cruz," the stranger said, pulling Padilla out of the car and up to the side of the road. "The ranch I handle is just up the road. Who are you?"

"Nelson Padilla." Padilla sank to one knee, overcome by dizziness.

"I've got to go to town and get the police." Cruz winced, noticing the blood on Padilla's face. "And you a doctor."

"I *am* a doctor. I just need a few minutes." Only one in twelve homes in Cuba had phone service, Padilla knew. Apparently Cruz's wasn't one of them. "Go ahead to town. I'll be fine."

"It's about three miles from here. I shouldn't be long."

Padilla glanced over at the cow, still kicking around in the brush every few moments. "Do you have something that could pull my car out of the ditch?" He motioned back over his shoulder toward the Chrysler. Hopefully, it was drivable. At least the engine still worked. "A tractor maybe?" He dabbed at the cut on his head. It was small, a few centimeters long. It wouldn't need stitches. He grabbed a couple of leaves off a bush and pressed them hard against the wound. "Something you can hook a chain to and drag me out."

"The ranch has a tractor, but the transmission is shot. I've been waiting on parts for a few weeks."

Padilla sighed. Typical. It seemed as if everything on the island were broken. Cruz would be lucky if he got the parts in a few *months,* let alone a few weeks.

"I'm going back to my place and get my car," Cruz explained. "You stay here. I'll be back as soon as I can."

"Yeah, okay."

As Padilla watched Cruz hurry away, the sound of a loud motor reached his ears and then a truck slowly rumbled around the bend. "Hey!" he called after Cruz. "Wait!"

The truck skidded to a stop fifty feet past Padilla and the accident scene. He watched Cruz climb up on the running board and speak excitedly to the driver, then jump down as the driver slammed the truck into gear and roared off.

"It's good," said Cruz, making it back to where Padilla was kneeling as the truck's lights disappeared around the next bend. "The driver says he knows a guy who has a tow truck and lives a few towns up. Says he'll stop in and see the guy after he talks to the police. Says he's pretty sure the guy will come and help, especially since you're a doctor."

Which meant the man who had the tow truck would want medical services in return for the tow out of the ditch, probably for a child in his family. But that was fine, barter was how it worked here. And Padilla always helped children in need, even if the parents had nothing to trade.

The noise of the truck had barely faded away when another vehicle's headlights swung around the curve. Padilla squinted into the glare, realizing that there were actually two vehicles coming at him, a second directly behind the first. As the lead vehicle skidded to a stop, he saw it was a jeep. An army jeep of the Revolutionary Armed Forces—the FAR.

Two men in uniform hopped out and moved smartly toward Padilla.

"What's going on here?" the driver demanded in a tough voice.

Padilla rose to his feet unsteadily, identifying the two men as *primer tenientes*—first lieutenants—by the shoulder bars with one red line in the middle of two blue ones sprinkled by three stars. Pretty senior to be out in the countryside at this time of night.

"The cow got out of the pasture," Cruz explained nervously, gesturing from the animal to the car in the ditch to Padilla. "Unfortunately this gentleman hit it."

"You all right?" the officer asked.

"Yes," Padilla said, watching another man move toward the scene from the second jeep. The man had a vaguely familiar stride. Deliberate, one boot directly in front of the other, each step carefully placed. "I'm fine. I just need to get my car out of the ditch. Do you men have a chain or something in the jeep you could hook up to my back fender and give me a pull?"

"Maybe," the man replied. "First tell me what you're doing out here."

The man who had walked up from the second jeep came into view over the lieutenant's shoulder. Padilla glanced away quickly and subtly covered his face with his arm. Not because he was afraid of being recognized, but because he didn't want Cruz or the two lieutenants to spot his expression of familiarity. The man who had walked up from the second jeep was General Jorge Delgado, commander of the FAR's western and central armies—40,000 troops in all—and a man Padilla had gotten to know recently. They'd met secretly three times in the past two months. Padilla wondered what the hell he was doing out here.

"Lieutenant."

The young officer who had been asking the questions turned toward General Delgado and saluted. "Yes, sir."

"What's going on?"

The lieutenant explained the situation.

Delgado pointed at the cow. "Shoot the animal, Lieutenant."

"Yes, sir."

The young officer strode to the side of the road, pulled an old Soviet-made pistol from his holster, and fired two bullets into the cow's brain. It collapsed into the brush and lay still, barely visible.

As the sound of the shots echoed away, Padilla noticed another shadow hurrying down the lane toward the scene. This time from the direction of the ranch Cruz ran.

"So that was your cow?" Delgado asked Cruz.

Delgado's voice was so sharp, Padilla thought to himself, it seemed to slice through the air like a rapier. A gravelly, penetrating tone that made you forget about everything else you were thinking of and pay attention solely to him. That had been Padilla's first impression of Delgado at their initial meeting, and it had stuck with him ever since. Haunted him, really. Gave him goose bumps because he realized that if the long-term plan succeeded, he would be hearing that voice a great deal more in the future.

"Yes, sir," Cruz answered respectfully. "A cow from the ranch I *run,*" he added carefully, aware that he had spoken too casually, implying that he actually owned the cow and therefore the ranch. No one owned anything here, and to even imply that you did could get you in deep trouble.

Padilla gazed at Delgado in the glare of the headlights. Tall, broad-shouldered, and fit, the general was an intimidating presence. Charismatic because of his handsome appearance, the way he carried himself, and his voice. A man you naturally wanted to emulate. Larger than life, like a movie star. The general was fifty-two, but looked ten years younger. He had an air of quiet confidence about him and would have been in charge of any situation, rank or no rank.

"The ranch you operate is right up the road?"

"Yes, sir."

"You have hands on the ranch?"

"Yes, sir. A lot of my family, but we also use ten men from the village. And their wives sometimes."

Delgado glanced at the dead cow. "I want you to slaughter this animal and use it for food. It shouldn't be wasted."

"Thank you, sir. I'll cart it up to the ranch right—"

"Wait a minute!"

Everyone's eyes shot toward the voice. It had come from the man Padilla had noticed a few moments ago stealing toward the scene from the direction of Cruz's ranch. He was scrawny and wore a cowboy hat that seemed much too big for his head.

"I have information you'll want to hear," the scrawny man volunteered.

Padilla snuck a glance at Cruz, who seemed suddenly uncomfortable, tugging at his shirt collar and dabbing at his wide forehead with a blue bandanna. He was sweating profusely.

"Who are you?" Delgado asked, removing a cigar from his shirt pocket, biting off the tip, spitting it into the brush, then slipping the bitten end into his mouth.

"Hector Rodriguez. I run the next farm down," he explained, waving with his left hand.

"Hector, what are you—"

"I'll ask the questions," Delgado interrupted, silencing Cruz. He lit the cigar and took several puffs. "What information do you have, Mr. Rodriguez?"

Padilla saw the hint of a satisfied smile crawl across Rodriguez's face, as if something he'd been plotting for a long time was finally coming to fruition.

"I witnessed this man lead the cow into the middle of the road," Rodriguez explained, pointing at Cruz. "He did it on purpose, then hid in the bushes. He wanted the cow to get hit so he could have its meat."

"No, no, I would never—"

"Quiet," Delgado ordered.

Cruz was breathing heavily, obviously aware of the penalties he suddenly faced. Obviously guilty of Rodriguez's charge. After all, Padilla realized, how could he have reached the Chrysler so quickly—just moments after the accident—if the cow had gotten loose on its own? Presumably Cruz wouldn't have known about the missing animal until morning.

Delgado moved to where Cruz stood, towering over the dairy rancher. "Is this true?"

Cruz swallowed hard several times and shifted from foot to foot, then jammed his hands into his pants pockets. "Yes, General, but I just needed food for my—"

"Lieutenant," the general interrupted.

"Yes, sir."

"Take Mr. Cruz into custody. Take him back to the house and wait for me there. Do not let him out of your sight until I get back."

"Yes, sir."

The general pointed at the little rancher wearing the big cowboy hat. "You, come with me." Then he glanced at Padilla. "You'll wait at the Cruz farm for me to come back, too."

Padilla was amazed. He hadn't caught the general glancing at him once during the entire exchange until just this moment. Now he understood that Delgado had been aware of who he was the entire time. He'd seen that flash of recognition in the general's eyes. "Yes, sir."

"Let's go, Mr. Rodriguez," Delgado ordered.

Padilla watched Rodriguez follow after the general like a puppy after its mother, then glanced at Cruz again. He looked like a man condemned as the young lieutenant snapped handcuffs on his wrists and led him toward the first jeep. Problem was, that could well be the case. Cruz might well be condemned to death for what he'd done. Or spend years in Quivican—which would be worse than death.

LUCK HAD BEEN with Steven Sanchez tonight. The obnoxious, whining young man from New York he'd been forced to sit next to on the plane to Miami hadn't had a limo waiting for him after all—as Sanchez had feared. He'd been forced to hail a cab like every other bloke—giving Sanchez a chance to stay with him. Taking a cab maybe meant the kid wasn't as wealthy as he'd bragged about—but that didn't matter. Being wealthy had nothing to do with anything at this point.

"You just want me to stay with this guy?"

"That's right," Sanchez said to his driver, digging into his bag for the photograph of Christian Gillette. He'd snagged the cab right after the young man had gotten his. "Don't lose him, stay right on his ass."

"Do you mind if I ask what we're doing?"

"I don't mind at all," Sanchez snapped, "but I'm not going to give you an answer. Not unless you're willing to trade it for your fare."

"No," the cabbie answered quickly. "I'm not."

"Then drive."

"Yes, sir."

Sanchez gazed down into his lap at the photograph. Gillette was a handsome man in his early forties who was reportedly worth billions. Now that was *real* money. He chuckled to himself. But even with all that money Gillette could never truly be safe. Not with men like me in the world, Sanchez thought proudly. He could get to anyone given enough time. Even the president.

He smiled as he watched the cab turn into a neighborhood ahead. Once they'd found the man's house, he'd direct the driver toward the poor side of town. He needed to rent that house.

4

GENERAL DELGADO drove the jeep himself, sending the lieutenant who acted as his driver along with the other two officers up to the Cruz farm in the first jeep to wait for him. When the little cowboy had hopped into the passenger side, Delgado turned the jeep around and headed back down the road the way he'd come. Roaring ahead through the darkness once he'd made it out of the S-turn.

"Thank you for your loyalty tonight, Mr. Rodriguez," Delgado spoke up after a few minutes of silence. He was convinced Rodriguez wasn't a member of Department-VI, the army's counterintelligence unit. Convinced the scrawny rancher with the big hat was simply guilty of making a selfish play tonight. "The Party appreciates what you've done, comrade."

"Yes, thank you, General. I'm very loyal." Rodriguez hesitated. "If the Party sees fit, I would be happy to take over the Cruz operation. Mr. Cruz is not loyal like me. He underreports his output, and he probably has double the number of cows on the farm as he claims. I would never do that."

Definitely not D-VI, Delgado thought to himself. If Rodriguez had been D-VI, he would have said something else. And the little bastard was probably selling at least as much milk as Cruz on the black market and probably had twice the number of cows he claimed to have as well. But Rodriguez had seen an opportunity and seized it. "I understand.

I'm sure you wouldn't." Delgado guided the jeep to the side of the road just in front of a small bridge that spanned a narrow creek.

"What are we doing?" Rodriguez asked, peering around as the jeep came to a jerky halt.

"I want to ask you about a piece of property I've been looking at for a few weeks," Delgado explained. It wasn't uncommon for senior Party members—especially senior FAR officers—to receive land as additional compensation. It wasn't actually deeded to them—it couldn't be since only the state could own land in Cuba—but they could do whatever they wanted with it. "It's up on a hillside overlooking this stream. I figure you know the land around here pretty well."

"*Very* well," Rodriguez bragged, jumping out of the jeep.

Delgado eased out, too, and strode around to the passenger side, making certain he'd been right about the terrain here. "It's that way," he said, pointing up from behind the little man with his left hand.

Rodriguez squinted, trying to follow Delgado's finger. It was late but there was a full moon, so he could make out the dark shapes of hills in the distance. "Where?"

Delgado pulled his pistol from his belt with his right hand, aimed it at the back of Rodriguez's head, and fired. The cowboy hat flew off as the little man tumbled limply down the ravine to the creek.

Delgado took a deep breath and slid the pistol back into his belt. He hated snitches, even ones who were just doing it for selfish reasons. Not as much as the D-VI people, but almost. This way of life—neighbors spying on neighbors—had to end if Cuba was ever going to be a place where people really wanted to live. He glanced down the ravine to see if he could spot the body—he couldn't—then turned and headed back toward the driver's side.

When he got back to the Cruz farm, he would order the three lieutenants out to the jeeps, then inform Mr. Cruz that Mr. Rodriguez had suffered a terrible accident and would no longer be able to manage his farm. That Mr. Cruz would now manage the Rodriguez farm, too. It was a small battle he'd won tonight—not even a skirmish, really—but you had to start somewhere. He'd learned that during his years as a military officer. You couldn't take Rome in a day. Or Havana.

Delgado slowed down as he neared the accident scene, easing to a stop when he spotted the dead cow lying beside the road, barely visible in the deep grass and brush. He jumped out of the jeep and hurried to the animal, kneeling down beside its head and pulling out a knife. Then he cut away the small metal tag that had hung by a leather strap from the animal's neck for many years, checking the state-issued serial number etched into it before slipping it into his pocket. This would be the sign.

MELISSA HART sat on the young man's lap—the seat filler she'd made eyes at before she'd won her Oscar. He was cute and nice and they'd hooked up at a party in Beverly Hills after she'd left Elaine's. She hadn't returned to her seat once she'd shocked everyone in the Kodak Theatre, so she'd sent him a message via another seat filler before taking off in the limo to meet her four friends. Now it was after nine thirty and the Oscars had just ended. She'd been up since early this morning, so nervous about what she was going to do, but she wasn't tired at all, just exhilarated. She couldn't remember how many glasses of champagne she'd drunk, but the hell with it, this was her night. Victory *and* retribution all at once.

God, she felt good. She'd won the Oscar and she'd gotten back at him—in front of the whole world. Now everyone knew what a real shit her father was. Maybe it would break his grip on Hollywood. Maybe people wouldn't be so damn afraid of him anymore now that the press really had something to dig their teeth into about him. There was more, too, more where that had come from—not just what he'd done to her mother. She intended to tell the press what that was.

As Melissa turned back toward the young man, someone tapped her on the shoulder. She looked up. It was Bo Martin, one of Hollywood's biggest directors and not a big fan of her father's, though Bo kissed the ring when he had to, she knew. "Hi, Bo." She'd been looking forward to his congratulations.

"Hello, Melissa." Martin smiled grimly. "Quite a performance tonight. Maybe even better than the one you got the Oscar for."

"Thanks."

Martin glanced around uncomfortably.

"What's wrong?" she asked.

"Right, look, here's the thing. I need you to send that script back to me. The one I overnighted you last week."

Melissa sat up, suddenly aware of how much she'd had to drink. Her head was spinning and she grabbed the young man's leg to steady herself. "*What?* Why?" She loved that script, mostly because she was going to be the star. No more supporting actress with a quarter of the screen time.

"You know why, Melissa. You don't embarrass the king in front of his court like that on national television and expect life to go on normally, even if you are his daughter." Martin turned to go, then stopped and glanced back at the seat filler. "Son, if you ever want to work in Hollywood, you better get your ass as far away from this young woman as possible. *Right now.*"

"HERE YOU ARE, VICTORIA."

Victoria Graham took the Scotch and water from Lloyd Dorsey as he sat down beside her on the couch. Close to her, so their thighs were almost touching. Closer than friends would. "Thank you."

They were relaxing in the second-floor living room of his impressive four-story Georgetown home just a few miles from the Capitol. Beautifully decorated with lovely antiques and expensive artwork, it was really his home away from home. He was a senator from Texas—the Republican minority leader and the most senior member of the Armed Services Committee.

"You look beautiful."

Graham smiled. "You're full of compliments tonight, aren't you, Lloyd?" He was gentle, kind, magnetic, and so handsome. The man she'd wanted for so long—ever since college. She gazed at him a little longer, then looked away and shut her eyes tightly. He was so perfect—and *so* married. "I do all right for fifty-seven."

"*All right?* You're incredible. You were the best-looking woman there tonight. By far."

"What did you think of President Wood's speech after dessert?" she asked, trying to change the subject. She loved Dorsey's compliments—and hated them. Loved them because they made her feel so good. Hated them because she heard them so infrequently. "I thought it was pretty interesting."

They'd been at a state dinner all evening honoring the new president of Brazil. Graham had come down from New York City this afternoon after Dorsey had called yesterday to invite her. Dorsey's wife was back in Dallas—where she was more and more these days after spending many years in Washington with him—but he'd still gotten an extra chair at his table. They'd arrived at the White House separately and done their best to make it look innocent all evening while they sat next to each other. Touching fingers beneath the table, never so anyone could see. Dancing with other people when the orchestra struck up its first tune and making certain they carried on long conversations with the other ten people at the large, round table. They'd even left separately. But now they were here alone, they didn't have to put on appearances anymore.

"Ah, I can't stand the guy," Dorsey muttered. "You know that. Spewing all that liberal crap all the time." He shrugged. "Of course, what can you expect from the first black president in the history of the United States? I mean, he doesn't have much choice about how to act. He's got to cater to his constituency." Dorsey's expression turned determined. "But we'll get him next time around. *I'll* get him next time around. There won't be any second term for Jesse Wood."

"You sound pretty confident."

"I am."

"But his approval rating is so high."

"Won't be for long."

"How do you know?"

"I just do."

She took a sip of the single-malt Scotch. It was smooth, smooth enough to cloud her vision—and her judgment. "I don't know, Lloyd. I heard a lot of support for the military in the president's words tonight. That isn't usually what a liberal would—"

"He knows they hate him. The whole national security team does. The military, the CIA, the NSA, everybody. He's desperate to get in their good graces, but it won't happen. They'll never be in his camp. They'll make him *think* they are, but they won't ever really be. They're establishment, *we're* establishment. He's the enemy."

"But I thought—"

"I love you, Vicky," Dorsey said softly, interrupting her again as he took her hand. "I always have."

She stared into his eyes for a few moments, then looked away again, pulling her hand from his. She couldn't bear it. He was going to ask her to stay the night with him, she knew that was coming next. It had played out exactly the same way last time she'd come to Washington, right here on this same couch. The same way it did every time. It was so predictable, but she couldn't resist him. She hadn't said it back yet, but she loved him, too.

"I know what you're thinking," he said.

"You do?"

"Of course. You think I'll never leave my wife." He wrapped his fingers around hers again. "You think I'm just giving you lip service. Well, I'm not," he continued before she could say anything. "I'm going to make it happen."

She wanted that so badly. *God,* she wanted it. And she'd do anything to get it—almost.

"Let me ask you a question," Dorsey said, picking up his bourbon and water off the coffee table. He'd been forced to make a separate trip to the bar in the next room for each of their drinks because he walked with a cane. "What do you think of Christian Gillette?"

She didn't have to think about her answer for long. "He's one of the most capable men I've ever known. All the hype about him isn't really hype. He's that good." She'd been expecting that question from Dorsey for a while. "I have a lot of respect for him."

"But I thought he screwed you a couple of years ago. On that Ohio deal. Almost cratered your career with your board of directors, right?"

Her eyes narrowed and she bit her lip. "Maybe."

"Then how come you like him so much?"

Her expression soured. "I didn't say I *liked* him, I said I *respected* him. There's a difference. A *big* difference."

Dorsey nodded. "Good. I'm glad to hear that."

"Oh?" She gazed at him over the rim of the glass poised beneath her lips. "Why?"

He took another sip of his Jack Daniel's. "Because I want your help with something. Something very important. Something that involves Gillette."

CHRISTIAN TAPPED the table as he waited for the other person to come on the line. Typically, he didn't put up with this. Didn't take a call from someone's secretary, then wait around while the other person took his time coming to the phone. He didn't do that to others, didn't like it done to him. But this was different.

"Hello."

Christian sat up in the chair. "Hello."

"Chris, is that you?"

Christian hesitated. "Yes, it is, Mr. President."

"Well, how the hell are you?"

"I'm fine, sir."

"Glad to hear it." There was a short pause. "I need an answer about that thing we talked about last week, Chris. Sorry to be so direct, but I've got the president of Brazil waiting on me downstairs. First time tonight we've had a chance to talk privately." There was another brief silence. "So, you going to help me out?"

PART
TWO

5

May

CHRISTIAN GAZED out at the Catoctin Mountains from a screened-in porch of Camp David's main lodge. It was a warm, crystal-clear, late-spring afternoon, and the trees blanketing the rolling hills of western Maryland were bursting with blossoms and new leaves—a lighter green than they would be after they were fully grown in.

"Can I offer you something to drink? A beer, maybe? I'd have one with you, but it's probably not a good idea."

"That damn nuke thing, huh?" Christian asked.

President Jesse Wood grinned. "Yup. You'd have to worry about it, too, if you'd been my running mate. One good reason to be glad you *aren't* the vice president."

"Hey, I've got my own issues."

"I know you do," Wood agreed, gesturing toward a Secret Service agent standing by the door, hands clasped tightly behind his back. "Mr. Gillette will have a bottled water. It's been a while and I forgot. He doesn't drink alcohol."

"Yes, sir." The agent disappeared inside.

Wood glanced back at Christian. "I know you're a busy man, Chris. Probably almost as busy as I am."

As chairman of Everest Capital, Christian had a lot on his plate. The

Manhattan-based investment firm owned thirty-eight companies that operated in a wide range of industries—from high-tech to pharmaceuticals to heavy manufacturing. Together, the companies had sales of more than $80 billion—which would have ranked Everest in the top twenty-five of the Fortune 500 if all the companies had been combined into a single entity. Along with running Everest, Christian also chaired twelve of the Everest portfolio companies, and six months ago he'd finished raising Everest's latest leveraged-buyout fund—a $25 billion pool of equity capital that had stunned Wall Street with its size.

"Which was one of the reasons I didn't want you on the ticket," Wood continued. "All those *issues*."

Jesse Wood had been elected president two and a half years ago—the first African American in history to occupy the Oval Office. His initial eighteen months as commander in chief had been rocky, made especially difficult by partisan conservatives who'd tried everything they could think of—ethical, unethical, even criminal—to derail him. But now Wood was riding a wave of popularity after crafting a Middle East peace accord that had gotten traction despite dire predictions, and being credited by many in Washington and the press with jump-starting a stagnant economy. Initially, Wood had chosen Christian as his running mate, then changed his mind a few weeks later, just before the Democratic convention.

"You still mad about that?" Wood asked quietly. "About me picking you as vice president, then changing my mind?"

In the months leading up to the convention, Christian and Wood had spent a lot of time together. But this was their first contact since Wood had won the nomination. They'd gone almost three years without speaking—not because of any lingering animosity, as far as Christian was concerned. But he'd been surprised when Wood had called. He hadn't held the decision to switch running mates against Wood—it had never been publicly announced. But it wasn't as if he'd been happy about the decision, either.

"Now why would I be mad about *that*, Mr. President?"

Wood rolled his eyes. "Call me, Jesse, will you? Like you did before. At least when we're alone like this. Besides, I owe you big-time. Hell, you're the one who pulled my ass out of the ringer."

Which was true. Christian had saved Wood's ass, then been kicked in the teeth. "Okay, okay. It's Jesse from now on." The Secret Service agent reappeared with the water. "Thanks." He opened it and took a quick sip.

Wood pointed at him. "You look good, Christian. Like you haven't aged at all since the last time I saw you. Still look like you're in your midthirties, not your midforties."

Christian was six-two, weighed a trim 190 pounds, and kept himself in good shape with daily workouts, even when he was traveling. He had straight, dark hair combed back over his ears—highlighted with silver now—intense gray eyes, and sharp facial features: high cheekbones, a thin nose—bent slightly thanks to a face-to-face rugby collision in college—and a strong jaw.

"Thanks." Christian wanted to say the same thing to Jesse, but he couldn't. Jesse looked as if he'd aged ten years since they'd last seen each other. His face had so many creases and lines that hadn't been there before, and his hair had gone from slightly to completely gray. The pressure had to be enormous. Not only as the leader of the free world, but as the first black man to hold the job. Christian kept thinking about the famous before-and-after pictures of Abraham Lincoln. Before taking office and having to deal with a divided nation—then afterward, just before his assassination. An energetic and youthful man in 1861, a tired and worn-down politician in 1865. Just as it seemed Jesse was going to be, especially if he won a second term. "You seem to be handling the stress of being the first—"

"Don't even try to con me," Jesse cut in. "I can't take looking at myself in the mirror anymore. I look like an old man now. But I guess that comes with the job, huh?" His expression brightened. "Hey, congratulations on selling Laurel Energy to Exxon. I saw that announcement in the *Journal* a couple of months ago."

"Thanks."

"How much did you get?"

"A lot. It was a nice transaction for us. So, why did you ask me out here to Camp David, Jesse?" It wasn't that Christian was being coy about the number, he just didn't like dwelling on his own good fortune. He was uncomfortable talking about his successes, always had been. Besides, he wanted to turn the conversation to what he was really interested in. What Jesse wanted from him. "I've gone through all the damn background checks." Three months' worth of them, including a daylong enema detailing his entire sexual history. "What do you want from me?"

Wood motioned for the agent to leave. When he was gone, the president leaned forward on the wicker couch. "It involves Cuba," he said quietly.

That sounded interesting. "What about it?"

Wood pursed his lips a few times. "Look, here's the thing. Our people in Cuba are fairly sure El Jefe is dead."

Christian glanced up.

"He hasn't been seen in public in a couple of months," Wood continued. "And we think the guy meeting people behind the scenes is a double." He chuckled. "The CIA has assassinated three of Fidel's doubles over the years, so they ought to know when they see one by now."

"Jesus."

"Yup. That's what they tell me anyway."

Amazing stuff, Christian thought to himself. There was so much the American people didn't know, so much they *couldn't* know. "There's been no announcement of the guy's death."

"I know. But we think he handed the reins over to his brother several weeks ago. Made him Cuba's new president for life right before he died. The thing is, the new man needs to consolidate power before he makes El Jefe's death official, so he's keeping the body iced down. But it's been harder for him to get control than he anticipated. Harder for him to get that same stranglehold on the country his brother had. The situation is just so bad inside Cuba. Food shortages, energy shortages, poverty. People are itching for change and they aren't mesmerized by him the way they were his brother, which is making it very hard for him to pull everything together. With some key factions inside Cuba's military, especially." Wood hesitated, letting out a long breath. "Which could be very good . . . or *very* bad."

"How sure is the CIA that El Jefe is dead?" Christian asked. Wood hadn't specifically identified "our people in Cuba" as the CIA, but Christian assumed that was whom he meant.

"Ninety-eight percent," Wood answered, smiling. "Same first question I asked." His expression quickly turned serious again. "Several of the country's highest-ranking officials have fled the country secretly in the last few weeks. Minister of tourism, minister of mining. A couple of others were caught trying to escape and were executed, families, too. People are really scared. More than they've ever been because the state has stepped up its spying activities on citizens. Which we think is more proof that El Jefe is dead. The paranoia level has heated up to a nuclear level and the crackdown's on." Wood paused. "A couple of years ago I'd have said we'd never have a chance to win back the Cuban people, but we may have a window of opportunity after all. We may have a chance to influence the island again, develop close ties to a new government that understands how helpful we can be."

"How do we do that?"

"Our guys on the ground there are telling me that the power struggle is incredibly intense. Several groups within the government are trying to take control, and a couple of them are actually trying to get rid of the Communists. Those groups are quietly getting support from some of the influential ministry honchos. People who want to see Cuba move away from Communism and come into the twenty-first century and who can do something about it. People who want to see the country open its borders to free trade and believe that capitalism is ultimately the way to go. I mean, it wouldn't be our kind of capitalism, at least not right away. It would be more like Argentina or Brazil, but at least that's a start. The problem is the support has to stay so quiet because people are worried about being hauled off in the middle of the night and never being seen or heard from again. So the progress isn't coming as quickly as we'd hoped." The president shook his head, as if he had a hard time believing what he was about to say. "We think the group that may have the best chance inside the government to wrest control from the Communists is one with ties to a guy named Alberto Ochoa."

Christian raised his eyebrows. "Sorry, Jesse, but I guess I'm not as up to speed on Cuba as I ought to be. Who's Alberto Ochoa?"

The president chuckled. "You mean you don't have time to run Everest Capital, all those portfolio companies Everest owns, have some sort of personal life, *and* be completely caught up on Cuban history?"

"I might if I had the entire State Department working for me," Christian muttered. A gibe, but there was a serious undercurrent to it. As he'd passed his fortieth birthday, his thirst for knowledge had dramatically intensified. He'd realized more and more how much he still didn't know about the world—but how much he *wanted* to know. He was trying to read something every week—a biography, a period piece—but it was tough with his schedule and all the reading he had to do for Everest.

"That does make it a little easier," Wood admitted. He checked the doorway, making certain the agent wasn't standing there. "Here's the abridged version. Along with Raúl and Che Guevara, Ochoa was one of the guys who made it happen for Fidel back in the day, back when the Revolution was coming to a head in the late fifties. When it was all said and done, Ochoa ended up being one of the most senior generals in the Revolutionary Armed Forces, in the FAR. He had a nice career going until the late eighties, when he suddenly found himself in Fidel's doghouse. It's not exactly clear what happened, but we think it might have had something to do with the fact that he supported the Russian brand of Communism, which ultimately couldn't fend off Big Macs and MTV. During the eighties, Fidel was demanding that all his top people strictly support his hard-line approach. When Ochoa wouldn't, the general basically bought his ticket to the execution train."

"Whoa."

"Yeah, they tied him to a post in front of a four-man firing squad in 1989 after a kangaroo court convicted him of treason. There were trumped-up drug charges and bribery allegations, but there wasn't anything to them. From everything the guys up the Potomac tell me, the only thing Alberto Ochoa was guilty of was defying Fidel."

But sometimes that was enough when the guy you were dealing with was a paranoid schizophrenic. History had proven that over and over. "First rule of living in a dictatorship. Don't piss off the dictator."

Wood nodded. "Too bad Ochoa didn't have you around, Chris. Maybe he'd still be alive. Maybe *he* could have led this thing."

"So there are still people around who are bitter about what happened to Ochoa?" Christian asked.

"Yeah, there are. Apparently Ochoa was a stand-up guy. Took care of his people and they were loyal back. They didn't take revenge for what happened to him because there wasn't much they could do. Castro isolated Ochoa's senior supporters very effectively. Paranoia has its positives." Wood winced. "Turns out Ochoa was a tough bastard. I mean, most of those senior FAR guys are, but listen to this. Ochoa had two requests at his execution. First, he didn't want a blindfold. Second, *he* wanted to give the command to fire. Fidel granted both requests."

"Damn." Christian tried to imagine giving a firing squad the command to shoot him. It seemed like one of those ultimate acts of bravery you never knew whether you were really capable of unless you were in the moment. "That's amazing."

"Yeah, right? Well, they ended up burying him in an unmarked grave in the hills outside Havana somewhere. Didn't even tell his wife where his body was for a while." Wood hesitated, gathering his thoughts. "Here's the bottom line. Now that there's weakness inside the regime, these people who were loyal to Ochoa are trying to take control. Turns out they haven't forgotten after all and they've formed an alliance with a group of civilians who are pro-capitalists. Maybe anti-anticommunists is a better way to put it. Chris, any way you look at it, you're going to need the Cuban military on your side to win the day down there. You'll need them afterward, too, and that's just the way it is. We've decided this combination has the best shot at bringing the Communists down and taking Cuba where it needs to go from both the military and private-sector perspectives. We also think this group is the most likely to stay loyal to us, which is probably the most important consideration of all. But we've got to act *fast*. We've got to let them know we're a hundred percent committed to them as soon as possible. We've told them we're almost there, but I have one more box I need to check before I dive into the deep end with them."

"Why *so* fast?" Christian asked.

"The problem, what we're all *really* worried about here, is that the people who are clinging to power in Cuba right now might look for help from the outside if they decide they can't hang on by themselves. If they sniff some kind of conspiracy they think actually has legs."

"*Help* as in a terrorist state," Christian suggested, anticipating where Wood was going with this. "Like Iran or Syria. Even China."

Wood pointed at Christian. "*Exactly. China*. I can't have China putting missiles on the ground ninety miles from Miami. Then I might start drinking something a lot stronger than beer on the job." Wood grimaced. "And our intel indicates there are those kinds of secret discussions going on. You probably know about that oil deal Cuba signed with China."

"Just what I read in the newspapers," Christian said. Which wasn't exactly true. He knew more than that, but he also knew the best way to get more information was to act as if you didn't know. Especially when the other person wanted something from you. "Which wasn't much."

The president nodded, as if he expected Christian not to know much because everything he was about to say was so hush-hush. "China and Cuba have signed a formal agreement to develop oil fields right off Cuba's coastline. They're big fields, too, bigger than what's being reported in the press. The right side of the aisle in Washington is going nuts on this, of course, but even some of my friends on the left side are getting nervous."

Which Christian already knew.

"What hasn't been reported," Wood continued, "is that we believe there are very secret discussions going on about China basically stepping into the old Soviet Union's role. Massive loans and subsidies, particularly with respect to the military and agriculture." President Wood raised his eyebrows. "We all know nations don't lend other nations billions and billions just to earn interest. There are other, very dark motivations here."

"Those missiles you mentioned."

"Right," the president confirmed. "*First-strike* missiles. Even today, that's a huge advantage."

"Jesus."

"Yeah, so basically what we're talking about here comes down to a defensive play. I mean, I would really like to help the Cuban people. They've suffered for a long time. But I absolutely can't have China getting a beachhead that close to us. That first-strike potential is terrifying."

"Of course." There was obviously a point to all this background and Christian could feel an excitement building, hoping he understood what Wood wanted him to do. "Why are you telling me all this, Jesse? Why did you have me come here?"

Wood stared at Christian for a few moments. "I need your help. I need you to meet with that group I mentioned, which includes some very senior ministry people who are secretly allying themselves with the Ochoa-legacy faction inside the FAR. But before I commit the United States to these people, I need you to tell me if they're real. If you think they can handle setting up a free-market economy in Cuba while the Ochoa people take care of the muscle side. And, if you think they are capable, I'll need you to advise them going forward. You'll be on the ground there for a while, starting when the whole thing breaks out. So you can advise them right from the get-go."

"You mean—"

"I mean right out of the box. You'll be in Cuba when the switch is turned on. When the general gives the order to take out the Party leaders and all hell breaks loose." Wood pointed at Christian. "You're the best person I can think of for this job. I trust your instincts completely." Wood picked a rose out of the arrangement of fresh flowers on the table and passed it beneath his nostrils. "As I'm sure you can imagine, there are a few major challenges with this thing."

Again, Christian could see the immense toll the day-to-day strain of being president was taking on Wood. The way the scent of a rose was such a welcome distraction—even if the distraction lasted only a few seconds. "Other than the possibility of me being killed, what?"

Wood slid the rose stem back into the vase. "Like I said, this thing is obviously top secret. If what I've asked you to do is ever uncovered by the press or people opposed to my administration, I won't be able to admit we had this conversation. I won't be able to say you had any backing from the United States government to do what you were doing. Hell, I won't even be able to admit you and I have spoken since I've been in office. If the rest of the world could prove we were supporting a new regime in Cuba, basically supporting a revolt, I'd have a massive diplomacy problem on my hands. Even our closest allies might line up against me."

Christian eased back in his chair, mulling over what the president had just laid out for him. "Well, I do have one specific concern with all that."

The president motioned inwardly with his fingers. "Tell me."

"United States citizens aren't supposed to do business with Cuban nationals. In fact, it's illegal to even have discussions with them." A few weeks ago, Christian had read an article about several Oklahoma businessmen being arrested for meeting with executives of Cuba's state-run oil company in Mexico City. They'd been arrested by federal authorities at the Tulsa airport at the entrance to the Jetway as soon as they'd returned. Then they'd been escorted away in handcuffs in front of a large crowd, which included their wives and children. "Even if you meet with them on neutral ground, it's a crime." He hesitated. "Unfortunately, I've made some enemies as the chairman of Everest Capital. It's been unavoidable and they might see it as an opportunity if they found out about it."

Wood acknowledged Christian's point with a quick wave. "I certainly understand the inevitability of making enemies."

"Right. Well, the problem is—"

"*The problem,*" Wood interrupted, "is that if one of your enemies found out you were meeting with people and alerted the local authorities, you'd have an issue. A potentially *big* issue because the local authorities would detain you, and the chairman of Everest Capital can *never* be detained *anywhere* for *anything* if he's going to keep his credibility with his investors."

"Detained might be okay. Convicted of something is out of the question."

"Already thought about all this," Wood assured Christian. "We'll make certain you're issued a valid license to meet with these Cubans. We'll arrange that through the Office of Foreign Assets Control. You'll get the license under an exemption for humanitarian projects and support for the Cuban people. It's pretty common stuff. You'll have a whole cover story, which will obviously have nothing to do with why you'll really be meeting with them. And you'll be carrying the license on you so there won't be a problem. I assume you'll take the right precautions such that no one will be able to follow you or be able to figure out where you're going in the first place," Wood said, his voice taking on a paternal tone. "Then we won't have to worry about this at all."

"I'll need help on that," Christian spoke up quickly. "I'll need to let Quentin Stiles in on this." Quentin Stiles was one of Everest's five managing partners—the five senior people who reported directly to Christian—and an expert in security, including physical protection. He was also Christian's best friend. "You remember Quentin, don't you?" Quentin and the president had met when Wood was considering naming Christian his vice president.

"Of course, I do. He's a good man." Wood smiled. "I also remember Allison Wallace." Allison Wallace was another of Everest's managing partners. She'd joined the firm after her family had made a huge financial commitment to the fund prior to the one Christian had just finished raising. "You and she still hot and heavy?"

"We were never hot and heavy."

"That's not what my Secret Service guys told me."

"Jesse, I don't think—"

"Okay, okay." Wood held up one hand. "Look, at some point I agree that you'll have to bring Quentin in on this, but don't tell him yet."

"That doesn't work. Quentin has to know right away."

The president thought about it for a few moments. "All right, I'll leave it up to you when you tell him. But *damn it*, Stiles better not—"

"I trust Quentin more than anyone else in the world. It'll be fine," Christian assured Wood.

"He'll need a background check, too."

"Fine." Quentin would raise hell about that, but so be it. "I assume, given his history, that'll be a quick process."

Wood nodded. "It'll be fast."

"You said there were a *few* challenges," Christian continued. "We've covered how I deal with the legal issue. What else is there?"

Wood grimaced. "Like you said, this thing could actually get pretty dangerous, Chris. If people inside the Party find out about it, there's no telling what they'll do. Ultimately you'll have to go to Cuba secretly. I'm talking Special Forces stuff to smuggle you in there. Choppers and a jungle-drop-at-night kind of crap. While you're in there, you'll be a hell of a target if somehow they smell you. If we've miscalculated and there's a spy inside the civilian group, for instance."

Christian took a sip of water. "I'm not worried." He'd never served in the military and had long felt a strange type of guilt about that. The possibility of being part of a Special Forces mission was exhilarating, even if he was just going to be the football. Maybe it would satisfy his growing hunger to do something bigger, something more important, than manage Everest. A hunger he understood more and more was being brought on by age. "Let me rephrase that," he said. "I'll be *plenty* worried, but I won't let it stop me from going." He'd earned a lot of money in his career because the United States was the safest place in the world to do business, but he'd never had any part in *making* it safe. "Plenty of young men and women went to Iraq. They didn't let the danger stop them."

"No, they didn't," Wood agreed. "Look, we'll have protection for you while you're there. A squad of Army Rangers *just* to protect you. And we'll be able to get you off the island quickly if the revolt doesn't look like it's going to succeed. If the general we're working with doesn't turn out to have the influence with his subordinates we think he does. We'll have plenty of ships right off the coast we can get you back to."

"Unless China has ships out there, too."

The president ran a hand over his hair. "I don't even want to think about that."

Christian knew this would probably be the most sensitive question he could ask. "Will we be supporting the revolt militarily?"

The president started to say something, then stopped. "I can't tell you that, Chris."

Christian nodded to let Jesse know he wouldn't dig any more on that issue. At least, not right now. "Okay." That Wood had gone silent spoke volumes anyway. The U.S. military would be there. And not just the Rangers who would be protecting him. "What else?"

Wood shrugged. "I don't know what to do for you in return. It's really hard to—"

"You don't have to do anything for me in return, Jesse," Christian interrupted. "If I do it, I'll do it because I think it'll help the country."

The president nodded slowly. "Thanks, Chris." He hesitated. "If there is anything I can do, you know I will."

"Yeah, sure."

They were silent for a few moments.

"Answer me this," Christian spoke up. "A few minutes ago you said that you wouldn't have thought this a few years ago, but that we might actually have a chance to win back the Cuban people. Has the embargo been that devastating?"

"It has," Wood confirmed, "but the root of the problem the Cuban people have with us goes further back than that. It really started back in the late 1800s when we won the war with the Spanish."

"I thought we granted Cuba their independence pretty soon after that."

"We did, but it wasn't without a lot of strings attached. Which is the problem," Wood explained. "There was something called the Platt Amendment that went along with their independence, which basically let us intervene in Cuban affairs anytime we wanted to. It gave us carte blanche to make things go our way whenever it suited us, and we did. That's really where the Cuban people's resentment toward us began."

"Mr. President." The Secret Service agent stuck his head out onto the porch. "Your next appointment is here."

"Tell him I'll be ready in a few minutes." Wood shifted his eyes back to Christian. "I need your help, Chris. Take a few days to think about it, but no longer. Like I said, we have to move on this. If it's not going to be you, I'll have to reach out to others."

Christian wanted to ask a few more questions, but an older man with a gray beard strode out onto the porch with a Secret Service agent right behind him.

"Hello, Jesse," the man said loudly.

Wood rose up off the couch. "Richard, hello. I'm not quite ready for—"

"It's fine, it's fine. Just finish up . . . quick."

"Yes," Wood said slowly. "Well, I—"

"I'm Christian Gillette." He held out his hand toward the man. "Nice to meet you."

"Richard Hart."

Christian recognized the name instantly. Richard Hart was a legend in the movie industry. "I've admired your films for years, Mr. Hart."

"So many people have," Hart said with a wave. "What do you do, Gillette?"

"I manage money."

"Ah. No wonder I don't recognize your name. I don't pay much attention to that financial stuff." He glanced at Wood, then back at Christian. "How much longer will you two be?"

IT WAS THE FIRST great lesson of Melissa's adult life: You can't defy the king no matter who you are—even if you're his daughter.

The night she'd won her award there'd been more than fifty screenplays stacked up on the dining room table of her apartment. Several she was extremely interested in, with roles she felt might win her the ultimate Oscar—Best Actress. The next morning her agent had called—again and again—to tell her that directors were demanding the scripts back. Then he'd called one final time at the end of the day—to quit, right on the phone. Richard Hart had struck with fury and force.

A month later she'd been out of money—and friends. Even the girls she'd gone to Elaine's with wouldn't return her calls. So she'd taken a job as a waitress and—nightmare of nightmares—been forced to sell her Oscar on eBay.

That's when they'd called, just when she was at her most vulnerable. With an opportunity to make a big pot of money—an amount that wouldn't have seemed like much a few months ago, but seemed like a ton now—and an opportunity for revenge. As poor as she'd suddenly become, the chance to one-up her father was almost as big an incentive as the money. Calling him out in public for being a failure as a husband and a father wasn't enough anymore. Now she wanted to take him down. She was still too young to understand that revenge never ended up tasting as sweet as you thought it would.

Melissa glanced into the sports car's rearview mirror. The long blond hair and blue eyes were gone. Now she had short dark hair and green eyes. She hadn't wanted to be recognized as that young woman who'd won the Oscar, then been banished from Hollywood.

Now she *couldn't* be recognized as that. They'd made that clear in no uncertain terms. They'd put so much emphasis on staying anonymous she got the feeling that if anyone ever found out who she was and these people heard about it, she might not be around long.

She shook her head. A few months ago she'd been on top of the world. It was amazing how quickly life could change.

6

ALLISON WALLACE looked around anxiously. It was like no other office she'd ever been to. It was more like the reptile house at a zoo. Not the conservative surroundings of a prominent Manhattan senior executive she'd been expecting. Lining two walls were shelves of aquariums and cages, filled with snakes and lizards of all shapes and sizes. And a three-foot alligator lay in a tank in one corner.

"Everything all right?"

Allison glanced at the plump, middle-aged woman wearing cat's-eye glasses who'd led her in here from reception. She'd barely heard the question because she couldn't focus. The whole scene was too distracting. "Um . . ."

"Never been here before, huh?"

"No."

"Don't worry, they usually stay put."

"Usually?"

The woman smiled. "Do you want anything to drink while you wait for Ms. Graham?"

"How about boric acid? In case I have to throw it at something slithering at me?"

"Sorry. The guy who was here before you got the last bottle. Good thing, too. That cobra over there would have nailed him if he hadn't."

Well, at least she had a sense of humor about it. "Pepsi would be great," Allison said, checking in the direction the woman had looked when she'd mentioned the cobra. Sure enough, there were eyeglasses on the back of the coppery hood. It was a small snake, but so what? Weren't baby snakes supposed to be even more poisonous than adults? "Thanks."

When the woman was gone, Allison took a closer look at some of the creatures, keeping her distance, especially as she neared the alligator. The teeth on the thing were already getting big and the tank didn't look that sturdy. It seemed as if it were smiling at her with those menacing pearly whites—not in a friendly way, either. More like he was hungry—and she was dinner.

"Like him?"

Allison whirled around. Victoria Graham stood in a far corner. She'd entered the office from an anteroom. Allison hadn't heard the door open.

"I call him Tricky Dick," Graham continued, moving toward Allison. "He reminds me of President Nixon. Powerful but sneaky. Got that sly look about him all the time. Like you never know what he'll do next." She held out her hand as she reached Allison. "Victoria Graham."

"Allison Wallace. Nice to meet you."

"You're probably too young to remember Nixon in any personal way," Graham said with a sigh. "He's probably nothing but a picture in a history book for you. Just those two quick vees as he stood in the chopper doorway that last time on the White House lawn." She held her arms up and fingers out in the classic Nixon stiff-upper-lip, farewell pose. "Maybe not even a picture for you, now that I think about it."

"I don't remember him," Allison admitted, "but I've read about him and Watergate, all about the tapes."

Tall and statuesque with pretty white hair swept back on both sides, Graham made a striking first impression. Fifty-seven, she looked her age, but was still beautiful—even sexy—for an older woman. She had a high forehead, a sharp chin, and her mouth seemed stuck in a mysterious semismile. She spoke in an aristocratic Katharine Hepburn croak and gestured with her hands a lot. Allison had done a Google search on Graham this morning and found several photographs of her. She was pretty in those pictures, but was much more impressive in person.

Allison's Internet search had also turned up a litany of testimonials to Graham's being a leader in the worldwide financial community as well as a ceiling-buster for women. The first woman to run a major U.S. insurance company, first woman to serve on five Fortune 500 boards at the same time, one of the first women to own a professional sports team. There were lots of firsts when it came to Victoria Graham, Allison had learned. Maybe Graham had the right to be a little eccentric about picking her officemates.

Graham gestured at the alligator. "I'm sure you'd like to hear the explanation."

In fact, Allison was interested. Not just in the alligator though. "Well—"

"I own a house on Marco Island down in Florida, and this little guy kept coming up out of the canal onto my lawn this past winter, scaring everybody half to death. We think he was after my cats because a couple of them disappeared. Almost took a chunk out of the pool boy's leg one afternoon. But he's so cute I just *had* to have him. So I had him trapped and flown up here. Unfortunately I'm not going to be able to keep him here at the office much longer. He's growing too fast what with all the rabbits we're feeding him. So, I'm building him a place out at my house in Connecticut. All climate-controlled. It's very nice."

Allison's eyes grew wide. "You feed him *here?*" This woman really was quite a character. Which hadn't come through in the news articles—nor had Christian mentioned anything like that. Of course, that was Christian. He usually let you form your own opinions about people. "In your office?"

"Well, of course. Where else would I feed him?" Graham asked. "You want to watch?"

"No, no." Instantly, Allison wished she hadn't been so quick to turn down the opportunity. It might be interesting to see the hunt. It would be sad to watch a cute little rabbit die, but the alligator was going to get his dinner whether she was here or not. "But thanks."

"Fine, fine." Graham headed to a big leather chair behind her desk. "Maybe one of the snakes when we've finished our meeting. The boa's a lot of fun to watch, too. But sometimes it takes him a while to strike after we put the rat in there."

Allison glanced at the thick, coiled snake as Graham's assistant came back in to deliver the soda. "Yeah, maybe," she murmured.

"I've always liked reptiles," Graham volunteered, sitting down. "In fact, I thought I was going to be a biologist or even a zoologist when I went to college." She raised both eyebrows, pursed her lips, and gazed out the window.

Almost longingly, Allison thought to herself. As though despite all the success she'd achieved, something inside her caused her to wonder what it would have been like to have had a simpler life. As though there was even the tiniest seed of regret about how her life had turned out.

"But I ended up in the insurance business," Graham continued.

"How?"

"My father owned an insurance brokerage business in Philadelphia. He died suddenly when I was a junior at the University of Florida, of a heart attack, and I had to come home and run the business because my siblings were too young to do it. Never went back to college," she said ruefully. "I sold the business four years later to a big firm, then took a job with Mutual of Pennsylvania." She fluttered her hand in the air and rolled her eyes. "The rest, as they say, is history."

"Things turned out pretty well."

"I suppose."

"What is it that you like about reptiles?" Allison liked digging into the psyches of successful people, especially older women. She'd been looking for a role model all her life.

"The fact that a lot of them haven't changed much in millions of years. I like that kind of consistency because I believe it's consistency that builds dynasties and longevity, which reptiles have certainly enjoyed." Graham smiled. "You're a beautiful woman, dear."

Victoria Graham was fascinating, not stiff and reserved as Allison had anticipated. Reputed to be tough as nails—she'd have to be tough to have been so successful in the male-dominated worlds in which she operated—she had a soft side as well. It seemed as if she said *exactly* what was on her mind, too. Something most people would never dream of doing. "That's nice of you to say."

"You're lucky." Graham shook her head and motioned toward the door. "I've done everything I can for Marcia. Poor girl. Plastic surgery, weight-loss spas, makeup specialists. But it hasn't done much good. She's the best assistant I've ever had and I love her like a daughter. But she's going to die a spinster if she doesn't watch out. She wants a husband so badly, but she's going to have to lower her sights if she's ever going to get a nibble." Graham smiled. "You, on the other hand, must be beating them away with a stick."

In her midthirties, Allison was pretty. Blond and vivacious with a body that still got those long whistles from Manhattan construction workers, Allison understood that she'd been blessed. She tried not to stick it in other women's faces during the day, keeping her outfits conservative for business. But when she went out clubbing on weekends, she loved dressing provocatively. It was fun and she didn't mind the stares. When the stares stopped, that's when she'd worry.

"Are those real?" Graham asked, pointing at Allison's chest.

Allison put a hand on her blouse and smiled self-consciously. *"Excuse me?"* Christian hadn't said much about Victoria Graham, but he had warned Allison that there wasn't a question the older woman wouldn't ask. Allison had just assumed he meant there wasn't a *business* question she wouldn't ask.

"They're just so perfect."

Allison burst into nervous laughter. "Jesus."

"Oh, I know, I'm direct."

"I'd say."

"But it's fun."

"Maybe for you, but—"

"And you don't have to worry, I'm not a lesbian. That's not why I'm asking."

"Oh, God."

Graham chuckled. "I'm a little peculiar, too, I guess."

"Well, I don't know about—"

"Christian probably told you."

Allison hesitated. She didn't want to get anyone in trouble. "He didn't say anything like that. All he said was that you've been one of Everest Capital's biggest supporters for a long time." Allison had been a managing partner at Everest for a while, but this was the first time she'd ever met Victoria Graham. Christian handled Everest's biggest and most important investors himself. "He has a lot of respect for you," Allison continued. "Says you made Mutual of Pennsylvania what it is today." Mutual of Pennsylvania—MuPenn, as the Street called the firm—was one of the biggest and most profitable insurance groups in the country. Graham had been CEO and chairman for nineteen years. She still ran the company with an iron fist, still got involved with decisions about what to do with the massive amount of premium dollars pouring into its coffers every day. "Says you've been with Everest from the start."

"That's right," Graham confirmed. "I invested a million dollars with Christian's old boss and mentor Bill Donovan, back in the early days, back in the mideighties. When Bill was just getting Everest off the ground. I wasn't even CEO of MuPenn at that point, just chief investment officer." She shook her head. "That first fund Bill put together was only twenty-five million dollars." She glanced at Allison. "How big is the fund Christian just finished raising? I can't remember exactly."

"Twenty-five *billion*."

"My Lord. That's incredible."

"MuPenn invested seven hundred and fifty million dollars," Allison reminded Graham. "You're one of our biggest investors."

Graham nodded. "I *do* remember that number. I signed off on the investment personally. The board doesn't usually ask me to do that anymore, but it's the biggest single investment we've ever made, and they wanted to make sure I rubber-stamped it personally."

"Just in case something goes wrong." A CYA move, Allison realized.

"Right," Graham agreed. "But nothing will. Christian has a great track record. He's the best in the business." She hesitated. "Which I'm sure is why your family invested so much with Everest."

The Wallaces were one of the wealthiest families in the country. Based in Chicago, they'd made their first fortune during the 1800s off railroads. Then it was real estate, parceling off and selling land they'd acquired from owning the railroad and developing other tracts themselves. Most recently, they'd struck it huge with the cell phone explosion. *Forbes* and *Fortune* put the family's net worth at $40 billion, but the number was actually higher. Several years ago the Wallaces had committed $5 billion to the last Everest fund—the one Christian had raised prior to the current $25 billion pool—and it was the largest individual commitment ever made to any leveraged-buyout firm. They'd sent Allison to Manhattan to watch over the massive commitment—and to learn.

"I thought you were going back to Chicago after that last fund was fully invested," Graham spoke up. "To set up your own leveraged-buyout business for your family. I remember Christian telling me that when he was first considering taking your family on as an investor. He was worried that you'd ultimately become his competitor."

Allison looked down. "I decided to stay."

"Why?"

"I like Manhattan." She liked Christian, too, a lot. Had since the moment they'd met. And he had the same feelings for her, she was sure. A couple of times it had almost gone to the next level, almost burst into something intense. But that they worked together always seemed to get in the way. "And I had a bit of a falling-out with my family."

Graham raised one eyebrow. "Tell me about that."

Victoria Graham could ask all the questions she wanted to, but there didn't have to be answers. Not when they dealt with Allison's personal life. Of course, she didn't want to aggravate one of Everest's biggest investors, either. Christian wouldn't be happy about that. "Things happen, you know?"

"Did you and Gordon Meade not get along?"

Gordon Meade had been in charge of the Wallace Family Trust—the vehicle the family used to make most of its investments—until a couple of years ago. After years of thinking Meade was a hired gun—an outsider who ran the trust because no one inside had that kind of experience— Allison had stumbled onto the fact that he was really a family member— with a dark secret. "We did . . . for the most part."

"I ran into Gordon a few times while he was running your family's money. It's a small world. Seemed like a nice enough man. But he died, right?"

Allison nodded.

"How?"

Now *that* was a tricky question. There was the official story—then what had really happened. "He had a stroke," Allison answered. She managed to keep her eyes locked on Graham's, but it wasn't easy.

"Who's running the family money now?"

"My brother."

"Is that why you had the falling-out with your family? They chose him and not you?"

Allison shook her head. "No." It was clear that Graham was expecting more of an explanation, but she wasn't going to get it.

Graham watched one of the snakes wrap itself around a limb inside its cage. "How many employees are there at Everest now?"

Good. Graham was off the family topic. "Almost eighty."

"How many partners? How many of you reporting directly to Christian?"

"Five."

"Are you the only female partner?"

"Yes. We had another one, but she left last year to have a baby. Her husband's an investment banker at Morgan Stanley so they didn't need her income and she hasn't come back. I doubt she will. Christian's keeping a slot open for her, but I think she's already pregnant again."

"That's our curse, isn't it?" Graham asked rhetorically. " *We* have the babies. It's very hard to do both. Work and be a mom, I mean. At least, effectively." She tapped her desk, as if she'd spent a lot of time thinking about that conflict but hadn't come up with any solutions. "How's your relationship with Christian?"

Allison glanced up. She'd been thinking about having a baby. It was something she was thinking about more and more lately. "Fine. We're good business partners."

"Any spark between you two?"

There it was again. Graham's habit of asking whatever was on her mind. Allison made a face, as if to say that there was no chance of that ever happening. "No way."

"Why not? You're both single, both good-looking, and you probably spend a lot of time together. That's a damn good recipe for romance." Graham laughed. "What's the matter, isn't Christian any fun? I've told him so many times he's got to start letting go a little."

Allison grinned. "He has his moments. Not many, but some." In all fairness, Christian didn't have much time for fun. People always needed him for something, and he was constantly having to make tough decisions. More and more she understood that because people were starting to pull her in so many different directions, too. "I just don't think it would do our business relationship much good if we ever started the other thing. And what if it didn't work? Then where would we be?"

Allison had tried to convince Christian several times that they could have romance without its getting in the way of what they needed to do every day at Everest—but she wanted to make certain Graham heard the party line. He'd come close to agreeing with her once, then backed off. She understood his point. It wouldn't be a good idea for the investors to think the chairman and one of the senior partners were hot for each other. If anything ever did happen between them, it would have to stay quiet. And she'd never been able to answer those questions he always asked. What if they tried it and it didn't take? What if the breakup wasn't mutual? Would they still be able to work together?

"And," Allison continued, "people would talk if we did start seeing each other outside Everest."

"The hell with *people*. It's not their lives." Graham put her head back and laughed. "Of course, at fifty-seven it's easier for me to say that than it is for you."

"You've never been married, have you?" The words had tumbled out of Allison's mouth abruptly, taking both of them by surprise. But she'd wanted to ask the older woman that question ever since reading this morning that Graham had never been married, never had children. Allison was starting to wonder if it was ever going to happen for her. The last ten years had blown by so fast. Pretty soon getting pregnant wouldn't be an option, at least not without risks. "Why not?" She smiled to herself. Graham's tendency to ask whatever question was on her mind was rubbing off.

"Never found the right man." Graham shook her head quickly and held up her hand. "That's not exactly true," she admitted softly. "I just never found the time. Life goes by so fast when you're in the trenches fighting it every day." She paused, her eyes narrowing. "Of course, maybe I didn't want to find the time. Maybe I was so busy battling men all day long I didn't want to be around one at night. Maybe that's why I have all these snakes in my office," she said, making a sweeping gesture. "To remind me of all the snakes I've dealt with in my career so I won't end up with one. At least not permanently." Graham's expression turned sad. "Anyway, I woke up one morning, I was fifty, and I was all alone." She pointed at Allison after a poignant pause. "Don't let that happen to you, dear. It's like they say: In the end, it's the wink of an eye."

"You're not near the end," Allison said firmly.

"I'm not near the beginning either." Graham clapped her hands to break the mood. "So, what's your favorite movie, Allison?"

Allison glanced at the alligator and thought for a few seconds. "Well . . . I . . . I mean, there's so many—"

The older woman banged a fist on her desk. "Don't give me that," she said loudly. "Just tell me what your favorite movie is, Allison. The one you'd pick if you were going to prison for the rest of your life and all you could take with you was a TV, a DVD player, and one DVD. Come on."

"It hasn't been made yet. And I doubt I'll have to go to prison tomorrow for the rest of my life."

Graham started to say something, then broke into a wide smile. "No one's ever given me that answer before. *A* for originality, but I still want to know what—"

"*Caddyshack.*"

Graham's eyes ballooned. "Oh, no, you can't—"

"Just kidding." Allison laughed. She was suddenly feeling very comfortable with Victoria Graham. "I have to say *Out of Africa*. With Meryl Streep and Robert Redford."

"I love that movie, too."

"Streep's so wonderful in any role, and she plays a very strong woman in that movie. And, well . . . Redford's very sexy. Even though he's older in it." Allison cringed, thinking of how that might sound to Graham. "Not that being old is bad."

"Please, Allison. I'm very aware of my age and I don't have any problem with it. In fact, I'm probably happier now than I've ever been. Well, maybe more at peace with myself is a better way to put it." Graham waved. "Enough of that. It's a wonderful question, isn't it? The movie thing, I mean. The answer says so much about you. And what's really interesting is that more often than not it's *men* who won't give you an answer at all. They get so defensive about it, too. Like the answer might be held against them in court or something so they aren't willing to open up."

"It is a good question." Allison was going to ask Christian the next time she saw him. The answer would be damn interesting now that she'd known him so long. "What does my answer tell you about me?"

"We'll talk about that next time. But right now let's get to the real reason I asked you to come see me today."

"Okay." Graham had called a week ago out of the blue—they'd never even spoken before. Allison had gone right to Christian to tell him about the call. He'd seemed a little surprised, but agreed that if Graham wanted to see her, she had to go. "What did you want to talk about?"

Graham gazed across the desk. "You."

"What about me?"

"I told Christian before I agreed to sign off on MuPenn's investment into Everest's new fund that he had to come up with a succession plan."

"Why?" Allison asked. "He's only forty-three. He's got a lot of years left."

"I've known Christian for a while now, and I'm worried that he might be burning out on Everest, on the financial thing in general. It's like he needs a new challenge."

Allison wondered if Graham somehow knew how close Christian had come to being Jesse Wood's vice president. Figured he'd been so interested in doing that because he was getting tired of all the headaches involved with running Everest. That he wanted a new set of headaches because at least they would be *different* headaches. After all, he'd done just about all there was to do in the financial world. People like Christian were constantly looking for new challenges, she knew. New worlds to conquer. She'd probably be in the same boat soon.

"Even if he isn't burning out," Graham continued, "at a firm as big and important as Everest Capital, you need to have a succession plan in place in case something happens."

"You mean . . ."

"Right. If Christian gets hit by a bus on Park Avenue."

Allison smiled. "He's a pretty careful guy. And besides, she laughed, they don't run buses on Park Avenue."

Graham's expression turned grave. "When you're as important and rich as Christian Gillette, sometimes that bus will find you wherever you are. Doesn't hit you by accident."

Allison tried to seem shocked, but she knew Graham was right. Being wealthy and powerful automatically painted a bull's-eye on your back—for a lot of reasons. That had been drilled into her head at a young age.

Graham leaned forward and put her elbows on the desk. "When I told Christian he needed a succession plan, I told him I thought it should focus on you. I've been keeping an eye on you since you came to Everest. You've done a great job. You've done more deals than anyone other than Christian, and, thanks to your family, you've got all the right connections. I told Christian that he should name you vice chairman."

A thrill burst through Allison's body. Christian had actually mentioned that possibility a couple of years ago, when it seemed that Jesse Wood was going to name him vice president. When Wood had backed off on that, Christian had refocused on Everest, concentrating on raising the latest fund. Apparently less concerned about succession at the firm since he wasn't going into politics after all.

"Is that something you'd want?" Graham asked.

"Absolutely," Allison answered quickly and firmly. "I'd love to run Everest at some point. There are some things I'd change, too. Not that Christian's doing anything wrong," she added quickly.

"I'd like to see more women get shots at running these big leveraged-buyout firms," Graham continued. "It's still such a good old boy fraternity in your world right now. The great thing is, Christian's a lot more open-minded than most of the execs at the other big firms." Her eyes glistened. "I think he'll do it. I think he'll name you vice chairman."

"I'd love it." Allison spotted a picture on a credenza to the right of Graham's desk. A small three-by-five photograph of Graham sitting at a table with a man wearing a tux, both of them leaning toward each other so their cheeks were almost touching. It was the only picture of Graham Allison had seen in the entire office. And it was half-hidden behind a small plant. "I really would," she said, rising from her chair.

"Let me ask you a question." Graham watched Allison walk to the credenza and pick up the frame. "This falling-out with your family. Does that mean you're out of the will?"

Allison didn't know which answer Graham wanted, but there was no reason to try to hide anything. Graham would be able to check out her story. People like Victoria Graham had connections everywhere. "I'm out of the estate, have been for two years," Allison said wryly as she looked at the man in the picture. He seemed familiar but she couldn't place him. "I need this job."

Graham clapped loudly. "Good." Her expression turned serious, the same way it had when they'd started talking about why Everest needed a succession plan. "Now we can get down to why I *really* called you over here today."

"Who is this?" Allison asked, pointing at the picture.

Graham gave her a forced smile. "A friend."

There was more to it than that, much more. Allison had known Victoria Graham for only a little while now, but she could already tell that there was probably an entire novel behind that forced smile. "I recognize him," she said loudly. "That's Lloyd Dorsey. The senator from Texas."

Graham nodded slowly. "Yes, it is."

Allison hesitated, wondering if she should be so forward as to ask. It would be a risk, but sometimes you built bridges much faster by taking risks. And Victoria Graham certainly seemed like the type of woman who respected directness. "Is Senator Dorsey the real reason you never got married?"

7

THEY CALLED THEMSELVES Los Secretos Seis. The Secret Six.

If anyone inside the Party loyal to the regime ever found out about them and their objectives, they'd be executed. Tortured first, so the authorities could learn as much as possible about what they were trying to do and whom they were trying to do it with, then murdered. Probably hung in a filthy, remote cell at one of the worst prisons—after being slowly castrated with a dull penknife—then buried in some mass, unmarked grave deep in the rain forest up in the mountains on the eastern end of the island. Where their remains would be found thousands of years from now by archaeologists of some future civilization who could offer only scant conjecture as to what might have happened to them.

The worst part was that their families would be kidnapped and tortured, too. The six men understood the risks going in. If they were caught and executed, so be it. A horrible outcome—however, that was the risk they ran. But their wives and children had no idea what was going on. No secret information about the inner workings or connections of the Six—no idea that the group even existed. However, the authorities wouldn't look at it that way. They'd assume the families knew something—that at least the wives did. So, of course, they'd torture the children in front of the mothers for maximum effect, to withdraw every shred of information possible—whatever the women made up as they begged for mercy and the lives of their offspring.

Still, the men were committed to their objective—freedom for Cuba and its people. Cuba had been operating in the dark ages of oppression for too long. It was time for it to come into the light. If sacrifices had to be made, so be it. If it got really dicey, they'd do their best to get their families out. They had assurances from their benefactors in the United States that their escapes could quickly be arranged. That choppers could get to pre-agreed remote locations on the island an hour after the coded SOS had been received. That there were ships out in the Gulf to support the rescues.

Which didn't mean they weren't scared to death and didn't take every precaution they could think of to keep their actions veiled. Going so far as to arrange meetings by means of placing used paper napkins in different sections of one of Havana's parks. The napkins were made to look like nothing but blown trash, but they were hung on specific branches of specific shrubs as code for dates and places of meetings. The men never got together in public, either, unless it involved a social function they would typically attend. A function authorities might consider it unusual if the men *didn't* attend. They also made certain their wives and children didn't become friends or acquaintances with the other wives and children. Made sure they never communicated unless it was a passing conversation at one of the functions.

Now the six men sat around a crude wooden table in the dingy basement of a cramped two-bedroom home in a lower-middle-class section of the city, conducting business by candlelight. The home had no running water and no electricity, but it was still coveted like another child by the family who lived here. One of the men in the group, a highly respected attorney at the Ministry of Justice who had midlevel connections within the government's housing department, had arranged for the destitute family who had been living on the street to move into it a year ago. After making *absolutely* certain that his connection at the housing department had no ties whatsoever to the regime's counterintelligence groups—the General Directorate for State Security or the D-VI inside the FAR. The connection at the housing department had enabled the family to skip over many others in the queue in return for just $5 U.S.— which he thought was an incredibly generous gesture by the attorney. Thankfully, the connection never dug for the hidden agenda behind the generosity.

The Secret Six needed places to meet and this house served as one of them. That was the attorney's real agenda, the real reason for getting the family in. He was glad to do a good deed, but the group had to have safe houses in which to conduct business. The state would never think of looking for treasonous activities of the upper-middle class here. Even if they did, the mother was so indebted to them they knew she would never give them away.

"What's the update, señor?" the attorney who had arranged for the house asked. They never addressed each other as anything but *señor* in these meetings. Just in case someone was listening. "What is our contact saying?"

Nelson Padilla took a long puff off his cigar, tapped the ash onto the basement's dirt floor, and leaned away from the table, clasping his hands at the back of his head as he blew a huge cloud of sweet-smelling smoke into the air above him. He was thinking about that night three months ago when his Chrysler had slammed into Gustavo Cruz's cow. How he had learned so much that night and how far the Secret Six had come since then.

Padilla had waited an hour in the main house of the ranch Cruz ran for General Delgado to return. Sat in the living room on an old couch opposite Cruz, who was sitting in a wooden chair, handcuffed and watched carefully by the three FAR officers—one with his pistol drawn. Padilla remembered the way Cruz had been slumped over, despondent, almost at the point of tears, as if waiting for his execution. And the way Cruz's expression had turned to absolute terror when Delgado had returned and ordered the officers and Padilla out of the room. Ordered the officers to drag Padilla's car out of the ditch and get him on his way, then to wait for him down on the road.

Twenty minutes later Padilla was driving home—after wiping the cow's blood from the windshield with a towel. Driving slowly because the transmission wouldn't go into any gear above first. It had taken him two hours to get home, but he'd never been happier to see his wife. They'd made love until three in the morning even though he had to perform that tonsillectomy a few hours later. Made love with mad passion, like teenagers. Like they hadn't done in years.

Remarkably, an army sergeant driving a tow truck had shown up at his door at 5 a.m. and taken the Chrysler away to be repaired, leaving the doctor a Ford station wagon to use in the meantime. He'd gotten to the hospital on time for the tonsillectomy, which had gone off without a hitch—despite just two hours of sleep. Magically, the sergeant had returned three days later with the Chrysler—in even better shape than before he'd hit the cow.

A week after the Chrysler had been returned, Delgado made contact about another rendezvous. Two days later they met in the darkness of a remote beach east of Havana. It was then that Padilla found out the fate of Cruz and Rodriguez. Cruz was now running both ranches, and Rodriguez—the little snitch wearing the oversize cowboy hat—was dead. Shot in the back of the head, his body lying at the bottom of a ravine a few miles from the Cruz ranch.

Delgado had explained all of that as if he were taking roll call—with no emotion whatsoever. Apparently not the least bit worried that Padilla would take the information to someone inside the Party and try to use it. Information that a high-ranking general was committing treason would have been prized by the state, and he would have been rewarded handsomely—if he could prove it was accurate. So Padilla very much appreciated the trust Delgado showed in sharing it. They were forming an alliance for the greater good of Cuba, and they needed to depend on each other at a high, high level if that was ever going to happen.

But Padilla also understood the reality of Delgado's willingness to give him the explanation. Ultimately, Padilla might risk as much by passing on the information as Delgado had giving it to him. Delgado might be able to turn the tables on Padilla—accuse Padilla right back of murdering the rancher—if Padilla tried to go to someone with the information. And Delgado probably had a good chance of making his accusation stick. Delgado commanded forty thousand troops and was a trusted member of the Party. Padilla, on the other hand, was just a doctor. One who nine months ago had come under intense scrutiny from the state for turning down a coveted position in one of the medical brigades—groups of physicians the Party sent to other Central and South American countries as emissaries to spread the word about the righteousness of Cuba's way of life. Padilla had begged off by citing the sickliness of his youngest child—which was documented—and the fact that he was doing so much other traveling for the state. His rejection had been accepted, but he knew he'd raised eyebrows downtown. Which was not a good thing. But if he'd been away on one of the medical brigade missions for several months, it would have seriously slowed the progress of the Secret Six because he was the lone contact between the Six and Delgado—as well as between the Six and the United States.

The news about Rodriguez's murder had shaken Padilla to his core because it made him understand the coldness of the man he was dealing with. But after he'd thought about it long and hard, he realized that Delgado had to be like that. It was the only way a man in charge of the western and central armies could act—and survive. He couldn't switch his coldness off and on; it had to be perpetually on. It was difficult for a doctor—a man dedicated to preserving life—to deal with Delgado, to try to make sense of the general's indifference to taking life—but there was no way the Secret Six could be successful without the military and, therefore, him. That was an undeniable truth that everyone inside the group agreed upon—as did their benefactors in the United States. Without that military connection, there would be no independence.

Padilla closed his eyes and inhaled deeply, not ready to answer the attorney's question yet despite the impatience he sensed building around the table. He wanted a few more puffs first. He'd never smoked cigars before the night he'd hit Gustavo Cruz's cow—now he did several times a week. The same brand Delgado smoked—a Dominican, because no one with any love of the old days—before Castro—would smoke a Cuban cigar, Delgado had explained. As a doctor Padilla knew better than most how bad cigars were for the lungs; he'd seen the damage they caused on so many X-rays. But there was something about the general that made Padilla want to emulate him in every way. Something about the way the general carried himself, how he was like ice when it came to tough decisions, how he was so effortlessly in charge of situations, how he had no compassion whatsoever for Rodriguez. Delgado's lack of emotion flew in the face of everything Padilla had ever believed in, was diametrically opposed to the way he'd lived his entire life. But it dawned on Padilla that caring and gentleness didn't have much chance of emancipating a nation. It had also dawned on him that he might be at the very core of a movement that could in the end bring a new, much better way of life to millions of people who'd never known it. But that the means to achieving those lofty goals might well involve a terrible level of brutality in the interim.

Over the last three months Padilla had accepted that awful reality and that he might even be a conduit to it in the short term. He'd taken a number of psychology courses at medical school in Toronto, and he was aware that his temporary change of attitude was manifesting itself in his daily routine in an increasing number of ways. Smoking cigars; eating foods that tasted good as opposed to being healthy for him; being shorter and stricter with nurses at the hospital and his children at home; asking Delgado to get him a gun at their last clandestine meeting; frequently demanding sex from his wife—once a few weeks ago even forcing her to have it with him when she'd said no at first.

Padilla's eyes narrowed, thinking about the intensity of that encounter. How his wife had actually fought him for a few moments as he'd held her down and pulled her clothes off—the first time that had ever happened in their seventeen-year marriage. How she'd admitted to him afterward as they lay wrapped in each other's arms that she hadn't been so aroused in years.

"Señor, will you please—"

"I'm sorry for taking so long, gentlemen," Padilla interrupted the attorney, pulling the cigar from his mouth. "I've been collecting my thoughts." He leaned forward, put his arms on the scarred table, and looked each of them squarely in the eye in turn: the deputy minister of foreign investment and economic development just to his left; the number four man at the Ministry of Science and Technology next to him; the attorney at the other end of the table who had been at the Ministry of Justice for twenty years; the deputy minister of agriculture to the attorney's left; and, directly to Padilla's right, the number three executive at the Central Bank of Cuba, who was also a former executive of the country's cartography company—a company owned and run by the army so that no military installations on the island ever made it onto a map of Cuba. "Forgive me, I have much to tell you about my recent trip."

The other men around the table nodded to each other expectantly.

Padilla had just returned yesterday from a weeklong trip to the United States, where he'd been a guest observer at eleven operations performed at Lenox Hill hospital in Manhattan. The operations had ranged from a triple-bypass procedure to brain surgery. It had been an intense schedule, but he'd still managed to slip away to meet his contacts twice. The primary reason he was a member of the Secret Six was because he was a doctor—he couldn't add much to what they were going to do after the Incursion, as they were calling it, but being a doctor allowed him to travel to and from the United States frequently. Which was invaluable to the group at this stage because it enabled them to keep in frequent touch with their U.S. intelligence contacts without having to use phones or e-mail, which could easily have been traced.

Despite the official embargo on products and services between the two countries, the United States wanted to be able to demonstrate to the rest of the world that it wasn't shirking its responsibility, as a superpower, to keep underprivileged nations up to speed on the latest medical procedures and technologies. So they allowed Padilla—and other Cuban physicians—to travel to the United States often. And Cuba had a history of being one of the most advanced Central and South American nations when it came to medicine—despite the country's other terrible problems—so Castro had been lenient in terms of allowing his doctors to travel to the United States.

"I had a very good meeting with our backers while I was in the United States," Padilla continued. "The support for us is very strong."

"What does *very strong* mean exactly?" the deputy minister of agriculture asked anxiously. "I'm still suspicious of these people." He looked around the table. "I think I have good reason to be; I think we all have good reason to be. Just look at history."

"It means," Padilla answered quickly and strongly, "that our efforts have been recognized at the highest levels of the United States government."

"Is it a firm commitment?" the deputy minister pushed. "I need to know that there are ships off our beaches with helicopters on them so I can get my wife and children out if I need to."

"They've chosen us, *only us,*" Padilla answered. "They will not back any of the other groups we believe are operating in the city." He watched the men around the table nod and smile. Suddenly the huge risks seemed worth it. They were helping Cuba—and themselves. In the island's post-Communist world they would certainly have esteemed status with President Wood's government and would be showered with significant economic favors from their American benefactors. "That's what my contact told me on my recent trip, señor."

"This is very good," the man from the Ministry of Science and Technology spoke up. His brother was a senior executive at Cuba's state oil company and would be the logical choice to become its CEO after the Incursion. The family would stand to make a great deal of money when the company was privatized. "But there is risk to that decision, too," he continued. "More eyes will be upon us, more people will know about us in the U.S. Because of that there is a greater chance now that we may be discovered by the spies in Washington . . . and here. We must be even more careful now."

Padilla shook his head. "I'm not saying we shouldn't continue to be as careful as possible, but I don't believe that the risk of spies in Washington uncovering our plans is as great as you may think."

"Why?"

"My contact tells me that President Wood is almost as afraid of being discovered as we are. For different reasons, of course. Us for our personal necks," Padilla said, bringing the hand holding the cigar ceremoniously across his throat, "him for his political neck. Apparently, he thinks if it comes out that he is supporting us in any way, economically, militarily, even just with advisers, the world will line up against him. So his people are going to be very quiet about this. Even after the Incursion."

"Does this mean that the help they give us will be enough?" the deputy minister of foreign investment asked, concern obvious in the lines on his forehead.

"It will be enough, but they are going to make sure we"—Padilla gestured around the table—"have the right stuff," he said, smiling, using the term his contact had used. One he knew Americans had loved since the early space-exploration days of John Glenn. He'd done his homework on America. "I will be having a preliminary meeting with one of their senior advisers in the United States very soon. If that goes well, that man will come here to Cuba to meet with all of us. Secretly, of course. Then the help will be plenty enough."

"Are you sure you weren't being followed when you met your contact in New York?" the attorney asked.

When Padilla traveled in the United States—anywhere, really—he was aware of being watched, but the surveillance was sporadic and easy to evade. He'd been exposed to it long enough now that it was easy to escape their eyes without seeming as if he were trying to. "Positive."

"Are you certain that our contacts in Washington know who we are allied with in the military?" the executive from the Central Bank of Cuba asked.

"Absolutely."

"Are we sure he's the right person?" the deputy minister of agriculture wanted to know.

There couldn't be a better officer in the FAR to be allied with than General Delgado, Padilla believed. His contacts in the United States couldn't agree more. Over the last several months they'd met with the general and one of his direct reports clandestinely on a farm outside

Havana—where Delgado had been coming from the night Padilla had hit the cow. But the men sitting around the table wouldn't understand how strong a partner the general was because they'd never met Delgado.

Suddenly the gravity of his situation hit Padilla, as it never had before. He was the conduit for *everything*. For the Six's contact with the United States and their contact with the FAR. If anything happened to him or Delgado, the Incursion would fail, or at least suffer a major setback that would delay it for years. For now, he was the key.

"We couldn't have a better partner," Padilla said confidently.

"Why?"

"He's in charge of a great many troops and has a senior level connection in the air force, which includes the Mi-8 helicopters. Once he's firmly in control, our contacts in the U.S. are convinced that the other six thousand Cuban troops will fall right into line."

"How do we know he won't get drunk with power once he's in charge?" the bank executive asked, aggravated. "Like all these military people do."

"He won't."

"But how do you know?"

"I just do."

"Perhaps we should all meet with him once," the attorney suggested.

Padilla shook his head. "No, he won't do that."

"Well, then maybe we should find someone else to—"

"Here's the way the general looks at this thing," Padilla cut in, intent on shutting this discussion down quickly. He didn't want the delicate balance of it all to spin out of control thanks to a snowball effect suddenly grabbing the group. "The way he looks at life, really. He believes that three people can keep a secret"—Padilla took a puff off the cigar—"as long as two of them are dead." That had been one of the first things Delgado had said in their initial meeting, and the hush in the room told him that it was having the same effect on the other men around the table as it had on him when Delgado had said it. The only sound was the faint cry of a baby upstairs. "He means it, too. Now, do you really want to meet him?"

"How did you meet this military officer?" the attorney finally asked.

"Four months ago a call came into the hospital late one night while I was on duty in the emergency room. A nurse took the call and told me that the man had demanded to speak to me immediately. When she informed him that I was in surgery, he said he didn't care. He told her there would be trouble for her if she didn't get me immediately. Then he told her he knew where her husband worked and the names of her children. Understandably, she was quite upset." Padilla had originally believed that his introduction to Delgado was a fluke, but he wasn't so certain anymore—which was the only thing that made him even the slightest bit suspicious of the general. "So I talked to the man. He told me his child was ill and that there was a jeep waiting for me outside that would bring me to his villa immediately. He then threatened me, too. I didn't want any part of that, especially when it became clear to me that he was a senior FAR officer."

The men around the table nodded in agreement. They all held senior posts inside the government, but even they weren't immune to the whims of their superiors or the FAR. Fear was a common denominator in Cuba.

"I was the only doctor in the emergency room at that point," Padilla continued, "but I knew my replacement would be there soon. So I got in the jeep and went with the lieutenant. The man on the phone turned out to be the general we are now in business with."

"Quite a coincidence," the attorney said. "Don't you think?"

"Perhaps, but his young son was actually very sick."

"Did he say anything to you about us that night?"

"No. It was a week later when he contacted me."

"Did he explain why he decided to contact you a week later?"

Padilla eyed the attorney. He was a small man, like Rodriguez the little rancher, with slicked-back silver hair. Padilla had always figured that if it ever turned out there was a traitor within the group, it was going to be the attorney. Padilla wasn't sure if he felt that way because the attorney was constantly asking lots of questions, or because he'd gotten an odd feeling about the little man the first time they'd met. The attorney had been brought to the group by the deputy minister of agriculture, who literally vouched for his loyalty on a Bible—and every man in the group was Catholic. Still, Padilla had wondered from the get-go about him. The attorney was smart and would play a vital role in the government if the Incursion was successful—as minister of justice, or whatever the successor organization was called. But for Padilla, there was always that doubt. Of course, it was too late to kick him out now, and the other men seemed to like him *because* he asked so many questions.

"No."

"Did you ask?"

"No." Padilla's temperature spiked when the attorney raised his hands and looked up to the ceiling, as if to say, "Why the hell not?" "Look, he did ask me when I was tending to his child if I had ever traveled to the United States. Asked if I was ever approached by people in that government when I told him I did travel there." Padilla took a puff off the cigar. "If you want my opinion, I think the connection was forged by people inside President Wood's government. I think the general we're talking about was already talking to his counterparts in the United States military and they knew about me. I think they put us together." He hesitated. "But I'm not sure."

The bank executive pointed at Padilla. "Do you know the name of this senior adviser who you're meeting with in the United States?"

"I do."

"Is he an important man in their country?"

Padilla nodded. "Yes." According to his contact in the States, you couldn't find anyone in the private sector more important than Christian Gillette.

8

"**WE SHOULD HAVE TAKEN** a helicopter," Quentin Stiles grumbled. "We'd be back in Washington by now, probably on the plane. Better than doing all this driving, that's for sure. Might have even convinced the pilot to go under the Key Bridge on his way to the airport, too. Now *that* would have been fun."

Christian glanced over at Stiles from the passenger seat. Stiles was behind the wheel of the Integra they'd rented at the airport after their short flight down to Reagan National from New York City this morning. "*Under* it?" The Key Bridge spanned the Potomac River from Rosslyn, Virginia, to Washington, D.C., right in front of Georgetown. It was a tall structure, but going under one of its six arches would still be risky as hell. Of course, that was Quentin. Into the extreme. Bungee jumping off cable cars in New Zealand, freestyle climbing in the Rockies, scuba diving with sharks. It was almost as if he had a death wish. They hadn't been able to get a key-man life insurance policy for him at Everest. He was the only managing partner who didn't have one. "Are you serious?"

Quentin nodded. "Yeah. I've done it once before. Got one of the navy flyboys to do it when I was in the Rangers. He could have gotten his ass kicked out of the service for it, but he said he'd always wanted to try it. It's a small fraternity of guys who've done it, and they all know who they are. Kind of a badge of honor to do it and get away with it, you know? Hell of a thrill, too, let me tell you. Looks like you're going to ram the damn bridge the whole way in, even when you're only a couple hundred feet away. Scares the crap out of everybody going across it, too, especially the pedestrians and the bikers." He laughed. "Should have seen the way the people scattered when we were about a hundred feet out."

"No commercial helicopter pilot's going to do that."

Quentin shot Christian an irritated look. "We were on our way to see the *president of the United States,* for crying out loud. I'm sure he could have arranged a military chopper if you'd asked him to. At least we could have gotten a limo," Quentin muttered.

"No. I told you, Jesse wanted us to be low-key about getting to Camp David." Normally they would have gotten a driver, but not this time. "He was very clear about that."

"Well, if you ask me, we were damn discreet. I just hope this rental car doesn't end up getting us killed. The steering on this thing stinks. I can barely keep it on the road going around some of these turns. Handles like a John Deere tractor."

"You're just too used to your high-performance cars. This is what most people deal with."

"If this is what most people deal with, then it's no wonder there are so many accidents."

Christian settled back into the seat. "Yeah, but this way we get to see more of the countryside, too." Camp David was eighty miles northwest of downtown Washington and Reagan National. This part of the twisting, turning drive back toward D.C. was through a remote rural area full of heavy woods. "It's a beautiful day. The sun is shining, the birds are singing." They had the windows down and Christian took a deep breath of the fresh spring air whipping through the car. The wind felt good in his face as he pulled off his tie and tossed it in the back. "If we'd taken a chopper out to Camp David, we'd have blown right over all this," he said, gesturing at the trees towering above the roadway. "We would have missed the experience." Out of the corner of his eye he saw an odd look cross Quentin's face. Well, this would *really* get to him. "Learn to appreciate life, my man."

"Don't give me that." Stiles snorted. "This is all about your fear of flying in something that defies the laws of physics, not communing with nature." He checked his watch. "It's three o'clock," he announced loudly over the air swirling around them. "We're going to hit Washington right at rush hour, and that rush hour is worse than New York's. I know, I lived there. After that we'll be stuck on the damn runway for an hour with everyone and their brother trying to get out of the city."

"That's all right. It'll give us more time to talk. Seems like we don't get to do that enough anymore."

"Jesus, where's the take-no-prisoners guy I know? What did you do with Christian Gillette?"

"I'll be forty-four soon, Q-Dog." Christian had given Quentin the nickname only a few months ago, even though they'd known each other for years. He seemed to like it. At least, he hadn't asked Christian to stop using it. "I'm trying to enjoy life a little more. Trying to take a look at what's actually around me instead of always trying to see what's around the bend."

Quentin shut his eyes tightly for a second, as if he couldn't believe what he'd just heard. "I give this new you a few days . . . at most. You're addicted to the game, Chris. It's in your blood."

Years ago Christian's father had founded a successful West Coast investment bank. And Christian had been working on Wall Street or at Everest Capital since graduating from business school. Doing deals had been his gig for more than two decades.

"Yeah, well, I'm trying to slow down a little."

"You don't know *how* to slow down. And if you figured it out somehow, it would drive you nuts."

"You might be surprised. I've been giving this a lot of thought lately and—"

"What happened?" Quentin interrupted. "You read some article this morning on the plane down here about how in the end it all seems to go by so fast and it finally got to you? What were you reading, like, *Psychology Today*? Or maybe it was *Woman's Journal*."

"You got a problem with *Woman's Journal*?"

"Nope, as long as other people read it, not you. Do me a favor, stick to *BusinessWeek* and *Sports Illustrated*, will you?" Stiles checked the rearview mirror uneasily. "I don't like your being out here like this with just me. It's not safe. We should have at least one more of my guys with us."

Christian waved. "We're fine. Don't be so worried about everything anymore. You've gotta start living life."

Quentin slammed the steering wheel with his palm. "What the hell's going on with you? Is this that midlife-crisis thing? You gonna blow me away in a second and tell me you've shacked up with a twenty-five-year-old?"

Quentin was a pit bull. Once he sank his teeth into a bone, he didn't let go. But that was one of the things Christian respected about him, too—one of many. Stiles was the most loyal, trustworthy man he'd ever known. "Sure would sell a lot of newspapers if I did, huh?"

Stiles put his head back and broke into a loud laugh. "I guess it would."

Christian patted Quentin's shoulder. "You're a good man, pal. There's darn few of us left."

Stiles was a strapping African American who'd made it to partner at Everest Capital after a long, hard road. No Ivy League diplomas or summers on the Cape for him. He'd grown up in Harlem, raised by his grandmother—he'd never known his father, and his mother had died of an overdose when he was young. When he was eighteen, his grandmother had forced him to enlist in the army after a bullet in a gang war almost killed him. He'd kicked and screamed all the way down to the recruiting office in Times Square, but he'd done it. And now he credited that move—and his grandmother—with turning his life around, probably saving it.

Quentin quickly became a star in the Rangers, had been involved in several highly classified operations inside the Defense Intelligence Agency, and ultimately became a Secret Service agent. After a few years at the White House, he'd left government and gone into the private sector, founding his own company—QS Security. Rapidly developing an A-list clientele that included sports stars, actors, and wealthy families. At one point Christian had retained QS Security—which was how they'd met—and bought the company because he was so impressed, merging it into a larger Everest portfolio company. Then he'd made Quentin a partner at Everest.

"You can put your mind at ease," Christian said reassuringly, gazing down at a gin-clear mountain stream as they zipped across a narrow bridge. He spotted a guy fly-fishing downriver. He'd always wanted to try that. "I doubt I'll be taking up with any twenty-five-year-olds." He made a mental note to start a list of "things I want to try." Lately, he'd begun to realize how many of those things there were. "That would probably be a disaster."

"Have you thought about it?"

"*What?* No, of course not."

"A lot of guys our age do."

Christian glanced over at Quentin again. "Have you?"

"Maybe. I mean, it sounds fun, you know? But I think it's one of those things that's a total disappointment when you actually do it. For both people." Quentin asked, "What about Allison? You two have been circling around each other like the earth and the moon for a long time. But you haven't talked much about her lately."

"Because I can't figure out which one of us is the moon and which one is the earth."

"What does that—"

"Hey, you're the one who's always telling me not to go there," Christian pointed out. "That I can't dip my pen in the company ink and expect to keep the fact that we're seeing each other under wraps for very long."

"I know, I know." Quentin guided the car through a sharp turn. The trees and bushes were heavy on both sides. They hadn't passed a car coming the other way in a while. "She really cares about you."

"What do you mean?"

"Exactly what I said, she really cares about you. Not just as a friend, either."

Quentin and Allison had known each other ever since she'd come to Everest, and it hadn't been any secret among the three of them that she wanted a deeper relationship with Christian. Still, it seemed like an odd thing for Quentin to say, if only because it was so obvious. "Why'd you say it?"

Quentin hesitated for a moment. "I took her out for drinks last week, after she closed that deal on the West Coast. You were in Europe."

"She told me you two went out." That wasn't unusual. Quentin and Allison had gotten to be good friends over the last few years. "So?"

"She had a whole bottle of champagne herself, then a couple of martinis."

She hadn't told Christian that. "And?"

"That woman's in love with you, pal. She started to unload on me after she finished the champagne. She was convinced you two were going to get together a couple of years ago, when we thought you were going to be Jesse Wood's VP. She wanted you to do that with him so badly because you kept telling her that then you wouldn't have to worry about the fact that you were both at Everest. She was really disappointed when it didn't happen, especially because you threw yourself into raising the last fund so hard and she said you two have kind of drifted apart. Told me you two haven't been out in a long time. At least, not by yourselves."

That was true, but it wasn't a conscious thing on Christian's part. It wasn't because he was avoiding her or dating anyone else. He'd just been busy, constantly traveling, constantly meeting with investors to raise the massive $25 billion pool of equity.

"She was talking about how much you two have in common on the family side," Quentin continued. "You know, now that her family doesn't talk to her anymore. She was thinking that might make you guys even tighter."

Christian's father, Clayton, had sold his investment bank to a New York firm for $100 million some years ago, then gone into politics. Ultimately becoming a U.S. senator—mentioned early and often as a possible presidential candidate—before dying in a small-plane crash on takeoff from Orange County Airport. Immediately after the crash, Christian had been cut off completely from the family by Clayton's wife, Lana. Christian was Clayton's son by another woman, a woman Clayton had had an affair with during his marriage to Lana. Something Christian hadn't known until he was a teenager. Until one night Lana had too much to drink and decided to blurt it all out.

Clayton had died right after Christian graduated from college, and Christian had been forced to ride freight trains home to California. Lana had closed his checking account and shut off his credit cards only hours after the crash, then refused to send him a dime. And no one else in the family would return his calls.

Christian hadn't spoken to his family in a long time. Now Allison was in the same boat.

"Allison met with Victoria Graham this morning," Christian said.

Quentin looked over, obviously surprised. "That tough old bird at MuPenn?"

"Yup."

"I thought you handled her seven-hundred-fifty-million-dollar investment by yourself."

"*She* called Allison. Didn't tell me she was going to, either. Allison came to me right after she hung up with Ms. Graham to let me know."

"Do you know why Ms. Graham called Allison?"

Christian wouldn't have told the other Everest partners anything about this, at least at this point, but it was different with Quentin. He knew if he told Quentin not to say anything, he could count on him to keep it completely to himself. You didn't find many people like that in life, even when they were your best friend. Most human beings *had* to tell *somebody*, and a lot of times telling that one somebody was enough to blow everything. "When I met with Ms. Graham about MuPenn's investment in our fund, she told me I needed to start thinking about a succession plan. She didn't make the investment contingent on having a plan in place, but she made me promise I'd have it ready to go soon."

"And?"

"And she wants Allison in that plan. In fact, she told me I ought to name Allison vice chairman of Everest. So Allison would be the person who takes over when I leave, or if anything happens to me. Said she'd been watching Allison's career develop at Everest and thought she was the best choice. I think that's why she asked Allison over to her office today, to tell her that." He grinned, thinking about Allison's reaction to the reptiles in Graham's office. Ally wasn't a big fan of snakes.

Quentin's face coiled into an irritated grimace. "Shouldn't Ms. Graham let *you* decide if you're going to name Allison vice chairman? And let *you* tell Allison what's going on?"

"Yeah," Christian admitted, "she should. But that's Victoria Graham for you. She didn't get where she's gotten by waiting around."

Early on as chairman of Everest, Christian would have forbidden Allison to meet with Graham. He would have fought being bulldozed like that on principle alone. But, over the years, he'd grown confident in his position. He'd learned when to pick his battles, and this wasn't one of those times. The thing was, he'd already been planning to make Allison vice chairman anyway. But he'd gotten sidetracked raising the fund after Jesse had named someone else as his VP. "Ms. Graham's been a good friend of the firm. Besides, I was going to name Allison vice chairman anyway."

Quentin snapped his fingers. "I knew it. I knew you were thinking about doing that. I can read your mind."

"Doesn't bother you, does it?"

"No way," Quentin said firmly. "Might bother a couple of the other managing partners, but I'm never going to run Everest. I don't have the connections Allison does, which is what you really need to be on the top rung of a firm like ours." He hesitated. "Plus, I've already way overshot where I thought I'd ever be in life. This is a long way from my gang days in Harlem. I've got you to thank for a lot of that."

Quentin was such a good man. And it was great—therapeutic, in fact—to be able to talk to him about what was going on at Everest and know he'd never tell anybody. "Your grandmother's more responsible than me," Christian said. "Without her, I have a feeling you and I never would have met. By the way, I'm going to announce the Laurel Energy distributions tomorrow." What each person at the firm received as a share of the profits on sold deals was up to Christian and Christian alone. No committees, no input from anyone else, just him.

"I heard about that," Quentin said, checking the rearview mirror. Eyeing a red sports car that had raced up on their tail.

"Nine hundred million is a lot to divvy up." But Christian had still been forced to make some tough decisions regarding a few people who weren't going to be happy tomorrow.

"I can't even imagine."

Christian waited for the obvious question: What's my share? But, of course, that question didn't come. Others would have asked it right away—but not Quentin. "I'm going to take a hundred of it and make some donations." Christian was on the board of one of the biggest hospitals in Manhattan, and they'd get the lion's share of that. "And I'm going to hold back another two hundred million for working capital." Life in the business world had taught him to always have reserves. He snuck a look at Quentin. He wanted to see the reaction to what he was about to say. "I'm giving you forty million of it."

Quentin stared blankly at the road ahead for a few moments, then shrugged. As if he didn't know what else to do. "Jesus Christ," he whispered, swallowing hard. "I . . . I . . ." His voice trailed off.

"Never seen you at a loss for words before." Christian laughed as the red sports car—an old Austin-Healey—buzzed past them on a short straightaway. The top was down, but he still couldn't see much of the driver. It looked like a young kid, but whoever it was wore a baseball cap and sunglasses so it was hard to tell. "Never."

"You're right, I don't know what to say. Except thanks."

"You deserve it." Christian watched the sports car disappear around the curve ahead. The car was flying. "I'm going to make sure most of the lower-level people make out well, too." He grinned to himself, thinking about calling Debbie—his executive assistant—into his office tomorrow morning to tell her she was going to get a check for a million dollars. He couldn't wait. She'd been loyal to him for a long time.

"I agree completely." Quentin's voice was still hoarse.

"Good. So, what's going on with you these days?" Christian asked. That was another good thing about their relationship. They both took a sincere interest in the other's life. "Is there a future Mrs. Stiles on the horizon? We haven't talked much about your love life lately."

"Not even a blip on the radar." Quentin laughed. "I'm having way too much fun." He jerked the steering wheel to the left, barely avoiding a squirrel that had scampered a few feet out onto the roadway, then frozen. "How did your meeting with Jesse go?" he asked when he'd brought the car back into the right lane. Quentin never wanted to talk much about the women he was dating.

"Fine."

"Anything you can tell me?"

"All of this has to stay *just* between us, pal." Christian knew he didn't really need to say it about this—Quentin would assume it in this case. Still, it made him feel better after he had. "President Wood asked me to help him with a very sensitive project related to Cuba."

"Really? That sounds pretty intense."

"I'll give you the full download later, but you're going to help me get a few places without anyone knowing. You're also going to help a few other people get where they're going. Even though the president doesn't know it yet, you're going to have full discretion over a couple of pieces of this project. If that doesn't work for Jesse, I won't help him on this thing."

"That's all right up my power alley, my man," Quentin said, smiling.

Quentin was smiling now, but he wasn't going to like this next nugget, Christian knew. "You're going to have to do the background-check thing." Predictably the smile evaporated.

"*What?* No way. They don't need to—"

"President's orders."

"Hey, I've been in the DIA, the Secret Service, the—"

"Then presumably, there won't be a problem." Christian had known this was going to be a big issue. "Humor me, okay? Jesse said they'd streamline it for you. No more than a day in Virginia, but he needs that."

"Okay, okay." Quentin held up one hand and nodded deferentially. "Was it tough to be friendly to him? I mean, you would have been vice president if he hadn't changed his mind at the last second. And, hell, if you hadn't gotten that video of him from those guys in Maine, he never would have been elected. You saved his ass, then he dumped you. Doesn't that still piss you off?"

Jesse Wood had been a professional tennis star in the early eighties, following his hero, Arthur Ashe, into a lily-white world and winning the U.S. Open and Wimbledon a couple of times. But he'd never used his victories as a platform for his political views, and everyone loved him, especially when he beat a Russian in the finals at Flushing Meadows one year—at the height of the Cold War. The win had ranked right up there with the U.S. hockey team's victory over the Russians in the semis of the 1980 Olympic hockey tournament. After his tennis days were over, Jesse had become a lawyer, then a senator—from New York—with backing from a powerful group of ex–Black Panthers who had a strict agenda for him to follow after he won election to the White House.

They'd also gotten possession of a video clip of Jesse bashing white voters—when he didn't know he was on camera. A clip that would have destroyed him if the public had ever seen it. Christian had managed to get that clip—freeing Jesse from the puppet strings. One of the first things Jesse had done after he was out from under the group's influence was to replace Christian as his running mate.

Christian could understand why Quentin might think he'd be angry, but he wasn't. "No, it doesn't really bother me."

"*Oh, come on.* I mean you—"

"Here's why. Let's say we hadn't gotten that clip, and I had been Jesse's VP. The guys who were backing Jesse didn't really want me for the long term. They were going to have me implicated in some trumped-up scandal in the second term. Which we ultimately found out."

"Well, you don't know if—"

"They just wanted to use me to get Jesse elected, wanted me to bring the white vote in. Then they wanted me out. They didn't want any chance of me being president after Jesse's second term. I wasn't really Jesse's choice, so I can't fault him for wanting someone else." All that sounded good, but not a day had passed that Christian hadn't wished he'd been on the ticket. Not for the personal glory, he didn't care about that. But it would have brought closure for him as far as his father's death went. It would have fulfilled a dream.

Quentin snorted. "I don't know, pal. Did he at least apologize?"

"He's the president of the United States. He doesn't apologize."

They blew past a small country store set back from the road, then came around a sharp curve and saw a man up ahead wearing a yellow hard hat and an orange vest. He was holding a stop sign and waving for them to slow down.

Quentin put down his window as they reached the man. "What's the problem?"

The man leaned over so he was on eye level. "Sorry, guys, but we've got a tree down just around this next bend," he explained, gesturing ahead. "I can't let you through right now. It'll be about five, maybe ten minutes."

Christian touched Quentin's shoulder. "Let's go back to that store we just passed and get something to drink."

"Yeah, sure." Quentin turned the car around and headed back the way they'd come. "Pretty deserted out here," he observed, looking around as they rolled into the gravel parking lot. The store seemed like an oasis in the forest. "Son of a bitch."

"What?"

Quentin pointed. The driver of the Austin-Healey had stopped at the store, too. "I ought to go over there and give that kid a scare. He was riding my ass before he passed us."

"Don't go looking for trouble," Christian pleaded, reaching for the door handle. That was the last thing they needed. "Please."

"Damn!"

Christian was about to get out of the car, but he recognized that tone in Quentin's voice: A pretty woman was somewhere in the vicinity. His eyes flashed back toward the Austin-Healey. The driver had climbed out of the car and taken off the baseball cap and sunglasses. He stared for a few moments, transfixed by the beautiful young woman standing beside the car. She had short, dark hair and wore a bright orange tube top above a white miniskirt. He watched her end a call on her cell phone, then toss it back into the car.

"I think I will go over there and talk to her about her driving," Quentin said with a grin, hopping out of the Integra and jogging across the gravel before Christian could stop him.

"Hey!" Christian called over the roof of the car, rising up out of his side. *"Hey!"* But it was too late. The woman was already laughing at Quentin's opening line—he was good with those. You had to act fast when Quentin was around, he thought to himself, heading for the store.

As Christian was coming back out a few minutes later, he almost ran into the young woman coming in. "Sorry." She was even prettier up close. And she seemed vaguely familiar, though he couldn't place her.

"My fault," she answered politely, stepping aside so he could come out onto the old covered porch that spanned the front of the building.

"No, no." Christian stepped back and held the door. "You first."

"Thanks." She give him a sweet smile and touched his arm as she moved past.

He watched her for a few moments as she headed toward the refrigerator cases in the back, admiring the way the white miniskirt swayed back and forth high on the backs of her toned, tanned thighs. He couldn't tell how old she was—she could be anywhere from twenty to thirty. If he had to guess, he'd say younger—twenty-two to twenty-three—but he'd noticed a hard edge hiding in those eyes despite the sweet smile. He wondered if she'd been through something awful somewhere along the way.

He took a step back into the store as she disappeared behind a tall display of soft drinks at the end of the last aisle. The wooden floor creaked under his weight and he glanced up at the elderly woman sitting behind the old manual cash register. She was glaring back, a mean expression on her face. He gave her a quick smile, turned around, and headed out into the sunlight, aware of what she was thinking. Too young for him and he shouldn't be ogling her.

Quentin was standing beside the open driver's-side door of the Integra, one foot up on the floor beside the seat, one arm resting on the top of the door.

"Here." Christian tossed him a cold bottle of Yoo-Hoo, then cracked a Mountain Dew for himself as he headed toward the passenger side. Quentin loved Yoo-Hoo. "Don't say I never gave you anything."

Quentin grinned. "Yeah, I mean, after all, forty million isn't what it used to be." He slipped in behind the wheel, shut the door, opened the bottle, and chugged the chocolate drink. "Damn, that's good."

Christian glanced up at the porch of the store as he eased into the Integra and took a couple of sips of Mountain Dew. The young woman was just coming through the front door. "How old do you think she is?"

Quentin shoved the empty bottle beneath the seat. "Mmm, twenty-three, twenty-four. But I'm bad at guessing ages these days. I'm usually way over or way under, and I don't know—" He stopped short, his eyes darting to Christian's. *"I knew it!"*

"What are you talking about? Knew *what?*"

"You're thinking about dating a younger woman."

"That's ridiculous. I just wanted to see if you thought she was the same age I did. I'm getting bad at guessing ages, too." Christian watched the woman bounce lightly down the steps and head toward the Austin-Healey. She was carrying a beer bottle. "That's all."

"Bull," Quentin retorted. "Look at you, you can't take your eyes off her."

"So what? She's pretty. Just because I'm looking at her doesn't mean I want to date her." Christian grinned. "And I'm envious. Must be awesome to be that carefree. Look at her, she's drinking a beer and driving a sports car on a beautiful spring afternoon. She doesn't have a care in the world."

"She'll have a lot to care about if she gets pulled over drinking that beer."

"Still. It must be nice not to have to worry about doing something like that. If she gets pulled over, she gets pulled over. Might lose her license for a while, but that's it. Me? Jesus, I don't even want to think about it."

Quentin nodded, understanding. "You're feeling old, Chris. That's what all this is about. The living-in-the-moment attitude, the not caring that Jesse dumped you as VP, the younger women. You want to feel young again. And who could blame you? Look at all the pressure you deal with. Any normal person would crack under it. You don't because mentally you're very tough, but even tough people need escapes sometimes."

Christian gazed at the young woman as she stood next to her sports car sipping from the can. "Come on," he urged. Maybe Quentin was right. Suddenly he was so tempted to go back into that store and get a beer for himself. "Let's get out of here."

The young woman waved as they rolled past, giving Christian a nice smile. He waved back, sad in a way that he'd been put off by the look the old lady behind the cash register had given him. It sounded crazy, but he felt that he might have made a connection with the young woman. There was something in the way she'd looked at him as he held the door for her that told him. He wished he'd at least found out her name.

"Jesus Christ! What the—"

Christian's eyes snapped away from the young woman as Quentin shouted and slammed on the brakes. The shoulder strap restrained Christian, but instinctively he reached out and braced himself against the dashboard just as a black sedan roared in front of them, missing the Integra by inches. As it came to a grinding halt in a cloud of dust in front of the store, four men jumped out.

Out of the corner of his eye Christian saw a flash of orange and white rush past his door. It was the young woman and she was running scared. The men were after her for some reason, he knew that right away. He grabbed the buckle of the seat belt and wrenched it back, shoved the door open with his shoulder, scrambled out of the car, and sprinted after her.

"Christian, don't!"

But he ignored Quentin's warning shout. He glanced over his shoulder as the woman reached the tree line and disappeared into the forest. Two of the men were coming after him, the other two were headed toward the Integra, toward Quentin, who was climbing out of the driver's side.

Christian hurtled into the brush after the young woman, holding his arms up as a shield against the low-hanging branches and thick sticker bushes. Following the sounds of her crashing over the dead, dry leaves covering the forest floor ahead of him. He caught glimpses of her through the trees as he ran. Bursts of the orange top and the white skirt, in between branches and new leaves ripping against his fingers and across his eyes as he tried to see where he was going.

Then he heard crashing sounds behind him. The two men from the black sedan who hadn't gone after Quentin—had to be. He felt bad about leaving Quentin alone like that, but Quentin had a pretty good chance of winning a fight, even when it was two on one.

He was almost to her now, only a few feet behind her as he dodged trees like a slalom skier dodging gates. He could hear her breathing hard as she tried to sprint across the soft, leaf-covered ground. It was like trying to sprint across dry sand, and it was sucking the energy out of her fast. Him, too.

Finally, he got to her. He grabbed her wrist and spun her around. Her hair was covered with shredded leaves and her face was scratched from the branches. "Why are those men after you?" Christian demanded in a low voice. He could still hear the pursuers' footsteps, but they were growing fainter, as if they'd lost the trail and were going off in a wrong direction.

"I don't know," she gasped. "I swear."

"Tell me."

She gazed up into his eyes. "I . . . I—"

"Tell me," Christian hissed. "I'll help you, but you have to tell me what's going on."

She put a hand to her chest, still trying to catch her breath. "All right, all right. I was having an affair with a guy in Washington. This morning his wife caught me in bed with him at the farm they own out here. She sent those guys after me." The young woman waved back in the direction of the store. "I thought I lost them, but obviously I didn't."

"The guy's wife must be pretty important if she can send four guys after you and you're that scared of them."

The young woman's eyes opened wide. "You got that right."

"Who is she?"

A frightened look spread across the young woman's face. "I can't tell you. I *really* can't," she repeated when she saw irritation in Christian's expression. "I—"

"Charlie, over here!"

In unison, Christian's and the young woman's eyes darted toward the sound of the voice. It was so close.

Christian grabbed the girl's wrist. *"Come on!"*

"**YOU KNOW,** Christian's handing out the Laurel Energy bonuses tomorrow."

Allison looked up from her computer. She'd been tapping out an e-mail to a lawyer she didn't care for, so it was a good time to take a break. Her tone was starting to get confrontational, which was the sinister part of e-mail—sometimes you wrote things you wished you hadn't because it was so much easier when you didn't have to say it to someone's face. So she always took Christian's advice and reread her e-mails at least three times before sending them. "I do know, but how did you find out?" Actually, Allison hadn't known that tomorrow was going to be the day. She knew it was going to be sometime soon, but she didn't have specifics. Here was another example of how she and Christian weren't as close as they used to be. Not too long ago she would have known that tomorrow was going to be the day before anyone else in the firm.

"Somebody found a copy of a memo in a trash can," Sherry Demille explained.

Sherry was an associate at Everest who worked almost exclusively with Allison—Allison had hired her away from another Manhattan investment firm a year ago. Sherry was only twenty-five, but she and Allison had become good friends despite the eight-year age difference. Sherry was big-boned but always managed to use just the right amount of makeup and wore clothes that accentuated her long legs and downplayed her wide shoulders and high waist. She had long, dark hair and a round face she broke up by wearing glasses she didn't really need.

"Somebody?" Allison asked in a leading tone.

Sherry held her hands up. "It wasn't me. I swear."

"Who was it?" Allison could see Sherry struggling, wanting to keep her source confidential but not wanting to aggravate her mentor. "Fine, you don't have to tell me. It doesn't matter anyway."

"When did Chris tell you?"

Allison didn't like the way Sherry referred to Christian so informally. She knew Sherry thought Christian was "dreamy"—she'd said it enough times, especially after a few drinks when they were out. It wasn't as if Christian would ever encourage Sherry's advances, Allison knew, but it seemed as though small things like that were bothering her a lot lately. "A couple of weeks ago." Allison didn't want Sherry thinking she and Christian weren't as close as they used to be. She'd never told Sherry how much she cared about Christian—because Sherry had a big mouth— but she wanted Sherry to keep thinking she was as close to the top as it got.

Sherry dropped her notepad down on the front of Allison's desk and clasped her hands together. "How much do you think he'll give me? Did he talk to you about it?"

"No." Sherry was as aggressive as a young associate came. Sometimes her attitude bordered on obnoxious, but she was also talented. Good at running numbers and doing due diligence. Fast and accurate with financial data and the other nuts-and-bolts stuff, which freed up Allison to think about the big picture. And Sherry was fun to be with outside of work. They'd been going out more and more together at night, to clubs in Manhattan. It took Allison's mind off Christian. "He makes those decisions by himself."

"He probably doesn't even know my name," Sherry fretted.

"Don't worry, he knows your name."

Sherry caught her breath. *"He does?"*

"He knows *everyone's* name," Allison said quickly.

But Sherry wasn't deterred. "Chris is so down-to-earth for being so famous and important, you know? Last week he held the door for me downstairs as I was leaving to go home, asked me if I needed a ride anywhere. I was meeting a couple of friends at a place right down Park Avenue, but I almost took him up on it just so I could get to know him better. It sure would have been nice to have the face time."

Allison gazed at Sherry. "He offered you a ride?"

"Uh-huh."

"In the limousine?"

"Uh-huh."

Allison glanced back at her computer screen. The guy she was e-mailing was forty-seven and had just divorced his wife. The rumor at the law firm was that he was dating a twenty-six-year-old bond trader at an investment bank downtown. A Paris Hilton look-alike. What was wrong with men? "But you didn't take him up on it?"

"I will next time."

Christian was just being nice, Allison figured. That was all there was to it. He didn't have designs on Sherry. He couldn't. "Let's go get something to drink at the deli downstairs," she suggested, standing up and grabbing a key off her desk. It was a spare one to Christian's office he kept on the molding above his door. Only she and Debbie knew about it. She had needed a file out of Christian's office early this morning and hadn't returned it yet. "My treat."

"So what do you think he'll give me?" Sherry asked, following Allison out of the office and toward Christian's.

"I don't know." As they approached, Allison saw that Debbie wasn't at her desk outside Christian's office. Allison didn't want to leave the key lying on Debbie's desk, so she reached up and replaced it on the molding. When she had, she turned around and pointed at Sherry. "Don't tell anyone," she warned.

"Of course not," Sherry said as they walked toward reception, rolling her eyes as if Allison really hadn't needed to say that. "Now come on and guess what Chris is going to give me. Jesus, Allison, don't be so uptight about this."

Allison pursed her lips. This was what happened when you socialized with your subordinate, she realized, when you didn't keep your distance. Maybe Christian was right after all. Maybe she couldn't work with him and date him, too. She let out a frustrated breath. It was too late. She couldn't turn off her feelings for him now. "You'll just have to wait for tomorrow."

Sherry scowled as they reached the elevators. "You know, someone told me they saw Christian out with a model last week at a restaurant on the Upper West Side."

CHRISTIAN HELPED the young woman along through the trees, at one point hauling her back to her feet when she tripped over a fallen tree. He had no idea where they were going—or where they were, for that matter—but he'd seen that terrified look on her face a moment ago and it told him they needed to run. Wherever, it didn't matter, as long as it was away from these men. His first instinct when he'd jumped from the Integra had been to catch her, then let the two men catch up and call their bluff. Surely they wouldn't do anything to her if he was there, especially if he told them who he was.

But that look of absolute dread had convinced him that a game of chicken was the wrong strategy. He'd spent a lifetime reading people's faces, taking his cues from subtle expressions in terms of when to push and when to give during negotiations, and his track record spoke for itself. She couldn't be *that* good an actress. He just wondered who in the hell could scare her so badly. The woman who'd caught her in bed with her husband had to be someone *very* powerful. He'd put Quentin on finding out who she was—if they saw each other again.

"This way." He could hear their pursuers, like a pack of dogs, crashing across the dead leaves behind them. It was a sick feeling. "Come on!"

"I'm so tired," she gasped.

"Don't think about being tired, think about being scared. And *run*."

Suddenly they were at the edge of a drop-off. At least two hundred feet down, Christian figured. At a sharp angle over big boulders, some jutting far out from the face of the hill. In the distance he thought he heard the sound of rushing water. "Damn it!" He made a snap decision. "We've got to go down there, we can't go back. They'll catch us if we do."

"I can't do it," she said fearfully. "I'll fall."

"Hey, I'm wearing loafers," he snapped, pointing at the hard soles, then her tennis shoes. "And I'm probably twice your age. If I can do it, you *definitely* can."

"I'm telling you, I can't do it."

It was time to act like a chairman. "No choice." He picked a route over and around the boulders, committing it to memory, then grabbed her hand and tugged her over the edge. "Come on."

"Oh, Jesus!"

They made it down the hill faster than he'd hoped, almost slipping several times, but they made it. He glanced up as they reached the bottom, half-falling, half-running the last ten feet through a small stream to level, dry ground. The men had just reached the brink of the cliff and were starting to climb down the slope after them. It looked as if one of them had shoved a pistol in his belt before scrambling down the first few feet, but Christian couldn't tell for sure.

He yanked her arm hard. *"Run, damn it."*

He pulled his cell phone out as they sprinted away. The LCD showed only one bar for an antenna, but he dialed 911 anyway—and got through. As he and Quentin had pulled into the store parking lot he'd noticed the name of the place—Grayson's Market—and he shouted it as loudly as he could to the operator as he and the young woman ran, hoping the men chasing them would hear him and understand that he was on his phone. He yelled that they were in the woods south and east of the store, and that they needed help fast. That they were running for their lives. That his partner was at the store and needed help, too. The men chasing them might figure he was just pretending to talk to someone, but that was all right. As long as he planted a seed of doubt in their minds, they might turn around. More important, help was on the way. Hopefully, it wouldn't get to them too late.

"What's your name?" he asked as he stuffed the phone back in his pocket. They were jogging along a narrow, faint trail, probably made by deer. The center of it didn't have leaves on it, so they weren't making much noise. He was planning to cut back into the woods in a few moments.

"Beth Garrison. What's yours?"

"Christian Gillette." He stuck his arm in front of her and pointed. "That way."

She put her hands in front of her face as they headed back into the heavy stuff. "Do you have any idea where you're going?"

"Do you care as long as we lose those two guys back there?"

She shrugged as she ran. "I guess not."

They took off through the underbrush, dodging thornbushes, branches, and roots. The sound of water was growing louder and soon Christian could see it through the trees, glistening in the late-afternoon sunlight. Then, suddenly, they were standing on the bank of a wide river, smooth, round, mud-colored rocks beneath their feet. It had to be the Potomac, based on the map of western Maryland he'd looked at on the way to Camp David. It was a couple of hundred yards across and appeared deep and fast in the middle. He was confident he could swim it, but not that she could—she seemed exhausted. And if the men chasing them had guns, they'd be vulnerable out there splashing across the surface. They might make it thirty or forty yards from shore before the men made it to the bank—a long shot with a pistol—but still he didn't want to gamble. For all he knew they were marksmen. He couldn't risk Beth drowning halfway across, either.

"What now, Columbus?"

Christian glanced over at the young woman. "Would you rather be on your own?"

Beth shook her head. "No, I wouldn't."

"Because it sure would be a hell of a lot easier for me if I were on my own out here. But, hey, it's like they say when the bears are chasing you in Alaska. As long as you can run faster than at least one other person in your group, you're safe. I'll bet I can run faster than you, even though I'm old enough to be your dad."

"I'm sorry. Please don't leave me here."

Christian scanned the far shore, searching for any sign of civilization, but there was nothing. Just an unbroken wall of fresh green leaves scaling the hills until they met blue sky. "We've got to keep moving," he said, heading back into the forest. "Sooner or later we'll find something." The bad part about this was that the farther they went downstream, the farther they got from the point of reference he'd given the 911 operator: the store. "I hope."

They moved through the underbrush quickly but didn't sprint, trying to stay as quiet as possible, keeping the river in sight through the branches. They stopped every hundred feet to listen, but the sounds of footsteps behind them had faded completely. Hopefully the two men had turned upstream when they'd reached the bank.

"Why are you helping me?" Beth asked, hunching over as she pushed a dogwood branch out of the way.

Christian was suddenly aware that the forest smelled good, full of sweet spring scents—and Beth's perfume. "To tell you the truth, I really don't know. I guess I've got this character flaw. When I see someone who needs help, I help."

"How old are you?"

He sighed. Why were people always asking that question? "Forty-three."

"*Wow.*"

His eyes moved to hers reluctantly. "Why'd you say it like that?"

"You don't *look* that old."

He didn't like forty-three sounding old to her. Of course, he liked that she didn't think he looked that old. She was probably just buttering him up to make sure he stayed with her while she was so scared. He winced. The investment world had jaded him. He was always looking for an ulterior motive, and sometimes there wasn't one. Sometimes people were simply being sincere. But not often.

"Really? I don't?" He tried to keep from asking the question—it might sound so pathetic—but he couldn't help himself. "How old do I look?"

"Forty-two."

Boy, he had that one coming. "Thanks a lot."

She laughed, glancing back over her shoulder nervously. "I'm just kidding. Really, you look like you're in your early thirties, max."

"You're just being nice."

"No, I'm not. I'm serious." She was quiet as they covered another twenty yards. "I like older men. I don't date young guys. They're too insecure, still too caught up in being macho. Still proving that they're better than everyone else and that they're right all the time. I like hanging out with men who already *know* they're better and don't have to show off for anyone."

She sure was a smooth talker. "How old are—"

"The man I'm seeing now is fifty-two," she interrupted.

"*Was* fifty-two."

"What do you mean?"

"Based on how his wife came after you, he's probably dead at this point."

"Oh, I doubt that."

"You going to tell me who she is?" he asked.

They came to the brink of a twenty-foot ravine. At the bottom was a small stream rushing its last few yards to the Potomac. Christian helped Beth down the slippery embankment—it had rained hard a few days ago and the slope was still muddy. At one point she fell against him and he noticed that she felt light as a feather. He found himself wondering right away if she'd fallen against him on purpose. She seemed coordinated. Not necessarily in great shape—she'd tired quickly running through the woods—but definitely athletic. And she was nice to look at.

"How old are you?" he asked as they climbed the other side, clinging to roots and saplings to pull themselves up to the top.

"I'm . . . oh, God."

Christian glanced at Beth, then in the direction she was looking. Standing in front of them was one of the men who'd jumped out of the black sedan back at the store. He wore military boots, jeans, a blue windbreaker, and sunglasses. And he was leveling a pistol at them.

"Nice try, Ms. Garrison." The man motioned with the gun. "Who's your friend?"

"I'm Christian Gillette."

The man stared at Christian blankly, no sign of recognition on his face. "Congratulations, Mr. Gillette. You picked a hell of a thing to get mixed up in. You should have left well enough alone." He pulled out a yellow phone and pushed the walkie-talkie button. "Jimmy, get down here fast," he said loudly. "I'm about a half a mile downstream from where we split up. They followed the river, just like you thought they would."

"On my way," the response crackled through the small speaker.

Christian watched the guy slip the phone into his front pocket, then suggested calmly, "Why don't we go back to that store and see if we can work things out?"

"Why don't you shut up?"

"I think once you find out who I am you won't want to do anything rash."

"I don't give a rat's ass who you are. I have my orders."

In the distance Christian heard a faint sound coming from the direction in which he and Beth had been headed. A *thump-thump-thump* that was growing louder by the second. He eyed the man holding the gun. The man heard it, too. Christian could tell by the way his eyes kept flickering toward the river and the noise, as if it made him nervous. A few moments later the sound was very loud, definitely headed right at them.

As the man looked up into the trees, he dropped the barrel of the gun slightly.

Christian grabbed Beth's hand and pulled her toward the river.

"Come on!" he shouted, racing down the gentle slope beside the ravine. He heard the *pop-pop-popping* of the man's pistol over the noise from above and bullets whining around them, pinging off branches and strafing through leaves. But he kept running, kept dragging her along until they reached the riverbank and the trees fell away. They stumbled out onto a point of smooth, round rocks and waved frantically just as the helicopter roared overhead, only a few hundred feet above them— MARYLAND STATE POLICE painted in bold, black letters on the bottom of the mustard-colored aircraft.

"Don't move!"

Christian and Beth whirled around. The man was behind them, at the edge of the trees, pointing the gun at them.

"Nice try—"

The sound of the helicopter had faded fast as it raced past them and upriver, but now it grew louder again as it made a quick, sweeping turn to the left over the river.

"*Shit!*" The man jammed the gun into his belt and disappeared back into the trees.

STEVEN SANCHEZ reviewed the Christian Gillette file for a fourth time as he sat on a chair beneath the palm trees enjoying the Florida sunset. The west coast was nice. The ocean was like a big pond here, barely even a ripple on the surface as far as the eye could see. Just small waves rolling the last few feet up onto the beach. He'd enjoyed bodysurfing as a younger man, so he'd hung out on the east coast when he came to the States then. But now that he was older—in his early fifties—Sanchez liked the calm, preferred lying on a float being rocked by the gentle swells while he read a book or reviewed a file. Now he went to Miami only when he had to.

As the orange sun dipped toward the horizon and a gentle evening breeze swayed the huge palm leaves above him, he put the file down on his lap and relaxed, taking in the last few rays of the day. He'd been on the west coast for the last two months, preparing—and doing a little stalking.

When the sun had almost disappeared, he saw the couple walking hand in hand along the deserted beach. An intense excitement surged through his chest. He'd been waiting a long time for this. After all these years, he still had it. Still had that incredible patience to wait for just the right moment. And that sixth sense when it came to hunting, when it came to anticipating which way the prey would go.

The young man could have gone south, toward town, but Sanchez had sensed he wouldn't, that he'd go north. The man was wooing a pretty girl he'd met on the beach today—while Sanchez watched—and Sanchez was certain the young man would try to make love to her out here. The public nature of it would excite him. Anyone with his money could have done it in a nice hotel suite, but he wanted to do it where they might be seen, maybe even caught, because that would be much more titillating for him—and her, though her feelings probably didn't matter to the little rich boy. Of course, he wouldn't do it where they would obviously be seen, he'd be careful about it. He'd go north, take her for a sunset stroll in that direction, then convince her to go into the trees back from the beach. Sanchez had analyzed it all so carefully. The way he always did.

As the couple moved past, Sanchez rose from his chair and dropped the file on the sand, still imprinting Gillette's image on his brain, trying to remember every detail of the face, every mannerism noted in the file. Sanchez stole through the trees, glancing ahead of the couple down the beach as darkness closed in. No one around, just the three of them. This was better than sex for him—now that he was older. Well, almost better.

When the couple stopped to kiss, he stole across the sand—already starting to cool now that the sun was down—until he was just a few feet behind the woman. She was an unsuspecting victim in this whole thing, but he felt no remorse. There were 7 billion people on the planet. The world wasn't going to miss one less.

Sanchez ran the twelve-inch, serrated blade into the woman's heart from the right side, from underneath her rib cage. She slumped forward instantly, dead.

For a moment the young man didn't realize what had happened, actually kept kissing her even as she went limp in his arms. Then his head came back and he allowed her to fall to the sand.

"Damn it," he cursed. "Shouldn't have let her drink so—" He saw Sanchez. "Oh, Jesus." He tried to run but it was too late.

Sanchez whipped the first two inches of the long blade across the front of the young man's neck with a deft, cat-quick move, slicing the throat wide open.

The young man gasped and brought his hands up as he slowly sank to his knees, unable to shout for help as blood gurgled out of him and poured down onto his pressed, white shirt.

Sanchez grabbed the young man's hair and pulled his head back, opening the wound wider at both ends. Then he let go and stepped to the side, allowing the man to fall face forward into the sand.

IT WAS DARK when Christian and Beth finally pulled into the Grayson's Market parking lot in the back of a Maryland state trooper car. In the headlights Christian could see Quentin leaning against another patrol car, arms crossed over his chest, talking to an officer. Christian hopped out even before the vehicle had come to a full stop and hurried to where Quentin was.

"One hell of an afternoon," Quentin said angrily. "Thanks for leaving me."

"Hey, I'm sorry, I—"

Quentin patted Christian on the shoulder and gave him a quick embrace. "Shut up, pal. I'm just glad you're all right. Is the girl okay?"

Christian nodded toward the trooper car he'd climbed out of. "She's fine. Her name's Beth, by the way." He saw the strange look Quentin gave him, as if to ask why he needed to know what her name was. "What happened here?" Christian asked as the trooper Quentin had been talking to stepped away to speak with the one who had given them a ride back. After the chopper had whisked them off to the closest barracks for questioning.

"It was weird," Quentin answered. "When you took off into the woods after the girl and the two guys chased you, the other two came at me. We got into a shoving match and we yelled at each other a little, but they backed off real fast. It was like they just wanted to make sure I didn't go after you. A couple of minutes of that and they were gone. I went into the woods looking for you, but there was no way I was going to find you at that point. I figured the best thing to do was come back here and wait. I called the cops while I was traipsing around in the trees and told them who you were and who you'd just met with at Camp David, and I guess we got action pretty fast."

"We sure did."

"What happened to you two?"

"Like you said, those guys were chasing us and I thought we'd lost them, but one of them caught up to us down by the river." Christian motioned in the general direction of the store, now closed. "Down the hill, past the store. Anyway, he had a gun and I thought we had a problem, but then this state police chopper showed up and scared the guy off."

"What the hell were those guys so pissed off about?" Quentin asked. "Why were they chasing her?"

Christian glanced through the darkness toward the Austin-Healey. Beth had headed over to the car to get a bag. "She was having an affair with an older guy and his wife found out," he explained in a low voice. "The Mrs. didn't take it too well. Caught them in the act, I think."

Quentin whistled. "Still. Seems pretty drastic to send four guys with guns after her. Not to mention just having four guys at your disposal to do that."

"Yeah, right?" Christian agreed. "She wouldn't tell me who it was. She was too scared. I guess it's a pretty powerful couple." Christian stopped talking when Beth walked up to where they were standing. She was wearing a windbreaker the police had given her at the barracks. It had gotten chilly since the sun had gone down. He introduced her to Quentin, then smiled at her. "You ready?"

"Yeah. I really appreciate this."

"What's going on?" Quentin asked.

"We're giving her a ride into Washington." He pointed at the Austin-Healey. "It's not hers. I really don't think she ought to be driving it at this point."

"HOW DID IT GO?"

Melissa Hart took off the windbreaker and laid it over a chair. It was warm in here. It felt good. "I'm sure you know by now."

"I've gotten reports, but I want your take. Obviously, I'm most in- terested in that."

Melissa sat down and crossed her legs carefully. She was still wearing the white miniskirt. "It went off perfectly. We connected. Christian even gave me a little kiss when he dropped me off at the train station."

"Good. You don't think he recognized you?"

Melissa shook her head. "No way." She smiled grimly. "If he had, he would have been the first. I guess this face doesn't make as much of an impression on people as I thought it did."

"Fame is fleeting."

She glanced down in her lap, wondering where her Oscar statuette was now. Probably sitting on someone's mantel, a conversation piece at dinner parties. "Yeah," she agreed quietly. "Fleeting."

"How's your money holding up?"

"Okay."

"Let me know if you need more."

"I will."

"When will you see Christian again?"

"Later this week," Melissa replied. "I told him I was going to be in New York seeing some friends. We're going to have dinner."

"*Very* good."

She shrugged. "It's what you wanted."

"Yes, it is."

Christian had risked his life for her. At least, as far as *he knew,* he had. She'd almost been convinced herself that she was running toward the river for her life this afternoon. Those bullets had come awfully close—*too* close. And he hadn't acted judgmental about her having an affair—a completely made-up story, but again, he didn't know that. Now she needed to get close to him so these people could spy on him, so they'd know his every move.

"Can I go now?"

"What's wrong?"

"What do you mean?" she asked as she stood up.

"You seem . . . distracted."

"Just tired."

"Don't feel anything for him. Do you understand?"

Melissa's eyes narrowed. "I don't feel anything for anyone."

THE GULFSTREAM took off from Reagan National toward the east, toward Chesapeake Bay. Christian sat on the left side of the plane in a big leather chair, looking out over the city lights.

"What are you thinking about?" Quentin asked. He was sitting on the other side of the plane.

"Nothing, really."

"Beth?"

Christian turned away from the window as the plane reached the cloud cover. A front had moved in during the last few hours, and as they'd been driving back from the store, it had started to rain. He thought about denying it for a few seconds. "Maybe."

Quentin wagged a finger at him. "Forget about her, man. She's trouble. She seemed nice in the car on the way back and all, but I'm telling you, she's trouble. It just follows some people, and she's one of them."

The thing was, Quentin was right. Trouble did follow some people. But there was something about Beth, something compelling that kept him thinking about her. Something familiar, too. "I'm having dinner with her later this week in New York."

Quentin groaned. *"What are you doing, man?"*

"It's not a romantic thing. I think I can help her, I think I can be her friend."

"You don't need another friend. Besides, men and women can't be just—"

"I know, I know." Christian had heard Quentin say it so many times. "Men and women can't be *just* friends." He hesitated. "Well, I guess we're going to test your theory."

9

"**WHERE WERE YOU YESTERDAY?**"

"Quentin and I had an errand to run," Christian answered. Allison seemed tired this morning, or worried. He couldn't decide which, but she was definitely on edge. Not her usual happy self. "You okay?"

"Not even going to tell me what part of the world you were in?" she pushed.

"Washington, D.C. I was seeing Senator Estes from Minnesota." Which was true. He had stopped by the Russell Office Building to see Estes—at the senator's request—before driving out to Camp David. Several months ago one of the Everest portfolio companies had announced plans to build a massive new manufacturing facility that would create thousands of new jobs. Minneapolis was one of the two finalist locations. "The senator wanted to tell me that he would be grateful if we built that plant in his state *and* to remind me three times that he'd been helpful in getting the Energy Department off its ass on the Laurel Energy deal. Claimed if he hadn't made a few phone calls, we *still* wouldn't have our money."

"Think he's telling the truth?" Allison asked. "Think he really called anyone?"

"I'm sure he made the calls. Whether it made a difference or not, I don't know."

"Well, there's no reason to get him angry."

Christian eased back into his comfortable office chair. It seemed like at this level, no matter how hard you tried not to, you pissed somebody off. The other possible location was outside Sacramento, and he'd gotten an earful from the California senators, too. "I agree, except that *both* of the distinguished senators from California called me several times in the last two weeks to let me know that they would look upon us building the plant in their state very favorably, too. *And* to remind me of the ways in which *they've* helped Everest Capital in the past and want to continue to help Everest in the future. How they don't want to see anything get in the way of their continuing to support us. Doesn't take a genius to figure out what they were saying."

"Well," Allison said with a sigh, "that's why you get the big bucks, Mr. Chairman. To make sure all the kids play together in the sandbox without killing each other."

"Speaking of big bucks," he said quickly, spotting an opportunity to change subjects, "I'm making the Laurel Energy distributions today."

"So I understand."

Christian heard aggravation in Allison's tone. Why the hell would she be aggravated about getting money? "What's that supposed to mean?"

"What?"

"Why'd you say it like that?"

She looked at him as if he were crazy. "Like *what*?"

"Come on, Ally, don't be like that with me. I've known you long enough to hear that tone in your—"

"It's a bummer to hear about your making the distributions from someone else," she admitted. "I thought you told me everything about what was going on at Everest."

"Who told you about the distributions?"

"Sherry Demille."

"That associate who works with you all the time?"

"Uh-huh. I guess I shouldn't be surprised that you remembered her so fast since you offered her a ride in your limo a couple of days ago."

"*What?*"

"That's what she told me."

"Well, she's lying."

"Why would she do that?"

Christian shrugged as he picked up his reading glasses and his to-do list off the desk. There were thirty items on it today—which actually wasn't too bad. Normally, there were twice that many. "I don't know. Ask her."

"Next thing you know she'll be telling me she saw you walking along Fifth Avenue arm in arm with some underwear model."

Christian looked at her over his glasses. "What the—"

"Are you telling me you didn't ask Sherry if she needed a ride?" Allison demanded, leaning forward in her chair.

"All I did was hold the door open for her downstairs as I was walking out." He put the list down. "Aren't you more interested in what your share of the Laurel distribution is than figuring out why some associate's trying to get a rise out of you?"

"I'll tell you what I'm *really* interested in. How you got those scratches on your face and hands."

Christian held out one hand and gazed at the thin, red lines zigzagging across his fingers. Plowing through sticker bushes while he was running for his life yesterday in western Maryland, that was how he'd gotten them. But he wasn't going to tell her that.

A Maryland State cop had called early this morning with some follow-up questions. Apparently Beth hadn't told the police much when they'd interviewed her yesterday evening at the barracks while he waited outside the interview room. They seemed keenly interested in getting to the bottom of why the men were after her. Christian had gotten the impression from the investigator who had called this morning that he thought the men chasing them might actually have been after him. Maybe because Quentin had told them over the phone from the store parking lot that he and Christian had been on their way back from Camp David at the time. Christian had asked the investigator several times not to call the Secret Service. He didn't want Jesse Wood finding out about this. He was excited about helping the president with the Cuba mission, and if Jesse found out what had happened, he might decide to use someone else, worried that Christian couldn't stay under the radar. If worse came to worst and the cops did contact the Secret Service, he'd get Quentin to call some of his old friends down at the White House and hopefully keep news of the whole thing under wraps.

"I was working outside at my house on Long Island over the weekend," Christian explained. "You know, clearing some brush." He grimaced and scratched his arms through his shirtsleeves. "Think I might have gotten some poison ivy, too."

"Clearing brush?" Allison asked incredulously. "Since when did you grow a green thumb? I thought you hated working in the—"

"Forty million bucks, Ally," he interrupted. "That's the number." Her reaction was almost the same as Quentin's. A blank stare for a few moments, then a deliberate shake of her head, as though suddenly she couldn't think straight. Since she'd been cut off by her family, money suddenly meant something to her again. And this was *real* money. This was flip-your-family-the-bird money. "That's what you're getting from the Laurel profits."

"My God," she whispered. "That's incredible."

"It'll be in your account this afternoon, and you better send half of it to the IRS right away. They'll get cranky if you don't, especially when it's this much."

"Chris, I don't know what to say. I mean, thank you, of course."

"It's the same thing I'm giving Blair and Tom." Blair Johnson and Tom O'Brien were two of the other managing partners who reported directly to Gillette. "Quentin, too. I'd say that you guys deserve it, but I'm not sure anyone really *deserves* forty million dollars. At least not for what we do. Kids who get shot up for their country maybe, but not us."

Allison tilted her head to one side. "You seem awfully patriotic lately."

"What do you mean?"

"You've been making lots of comments about the military and Iraq and kids getting killed in the line of duty."

Christian shrugged. "Yeah, well, maybe I feel guilty."

"Why would you feel guilty?"

He thought about the question for a moment. "I've made a lot of money thanks to the fact that kids are willing to lay down their lives to protect my ability to do it. I've never done anything like that in my life." He hesitated. "Maybe I should have."

"You've paid a lot of taxes."

Taxes. Somehow that didn't make him feel any better. Which was one big reason he was so intrigued by Cuba: It would be a chance for him to give something back. "That's not quite the same as risking your life."

"Agreed, but you can't feel bad because you didn't volunteer to invade Iraq, Chris."

"I know." But he was thinking that helping Wood with Cuba was perfect. That it might satisfy his hunger to make a difference. To *really* make a difference.

"What about Jim?" asked Allison. Jim Marshall was the fifth managing partner. "What are you giving him?"

"Nothing," Christian replied bluntly.

"Wow." Allison winced. "That's kind of harsh, don't you think?"

"The portfolio companies he's responsible for are sucking wind, Ally. You know that. Last year, four of his six companies did worse than they did the year before. The other two *lost* money. I can't give him money from the Laurel profits with that kind of track record. Besides, he's making a million a year in salary." Christian tapped the desk. "Most important, he's got to clean up his act."

"What do you mean?"

"He's got a drinking problem."

She looked up, amazed. "How do you know that?"

"I smelled something on his breath one day a few months ago, so I had Quentin put one of his guys on him. Tail Jim when he went out, you know? Turns out he's drinking at lunch almost every day. Three or four Scotches with some accountant friend of his, a *female* friend. Quentin's guy told me they've been holding hands, making out like teenagers in Central Park. The guy's married with kids, for crying out loud. Look, I'm not naïve, I know this stuff happens all the time, but he's not some low-level clerk who pushes paper for a living, either. He's the chairman of six companies. He can't be doing that kind of crap." Christian saw that Allison was going to say something. "*And,* I found a bottle of Scotch in his desk," he spoke up before she could. "He's drinking here at Everest. That's ridiculous."

"*You went through his desk?*"

"I sure did."

"Have you ever gone through *my* desk?"

"No."

"Why not?"

"You haven't given me any reason to."

"But you would if I did?"

"Absolutely."

Allison gritted her teeth. "I think people are entitled to their privacy, Chris. No matter what. For me, a person's desk comes under the privacy heading."

Christian shook his head firmly. "Not when they're handling billions of dollars of other people's money. Check out the contract you signed when you joined Everest. It says I can do whatever I think is necessary to protect the integrity and the reputation of Everest Capital. If you're going to run this place someday, you better get that same attitude fast because ultimately the investors will blame you if things go wrong around here. They won't want to hear that somebody else is responsible, even if they are. They blame the chairman. *That's* why I get the big bucks." He saw that his comment about her running the place someday had taken her by surprise. They hadn't talked about that possibility in a couple of years, and she probably figured he'd decided not to name her vice chairman. "Fortunately everyone else's portfolio companies are doing all right. Making four and a half billion dollars off the Laurel deal tends to keep our investors happy, too, even when we keep nine hundred million dollars of it. But it wouldn't be fair to everyone else if I gave Jim a big chunk of the ups when he doesn't deserve it."

"But *nothing?*" she protested. "I mean, he's got older kids. One in college, I think."

"If you can't get by on a million bucks a year, something's wrong."

She took a deep breath. "He just got divorced, Chris," she said in a low voice.

Christian looked up. "Oh?"

"That's what's going on. That's why he's drinking and meeting another woman. It wasn't like he was running around with her before the divorce, either."

"I had no idea."

"The divorce was finalized at the end of last year, and he really got screwed. He's paying his ex something like fifty grand a month for life with no tax deduction for the alimony."

Christian ran a few numbers in his head. Fifty grand a month would be six hundred thousand a year. If Jim wasn't able to deduct those payments, he was being taxed on his gross earnings, on the whole million dollars. Federal taxes alone on that amount would be almost four hundred grand. As incredible as it seemed, Jim Marshall was losing money every month.

"Did you give him a bonus last February?" Allison asked.

"No."

"So he's actually losing money every month."

"I know, I just did the calculation."

"The problem," Allison explained, "is that the court looked at his income as a whole, with his bonuses. What he's averaged over the last few years. Apparently his lawyer convinced the judge not to consider the ups payments, like Laurel, in terms of calculating the monthly alimony because they weren't predictable. But he still has to give her half of those whenever they're paid to him."

"How do you know so much about his divorce?" Christian wanted to know.

"I asked him. How do you *not* know?" Allison waved her hand. "That's not fair. I'm sorry."

Maybe this was why Victoria Graham wanted Allison to be vice chairman of Everest Capital, Christian thought to himself. Maybe Allison was more in touch with the staff. Maybe Graham had gotten sentimental as she got older. Hell, he was getting more patriotic. And it wasn't that he *didn't* care about the people here, he just couldn't seem to find the time to dig that deeply into their lives. He wasn't sure they really wanted him to, either. A year ago he'd hired a human resources expert to help him figure out why Everest was experiencing what he thought was a high employee-turnover rate. Maybe that was the wrong approach. Maybe there was a simpler solution. Understand people's personal lives.

Christian shut his eyes tightly and rubbed his forehead. Don't be distracted, he thought to himself. His job was to make money for his investors. Ultimately, while some of them might be sympathetic to Jim Marshall's plight—because statistically at least half of them would have gone through divorce themselves—they invested with Everest to make money, not to solve personal crises. As far as Christian was concerned, paying $40 million to someone who was having a liquid lunch every day and shirking his responsibilities set a bad precedent. No matter what his personal situation was.

"How did your meeting with Victoria Graham go yesterday?" he asked.

"Fine, but don't change the subject. I'm worried about Jim. Don't leave him out in the cold on Laurel, Chris. He's counting on this money."

Christian shook his head regretfully. "I'm not giving him any of the Laurel ups, Ally. It wouldn't look good."

"Throw him a few million dollars," she countered, "to help him get back on his feet."

"No. But what I will do is send him to AA, and I'll give him paid leave. Enough on top of his regular salary that he'll be able to pay his bills." Christian didn't like that Allison had gotten close enough to Jim Marshall to know the details of his divorce. Getting to that level implied that Jim and Allison had become more than just coworkers. The receptionists seemed to find Marshall attractive—Christian had overheard them talking once. Maybe Allison did, too. "How much time have you been spending with Jim anyway?"

"Enough. *You* haven't been around to spend any time with."

There it was again, that aggravated tone she'd used when she first sat down. "What's wrong, Ally?"

"Nothing."

"Come on, we've known each other too long for this kind of stuff. Don't hold back on me." Christian caught the glare in her eyes.

"Isn't that the damn point?"

"What?"

"You've been holding back on *me* lately. I thought we were closer than that."

"How have I been holding back on you?"

"When my associate knows that you're going to make the Laurel distributions before I do, I call that holding back. And it isn't just things like that, Chris," she said loudly, standing up. "It's the fact that we hardly ever talk to each other anymore."

"We talk all the time," he protested.

"About business."

"That's what we're in together," he said, gesturing around the office. *"Business."*

Allison gazed down at him. "Silly me. I thought it was so much more." She turned and stalked toward the office door.

"Ally," he barked, standing up, too. *"Ally, stop!"*

But she didn't, slamming the door loudly behind her.

FOR A BASE CAMP, it wasn't much. Just a few run-down, rotting wooden shacks with corroding tin roofs at the edge of an overgrown, brackish canal in the middle of the sultry Florida Everglades. Glittering downtown Miami with its chic nightclubs and beautiful women was less than seventy-five miles away—he'd enjoyed one of those clubs and two women he'd met in the club last night. But you'd never know how close all that was by looking at these dilapidated ruins. Rumor was this place had served as a training and staging area for the Bay of Pigs invaders back in the early 1960s. Men who had died at the hands of the Cuban revolutionary forces when the U.S. air cover they'd been counting on hadn't materialized.

Antonio Barrado glanced around the desolate place with his one good eye—he'd lost the other in a knife fight years ago and now he wore a glass eye and hid that the pupil didn't move behind polarized sunglasses. For a base camp, it would have been almost useless. Looking around, he concluded that if the entire effort had relied on camps like this, the invasion would have failed even if the air cover had shown up. But, for what he needed, it was perfect.

Barrado looped the bowline of the small outboard motorboat around what he judged was the sturdiest of the rotting pilings and pulled himself up onto the pier's brittle planks. He was a small man—just 145 pounds—so, as long as he was careful, he could move along the old boards without worrying too much about falling through. He glanced to the right, toward deeper water, toward where the planks ended but the pilings continued out into the murky water like soldiers in a column two across. Hurricanes had destroyed the pier in the deeper water, as the storms had also destroyed most of the shack roofs. No worries, they could repair the place quickly. A few hours of work and it would be fine for the short time they'd need it. The only other thing they had to do was find a place for the clearing.

Barrado's good eye narrowed as he noticed a subtle movement on the surface of the water near the far bank. Two round bumps emerged slowly from the depths, followed by a third that was slightly larger—the size of a doorknob—and about a foot in front of the other two. Alligator eyes—and its nose. Seventy-five miles from Miami, from a bustling civilization where man was supreme, but here the animals still ruled. He tapped the .44-caliber magnum pistol hanging from his belt, making certain it was there. It was the great equalizer. A piece of equipment that made him just as deadly as a ten-foot alligator—or a man twice his size.

He stared back fiercely across the canal at the alligator for a few moments through the bright sunshine. A natural instinct to try to communicate to the predator that he wasn't scared and that it better keep its distance. Finally it slipped back into the depths, leaving several faint swirls on the surface that slowly evaporated until everything became calm again. The fine hairs on the back of his neck rose as the last eddy died away. He was accustomed to being the hunter, not the hunted.

It smelled awful out here, like rotting eggs. The only thing about the

Everglades Barrado couldn't stand. He could take everything else: the intense heat and humidity, the isolation, the predators, the two-o'clock thunderstorms you could set your watch by. He just hated the stench. And it wasn't bad while you were cruising along in a motorboat with the wind whipping past your nostrils. Only when you stopped and stayed in one place for a while did you notice it. He pulled the bandanna up from around his neck and put it over the tip of his nose. He'd dipped it in lemon water this morning before taking off in the boat from the put-in on Interstate 75—what they called Alligator Alley down here.

As Barrado stepped into the first shack and pushed aside the vines that had overtaken the insides, something slithered beneath his boot. He stepped back quickly and whipped out the huge revolver, then pushed aside the brush. The cottonmouth had already coiled up to strike, tongue flicking in and out quickly as it dared him to come any farther. He hated snakes, especially poisonous ones.

He aimed and fired, and the report thundered through the tiny enclosure. One less snake in the world. That was a good thing.

ALLISON SAT on a bench in Central Park, staring out over the reflecting pond in front of her. She'd come here straight from Christian's office because she didn't know what else to do. She had to get out, had to get away. It had been as if the walls of Everest were closing in on her. For the first time in her life she felt trapped.

She wanted it to be fun and easy with Christian. Wanted to talk to him about things like what his favorite movie was. Then, after giving him a hard time for his answer—no matter what it was—take him to dinner. She wanted it to be the way it had been—the way she'd hoped it *could* be all along. But apparently it wasn't going to happen—because Christian wasn't going to let it happen.

She leaned forward and put her face in her hands. Maybe she ought to listen to Victoria Graham after all. As shocked as she'd been by what the older woman had laid out for her yesterday, maybe that was the only alternative left.

10

VICTORIA GRAHAM watched the thick, twelve-foot-long, brown, gold, and yellow Burmese python approach, sizing up its prey through the underbrush, barely moving a leaf as its wide head slid forward menacingly. When the huge snake hesitated, collecting itself into several tight S-shapes, she felt a rush of exhilaration surge through her body. It wouldn't be long now.

Her eyes flashed to the white rat. It was hunched down behind a small bush in a corner of the twenty-by-twenty-foot glass enclosure—which she'd had constructed in one of three climate-controlled barns on her hundred-acre Connecticut property. The rat's pink eyes flicked left and right, searching desperately for the danger it knew was somewhere out there, trying to convince itself it was hidden from the python's view. With no conception that the snake sensed its presence by the heat it emitted, not by the way the rat saw the world.

There was no way for the rat to hide—and now that it had gone to a corner, nowhere for it to run, either. It rose up cautiously on its hind legs to get a better view, drawing its front feet together, as though it were praying. Which was the right thing to do, Graham thought. Because only God could save it now.

She glanced over her shoulder at the man who'd come to visit. He was standing twenty feet away, his back to the barn's cinder-block wall, looking around anxiously at all the cages. The same way Allison Wallace had looked around nervously in the office. Graham motioned for him to get down on his knees and crawl to where she was, silently warning him with a finger to her mouth to move slowly so as not to disturb the life-and-death struggle playing out before them. She was vaguely amused by the aggravated expression he gave her. Obviously he hadn't come all the way from Washington for a display of reptile predation and wanted her to understand that. But she didn't care. In fact, she was a little put off by his showing his aggravation at all—*he'd* asked for the meeting. Of course his attitude was all wrapped up in his mind-set. He wasn't used to being treated as an afterthought. He was used to being the center of attention. At least, one step away from the man who was.

He wasn't dressed for a safari, either, which was probably bothering him, too. She was wearing jeans and a sweatshirt, but he had on a suit and tie. The barn's floor was covered with dried mud and straw, and the elbows and knees of his suit were quickly getting filthy as he crawled along. Even the end of his red silk tie was picking up dirt. She grinned as the pun crossed her mind: All this was bringing him back to the earth, so to speak.

Finally he was kneeling beside her so that both of their faces were just inches from the glass, from where the rat was trying to hide.

"You're going to like this," she whispered, admiring the perfectly shaped diamond patterns along the snake's sturdy body. Speaking loudly wouldn't bother the snake—it sensed vibrations from the ground, not from sound—but a loud voice might spook the rat, somehow enabling it to escape by startling the big snake. Even though the python was hungry, it might be another hour before it was ready to strike again because it was a careful and precise hunter. One reason she admired these snakes so much: Nothing happened until they were ready for it to happen, until the kill was all but assured and they were certain the angle of attack was perfect. So there was little chance that they'd be injured in the ensuing struggle. They almost never missed when they struck. "It's incredible to watch, Grant."

Grant Bixby was chief of staff for Senator Lloyd Dorsey. Short, pudgy, and out of shape, Bixby was already perspiring profusely from his crawl across the dirty floor—and the fact that it was eighty-five humid degrees in this first-floor room of the barn.

"I've seen this a million times on the Discovery Channel with my kids," Bixby complained. He was forty-four with a twelve-year-old son and a nine-year-old daughter. "We need to talk, Ms. Graham. I don't have time for this. We've got a lot to go over, and I've got to be back down in Washington by six thirty." He checked his watch. "I'm on the five-o'clock shuttle."

Bixby seemed harmless, but Graham knew better. Lloyd Dorsey didn't hire patsies. Dorsey was an ex–navy pilot who'd been shot down over Vietnam in 1966 and spent two years in the Hanoi Hilton, enduring insidious Asian torture methods. He still walked with a limp and a rattan cane as a result, but, unlike his fellow Republican senator from Arizona who'd also spent time in the North Vietnamese prison camp, Dorsey hadn't forgiven *anyone*. His experiences had only cemented his resolve that the United States needed to have the greatest war machine on earth.

Bixby seemed benign enough with his unkempt curly blond hair, his paunch, and his poorly fitting suits, but his reputation was decidedly otherwise. He was the heavy hand in Senator Dorsey's camp—the bad cop—so the senator could maintain his reputation as tough but smooth, the iron fist beneath the velvet glove. Never getting directly involved in a Capitol Hill dispute until Bixby had basically presettled the matter.

An ex Dallas lawyer, Bixby was one of the most hated men in Washington. He threw Dorsey's weight around with impunity, sometimes with obvious aggression that bordered on enjoyment, making enemies left and right. Bixby made no bones about the fact that as Senate Minority Leader, Dorsey could make things difficult for party senators who didn't toe the line. Bixby was hated—but no one dared tell him that to his face. Especially since it looked as if Dorsey would be taking on Jesse Wood in the next presidential election and Bixby would become the most important and influential chief of staff in the country—assuming Senator Dorsey could pull off the upset.

"This is nothing like seeing it on the Discovery Channel," Graham assured Bixby. "I promise you."

"Ah, I don't buy that," Bixby snapped. "The stuff on TV these days is pretty close to virtual. It's just like you're there in the jungle—*Jesus Christ!*" he shouted.

The snake had struck with lightning speed—impossible to see with the naked eye. Nothing but a dark blur against the green background of the enclosure. One moment the serpent was stone-still, the next it was balled around the rat so completely that the only visible part of the rodent's body was its limp tail sagging down one of the snake's coils. Every few seconds the tail would spasm as though it had been hit by an electric shock, extending straight out and shaking spastically.

"You all right?" Graham asked, laughing as she rose quickly to her feet. She was still spry for fifty-seven and damn proud of it. She did yoga first thing every day to stay limber. "Come on, Grant, get up." She reached down and helped Bixby to his feet. He'd fallen backward on the floor, the snake's strike had scared him so badly. "Just like on TV, huh?"

"Yeah," Bixby growled, clearly embarrassed. "Why's the rat's tail doing that?" he asked, bending over and dusting himself off. "Looks like it's being shocked."

"The snake senses when the rat inhales," she explained, "and that's when it tightens its coils for maximum effect, so the rat can't exhale. Causes the muscles inside the rat to go haywire with the pressure, too. The tail going nuts like that shows you when it's happening. Ultimately, the rat suffocates."

Bixby winced, then took a deep, exaggerated breath, as if to reassure himself that he still could. "Now that I've seen the noon feeding, can we get started?"

"We'll chat while we walk," she said, heading off toward the far end of the barn. "I want to check on my new alligator pen. It's in the next barn over. Come on."

Bixby jogged after her. "You want to talk *now*? *Here*?"

"You're the one who's got to make a flight back to Washington. So, what do you need?"

"You know what we need, Ms. Graham—what Senator Dorsey needs."

Bixby was right. She did know what Dorsey needed—more than she wanted to know about what he needed, actually. But she was in it up to her neck at this point, so she might as well see if she could get more out of Bixby since she had him to herself. Usually, he and Dorsey were joined at the hip. "Specifically." Graham slammed the pointed toe of her cowboy boot down on a large beetle scurrying across the floor in front of them.

Bixby gasped and pulled back, startled by Graham's sudden attack. "It's not just Senator Dorsey and me," he explained. "It's the Republican Party as a whole that needs you."

Bixby was a city boy, Graham knew. Born and raised on the streets of Manhattan, so he wasn't comfortable in the country. Which was good.

She always liked having an advantage. The only reason Bixby had left the sophistication of New York for what he undoubtedly considered a cow town after law school was that Dorsey—who was a senior partner at a prominent Dallas firm at the time—had promised Bixby that they would work closely together. *And, more important,* that he'd take Bixby to Washington if he won the congressional race he was planning to run in. Dorsey had entered the race two years later and won—then made good on his promise to bring Bixby along. Now they were fixtures in Washington.

"Sounds important," she said.

"It's *very* important. You know that. Why are you—"

"And ominous." As they reached the other end of the barn, Graham grabbed two metal handles protruding from the wooden wall and slung them to the left. Instantly they were hit with warm May sunshine as the ten-foot-high planked door slid to the side on its rails. She hid a grin as she stepped down to the ground and moved off. She'd seen Bixby's impressed look. "I've known your boss for a long time, Grant," she called over her shoulder, marching across the field at a steady pace. She took a long sniff. One of her workers was cutting an adjoining field for the first time this spring. The freshly mown grass smelled wonderful. "Lloyd Dorsey is a good man, and a hell of a patriot."

"He thinks the same of you, Ms. Graham," Bixby said, huffing as he tried to keep up. "He needs you to—"

"You, on the other hand, well, I know you only by reputation." She wagged a finger at him as she walked. She and Bixby had met only a few times, but she knew Lloyd was intensely loyal to his COS. Still, she wanted to keep Bixby at a distance, wanted his respect. "Which isn't good."

"Yeah, but I—"

"I understand the game, Grant. Believe me." She tore off a milkweed flower as she moved along. "What does Senator Dorsey need me to do? Exactly."

"But I thought you and he had already—"

"In general terms, we did, but I need specifics. I need the whole story. Everything."

"I can't tell you everything," Bixby said quickly. "I doubt I know everything. Hell, Senator Dorsey may not know everything."

"Then everything you can tell me," she said, getting exasperated. "Everything you know."

"Okay, okay." Bixby looked around nervously as they walked. "Are you sure we should talk out here?"

Graham turned around sharply, expecting Bixby to run into her—but he didn't. He'd already stopped. She grimaced. Never underestimate anyone, she reminded herself. He'd anticipated that she would turn around suddenly. Maybe he didn't understand a real python stalking a real white rat—but he understood how people stalked each other politically. He'd known his question would elicit her response. "Is all this really *that* sensitive?" She knew it was, but she was trying to get every crumb of data she could. She wanted him to start from the beginning.

He nodded. "Absolutely."

She spread her arms and looked around the sprawling landscape. The only other human in sight was the guy on the tractor in the next field. "Can you think of a better place than this to talk about something sensitive, Grant? Are you really worried about microphones in the weeds?"

Bixby loosened his tie, then held his hand up to shield his eyes from the bright sun. "I'm paid to worry."

At least she had the sun behind her, at least she had that advantage. Always have every advantage you can. She'd lived by the mantra—it had served her well. "Talk to me, Grant."

But he still took his time, looking around again before finally starting. "Okay, here's the deal. The conservative brass is worried that President Wood is doing too well. They're worried that he's becoming untouchable, that everything he proposes is turning to gold. They're worried that—"

"They're worried that they've lost control," Graham interrupted. "They're worried that they're heading toward that twilight zone of becoming a permanent minority, a party that doesn't matter anymore, a party with no clout. Your boss is worried that he'll actually get the Republican nomination for president next time around and make a fool of himself by running. That he'll become a John Kerry or a Bob Dole. A footnote in someone else's biography."

Bixby looked out over the fields. "You know how much Senator Dorsey values your friendship," he said in a low voice. "Well, it's more than just friendship. We both know that."

Graham swallowed hard and looked down. Damn, Bixby was good. He'd taken her completely off guard with that little machine-gun burst and now he had the pleasure of seeing her reaction.

"He's *very* fond of you," Bixby pressed. "We talk about you a lot."

Graham had been nagged incessantly by Allison Wallace's question. *Is Senator Dorsey the real reason you never got married?* Graham had cursed herself for leaving that picture of Lloyd and her out on the credenza the other day for Allison to see, for being so weak, but she loved it. It had been snapped during that White House state dinner a few months ago. It had been a night she'd been waiting a lifetime for and she'd convinced Lloyd to give her the film as a keepsake. They should have had so many nights like that.

Graham and Dorsey had met more than thirty-five years ago when she was a student at the University of Florida. She'd been auditing a class in the law school on oceanographic regulation—to prep herself for her plans to save *all* the whales—and Lloyd Dorsey had been a guest speaker one day because he was a friend of the professor's. She and Lloyd had locked eyes at the beginning of class, and it had been as if they were the only two people in the room for the next ninety minutes. She hadn't agreed with his conservative view on eminent domain, especially his opinion that the president ought to be able to unilaterally sell drilling rights to the big oil companies if he wanted to. *Texas* oil companies, he'd emphasized with a sly chuckle, eliciting a loud laugh from the students, who understood his loyalties thanks to the professor's long introduction. But for the first time in Graham's life, a contrary environmental view hadn't mattered much. Not nearly as much as having the attention of this handsome young Texan.

When class was over, he'd subtly motioned for her to come up to the lectern and, while everyone else was filing out, asked her to lunch. Told her directly in his smooth drawl that he'd never seen a woman so beautiful on the outside and wanted to find out if she was the same on the inside. She'd hesitated, not exactly certain what he meant, aware that she might be naïve and not realize he was referring to sex and not matters of the heart. Then he'd smiled warmly and touched his chest, reassuring her. She'd melted.

It had been the most intense four months of her life. Lloyd had flown her to Dallas almost every Friday from the University of Florida. Wining and dining her all weekend until that long kiss at the airport on Sunday afternoons, tears streaming down both cheeks as she turned and ran for the plane back to Gainesville. But they'd never made love. He'd asked once—at the airport, as they were saying good-bye one Sunday—and she'd said no, said she wasn't ready. She'd figured he would never call again after that, but she'd figured wrong. Five minutes after she'd gotten back to her dorm room from the airport, the phone was ringing and it was just as it had always been. He'd never asked her to have sex with him again—until just before a delicious chocolate torte dessert was served at that state dinner a few months ago. That time, she'd said yes.

Four months into her relationship with Dorsey, her father had died of a heart attack. She'd dropped out of the University of Florida immediately to run the family insurance brokerage business, and she and Lloyd had fallen out of touch. Not that Lloyd hadn't tried to keep the fire burning. He had, even flying to Philadelphia one weekend, but she'd been too distracted to be any fun. The next thing she knew she was thirty and Lloyd had been married to Betty for seven years and had two children. It was still the biggest regret of her life. Maybe Allison was right, maybe Lloyd Dorsey was the reason she'd never gotten married. Maybe she'd always wanted to be married to Lloyd. Maybe she *still* wanted to be married to him. But that was impossible now. Lloyd had promised her in Washington that night he was going to get divorced, but he hadn't said anything more about it since.

"Why does Lloyd want me to help him?" she asked, still awash in her memories. "Why has he asked me to arrange this whole thing? Every time I've come down I've been expecting the whole story, but I haven't gotten it. Even in bed." There was no reason to dance around the fact that she spent nights at Lloyd's house in Georgetown. Bixby had given her a ride from the White House to Dorsey's house after the state dinner that night a few months ago. He knew everything Dorsey did. Almost. "What's this all about?"

"Senator Dorsey wants you to help him expose something President Wood is involved with." Bixby's voice was low.

She glanced up. Finally. "What?"

"*Cuba,*" Bixby replied, his voice strengthening. "Basically, helping the Cuban military lead a coup against the old regime. Armed aggression using U.S. forces."

Graham gazed at Bixby for a few moments, her eyes transfixed. "*Are you serious?*" She already knew all this, but she'd always been a good actress. You had to be at board meetings.

Bixby nodded. "Yeah. Amazing, huh?"

"How did Lloyd come up with this one?"

"A deep throat in the Pentagon. It's one of the most sensitive projects ever parked over there, but it's parked in a cave in the basement of D-ring so it's all but invisible. Most of the people working on it don't even know they are. The senator's contact couldn't tell him much, but what he did say was incredible. Apparently—"

Graham held up her hand, cutting Bixby off. "Is Lloyd trying to use this thing to get President Wood caught up in some kind of scandal?"

Bixby hesitated. "Yes. As you might imagine, there are others involved as well."

She furrowed her brows. "I don't understand how that's going to work. I think Lloyd's barking up the wrong tree."

Bixby seemed perplexed, as if his entire understanding of the world had suddenly been called into question. "Why?"

It seemed obvious to her and she couldn't understand why it wouldn't be to him. He wasn't likable, but he was savvy. Maybe he was just too close to the situation to see it. "The American public knows we've been trying to take down the Communist government in Cuba for fifty years. They just assume every president since Kennedy's been trying to do it, whether it's been advertised or not."

Bixby bit his lip.

Obviously because he wasn't sure how much to say, Graham could tell. That in itself told her how secretive this thing was. Usually Bixby knew exactly what to say—and what *not* to say.

"Sometime early this year or late last," Bixby began, "President Wood signed a top secret directive giving a small cell inside the United States military permission to covertly assist and support a senior Cuban army leader with taking down the regime, with leading a revolt against the Communist Party. A *very* senior general, code-name Zapata. In turn, this general is working with a small group of senior Cuban officials in the important government ministries who will take over high-profile roles in the new government if the coup succeeds. President Wood gave this U.S. military cell the authority to covertly support the general and the secret group of officials with the coup. That coordination and support includes the possibility of a U.S. invasion of the island immediately after the coup is initiated to make certain Zapata's people are successful. At the very least there will be U.S. Special Forces people on the ground in Cuba when the revolt starts. Rangers, Seals, etc."

"I still don't see how that puts President Wood in hot water," Graham argued. "At least until something happens." She thought about it for a few moments. "Probably not even then. Heck, he might even be a bigger hero afterward."

Bixby looked around, then reached down and picked a blade of grass. "There's an assassination list, approved by President Wood himself."

"But—"

"That list includes civilian targets," Bixby went on. "The top people at the important ministries and at the Central Bank of Cuba, most of whom are hard-core Party members. The plan is to kill them in the first few days of the coup so the next level down—the people Zapata is working with within the ministries—can take over and not have to worry at all about the regime regrouping or about reprisals."

Graham ran her fingers through her hair. It was one thing to approve a plan to work with Cuba's military to engineer a coup. *Quite* another to approve assassinations of civilians, even if they were members of a Communist regime that had been committing awful atrocities against the Cuban people for half a century.

"It's actually a crime to do that now," Bixby spoke up. "For the president to approve assassinations of any kind. Not to mention civilian assassinations."

She knew that. It was a function of the new politically correct landscape where people thought they had the right to know everything their government was doing. Which, in her opinion, was wrong. It would be just like every shareholder knowing everything she was doing. Sometimes you couldn't tell people how you made the money because then you wouldn't be able to make it. Some things had to be done in the dark and you just hoped they never came into the light. "Do you have proof President Wood has done that? Ordered assassinations?"

"We're working on it. We're almost there. Our contact inside the Pentagon is scared to death to say anything, and he should be. Even more scared to make a copy of a presidential assassination order. I think you can understand. We think he'll get us what we need, but we're trying to find other ways to get confirmation of it, too. That's part of the reason I'm here."

She had a feeling she knew what was coming.

"We think President Wood has recruited a very prominent individual from the private sector, as well. A man who—"

"Christian Gillette," she broke in.

Bixby gazed at her, dumbfounded. "How did you know?"

Graham's expression turned grim. "I have friends on both sides of the aisle in Washington." Actually, Senator Dorsey had told her himself that the man he was interested in was Christian. He'd told her the night she'd been at his town house months ago, and several times since. That he needed to follow Christian closely, and he needed Graham to help him with that. That he couldn't arrange it himself—or have Bixby arrange it—because if that was uncovered, he'd be expelled from Congress for spying on a U.S. citizen. But he'd told her in no uncertain terms that he needed to know everything Christian did before he did it, everywhere he went before he went. "You don't get where I've gotten without that kind of help, especially when you operate in a very regulated business like insurance."

"Well, of course but . . ." His voice trailed off.

She appreciated that he didn't press her for how she'd gotten her information. It was a sign of respect, probably newfound because she'd known about Christian working with President Wood before he'd told her. "A lot of people in this country think President Wood is doing a damn good job, Grant."

"No one can look at what he's planning to do in Cuba and approve of it," Bixby said. "You can't target civilians for assassination, you just can't. And the order is very clear, according to our contact. These people are not to survive the coup. There's to be no chance of them somehow reforming and retaking control. No trials for human rights violations because there won't be anyone to try."

"Sometimes a president has to do things the public doesn't approve of."

"You mean like introduce legislation to force big insurance companies to offer health insurance to inner-city populations for next to nothing."

Graham had been watching the tractor in the distance as it moved around the field, slowly making the uncut rectangle in the middle smaller and smaller. "What are you talking about?" she asked, catching a triumphant tone in his voice.

"President Wood has been quietly working with several congressmen from inner-city districts in New York, Houston, and Los Angeles on this legislation for the last three months. It's designed to boost his support with Hispanics without pissing off whites. At least, not in the short term," Bixby said. "He's already got the black vote, of course, but he's trying hard to increase his support with the biggest minority group. He didn't get as much of the Hispanic vote last time around—they usually do vote conservative. But he's trying to change that. And he won't really piss off whites with this thing. The only whites who'll know what's going on are the executives at the insurance companies. Like you," Bixby said, pointing at her. "I mean, ultimately you'll end up raising your rates on everybody else to pay for this, which President Wood knows. They'll understand how bad it is when their premiums go up or companies start charging them for their health benefits because carriers are suddenly charging so much. But by that time Wood will already be reelected. It won't matter then. He won't care what whites think at that point."

"Are you serious about this?"

"Absolutely. I can confirm that President Wood is working with these guys, a couple of black guys he's gotten close to in Congress, to introduce the legislation. We'll show you the preliminary draft. We lifted it out of one of their offices last week."

"How far along is the president with this thing?"

"Another couple of weeks and he'll announce it. That's so there's enough time to get it passed and start implementing it before the election."

"What are we talking here?" Graham asked. "What kind of premiums?"

"I believe I heard that under the proposed plan a single mom will be able to buy full coverage with only minor deductibles for a hundred dollars a month. Each kid she has will be covered for just another twenty-five dollars."

"What?" That was absurd. No one could offer health insurance at those rates and make any money, especially to people in the inner city. "The carriers simply won't do it."

"They won't have a choice," Bixby retorted. "If they don't comply, they'll have to pay a penalty tax of some sort, which will be just as expensive as offering the coverage or not be allowed to operate in the state in which they refuse to make the offering available. Not be able to sell *any* insurance in that state. Not just be barred from selling health insurance."

Graham thought it over. The insurance industry would fight it hard, but ultimately there'd be a compromise—or Wood might just win flat out. Plus, he had the majority in both houses at this point. However it turned out, the president would gain a lot of points with inner-city voters, especially, as Bixby had suggested, Hispanics. "What does President Wood want Christian to do for him as far as Cuba goes?" she asked.

"You don't know?"

She shrugged. "How would I?" She was still digging, still taking advantage of the fact that Bixby and Dorsey hadn't gotten their stories straight.

"You just told me you knew they were working together."

"All I know is that Christian met with President Wood not long ago and that the whole thing was very hush-hush." Dorsey *hadn't* told her this. This had come from another source—the one Dorsey wanted to know about. "Even how he got to wherever they met was kept quiet. I don't know exactly when it was or where it was, and I didn't know it was about Cuba." Graham could tell it was killing Bixby not to ask her how she knew Christian had met with Wood. "It's the first time they've met since Wood almost chose him to be the vice president." She knew Bixby was aware of that—Christian almost being Wood's VP—as this was another thing Lloyd had told her. And at this point she was really just messing with Bixby. Now he couldn't figure out what Dorsey was telling him and what Dorsey was telling her. It was beautiful. "How did Lloyd find out about Wood almost choosing Christian to be his vice president?" This would tell her how much they really wanted her help.

"Are you going to help us?"

"I don't know, Grant. Christian's made a lot of money for me at Everest over the last ten years. I get the feeling he may get caught up in what you're trying to do to President Wood. If you could prove he was somehow passing information about the coup and the assassinations to this general, to this Zapata character, I suppose he'd have a problem as well."

"A *big* problem," Bixby confirmed.

"Am I right? That this isn't just about President Wood?" Graham had sensed over the past few years that Lloyd wanted Christian's head, but he'd never explained why. "That Lloyd wouldn't mind seeing Christian crash and burn, too?"

"Priority number one is Jesse Wood," Bixby said firmly. He hesitated for a few moments. "But you're right, Senator Dorsey would love to see Christian Gillette go down in flames, too."

"Why?"

"Long story."

Graham crossed her arms over her chest and stuck her jaw out. "I've got plenty of time. You're the one with the plane to catch."

After a few seconds Bixby gave in. "Look, Christian's been a pain in the ass to the establishment for a while. For starters, a few years ago some senior people inside the government, inside a very clandestine cell of the intelligence sector, were carving a cutting-edge technology out of a secret government research group. So they could move it into the private sector and clean up financially."

Graham had heard rumors about those kinds of diversions— government insiders secretly transferring federal research projects to friends in the private sector, then getting shares of stock in the company so they could make tons of money in the IPO—but, until now, she hadn't heard of a specific example. "What did the research deal with?"

"Nanotechnology, specifically on the bio side. It was unbelievable, it would have been a blowout IPO with just a year or two more of development. A lot of people were going to be paid back for a lot of years of crappy government wages when they could have been in the private sector making millions all their professional lives. Anyway, Christian screwed that whole thing up. He found out about what was going on and ruined it. Pissed a lot of people off and cost a couple of men their reputations."

That sounded like Christian. Black-and-white—no gray. By the book or bye-bye. "I can see him doing that."

"Well, the establishment didn't like it," Bixby retorted angrily. "And what made it really hard for people, what people couldn't understand, was that his father, Clayton, was a big conservative before he died in that plane crash."

"I remember," she said, brushing a few strands of hair from her face. A slight breeze had picked up. "They were talking about Clayton being a lock to win the Republican nomination for president at some point."

"The men in charge thought Christian understood that, thought he got it, so they couldn't understand what the hell he was doing by getting in the way of a little payback to their friends." Bixby looked around.

As if he thought there might actually be microphones out here, Graham mused, wondering how people could become that paranoid. Maybe that was just what happened to you when you'd been in Washington for so long.

"There's more," Bixby continued.

"What do you mean?"

"Do you remember a guy named Sam Hewitt?"

Graham rolled her eyes. "Of course I do. Samuel Hewitt was chairman and CEO of U.S. Oil for a long time." U.S. Oil was a Texas-based energy company, the biggest industrial company in the world. "He was the only person ever to be the *Forbes* most admired executive more than once, I think."

"Exactly right," Bixby confirmed.

"Hewitt died a couple of years ago, didn't he? Of a heart attack or something?"

"Well, that was the *official* story."

Graham glanced up. "Oh?"

"I know you remember Senator Massey from Texas."

"Sure," she agreed, wondering where all this was leading. "Massey was actually Lloyd's mentor. He was the one who got Lloyd interested in politics in the first place. Got Lloyd to consider running in that first race." She put a finger to her chin, trying to remember the news account she was thinking of. "Massey drowned in a boating accident or something."

"He was fishing at a lake in Oklahoma, by himself. The lake was way back on a friend's property, in a very remote area. He did die by drowning, but he was murdered, just like Sam Hewitt was murdered. There was indisputable evidence proving murder in both cases," Bixby said. "Nothing the public ever heard about, of course. The bottom line is that Hewitt and Massey were working together to keep Jesse Wood out of the White House. They'd gotten hold of something that they were certain would destroy him. A film clip or pictures of him, and they were going to release it to the press." Bixby paused for a few moments. "But they were murdered first . . . and Christian Gillette was involved."

"I don't believe it," Graham said firmly. "Christian would never be involved with something like that. It's not in him."

"If you don't believe me," Bixby said sharply, "then I suggest you talk to my boss. He has the details. He spoke to Samuel Hewitt just before he died. He's also seen the evidence that proves Hewitt and Massey were murdered."

Graham gazed across the fields. The man had finished cutting and was steering the tractor back toward the barn where they were heading. "I will talk to Lloyd."

"He was hoping you'd want to. In fact, he was hoping you'd come back to Washington with me tonight. He was hoping you might be able to stay a few days as he's, well, free."

Graham knew what that meant. It meant the senator had enjoyed their night together after the state dinner. Enjoyed the two other nights she'd spent at his house in Georgetown since then and wanted more. "I may be able to help Senator Dorsey," she said, "may be able to get him the information he needs on Christian Gillette. I've arranged for someone to be very close to Christian." She watched a smile creep across Bixby's face. Suddenly he seemed like a completely different man.

"Great," Bixby said happily. "So, will you come back to Washington with me?"

11

"**JIM MARSHALL** is waiting for you."

"Thanks, Debbie, send him in."

Christian switched off the intercom and closed the file he'd been looking at. It was a file he'd been handed on his way out of the lodge at Camp David by a man President Wood had introduced him to—Dex Kelly—after they had left Richard Hart on the porch. Kelly had informed him that the contents were strictly for his eyes only, that he was to look at it only when no one else was around. The file wasn't thick—just five pages—and he'd gone through it twice in the last ten minutes. Not extensive, but what was there—a summary of President Wood's plan for Cuba—was incredible. Sensitive information about how the initiative would be carried out—coordinating with both the Cuban military and the civilian sectors—and who would be involved. Including the name of the civilian Christian would meet with soon—a surgeon named Nelson Padilla—who was clandestinely working with a general in the Cuban army, code name Zapata. According to the file, the doctor was heading up a group called Los Secretos Seis, which included high-level civilians from several of the major ministries who would take over after the coup had been carried out.

It had surprised Christian to actually see a name in the report because he hadn't officially committed to helping President Wood yet. He had every intention of doing so, but it seemed odd that Wood's people would jump the gun like that. Of course, you could never really be sure what was going on when intelligence people were involved—he was well aware of that because the CIA had used two of Everest's portfolio companies as conduits. Secretly paying intelligence officers in foreign countries using portfolio company accounts to transfer the money. Maybe the name of the Cuban doctor wasn't real. Maybe Wood was using Christian as a decoy, hoping someone would get the file and see the name, sending them off in the wrong direction.

His eyes narrowed. The file even mentioned the city where he would meet Dr. Padilla: Miami. Well, that was going to change. Quentin Stiles would see to that. No one would know where the meeting would take place until the last minute—that was how Quentin worked. And it sure wouldn't be in Miami. Who knew how many people had gotten this file? If Dex Kelly and the president didn't like that, too bad. He was willing to take chances, but not stupid ones.

Just as Christian locked the drawer, the office door opened—sooner than he'd anticipated—and Marshall appeared. Maybe it was just his imagination, but it seemed as if the other man had glanced at his hand as it moved away from the handle. "Come in." Christian motioned toward the chair in front of his desk as he slipped the drawer key into his pocket. "Have a seat."

Marshall was older than Christian—fifty-one—and Christian had always sensed that Marshall was uncomfortable reporting to a man eight years his junior. Marshall looked his age—he had a full head of hair, but it was completely silver. He was tall and distinguished-looking, and, until the last year, he'd been a solid performer. The Everest portfolio companies he was responsible for had always done fine—nothing spectacular, no grand slams like Laurel Energy—but they'd always hit singles and doubles, as people in the firm referred to solid but not outstanding results.

"How are you, Jim?"

"Fine, thanks," Marshall answered in a subdued voice.

As if he knew what was coming.

As Marshall sat down in the chair in front of the desk, Christian couldn't help wondering again how well Marshall and Allison had gotten to know each other in the last few months. Christian knew it wasn't fair, but he couldn't help feeling a twinge of jealousy, either. Allison was right, he hadn't been paying much attention to her lately, so it wasn't as if he could say anything about her looking elsewhere for attention—if there was anything going on between her and Marshall, or her and *anyone* else for that matter. Still, he didn't like thinking about the possibility that she and Marshall had become more than just friends now that Marshall was divorced. A few times in the past she'd mentioned having a thing for good-looking, older men. Marshall fit that bill. A bit plastic-looking in Christian's opinion, but he could see how women might be attracted to him. "Thanks for coming in," he said.

"Sure." Marshall fiddled with his cuff links for a second, making sure they were fastened securely.

Marshall always dressed nattily. Today it was a blue shirt with a white collar, French cuffs, those sporty cuff links, suspenders, a sharp tie, and a chalk-stripe suit. Too much for Christian's taste. He liked things simple and straightforward, didn't like all the extras. "I'm making the Laurel distributions today."

Marshall nodded. "I know. The word's out all over the firm. Not much work getting done out there." He waved toward the office door. "People are excited about it, including me. It's the whole reason I came to Everest, the whole reason I gave up my career at KKR." Kohlberg Kravis Roberts was another large private-equity investment firm based in Manhattan. Marshall had forfeited his small piece of the KKR partnership to join Everest. "I left a lot of money on the table over there when I joined this place, Christian," he said, his voice rising. "I didn't have a big piece, but even a small piece of KKR is like winning Lotto. Pissed some people off when I left there. Can't go back, that's for sure."

Marshall was making his case, trying to preempt the bad news he was clearly anticipating. Trying to make it as hard as possible for Christian to leave him out in the cold on the Laurel profits. "Jim, I want you to—"

"Got a kid in college, too, and I—"

"Just got divorced," Christian cut in.

Marshall's expression sagged, as though that wasn't what he'd been about to say. As if he didn't want Christian to know about the divorce and was shocked that he did.

"Yes, I heard."

"How?" Marshall asked.

"Those things are tough to keep quiet. People talk. You know that."

"Damn it, did Allison tell you?"

"No," Christian replied flatly. He couldn't roll over on her like that. "Jim, you aren't getting anything out of Laurel." It was better to get the bad news out there right up front than to let this go on any longer.

Marshall gazed at him for several seconds, mouth wide-open, as though he were about to gasp for breath. *"Are you joking?"*

"I'd never joke about something like that, Jim. It's tough to hear, but we both know your companies haven't been doing well lately. Which is why you didn't get a bonus this past February."

Marshall gritted his teeth. "You can't leave me out in the cold like this, Christian. I've been counting on this money. I've gotta have it."

"You're going on paid leave, Jim." That one hit Marshall like a freight train. Christian could see it all over Marshall's face. Anger, then panic, then fear—all the emotions registering on his face one right after the other in a matter of seconds. "You need to get your life back on track, you need to dry out. I'm going to send you to one of the best clinics around, and I'm doing it on my own dime. I'll throw you an extra three hundred grand while you're in there so you can pay your bills. I know about everything. We're going to get you well again."

"Well again? What the hell are you talking about?"

"You know what I'm talking about. You're a drunk."

Marshall leaned forward in his chair. "My God," he whispered, "are you really that greedy? Don't you already have enough?"

"Wait a minute—"

"You're going to make up some ridiculous story about me drinking so you can take my share of the Laurel profits? That's it, isn't it?"

"Don't even go there, Jim."

"This way it doesn't look so bad," Marshall continued, eyes bulging. "How much are you taking, Christian? What, half? Four hundred fifty million?"

"I'm not taking any of it. Not a damn cent."

"Bullshit! It'll get to you somehow, probably through a charity or something. You'll make a big donation to it for the cameras, won't you? Get lots of pub about what a great guy you are. Picture of you in the *Times* handing somebody a big check and all that. Then you'll suck every drop of it out the back door and into your pocket so you can buy another mansion somewhere."

Christian's first instinct was to lay into the other man, to rake him over the coals. But he held back, reminding himself that denial was usually the first reaction. "That'll be all, Jim," Christian said curtly, pointing to the door. "Maybe we'll talk later, when you've cooled down."

Marshall shot up out of his chair. "You better pay me, Christian!" he roared.

"I told you what I'm doing, Jim. Be glad I'm not firing you." Christian stared up at Marshall, knowing he shouldn't say this. "We found your stash. I know you're drinking on the job."

"You went in my desk?"

The office door opened and Debbie leaned in. "Everything all right?"

"Everything's fine, Deb." Christian motioned for her to close the door. "Yeah," he admitted when she was gone, "we—no, *I*, went through your desk. You didn't give me a choice."

"You'll be hearing from my lawyer. I'll bury you, you prick."

"Calm down," Christian warned, his anger starting to boil over.

Marshall smiled slyly. "There're a lot of people who want to know about you, Christian. You shouldn't make enemies so fast right now."

Christian stood up, too, not taking his eyes from Marshall's. "Jim, go back to your office and get whatever you want to take with you. I had Debbie put a couple of boxes in there while we were talking. Pack them up, and we'll have them delivered wherever you want. When you're off the sauce for good, you'll still have a place here." The intercom went off. Christian assumed it was Debbie giving him an excuse to cut the meeting short, but he pushed the button down anyway. "Yes?"

"Pick up."

Christian reached for the receiver and brought it slowly to his ear, still staring at Marshall, who hadn't looked away either. "I've got everything under control in here, Deb. There's no need to—"

"That's not it. That person is on the phone," she explained. "The one you told me to put through no matter what you were doing or where you were."

THE AMTRAK TRAIN pulled slowly away from the Philadelphia station heading north, clattering and shrieking as it negotiated the labyrinth of switches at the head of the yard, bouncing passengers around. It would have been nice to take a speedier and more comfortable Metroliner to New York, but Melissa was surviving on a much smaller budget these days—a long way from the limousines and champagne she'd grown accustomed to in Hollywood. She couldn't afford the extra several hundred dollars a round trip on the Metroliner would cost. Her benefactors had her on a fixed monthly allowance, and when she exceeded it, she needed a good explanation. Even when some of her expenses involved playing the role of Beth—as they would tonight. The big payday wouldn't come until the end, they'd told her. Until then the stipend would only be enough to get by on.

She hated being beholden to these people, but right now she had no choice. She'd put calls in to a few Hollywood agents this afternoon, before she'd boarded the train—lesser agents she knew would have done anything to represent her a few months ago—just to see if she got a nibble. But she hadn't heard back from any of them. One of them had been in his office when she'd called—she'd heard him in the background, asking his assistant who it was. When he understood, he'd told his assistant to cut the call off immediately. Her father had been frighteningly thorough.

Melissa gazed out the window at the urban landscape as the train picked up speed, wondering how many people out there had seen her Oscar-winning performance. Wondering if she'd ever have a chance to get back what she'd had. God, she missed California. Missed the life. It had been fun, and profitable.

An eerie chill suddenly enveloped her like a cold fog, and she glanced around quickly, looking for whoever was staring at her. She'd gotten good at picking up on that—when someone was watching her. Probably because she'd been stalked several times in Santa Monica. But she didn't see anyone suspicious, just an elderly woman on the other side of the train reading a magazine.

MARSHALL WAS SITTING on the edge of the hotel room bed in just his boxers when the knock came. It had taken longer than he'd anticipated for her to get up here, and suddenly he was relieved—and very turned on. He jumped up and trotted across the carpet, yanked open the door, grabbed her roughly by the wrist, pulled her into the room, and pinned her against the wall beside a painting, pulling the leather purse strap from her fingers and dropping the bag to the floor. It had been a long time and the taste of her soft lips was delicious thanks to the flavored gloss she had on. They'd spent an hour at the bar downstairs, way in the back, drinking martinis and flirting, until he'd finally suggested this. To which she'd quickly agreed.

The trendy little hotel was in TriBeCa—just a hundred rooms, used mostly by German and Austrian tourists—so he was fairly certain they wouldn't run into anyone from Everest. Especially that bastard Christian

Gillette. Still, Marshall had insisted that they leave the little table in the back corner separately, in case anyone was watching. He was worried about that these days, about being watched, and for good reason. From what he could tell, this thing was crazy, much bigger than he'd initially thought. They hadn't given him many details, but the way they were acting and whom they claimed to be made him suspicious and careful.

That Christian had put him on leave this afternoon was too coincidental. Christian had to suspect something. It couldn't be just that he was pissed off about the drinking. Especially because he'd made such a big deal to his assistant Debbie about getting Marshall's key to the Everest front door, and his magnetic swipe card that activated the elevator to the floor. Losing the key wasn't a problem. Marshall had already made a copy of that and it was back at his apartment. But losing the swipe card was a problem. He'd tried to order another one last week, just in case Christian fired him, but it hadn't come. He had to be able to get back into Everest, if for no other reason than to go through Christian's desk. The men who'd hired him last week would find out quickly that he'd been dismissed. He needed to have something to trade with right now.

She moaned as he reached beneath her pinstripe skirt, lifted it, and pulled her thong to one side, then smoothly slipped a finger into her. Her fingernails dug into his back as he moved it in and out several times quickly—she'd told him downstairs that was how she liked to start. Then he led her to the bed and pulled the clothes from her body, pushed her down onto the mattress hard, stepped out of his boxers, knelt on the bed, hiked her legs up over his shoulders, and thrust inside her.

She arched instantly, pushing her chin back and her throat up. He ran his lips and tongue along the soft skin of her neck, then bit, causing her to moan loudly and thrust up against him several times in rapid succession. She was beautiful, but he wasn't going to be selfish. He wanted to feel good—and he would—but there was another, more important agenda to this afternoon. Thank God he'd been flirting with her for a while, bringing her into his confidence. He'd picked just the right day, too: Laurel distribution day. She'd already been high as a kite on the money before ever getting the first sip of that martini.

He made love to her for a long time, growing gentler and gentler by the minute. She'd consumed four tall martinis during their hour downstairs and was drunk, probably unable to have an orgasm at this point—he'd found that, like men, most women lost that ability when they had too much to drink. But unlike men—who wanted it even more when they were drunk—women didn't care. They derived pleasure from simply being intimate.

Marshall kissed her breasts, drawing circles around her nipples with his tongue as he pulled out of her and moved to one side, running his fingers down over her soft belly, then lower, stroking her lightly the way his wife had always wanted him to.

"Oh, Jesus," she murmured, kissing his forehead. "I love older men, I just *love* older men."

He whispered in her ear as he manipulated her, telling her how beautiful she was, telling her the different things he wanted to do to her. How he'd been fantasizing about her ever since he'd come to Everest. He kissed his way down her stomach, then knelt between her legs and tongued her gently for a long time, until she was moaning to him that she couldn't take any more. He rolled her over gently and brought her to her hands and knees, pushing himself inside her again. Until she was lying flat against the mattress, arms and legs spread wide. Moving in and out more and more slowly, massaging her upper back and neck as he followed her down.

Finally he hesitated, still half inside her, and listened to her breathe. Slow and deep, slow and deep. She'd passed out. He chuckled as he got out of bed and stole across the room to the door. There, he knelt down and went through her purse carefully, trying not to disturb anything. It had taken all his self control not to explode several times, but that self-control had paid off, he thought to himself, picking up the woman's magnetic swipe card to the Everest elevator and holding it up in front of his face. Bingo. Now he had something to bargain with—or at least the opportunity to find something.

He moved to a far corner of the room and picked up his suit coat, which lay across the back of a chair, and slipped the card into an inside pocket. Then he moved back to the bed, rolled the woman onto her back, and shook her chin until her eyes finally fluttered open. "Hey, wake up." He'd gotten what he needed, now he was going to get what he wanted.

MELISSA AWOKE with a start as a Metroliner burst past in the other direction on the next track over, causing the window she was resting her head against to shudder. She'd been having an awful dream about her father leaving her and her mother eight years ago. He'd been flaunting his bimbo in front of them, and it had turned out to be one of the girls she'd been having drinks with at Elaine's the night of the Academy Awards.

As she came to full consciousness, she had that eerie feeling of being watched again, but she wasn't sure if it was just what was left of the dream. She glanced back over her shoulder just in time to see a man moving through the doorway at the end of the swaying car, headed for the bar, which was in the next car back. No way to tell how long he might have been staring at her—or who the hell he was.

She glanced at her watch. She'd be in New York in an hour. She had to keep telling herself not to have feelings for Christian, to treat this like any other acting gig. But those gray eyes of his kept haunting her.

She moaned and eased back in the seat, irritated with herself. It seemed as if everything were haunting her tonight.

12

IT WAS AN ODD FEELING for Christian. Sitting down to an intimate dinner with a woman who was probably half his age and realizing that, despite all his attempts to ignore it, there was a spark of romance for him. *And* realizing that he was more than just a little interested to know if there was a spark for her, too.

Beth hadn't been specific about her age—she'd joked about the big 3-0 being right around the corner—but Christian figured she couldn't be more than twenty-five. She was probably trying to make herself seem older so the age difference wouldn't loom so large. Wouldn't be that big gorilla sitting in the corner that neither of them wanted to talk about.

Beth hadn't been specific about a lot of things. Maybe "not forthcoming"—as Quentin had put it—was a better way to describe how she'd been on the way back to Washington in the car. Quentin had said something about how evasive she'd acted as soon as they'd dropped her off. Said the hour they'd spent with her had reminded him of times he'd tried to interrogate captured enemy intelligence officers: She'd never directly refused to answer any of their questions, but she'd always managed to divert the focus to something else, turn the conversation back on them before they could say anything or tease them about how they were so interested in her. She was mysterious—which only made her more attractive to Christian. He had to admit that to himself. Beautiful and mysterious. A spellbinding combination.

He'd chosen a small Italian place on the Upper West Side for dinner. He knew the owner—had personally loaned the guy money to start the place a few years back—so he had his own table in a quiet corner whenever he wanted it and, more important, he had privacy. No one would bother them while they were eating. No chance one of the waiters would tip off a cameraman at the *Post* or the *Daily News* that he was there so the guy could snap a picture as he came out, either. Which had happened a few times at other places.

Much to the delight of people at Everest—and much to his own irritation—he'd turned up constantly over the last few years on the city's most eligible bachelor lists. So, like others on the list, he sometimes found himself the object of the paparazzi, each one trying to be the first to break the story of whom he was with. It wasn't anything like the chaos that followed movie stars and pop singers when they went out in Manhattan, but it was still annoying.

He shuddered at the thought of a photo of Beth and him making it into one of the daily newspapers. Shuddered even harder thinking about the captions: "Gillette Robs the Cradle" or "Girlfriend . . . or *Daughter*?" His investors would be shocked, and he'd be explaining the pictures for months.

So the question that kept gnawing at him was, why was he here? Beth Garrison was at least twenty years younger than him, and he didn't know a damn thing about her. Sure, he loved mystery, but he could find that a lot of places. And despite the privacy he felt confident he'd have at this place, there was still a chance that someone might recognize him and the word would get out. Then he'd have all that explaining to do—including to Allison. And the explaining to Allison wouldn't have anything to do with the age difference.

There wasn't anything official between Allison and him, but they both felt a deep affection and attraction for each other. They'd never actually said that to each other, but they both knew it was there. And there'd been a kind of unofficial understanding between them that they wouldn't see anyone else, at least not regularly, without telling the other—which was what had bothered him about her being *so* up on Jim Marshall's divorce. It made him think that she was closer to Marshall than she was letting on, maybe even dating him.

In fact, Christian had told Allison that if it turned out he was Jesse Wood's vice president, it would be a perfect chance for them to start a romantic relationship. He'd even pictured her as the first lady eight years down the road, if he'd been fortunate enough to go on to be president. But that hadn't worked out, and she'd been disappointed. So had he—about not being VP and not being able to get closer to her—but he'd never told her, never let on. Just buried himself in his work.

When he was being completely honest with himself, he knew they would make a great couple, knew Allison could be a perfect match for him. Intelligent, fun, reliable, generous, a person who despite the wealth she'd been raised with didn't take herself too seriously and didn't let those around her take themselves too seriously—she was all the things he valued in a woman. Basically, she was perfect for him.

So then *why* was he here tonight?

He couldn't come up with a good answer—with any answer, really—but he knew one thing for sure: He'd been looking forward to tonight a lot. He'd been checking his watch all afternoon—the minute hand had seemed to *crawl* from Roman numeral to Roman numeral—he'd changed his tie three times, and he'd ended an important conference call early, well before he should have. Ended it before there'd been a resolution with the portfolio-company management team, telling everyone on the call that they'd have to pick up where they left off tomorrow. He'd overheard one of the Everest vice presidents in the conference room saying something about how "Christian doesn't do *that* every day" to another VP as they were walking out.

Well, Christian didn't have a date with a twentysomething knockout every day, either. Of course, it wasn't really a date. As he and Quentin were getting close to where she'd asked them to drop her off in Washington the other night, she'd mentioned that she was going to be in New York, and his dinner invitation had just sort of tumbled out. She'd accepted right away. Quentin had given him so much heat for it on the way back to New York, flat out telling him to cancel the dinner several times, but he hadn't folded. Which was more proof of how interested he was in tonight. Usually he listened to Quentin. In the past, when he hadn't listened, he'd ultimately wished he had.

Maybe doing this whole thing was just a way to prove to himself that it could never work out with a woman who was so much younger. He'd see by the end of the evening that they had absolutely nothing in common and be done with the fantasy. Or maybe it was to reassure himself that someone as young as Beth could still be interested in him. It was a tough thing to admit, that he could have that insecurity, but at least he could admit it. Hopefully she'd say something nice, something that made it clear she wouldn't mind this going further, and that would do it for him.

He took a deep breath. This was so unlike him. But somehow that was what made it so compelling.

God, getting older was tougher than he'd anticipated. His father had mentioned how bad it was a couple of times when Christian was younger, but he hadn't really listened. Be nice if his father were around now. Be nice to talk to him about all this.

"Thank you." Beth smiled at him as he held the chair out for her. "You're such a gentleman."

"You should really thank my dad," Christian said. "He was a stickler for manners, especially when it came to how to treat a lady. Taught me everything. He probably should have been born in a more chivalrous time, not twentieth-century America. He liked being an investment banker and all, but I think he would rather have been someone's knight in shining armor."

"My mother was the same way," Beth said as she sat down. "She always wanted to be the princess in the tower, wanted the knight to come rescue her. But my father never did."

Christian heard naked truth in Beth's voice for the first time, something he hadn't heard in the car on the way to Washington—and he liked it. "It's interesting you say that. My mother never cared that my father held doors for her, got her coat, or that he made a point of walking closest to the street on the sidewalk. All she cared about was the money."

"Mom never cared about the money. All she cared about was my father."

They locked eyes for a second. Damn, she looked nice. Typically, he preferred blondes—like Allison—didn't usually go for brunettes, especially when they wore their hair short. But Beth made it work, she definitely had the look. And those smiles of hers were killers. He'd already noticed about ten different ones. Most people he knew gave away their emotions with their eyes. With Beth, it was her mouth.

"Sounds like *they* should have been together," he said after a few moments. "You look really nice."

She touched his hand gently as he sat down next to her. "Thanks."

"What would you like to drink?" he asked.

"I'll have a glass of cabernet."

"She'll have that Rothschild you serve by the glass," he said as the waiter made it to the table. Allison had liked that wine very much the last time they'd come here—about six months ago.

"Sure." The young man smiled smugly and glanced down at Beth's bare legs. She was wearing a short dress. "I'll need to see your ID, ma'am."

Christian had caught a curious expression on the young man's face, too. As if he couldn't figure out what the relationship was here. Father-daughter? Boss-employee? An expression that told him the waiter figured something was going on other than just two people enjoying a nice dinner.

Beth shrugged apologetically. "I don't have it with me, Christian. I left it in my other purse. It's back at the apartment where I'm staying."

Christian waved to the owner, who was at the maître d' stand checking the reservation list. There were only twenty tables in the entire place so the little man got to them quickly.

"Yes, Christian?" he asked in a thick Italian accent. "Anything at all I take care of?"

"Vincent, Beth left her ID in her other purse," Christian explained, gesturing toward her. "I'm sorry to ask but—"

"No problem," Vincent assured them, waving both pudgy hands in front of his face. "I take care of everything," he promised, tugging the waiter away from the table.

Beth leaned toward Christian. "I take it you have some pull here."

"Vincent likes me."

"Vincent *owes* you."

"Why do you say that?"

"When people like you, they pat you on the back and tell you they just had a warning from the local alcohol control board and their hands are tied. That there's nothing they can do about your ID issue, whether they really just had the warning or not." She nodded at the waiter, who was already headed back toward them with a glass of red wine on his tray. "When they owe you, they can't do favors for you fast enough." She nodded at the waiter. "All of a sudden our waiter's gone from leering at me to being your personal black Lab."

The waiter placed the glass in front of Beth. "Signorina."

"Thank you."

"I'm sorry about the mix-up," the waiter said to Christian. "I make sure everything is very good for you tonight, very good. What can I get you to drink?"

"Bottled water, please."

"Yes, sir."

"Don't you want some wine?" Beth asked as the waiter moved off.

"I don't drink."

"Why not?"

There she went again. "No, no. We're going to find out about you first. Quentin and I talked a lot about you after we dropped you off in D.C., and we both agreed that you're very good at avoiding questions."

"Well, thanks. Now tell me why you don't drink."

She had a way about her, that was for sure. A way of getting what she wanted when she wanted it. She was feisty in a sexy way. That little pout was mesmerizing. "I wrapped my father's car around a redwood tree one night when I was in high school after drinking a case of beer, and I almost died. He and I had a long talk when I got better, when I was ready to drive again. He didn't read me the riot act or put me on a guilt trip about it, just told me he'd done the same thing when he was my age. And that he'd never had another drop of alcohol after that. He was a damn successful man, so I listened to him. I'm glad I did." Christian nodded at her glass. "But I don't have any problem at all with people who do enjoy a drink. In fact, sometimes I wish I could, too. Sometimes it's all I can do not to order a drink. But I made a choice, and I've stuck to it."

"Sounds like your dad's had a big influence on your life."

They'd have to spend the rest of dinner talking about it for her to really understand *how big* that influence had been. "Yeah."

"Do you still see him a lot?"

"He died, Beth. A long time ago."

The corners of her mouth dipped and her face stiffened. "I'm sorry."

He thanked her, then noticed that she was looking at a painting on the far wall, but that her focus was miles beyond it. He thought he could see moisture building up on her lower lids. "What's wrong?"

"Nothing."

"Come on, don't stonewall me already. We just sat down."

"That's what they say about *you*, isn't it? You're the man who can handle anything, the man who never loses his cool when everyone else is flipping out. But it's impossible to get behind that stone-wall surface."

There it was *again*. Her ability—maybe it was an instinct now that he thought about it—to volley the focus of the conversation right back on him.

"At least, that's what a lot of interviewers say about you," she added.

"Did your research, huh?" But she must not have done it too thoroughly. If she had, she would have known about his father. There were all kinds of articles about the plane crash out there. "Went right to the Net?"

"Of course, I always go right to the Net when I want to find out something. After all, I'm twenty-two. I've grown up with it." She hesitated, realizing how that might have sounded. "Not that you wouldn't, too."

Well, at least he'd gotten a specific age out of her, and at least for the time being she wasn't quite half his. "But not as fast as you would," he said, "because, after all, I'm forty-three and I *didn't* grow up with it."

"I didn't mean anything by that, I was just saying—"

"It's okay." He slid the salt shaker back and forth on the linen tablecloth for a few moments. "What were you thinking about when you were looking over there?" he asked, pointing at the painting. "When I told you my dad was dead."

She took another sip of wine. "Are you uncomfortable?"

"Beth, I asked you a question and I—"

"Are you uncomfortable?"

"What about?"

"Our age difference."

He liked that, getting right to the heart of the matter, even if she had changed the subject. "I'm not sure. Are you?"

She started to giggle—and after a moment it made him laugh.

"What's so funny?"

"How you don't want to tell me you're uncomfortable about it, but at the same time you do want to tell me." She reached for his hand and wrapped her fingers around his. "How you don't want to admit that you're interested in me, either. Because you're worried that I'm not interested in you in the same way." She squeezed. "So, I'll go first. Even if all this makes me feel like I'm in high school again."

He winked at her. "At least you said *again*. I thought you were going to tell me tonight you were *still in* high school."

"Very funny."

"I'm not kidding. When the waiter took your drink order, he looked at me like I was the dad and you were the babysitter."

She was laughing hard now. "He did not. Stop it," she ordered when she saw he was going to make another crack. "Look, I'm very attracted to you, and not because of who you are. Not just because you saved my life the other day, either."

"Not *just* because I saved your life? You mean there's something else?"

She shot him a coy look. "Maybe."

"What?"

She gave him the once-over, eyeing him up and down. "Well, your looks would do in a pinch," she kidded, "but there was something else that got me while we were running through the woods. Maybe it was those gray eyes. I've never seen anything like them."

He'd heard that before.

She shrugged. "I don't know for sure, but that's okay."

"It is?"

"Yeah, I like mystery. I like to wonder why I'm attracted to someone."

So did he. "Are *you* uncomfortable about the age thing?" he asked directly.

"Not at all. I already told you that. The guy I was seeing before I got chased around the woods by those goons was almost fifty-two. I like older men."

It was the same thing Allison had said a number of times. "Why?" He wanted to see if Beth gave him the same answer.

"They know what they want. Most men who are younger than forty don't. They're still immature. And they don't know how to treat a woman, either. I'm a lot like my mom. I like being pampered."

Christian gazed at her for a few moments. Yep, same answer. "What were you thinking about after I told you my father was dead?"

Beth slid her hand from Christian's. "Nothing."

"Come on, Beth."

"Hey, I barely know you."

He realized he was going too fast, but it was a habit he had a hard time breaking. Time was such a precious commodity. He always felt that he was running out of it, that he had to go faster and faster. Especially as he got closer and closer to the age his father had been when he died. "Sorry, I'm just—"

"I was thinking about my mother being sick."

Smooth move, Gillette. He should have realized something big was going on. He shut his eyes for a moment. He spent all day trying to understand the psyches of the senior executives who ran the Everest portfolio companies for him so he could understand how to motivate them, and he'd forgotten that he ought to be doing the same thing here. He'd missed the signs because he'd been trying too hard to make a connection. "What's wrong with her?"

"Breast cancer."

Christian winced. "I'm sorry." He pulled the folded white handkerchief from his suit jacket pocket and handed it to her as a tear ran down her cheek. "What's the prognosis?"

"It's terminal." She shrugged, trying to seem strong. She took the handkerchief and dabbed her eyes. "It spread to her lymph nodes before they could get it all out. It's all through her body now."

"Jesus."

"And my father left her for another woman a year ago. A month after she was diagnosed." She looked over at him. "All she has is me."

He gazed at her. Suddenly she was just a vulnerable kid facing the toughest time of her young life. He'd pushed her to open up and she had—even though she hadn't wanted to. Now it was his responsibility to help.

"Christian," she said softly, "I'm scared."

"**THIS IS ALL GOING TO** work out very nicely, isn't it, Victoria?" Lloyd Dorsey limped back into the great room of his Washington town house with a Scotch for her. "I get to run Jesse Wood out of the White House, and you get total control of Everest Capital. You won't ever have to worry about Christian Gillette snubbing a deal of yours again. Allison Wallace will do whatever you tell her to do." He handed Victoria Graham her drink as he sat down beside her on the antique sofa. "*And* you won't have to worry about this ridiculous health insurance thing Wood's trying to push through. Once he gets caught up in the Cuba scandal, he'll forget everything else. He'll just be trying to survive at that point, which he won't. I'll personally see to that." He smiled and held his glass up. "To us."

She touched her glass to his. "To us." He was still so damn handsome, still so damn charismatic. Still had the same effect on her he had had that day in the University of Florida law school classroom, when they'd seen each other for the first time. "Yes, it all sounds very good," she admitted, taking a long sip of the honey-colored liquid. "Lloyd, what's actually going to happen to Christian?"

"Don't ask."

"I want to know."

"Why?"

She put her glass down on a table beside the sofa. "He's made me a lot of money over the years."

Dorsey groaned. "We've been through this so many times. Didn't Gillette basically tell one of your board members he thought you were off your rocker? That he thought you were going over the legal line with that Ohio deal?"

She didn't answer.

"Vicky."

A few years ago she'd gone to Christian and asked him to buy an Ohio insurance company for her. MuPenn was competing directly with the company in a couple of big markets, which was driving premiums down for both firms, she'd explained to him. And she'd already gone to the insurance regulators seeking permission for MuPenn to acquire the Ohio company, but had been turned down by both states. So she wanted Christian to buy the company using Everest so they could "rationalize prices," as she'd termed it, in the competing markets. Basically, have an informal agreement—after Everest did the deal—between MuPenn and the Ohio company not to compete on price. In fact to raise prices and keep them equal because they were the only two big carriers in the region. Which was completely illegal. A clear violation of the Robinson-Patman Act, punishable by years in jail.

Technically, there wouldn't have been anything the regulators could have done or said if Everest made the acquisition because MuPenn was just a limited partner with Everest, with no "official" control over anything Everest did. At least, that was what she'd initially thought—she'd found out later that the Feds could actually have prosecuted her if they'd been able to prove complicity between Christian and her. It was the only time she'd ever asked Christian for a favor, but he'd treated her like any other Joe off the street despite the huge amounts of money MuPenn had invested with Everest over the years. And it had made her as mad as she'd ever been, though she'd never told Christian. Of course, he'd quickly figured out *why* she wanted to do it.

Christian had his young people at Everest do the acquisition analysis—

run the numbers—of the Ohio company, then told her it wasn't going to happen and, in so many words, told her that there wasn't going to be any further discussion about it. Even today, the Ohio firm was still a thorn in her side, driving MuPenn's earnings per share down a couple of percentage points each quarter. But what had really gotten to her at the time—what had *really* irritated her—was that she had believed Christian had seen one of MuPenn's board members at a dinner party and told him that she had tried to skirt the law. He'd been right—she had been trying to skirt the law—but he hadn't needed to tell her board member that, hadn't needed to rat her out. She'd been forced to address the issue in a closed session of the executive committee a few days later, and while nothing had come of it—the board hadn't taken any kind of punitive action—she'd almost had to live under a dark cloud for a while.

"I'm glad you're here," Dorsey said softly, leaning over and kissing her on the cheek. "Why don't we finish these drinks upstairs?"

She gazed at him as he pulled back. "You've got everything all planned out, don't you? How to take Wood down, make yourself president, and keep me happy without having to lose half your net worth in a divorce. You're a smooth operator, Senator Dorsey."

Dorsey gave her a hurt puppy-dog look. "That was a mean shot, Vicky. You know I'm going to tell my wife soon. I can't just sit her down and tell her we're getting a divorce. It has to be a gradual thing, almost her idea, you know? I wish you wouldn't treat me like—"

"Oh, stop your whining," she scolded, standing up. "Come on, let's go. I can't believe I'm doing this, but I can't resist you."

CHRISTIAN CHECKED his watch: eleven thirty. He'd just said good-bye to Beth. He'd offered her a ride wherever she wanted to go, but she'd politely turned him down, saying she didn't want to bother him, and he hadn't wanted to press. The dinner had gone too well and there was no reason to push it. They'd already made plans to see each other again in a few days.

"So, Romeo, how'd it go?" Quentin asked.

Quentin had picked Christian up in front of the restaurant right after Beth had caught a cab. "I'm sure we won't see each other again," Christian answered. He could tell that Quentin was relieved. "Not anytime soon anyway."

"Why not? What was the death blow? Her dad call while you were having dinner to remind her she had a midnight curfew? Find out he was younger than you are when he called?"

"Very funny."

"Come on, what was it?"

"She didn't know who the Beatles were."

Quentin nodded triumphantly. "I told you. You don't have anything in common with that girl, do you?"

Christian shook his head as they passed through Times Square, headed downtown on Broadway in Quentin's BMW 760. "Let's put it this way, dinner went four hours. You know me, I've got the patience of an empty hospital."

"Ha ha."

"If it was obvious we didn't have anything in common early on, don't you think I would have been out of there after the appetizer?"

"But what about the Beatles?" Quentin grumbled, obviously disappointed. "I thought you said she didn't—"

"She knew more about them than I did. She's up on music, sports, politics, movies. Our vintage, too. She's amazing."

"What does she do?"

Christian cocked his head to one side as Quentin dodged a cab at Thirty-sixth Street. "I don't know." He'd completely forgotten to try to pin her down on that stuff, he was having so good a time. Quentin had reminded him on the phone right before he'd gotten to the restaurant to dig for answers at dinner, answers they hadn't gotten in the car in Maryland. Answers to such basic things as where she was from, where she'd gone to school, what she did for a living. But somehow all that had slipped his mind. "I figured you'd get answers to all that stuff."

"Well, I didn't," Quentin muttered. "I couldn't find anything on a Beth Garrison anywhere. Not one that fit her description, anyway."

"Did you talk to your buddies down in D.C.?"

"Not yet, but I will."

"What about the Maryland troopers who interviewed her the other day?"

"I tried. I'll be able to get that file, but it's going to take a little longer than I hoped. They weren't real helpful." Quentin shook his head. "I don't like this. I don't like that it's so hard to find out anything about her."

Christian waved. "Ah, it's nothing. She's probably just a small-town girl who went to Washington to try to spice up her life and got caught up in something she couldn't handle. She's probably an embassy secretary or something. I think you ought to be more worried about this." He gestured ahead, toward downtown and the clandestine meeting they were going to.

Strange thing about dinner tonight, Christian realized, was that, in a way, Beth had reminded him of his half sister, Nikki, who'd passed away a few years back. He and Nikki had been close growing up until Clayton had died and Christian's stepmother, Lana, had cut him off from the family. Then they'd reconnected when she'd gotten sick. Christian had actually paid for Nikki's treatment because she didn't have insurance and Lana had pleaded poverty—which was a joke. Beth had the same joy for life as Nikki, even some of the same mannerisms. He'd realized that early on during dinner when she'd lifted her left eyebrow and leaned back slightly—the exact thing Nikki always did.

"So this is the guy from Camp David?" Quentin asked.

Christian shut his eyes for a few moments, still mentally at dinner.

"The same guy that handed you the file on the way out of there?" Quentin pushed.

"Yeah." Debbie had interrupted Christian's meeting with Jim Marshall to let him know that the special caller was holding. The man Christian had told her was to have priority access all the time. A man she should put through to him anytime, no matter what he was doing. "Dex Kelly."

"You should have had a rolling code or something, not just a name. People forget faces pretty quick, and it'll be real dark."

"A name like that's good enough. Besides, I'll recognize him." Kelly had one of those faces you didn't forget. Dark eyes, straight, dark eyebrows, defined features: a turned-up button nose, thin lips, hollow cheeks, and a pointy chin with a deep cleft. He was older, midfifties probably, with a paunch that bulged over his belt. "If it isn't him, I'll know fast. Besides, you'll be watching. You'll see if I'm in trouble."

Quentin shook his head worriedly. "These guys are good. I may not know."

"Why would the president's people want to screw with me right now?"

"It's not government people I'm worried about. Not *U.S.* government people anyway."

Christian had gone ahead and given Quentin the full download on his meeting with President Wood at Camp David. Done it this afternoon when Quentin had gotten word about passing his background check. And it had been a big relief to do it. What had happened on the way back from Camp David had shaken him. He hadn't let on to Quentin, but it had. That Maryland troopers had speculated that the incident might have to do with him and not Beth had gotten him thinking. "What are you saying? You mean—"

"Yeah, I mean Cubans," Quentin interrupted. "I'm worried because that file you got from Kelly has so much sensitive information in it. And from what you told me, you haven't committed to help President Wood yet. If you got that file, the Cubans might have it, too. Doesn't sound like Dex Kelly's running a real tight ship."

"I doubt anyone else got it."

"Why not?"

Christian shrugged. He really had no idea how good—or bad—Wood's people were. He didn't even know if Dex Kelly was Secret Service, CIA, or something else, and he sure didn't have any idea how experienced the guy was.

"One thing I can tell you is that the first meeting won't be in Miami," Quentin said quickly. "Not now that it's been in a memo like that. Really, anyone could have gotten their hands on it."

Christian smiled. He knew Quentin so well.

"Look, this is a dangerous thing you're getting into," Quentin continued. "Personally, I recommend that you *not* get into it. I recommend that you get yourself *as far away* from it as fast as you can and stick to things you have experience with, like running Everest Capital. Make me and the other partners more money, like the forty million bucks I just made off Laurel Energy." He hesitated. "Seriously, you have no idea how the Cubans might go, what they might do to you if they figure out you're involved. They've got to be paranoid as hell, got to try as hard as they can to infiltrate every administration as fast as they can because they know every U.S. president, Republican or Democrat, is out to get them. The island's too full of politics. Just like China hates us being close to Japan, we'd have a psychological meltdown if we thought China and Cuba were getting to be buddies. Especially now that we've had fifteen years of the Soviet Union out of there. We've gotten used to feeling that there's no threat from Cuba." Quentin coasted to a stop at a red light at Canal Street. "I don't give a damn about the money, Chris," he said, his voice turning somber, "you know that. About forty million or four *hundred* million. I care about you. This is dangerous."

"I'll be careful, *believe* me."

"That won't be enough, believe *me*," Quentin said, accelerating through the intersection when the light turned green.

"I can handle myself."

"Said like a true babe in the woods."

"You've seen me in a fight. You've seen what I can—"

"These people won't be out just to kill you, Chris, these people will be out for information. If they catch you, they'll want to know who you're working with, and they won't stop until they find out. Killing you will be an afterthought, something the low man on the team does. A bullet to the head and an unmarked grave in a rain forest somewhere in Cuba where no one will *ever* find your body. *Do you understand what I mean? I'm talking about torture.*"

Christian glanced up. They were through TriBeCa now, almost down to the financial district, just passing the Woolworth Building. Maybe he was still harboring some resentment toward Jesse Wood for passing him over as vice president—as Quentin had suggested when they were down in Maryland. For getting his hopes up so high when Wood had asked him to take the job, then having them dashed when Wood changed his mind. Especially because he really had saved Wood's ass. Maybe he was out to prove to Jesse Wood that he'd made the wrong choice, that he should have chosen Christian as his VP. Maybe that was part of what this was about after all.

"You think I'm just trying to show Jesse he was wrong to drop me? You think that's what this is all about?"

Quentin was checking street signs. "Maybe."

"It's up on the left across from the Trinity Church," Christian said. It hadn't occurred to him that Quentin wouldn't know exactly where Wall Street was. Everest's offices were in Midtown, so Quentin rarely came down here. But it was second nature for Christian. He'd started his career at Goldman Sachs, which was on Broad Street right off Wall and down from the Stock Exchange. "You can't miss it."

"I know where it is," Quentin shot back.

Christian grinned. "*Suuure* you do."

"Yeah, I think that's *exactly* what this is all about. Absolutely you're out to prove something to Jesse. Just like you were out to prove something to yourself tonight by going out with Beth. You were out to prove that a girl who's barely out of training bras could find you attractive. That you're still attractive to younger women. And you're out to prove to Jesse that he made a mistake."

"Bullshit. To both."

"Don't 'bullshit' me, pal. You know it's true." Quentin spotted Trinity Church on the right, then the parking garage beyond it in the next block.

Maybe Quentin was right about proving something to Jesse, though Christian would never admit it. But there was that other, more important reason driving him to take the huge risk. He wanted to be part of something, something big. Selling Laurel Energy for all that money wasn't enough anymore, just more dollar signs in an account. He wanted more, wanted to satisfy that hunger. Of course, that was the problem—he always wanted more. Had since he was a kid. In this case, to have an impact on history. He shut his eyes, careful not to let Quentin see his frustration. Getting older was turning out to be a real bitch. "You want to know the real reason I'm not worried?"

Quentin looked over. "Why?"

"Because you'll be there every step of the way. You'll have approval over everything I do. I'll tell Dex Kelly that tonight. If he doesn't like it, then I'm gone. I won't be part of this. I trust you that much."

Quentin reached over and patted Christian on the shoulder. "You should, too."

"I know."

"Promise me you'll really say that to Kelly."

"Absolutely."

"Good. That makes me feel better."

"I knew it would."

Quentin pulled into the all-night garage and tossed the attendant the keys as they both climbed out of the car. "We won't be long," he said to the guy, "an hour tops."

Outside the garage Christian took off ahead of Quentin, heading up Broadway until he reached Wall Street, then turning right onto the narrow little lane. Christian had always enjoyed bringing friends from out of town down here when he worked at Goldman Sachs—before going to Everest Capital—because they were always so surprised when they saw it. They assumed Wall Street was a massive avenue, like Park or Fifth, but actually it was barely wide enough for a car to pass a delivery truck parked at the curb.

He headed east toward the Stock Exchange, then crossed over to the north side of Wall Street, taking a left at Federal Hall and moving up the darkened side street. Halfway up the block he spotted a solitary figure in the shadows, leaning against the building. It was a chilly night for late spring and the figure was wearing a long trench coat. As Christian neared the man, he saw that it was indeed Dex Kelly.

"Hello, Christian." Kelly held out his hand as they came together. "Thanks for meeting me all the way down here. It was easier for us to make sure it was clear down here than in Midtown. Almost no one down here after around ten o'clock at night."

Christian glanced around, looking for any others who might be with Kelly, but he didn't see anyone. "No problem."

"We can't talk on the phone about anything important after this." Kelly spoke brusquely, and Christian detected a slight New England accent. "Got it?"

"I got it."

"You look at that file we gave you in Maryland?" Kelly asked, checking up and down the darkened street.

It was funny how the brain worked, Christian thought to himself. His mind had been in a completely different place because something strange had just struck him out of the blue. He'd been thinking about Beth's response to the waiter's request to see her ID. How she'd explained that it was in her other purse at the apartment where she was staying. A reasonable explanation because usually women did use a different purse from their everyday bag for a nice dinner. A reasonable explanation except that Beth had come straight from the train station, small rolling suitcase in tow. He'd checked it for her himself with the owner's daughter. "Yeah, I looked at it."

Kelly gritted his teeth. "There was a lot of information in there."

"I noticed."

"Information that shouldn't have been in there, and I'll take accountability for that."

"So what happened?"

"We had a miscommunication internally. We thought you were already committed. Sometimes President Wood gets ahead of himself."

It was Christian's turn to glance down the street. Quentin was down there somewhere. "I *am* committed. You can tell President Wood that. A hundred percent." He thought he noticed a subtle slump of Kelly's shoulders and a quick smile cross the older man's face through the darkness.

"Good man. Good to have you aboard. The chief executive says you can be trusted."

When they'd met at Camp David, Kelly had referred to President Wood as the "chief executive" then, too.

"And that's good enough for me," Kelly went on. "When you've been in this business as long as I have, you realize that sometimes the only thing you can do is trust people, most importantly yourself, your own instincts. You can try to confirm, try to do all that fancy due-diligence stuff. But when it really comes down to it, you have to trust your gut. What you see in the other guy's expression."

"What business is it exactly that you're in?" Christian asked.

"You *know* what business I'm in, Mr. Gillette. Don't play me, young man. What you meant to ask was, what *branch* of the business am I in? Right?"

"Okay."

"I'm not going to tell you, but I will tell you this." Kelly stuck a finger in Christian's face. "I know you have experience with the intelligence cells of the United States government. I know this because I've been through the background check that was done on you during the time the chief executive was thinking about making you his vice president. That background check makes it clear that you knew that a couple of the Everest portfolio companies have been and still are being used by the CIA and the DIA." Kelly chuckled. "And by one group you *don't* know about." Kelly leaned in close. "I'll tell you this, too, just to give you a little hint on who I run with. I knew well before I went through that background check of your familiarity with the U.S. intelligence operations. Maybe nanotechnology rings a bell?"

Christian froze. He'd already paid the price for messing with that nest of vipers once. Didn't want to pay it again because this time the price might turn out to be a lot higher.

"But don't worry, son, I don't care about that. The people you screwed were scum. I was glad you outted 'em. Point is, don't underestimate me. You got that?"

Christian hesitated for a moment before answering, "Yeah."

"Good. Now, I'm going to need you back down in Washington early next week. Actually, just outside it. As the chief executive made clear, we need to move quickly. Can you be there? I need your total commitment."

"I'll be there," Christian agreed, suddenly understanding that this was getting real as Quentin's warning in the car on the way down here played in his head over and over. About the danger involved, specifically the possibility of torture if he was ever caught. "Don't worry."

"Good, we'll communicate by code from now on." Kelly reached into his pocket and produced a laminated card with tiny writing on both sides. "These are phrases we'll use by phone and e-mail. Beside each phrase is its real meaning. *Do not lose this. Do not let it out of your sight. Sleep with it under your pillow.* Do you understand me?"

"I understand." Christian took the card and slipped it into his pocket.

Kelly grabbed Christian's arm. "But if you do lose it, let me know right away. Okay?"

"Okay."

"E-mails will come to you from your portfolio company in Minneapolis. The sender will be a JRCook. Got it?"

"JRCook," Christian repeated, suddenly feeling a chill. It was getting very real very fast.

"All right," Kelly said, taking on a less authoritative tone, as if he were finished with the important stuff. "It'll probably be Tuesday and Wednesday next week when we'll need you."

"Yeah, sure. One more thing." Christian knew this was going to piss Kelly off.

"What?" Kelly growled.

"I told the president this when I saw him, but you need to hear it from me, too. Just in case President Wood forgot to say something."

"What's that?"

"One of my partners at Everest is a man named Quentin Stiles."

"Yeah, yeah. The guy we just finished the background check on." Kelly waved. "But I knew about him way before that."

Which didn't surprise Christian. Quentin had a hell of a reputation inside the government even though he'd been out of it for a few years. Of course a senior guy like Kelly would still remember him. "Quentin's going to be advising me on this. He'll know every detail of what's going on. I won't do anything unless he approves." Even in the dim light, Christian could see Kelly's face twisting in irritation. "I'm absolutely serious about this."

"That's impossible. I can't agree to—"

"Then you don't get me. And you can tell President Wood that."

Kelly's eyes flashed. "Is that file I gave you in a safe place?" he snapped.

JIM MARSHALL moved confidently past the guard desk in the lobby of the Everest building. It wasn't unusual for Everest employees—even managing partners—to come and go at late hours, so the two guards simply nodded and waved him toward the elevators without making him sign in, recognizing him, unaware that Christian had put him on paid leave. Marshall pushed the button for the elevator, giving them a quick nod as the doors opened and he entered the car. Then he took out the woman's magnetic card—he assumed she was still back at the hotel, passed out—and swiped it through the slot, now able to access the Everest main floor. The card was the other reason the guards hadn't made him sign in. Using it left a recognizable set of fingerprints that Christian could check—which he probably did every morning. The prick, Marshall thought to himself. Probably had a detailed report sent to him by the building's property manager just so he could see who was working late, whose fingerprints showed up. Marshall chuckled as the car rose. The good thing was, *his* fingerprints wouldn't be on there.

The car slowed and opened to the main floor of the Everest Capital offices. The firm had three floors in the building—including the two directly below this one—but you had to enter on the main floor, then head down the staircases to get to the other two. He pulled out the key he'd retrieved from his apartment and slid it into the lobby lock. He was inside quickly, past reception and heading toward Christian's office, which was in the very back. Moving through the dimly lit space past other offices—managing directors, then the managing partners. Blair's, then his, then straight to the back past Debbie's desk.

"Send me to a detox center, will he?" Marshall muttered as he reached Gillette's door, pulling out a set of lockpicks from his pocket. "He'll be sorry he screwed with me."

One of Marshall's portfolio companies at Everest was the largest wholesaler of hardware in the country. A couple of weeks ago he'd gotten a lesson in lock picking from one of the top salesmen when he was visiting the headquarters in Stamford, Connecticut. Telling the guy he'd always wanted to know how those TV detectives did it so easily, unconvinced that it really was so easy. Only too willing to please, the salesman had retrieved the lockpick set and shown Marshall how to do it.

Marshall was into Christian's office in no time. He went straight for the desk, for the drawer he'd seen Christian pull his hand away from as if it were electrically charged when they'd met earlier. Marshall used the same pick set to unlock the drawer and smiled when he heard the gentle click from inside indicating that it was open. Then he stowed the pick set in his pocket and pulled the drawer open. His eyes narrowed and he leaned closer. Nothing but blank loose-leaf pads.

"Damn it!"

Hopefully he'd find something else in here and hopefully he'd find it fast. He didn't want to be in here too long.

"HEY, GUYS." Christian waved to the guards behind the lobby desk as he hurried past.

"Hello, Mr. Gillette," one of them called. "You all sure are busy tonight."

"Always," he called back, moving into one of the elevators and pulling out his swipe card. He liked hearing that, liked knowing people were burning the midnight oil. "Have a good night."

Moments later he was in the Everest lobby, opening the main door with his key, then hurrying back toward his office. Kelly and Quentin had gotten him nervous about the Cuba file and he was going to grab it—even though it was after one in the morning. He was going to keep it with him at all times now, maybe even destroy it—he'd memorized every word and there had to be a duplicate with Kelly's people. He slid his office door key into the lock, turned the knob, and trotted to the desk, flipping on a green-shaded banker's lamp, then unlocking the drawer with a third key. He let out a long, low relieved breath when he saw the file. He grabbed it and headed out.

The young woman finally exhaled when she saw the small shaft of light at her feet go out and heard Christian's door shut. It seemed as if she hadn't taken a breath since she'd heard him unlocking the office door and bolted for the closet, the copy of the Cuba file pressed to her chest. She'd barely had time to slip the original file back and lock the drawer when she'd heard the rustling at the door.

Just to be safe, she was going to wait another few minutes before coming out.

13

THE SECRET SIX were meeting in Gustavo Cruz's barn, in an office
the cattle rancher had set up in a corner room to manage the farm. A
room where he kept all his falsified records of milk production. File cabinet after file cabinet of meticulous reports—that were completely bogus.

Nelson Padilla shook his head as he gazed at the cabinets, monu-
ments to one of the things that were wrong with Cuba. As General Delgado had explained in detail to Padilla, there were no authentic records
anywhere on the ranch, nothing that could incriminate Gustavo Cruz if
the D-VI suddenly showed up. The 40 percent of production Cruz sold
on the black market was all done in cash, and that cash was kept in a wa-
tertight safe buried at the corner of two fields. Only Cruz and one of his
sons knew the safe's location—Delgado hadn't forced the location out
of him, or so he had maintained. The cash was used to buy food and
spare parts on other black markets so there were no records of it ever
running through an account anywhere. And Cruz made certain that he
never kept more than 50 percent of his herd in the fields near the barn.
The rest were on back fields, well away from the barn through the jungle, splintered into miniherds.

Cruz could have been caught in only two ways, according to Delgado. The first was by the intelligence people checking his falsified
records, then getting in a helicopter, flying over the entire ranch, and literally counting cows. The good thing was that the cows in the back

fields often went into the jungle during the day to escape the heat, so it would be difficult for the D-VI to spot all of them from the air—Cruz assumed they wouldn't actually go look for cows in the jungle on foot. That would be incredibly time-consuming and, he hoped they would feel, not worth the trouble. That there were easier fish to fry.

The second way Cruz could have been nailed was by having a spy in his midst. One of the men or women from the town whom he employed, even one of his own family members. There was nothing he could do about that except watch them closely. Which was why he paid his bribe. So that the man he paid would tell him if someone was passing on information.

General Delgado had told Padilla all of these details about Gustavo Cruz several weeks after the night Padilla had hit Cruz's cow on the darkened lane. General Delgado had also confirmed for Padilla that Cruz had in fact done exactly what Rodriguez had accused him of. Cruz had led the cow to the road to be killed so he could have its meat without worrying about going to jail for slaughtering state property without authorization.

After relaying all that, Delgado had then informed Padilla that they could use Cruz's ranch for Secret Six meetings whenever they wanted. As Delgado would use Cruz's ranch for clandestine meetings with his U.S. military contacts. That in exchange for not saying anything about Cruz's true motivation that night on the lane *and* enabling Cruz to take over Rodriguez's ranch, Delgado had made it clear that the ranch could be used for these kinds of activities. Cruz had immediately agreed and promised absolute loyalty. Delgado believed Cruz would never be a problem.

"You'll keep watch for us," Padilla said to Cruz as they walked out of the barn into the darkness. It was after ten o'clock at night. "Until we're done."

Cruz nodded solemnly. "Yes, sir."

Padilla sensed that Delgado's analysis of the situation was exactly right. Cruz would never be a problem—he was shaking in his boots. The rancher had patiently waited in the house until all the men were in the barn before coming out, kept his family in there, too. Even suggested a clearing in the woods a quarter mile down the lane to hide the van they'd all taken out here together. Which was a risk. But Padilla had decided that trying to hide six cars with registration numbers that would lead directly to them was an even bigger risk.

If they'd told Cruz what the meeting was all about, he would probably have been even more committed to what they were doing. Padilla had checked on the rancher's family history. Before the Revolution, they had been wealthy, one of the wealthiest on the island and extremely influential in politics. But like everyone else, they'd lost everything when Castro had come to power. Cruz would probably figure that if he helped the group and the Incursion was successful, he would get his land back. But they couldn't tell him what it was about, couldn't take the chance that he might inadvertently give them away. Couldn't take the chance he might name names in a torture session because some D-VI hard-ass had figured out that he was cooking the cattle books.

They moved to the head of the driveway, near the barn, frog and insect calls loud in the warm, humid air. From here, Cruz would quickly see any cars heading up his driveway and get to the meeting fast so the men would have plenty of time to scatter into the jungle.

"Don't leave this spot until we're done," Padilla ordered.

"Yes, sir."

"And don't let your family or your workers come out of the house."

"I won't, sir."

Padilla smiled. He had to admit that it was a little psychologically intoxicating to have this man address him so deferentially, but it wasn't right. In fact, it was what they were fighting. "Don't call me, sir," he said gently. "Please."

Cruz put his hand on Padilla's shoulder. "I don't know exactly what you are doing, but I hope you are successful."

Of course, Cruz had guessed. But that was all right. He didn't know who they were, couldn't name names. Padilla thanked him. "I'll see you when we're done."

"Okay."

Padilla turned around and headed for the barn.

The other five were already seated around a makeshift table when he entered the room. Like most of the other places they'd met, this room was lit only by candles. He was instantly irritated because the attorney from the Ministry of Justice had taken one end seat and the Central Bank executive the other. Even more irritated when they both offered smug smiles when he made eye contact with them, like children who'd found seats in a game of musical chairs smiling at the one left out. They knew he felt that he deserved an end seat—a traditional seat of power in any culture—and he could see they were taking pleasure in shutting him out. But he didn't show his emotion, simply sat in the last seat available—a wooden stool.

"The meeting will come to order," Padilla said loudly, sitting down on the uncomfortable stool. Amazing, he thought, that even a group with as noble a cause as theirs could have ego issues. Just the natural result of testosterone, he knew.

"It stinks in here," the deputy minister of foreign investment and economic development spoke up.

The deputy minister of agriculture laughed. "No, it smells good, señor." He took a deep breath for effect. "Ah, manure. The sweet smell of success."

"All right, all right," Padilla said. "Enough."

"When are you going to the United States?" the man from Science and Technology asked. They all knew things were heating up, that the time was getting close.

"Soon," Padilla answered. "I don't know exactly what day it will be, but it will probably be in the next two weeks. If that goes well, the man I meet with will come here to meet all of us and the general. In fact, we'll probably use this place for both meetings."

"Can you tell us any more about this man you're meeting with?" the attorney asked. "More about his standing in America?"

"He's in the private sector but has the ear of the president. Most definitely."

"Who tells you that?"

"My contacts in the United States. As do the general's."

"It would be very disappointing if when you met him you found out he was not of stature."

"Well, I—"

"But you would tell us right away if that was your feeling," the deputy minister of agriculture pressed. "Wouldn't you? Because if he is not of stature, that will tell us that we may not be able to depend on these people. That we're putting ourselves in a lot of danger for no reason."

"Or that they are working with others here on the island," the man from Science and Technology added, "and that we're the second team."

"We're *not* the second team," Padilla assured them.

"But how do you know?"

"We must have faith. We must—" Padilla interrupted himself as he heard the sound of running footsteps.

Gustavo Cruz appeared at the door, fear all over his face. *"Señores, there is a vehicle stopped at the end of the driveway."*

STEVEN SANCHEZ had been in Spain working on another project, one that was much broader in scope and would require a large team. Which meant the pay was better, but also meant that there were many more headaches—and more ways to get caught.

Now he was back in Miami, just off the plane from Barcelona and at his hotel in South Beach. It was late—eleven ten—and he was dead tired, as he'd been up since early morning yesterday Europe time. But he had one more meeting tonight before he could go to sleep, before he could let his head hit that soft, soft pillow of his suite in the Ritz Carlton. He planned to crash for at least twelve hours to completely recharge his batteries, then hang out on the beach under the palm trees and the warm sunshine until the thing with Christian Gillette went live. Which wouldn't happen for at least a few days and might not happen for as much as another two weeks.

In a way, despite his exhaustion, Sanchez was looking forward to tonight, to finally finding out who was behind this whole thing. He'd been operating on this project through an intermediary—which he hadn't understood until yesterday. Until the intermediary had told him that, and that the person pulling the strings wanted to sit down with him to go over a few final details as quickly as possible.

"Here is your suite key, Mr. Emilio."

"Thank you." The young woman checking him in was quite pretty. A Latina, no more than twenty, with long, straight, jet-black hair, unblemished caramel-colored skin, pretty facial features. And he was a sucker for those big brown eyes. He glanced at the name tag pinned to her blue blazer: Mariposa. "Tough to work the night shift, huh?" he asked, picking up the plastic card and the bar key. He and the girl were the only two people in the lobby.

She shrugged and gave him a polite smile. "What am I going to do? I have to earn money, you know?"

Suddenly Sanchez realized that he hadn't had sex in six weeks, and that the last go-around hadn't been very good. A midthirties woman he'd picked up in London who'd looked a lot better dressed in the dim light of the club bar than undressed in his hotel room. And who'd demanded $100 to stay before she'd take off her clothes. He hated ever paying for it—especially when he hadn't anticipated that the woman was a hooker—but he had anyway. And he'd been sorry. She'd been completely boring about the whole thing, even after he'd paid her.

He'd thought about killing her, but too many people had seen them together. Including the doorman at the club who'd put them in a cab when they left. And the woman had made a big deal about his getting her door for her, too, so he'd probably remember her. The security camera Sanchez had spotted above the door would have, too. Discretion had won the day, but the interaction had whetted his appetite.

"You should be in movies, Mari."

She'd been tapping something on her computer, long fingernails clicking on the keyboard like someone in an old movie sending something over the telegraph. She stopped and looked up. "How did you know I was taking acting classes?"

What luck. "Well, it was either the movies or modeling. You're quite beautiful."

"Aw, thank you."

Sanchez turned to go, then hesitated. "I know a man in Europe who makes movies. I know him pretty well, actually. Perhaps I could introduce you to him." He ticked off a few of the films the man had produced, and her eyes opened wider and wider with each title. "Would that be something you'd be interested in?" he asked, knowing what her answer would be. Knowing what any pretty young woman who was taking acting classes would say.

She put her hands to her mouth. "My God, yes," she exclaimed. "Would you really do that for me?"

"I'd need to know a little more about your background first. Let's get together tomorrow and talk." He saw her enthusiasm dampen slightly when she realized there'd be a quid pro quo for his help and that she'd have to assess whether he was real. But her dejection didn't last long.

"I work again tomorrow night," she answered. "I start at ten."

"Why don't you get here early?" He wanted to give himself plenty of time to lure her to his room. "Say around six."

"Okay," she said hesitantly.

Beautiful. She had to know it wouldn't take four hours to go through her background. She had to understand what he wanted. "I've done this only once before," he told her reassuringly. "Arranged for a woman to meet my producer friend, I mean." Which was true. And he would actually make the introduction for Mari if she was good to him. Maybe. The other girl he'd made an introduction for was doing well in London now. She'd played bit parts in a few movies and was a minor character in a nighttime TV drama. "I'll meet you over there," he said, pointing toward several couches in a far corner of the lobby.

"All right. Oh, Mr. Emilio," Mari spoke up as he was turning to go. "I almost forgot." She handed him a note. "This was on the message board for you."

"Gracias." He'd been wondering how the contact was going to work. The intermediary had told him the person he was working for was extremely sensitive about confidentiality. Which told him it was his first time. Not that everyone wasn't worried—no matter how experienced or inexperienced—they just didn't make it so obvious. "Thanks, Mari. I'll see you tomorrow."

Sanchez made a quick trip to his suite to drop off his luggage and to splash some cold water on his face. Then he headed back to the elevators, up two floors and down the corridor to the designated room. He knocked three times—as the note had directed—and waited.

Moments later he heard the person inside unlock the door. Then it opened, just a few inches—as far as the door could open with the chain still in place. He couldn't see anything but darkness, then the door closed and reopened. He grinned slightly when he saw the person standing before him. This was going to be a new experience.

CHRISTIAN HELPED BETH out of the limousine, then reached back inside and grabbed her bag off the bench seat next to the bar. She had come up from Washington on the train again this afternoon to see her "friend" here in New York. She still wasn't being forthcoming about things, and Quentin wasn't coming up with much of anything, either. Christian had pressed her on one simple question—where she'd gone to college—but she'd managed to avert the answer to that one, too. He couldn't decide if she was just that unegocentric—which was great—or really didn't want him to know things about her for some reason.

At least she'd told him tonight what she did for a living in Washington—she was an administrative assistant for a Maryland congressman. He'd excused himself after they'd finished their entrées to go to the restroom, where he'd called Quentin to let him know about her job. Quentin text-messaged back a few minutes ago that he'd confirmed her story with a friend and that he'd follow up in the morning with the congressman's office to get more details.

"I had a great time tonight, Chris," she said as they moved to the top step of the stoop in front of a six-story walk-up. The building was on Fifty-third on the east side of Manhattan.

"I'll carry your bag upstairs," he offered.

She shook her head. "No, I can get it."

"I'd like to meet your friend."

Beth grinned. "No way. She's very pretty and *very* money hungry. She'd be all over you the minute I left New York. I'm not letting her anywhere near you."

He gazed at her. They'd had another wonderful dinner, full of laughs and light touches. "She can't be any prettier than you." He watched her smile disappear, replaced by a soft, searching expression. As if she was trying to figure out what he was looking for and what he was really about, he thought to himself. The problem was, he still hadn't figured that out himself.

"Thank you," she said, moving close, kissing him on the cheek, then hugging him. "I had a really cool time tonight."

He smiled at her use of the word. It reminded him of the young lawyer at the Laurel closing. "Me, too," he said, slipping his arms around her. She was so small and delicate, and he thought he could feel her slim body shaking.

She leaned back and looked up at him. "Would you . . . well, um, would you . . ." She moaned. "No, I can't ask you to do that."

"Do what?"

"No."

"Come on."

"You're too busy."

He shook her shoulders gently. "Spill it, will you?"

Still she hesitated. "I was hoping you'd come down to Washington," she finally admitted. "Well, Baltimore actually. That's where my mom's in the hospital. I was hoping you'd come with me to the hospital to meet her," she said, her voice rising with excitement. "I've been telling her all about you, and she'd love to meet you. She's never met a celebrity before."

He put his hands up. "I'm not a celebrity."

"Oh, yes, you are. She's been reading all those articles about you in *Forbes* and *Fortune*. I think she's started her own Christian Gillette fan club. You'd make her millennium if you'd come to see her, believe me." Beth paused. "You'd make me very happy, too. I know it's a lot to ask, but . . ."

He nodded. "Of course, I will. I'll check my calendar in the morning. Call me before noon, okay? We'll figure it out."

She grabbed him tightly again. "Christian, you make me so happy."

"Easy, easy," he chuckled. She seemed ecstatic, like a child on Christmas morning. And there were always people he could visit down in Washington anyway—senators, congressmen. Maybe he could combine seeing Beth and her mother with that trip he was going to have to make to see Dex Kelly. "We'll have fun."

She kissed him one more time on the cheek, grabbed her bag, and headed inside the building. As if she didn't want to give him a chance to change his mind. Well, he wouldn't. He'd make that trip no matter what. If he could raise her and her mother's spirits a little bit, hey, that was the least he could do.

Before he eased into the limousine he gave her one more wave—she was still waiting inside the foyer for her friend to buzz her inside the second door.

"Where to, sir?"

"Everest, Wayne." Wayne Tyson was one of Quentin's men. Wayne was sitting up front with the driver.

"Everest? It's almost eleven thirty. Don't you want to go home?"

"I sure do," Christian answered, taking out his cell phone as they pulled away from the curb. He glanced up the stairs one more time. Through the door window he could see Beth still standing there. "But I've got some things to finish up at the office first."

"All right."

Christian relaxed into the seat, thinking about dinner. It was almost overwhelming how much Beth reminded him of Nikki. Which made anything romantic impossible. It just wouldn't work now. But it didn't make him want to see Beth any less. In fact, more. He'd loved Nikki, but he'd missed all those years with her because Lana had cut him off. Maybe this could be a way to reconnect.

He took out his cell phone and text-messaged Quentin, asking him to make certain he didn't raise any eyebrows when he spoke to the congressman's staff about Beth in the morning. He didn't want Beth find-

ing out that they were checking up on her. By the time he'd sent the
message and looked at his new e-mails on his BlackBerry, they were back
to Park Avenue and Everest Capital.

"Wait down here for me, okay, Wayne?" Christian said. "I won't be
long. No more than twenty minutes."

"Yes, sir. But I am walking you to the door. Stiles's orders."

Christian climbed out and moved to the front entrance of the building with the young man, who nodded to him and stayed by the door
once they were inside. As Christian moved through the revolving doors
into the lobby, he noticed a young woman talking to the guards behind
the security desk. A few strides closer and he recognized her: Sherry Demille. She was casually dressed in a T-shirt and jeans. As he neared the
desk, he realized some kind of argument was going on. He didn't know
Sherry that well, but her voice seemed high-pitched, irritated. And the
guard was definitely mad, sticking his chin out, arms crossed tightly.

"Hello," Christian said calmly as he reached the desk. He caught
Sherry's surprised look when her eyes snapped to his. "What seems to be
the problem?"

"Nothing," Sherry said quickly. "Everything's—"

"Miss Demille forgot her swipe card, Mr. Gillette," the guard interrupted. "She wants me to let her upstairs anyway."

"You know I work here," she said angrily to the guard.

"No tickie, no laundry," the guard retorted, aggravated at the young
woman's attitude.

"I'll take her up," Christian said, glancing at the guard's name tag. "I
appreciate your being so careful."

"Rules are rules, especially in this day and age."

"Absolutely. Keep up the good work, Henry."

"Thank you, Mr. Gillette."

Christian smiled at Sherry and nodded toward the elevators. "Come
on."

"Thanks for saving me," said Sherry as they moved into the waiting car.

Christian swiped his card through the slot and pressed the button for
the Everest floor. "No problem." He could tell she was nervous. She was
twirling her hair like mad. "Where's your card?"

"At home. I left the office around eight tonight. About a half hour
ago I got this idea about a deal I'm working on with Allison, right before I was going to bed, and I couldn't wait to see how it worked

through my projection model. But I left so fast from my apartment to get over here I forgot my card. I tried calling upstairs from the security desk. I thought maybe someone might still be working, but I couldn't find anyone."

Christian smiled. "I like your dedication."

"Well, I love Everest. It's the best place in New York to—"

"Let me ask you a question," he interrupted. "Did you tell Allison Wallace I offered you a ride in my limo last week?" He almost had to hide a grin because her face went white so fast. She was suddenly caught in a bad spot. She didn't want to lie, but she didn't want to admit to him that she'd made up something to make Allison jealous, either.

She nodded slowly. "Yes. That's what I thought I heard you say. Didn't you?"

Christian stared at her for a few moments as the elevator doors opened to the Everest floor. She actually seemed as if she believed what she was saying. It was like a friend of his had said to him one time: *It's really not a lie if you believe it.* Clearly, Sherry Demille adhered to that misguided theory. He'd have to have a conversation with Allison about her. Couldn't have a liar working at Everest.

He gestured to her. "After you."

ANTONIO BARRADO gazed up into the crystal-clear night sky at the vast array of stars above him and his Everglades camp. He was lying on his back, hands behind his head, inside one of the roofless shacks. He was cozy inside his sleeping bag—it still got cool at night out here in May—on top of his canvas cot. He'd brought a cot for each of the other men who were with him now, and he made sure they used them. The cots weren't very comfortable—in fact, the ground would have been a lot softer—but they were necessary. If you slept on the ground out here, snakes could easily crawl into your sleeping bag, seeking warmth, and coil up beside your legs. If they were *poisonous* snakes—water moccasins, corals, rattlers—and you rolled over during the night or kicked in the morning getting out of the bag, you had a problem. Being bitten by a poisonous snake wasn't good anywhere, but out here, a long way from help, it could easily be fatal.

Tomorrow's project would be to repair the roofs of the three shacks. Pretty soon thunderstorms would start rolling into the Everglades like clockwork every afternoon at two, and the downpours could be monsoonlike. There was no telling how long they'd be out here, and he wanted to be comfortable. He'd been involved with a couple of these things down in the rain forests of Central and South America, and he knew what it was like to be wet for a week at a time. He didn't want to live that experience ever again.

He smiled and shut his eyes. It was all going well. Now they just had to wait for the word.

VICTORIA GRAHAM closed the hall door of her hotel room and locked both locks—doorknob and dead bolt—making certain three times they were securely latched before she finally turned away. For a moment she even considered switching rooms so he wouldn't be able to find her if he decided to come back for some reason.

She'd never met a scarier individual than Steven Sanchez. If she'd known what she was in for, she would have had half a dozen armed security guards with her—and she still might not have felt safe. Something about him told her he was one of those few men who could never be killed by anyone but God. Of course, that scariness convinced her he knew what he was doing, too. And, hopefully, this would be the only time she'd have to meet with him.

She swallowed hard as she moved through the dark room and climbed into bed, wondering if Dorsey had gotten that other thing right. Making certain that the man who was to die tonight wrote a suicide note blaming Christian Gillette. She hated that he had to die, but there was no other way.

NELSON PADILLA peered out from behind the smooth trunk of a palm tree, trying to see if it was all clear. Trying to see if there were any unfriendlies milling around the van he'd parked in the clearing that Gustavo Cruz had suggested.

"See anything?" The deputy minister of agriculture stood behind Padilla, looking over his shoulder nervously, back the way they'd come.

Padilla wiped his forehead with a handkerchief. "No." He was sweating profusely. They'd been feeling their way through the jungle for over an hour now, pushing huge ferns and broad leaves out of the way as they snuck ahead. Wondering the whole time if they were suddenly going to be blinded by brilliant spotlights and ordered to throw their hands in the air by rifle-wielding FAR soldiers. "It's too dark," he whispered, holding his hands up in front of his face. His fingers were bleeding from the sticker bushes that had been clawing at him.

After Cruz had burst into the meeting to tell them that he'd seen a vehicle at the end of the driveway, they'd all raced from the barn and scattered into the tree line behind the building. Padilla and the deputy minister had literally bumped into each other a few hundred yards into the forest—scaring each other to death—then stayed together, slowly moving back toward the clearing, giving the barn and the driveway a wide berth. Stumbling onto the paved lane just as a pair of headlights swung around a curve. They'd raced back into the brush and watched as an army transport vehicle had roared by, ready to spring from their hiding place and sprint away into the woods if the truck looked as if it were going to stop. But it hadn't stopped. They had no idea if the truck was headed to the Cruz ranch as part of a team that was trying to find them, or if the vehicle was simply headed from one FAR installation to another or was on a normal patrol.

They had come out onto the lane too far from the Cruz ranch, had given the driveway too wide a berth. So, once the truck was gone, they'd headed back into the woods and cautiously made their way toward the clearing. It would have been easier to head down the lane to the dirt road that would lead to the van, but they didn't want to be out in the open like that.

Padilla knelt down, wiping his forehead again as he gazed through the darkness at the faint outline of the van fifty feet away. The humidity, combined with the physical exertion of fighting through the jungle and the terror that shook him, was nearly melting him.

It was the first time during this whole thing he'd come face-to-face with the reality of what they were doing, and of what they could accurately be accused of—treason against the state—and for which they would be executed. Until now, the Incursion had seemed like a romantic mission. Fraught with danger, but nothing he couldn't handle. However, as he'd been stumbling wildly through the trees in those first few seconds after Cruz had burst into their meeting, branches ripping at his face and hands, he'd imagined men like General Delgado on the other side. The side loyal to the Communists. Men just as cold and just as driven as Delgado who would think nothing of torturing him for information, then shooting him in the back of the head and throwing him down a ravine—the same way Delgado had the little rancher from the next farm over.

"What are we going to do?" the deputy minister whispered. "I don't think we should stay around here too long if we aren't going to go to the van."

The problem was that the FAR might have found the van before they'd gotten to Cruz's driveway, Padilla realized. They might have found it, then left several soldiers here to wait for members of the Secret Six to show up. They might be hiding in the bushes at the edge of the clearing, just as he and the deputy minister were. Fear gripped Padilla. They might be equipped with night-vision capability, might be watching the two of them right now.

Padilla gritted his teeth. The attorney from the Ministry of Justice. Bastard. It had to be him, he had to be the spy. Padilla had always suspected the man, and now he replayed those first few moments of chaos back to himself. He remembered glancing over at the attorney right after Cruz had burst into the room and shouted about the lights at the end of the driveway. The man hadn't seemed that flustered—not the way the rest of them had been. He'd raced out of the meeting, too, but he'd been the last one out the door.

"Dr. Padilla, what are we going to—"

"Shut up!" Padilla hissed. "What are you doing saying my name?"

"Sorry, sorry, but I—"

Padilla stood up and pressed his hand hard over the other man's mouth. "Shut up." The deputy minister nodded and Padilla slid his hand away from the man's face. The deputy minister was sweating, too, and Padilla wiped the perspiration off his fingers onto his pants, feeling the van's keys in his front pocket as he did. He'd driven. It was a hospital van. "Maybe we should—"

Then Padilla noticed two dark figures break into the clearing. He squinted, trying to make out who they were.

FROM INSIDE the foyer of the walk-up, Melissa watched Christian pull away from the curb in his limousine. Every day she was hating Beth Garrison more and more—because every day Melissa Hart was falling more and more in love with him.

The magazines were right about his business acumen, at least from what she could tell. He was brilliant; she knew that even though she didn't understand much about business. He knew so much about so many things, but she loved the way he never made her feel stupid, didn't try to intimidate her when she didn't understand. Just took the time to explain to her what he was saying when she didn't get it, just let her find him attractive at her own speed. And the more he explained, the more she was intrigued by what he did, by the immense power he wielded. And, understanding him as she did now, she knew he wasn't telling her half of how much he influenced. Partly, because he probably couldn't. More important, because he didn't want her to think he was impressed with himself.

She'd always adored that in a man—not needing others to be impressed with him. Maybe because for years she'd witnessed her father's desperation. Even from an early age she'd realized how incredibly insecure he seemed and how silly that was because he didn't need to be. He was already one of the most important men in Hollywood by the time she was ten years old.

The magazines were right about Christian's ability as a businessman, but they were wrong about his coldness. He definitely wasn't a man who opened up easily—so maybe the reporters were justified in what they'd written about him—but he was a warm and genuine man when he did. A man who couldn't do enough for his friends, Wayne had told her as they'd waited in the limousine outside the restaurant for Christian to come out. A man who was color-blind when it came to race, who made certain that women got every opportunity they could. And it wasn't as if he hoarded all that money he made like some kind of Scrooge, either. Quite the opposite. He gave to charities frequently and generously.

She grimaced and looked down at the tiny tiles of the foyer. The man was so busy, but he was going to come all the way to Baltimore to see her sick mother—a woman Melissa had never met. A woman the people behind all this were paying a lot of money to for her cooperation. Melissa bit her lip. Christian was going out of his way to make time for her, and she was screwing him. And getting paid to do it.

"You ass," she hissed at herself, moving back out through the first door and down the steps. "You total ass." All of a sudden she hated herself.

Hated herself because she was allowing herself to be played, to be tempted by money. Just as she'd thought about turning her back on it all and losing herself in some small town in the Midwest, they'd come to her with a bigger, better offer. It was as if they could read her mind. Now she was making real money again. Not what she'd make as an Oscar-winning actress, but not too bad, either. And they were still promising her a huge bonus when it was over. They hadn't been specific, but "seven figures" were mentioned.

She'd been thinking of losing herself in that small Midwestern town with no idea what she would do to earn a living. And she'd found out that not knowing how you were going to support yourself, not knowing where your next meal would come from, was scary. Something she'd never experienced. So she'd sold out again, agreeing to this charade, agreeing to the money.

"I hate you," she muttered to herself as she moved slowly along the sidewalk toward Third Avenue.

They hadn't told her what this was all about, why they were so damn interested in Christian Gillette. Just that she was to get as close as possible to him and *stay* as close as possible to him so they could track his every move. They hadn't told her what was going to happen to Christian in the end, either. Whatever it was, she knew it couldn't be good.

PADILLA PEERED through the darkness from behind the palm tree, with the deputy minister of agriculture breathing down his neck. He was trying to determine who was standing by the van. In the back of his mind he was still thinking about the Communists who'd torture him, then cut him up into little pieces, if they found out what he was doing. Then one of the men by the van coughed and swore and instantly Padilla recognized the voice. As Padilla stepped out from behind the tree and into the clearing, the deputy minister tried to grab him, tried to hold him back.

"What are you doing?" the deputy minister demanded under his breath. "Come back here."

Too late. The figure by the van had already spotted the movement through the gloom and smoothly drawn a pistol.

"Hands up!" he shouted.

"Mr. Cruz!"

The figure froze. "Amigo?"

"Yes, yes."

"Oh, Jesus." Cruz shoved the nose of the pistol back down into the holster he was wearing on his leg. "I almost shot you."

They shook hands, more out of relief than anything. "It's okay," Padilla said soothingly. He could tell that tonight had been almost more than the gentle rancher could handle. "What the hell's going on?"

Cruz shook his head. "It was nothing, all my fault. The car at the end of the driveway was an old man's. He had a flat tire. I helped him put on the spare, then got him going again. I'm sorry I caused you all so much panic."

Padilla waved. "It's okay, it's what we asked you to do. Don't worry about it. Do you know where the others are?"

"Everyone else is back up at the house." Cruz glanced past Padilla as the deputy minister moved toward them. "They are all fine."

"Good, good."

The deputy minister put a hand on Padilla's shoulder. "Well, Doctor, you gave me quite a scare."

Cruz's eyes flashed to Padilla's. "You are a doctor?" he asked quietly. Padilla hesitated. "Yes."

Cruz leaned close to Padilla and whispered, "My son's boy is sick, he has a fever. My grandson, it's the little one. He's just four. Would you mind seeing him for a few moments?"

Padilla's eyes narrowed. A slip of the tongue by the deputy minister that could cost him his life. "I'm happy to take a look at him."

"**CHRIS?**"

Christian glanced up quickly from his computer screen at the sound of a soft knock on the open door, startled. It was after one in the morning, and he'd thought he was the only one still left here at Everest. He'd called Wayne on his cell to send him and the driver home. Wayne had sent the driver home but was still waiting downstairs in the lobby. Quentin was clearly worried about something.

"*Ally!* Jesus."

"Sorry. Didn't mean to startle you."

"What are you doing here?" He motioned for Allison to come into the office.

"Just taking care of a few things," she answered, sitting down in front of him. "I couldn't sleep."

Still, she seemed tired. Distracted, too. He'd been in the office plenty of times with her at one in the morning over the past few years and she was usually more upbeat. Joking, telling a story, something.

"What are *you* working on?" she asked.

He grinned and reached for the printer on a small table beside his desk. "Something I think you'll be excited about."

She gave him a curious look.

"Here." He handed her a copy of the memo he'd been drafting. "That'll go out later today to every employee and all of our investors."

Allison's eyes widened as she read the three paragraphs. "I can't believe it," she said, her voice growing stronger. "You're really going to make me vice chairman?"

"It's official. The documents are already drawn up. I just have to sign them in the morning. So do you."

"Thank you. I . . . I don't know what to say. I really appreciate your faith in me."

"Well, I needed a little push from Victoria Graham, but that's all right. I need a push sometimes. You know that." He gestured at the memo shaking slightly in her hand. "You'll be number two around here from now on. With this promotion I'm going to ask you to take over a lot of the admin stuff. Which won't be a lot of fun." He chuckled. "Maybe you want to reconsider."

She shook her head. "No. I want to help you with that. It's nuts and bolts and not very exciting, but you need a break from it, Chris. Everyone thinks so. And I'm more than happy to do it. I'll take care of it, I promise."

"And I didn't even have to give you a raise."

"Of course not. You know I'll do it—"

"But I *am* giving you a raise," he interrupted. "A hundred thousand bucks a year. You deserve it, you've done a great job. Of course, after the Laurel Energy payout, a hundred grand won't mean much to you."

"It means plenty. And it's got nothing to do with the amount." Allison gazed at him for a few moments. "You're amazing."

"Nah. This should have happened a while ago. I shouldn't have taken so long." He laughed loudly. "Maybe it was just that I didn't want to draft the memo. You know how much I hate doing that stuff."

"Some of the managing partners might not feel very good about this," she said, holding up the piece of paper.

He waved, as if she shouldn't be worried about that at all. "It's okay. I talked to all of them except Jim Marshall, and they're fine with it." He snapped his fingers. That was another memo he needed to draft. The one letting everyone know Marshall wouldn't be around for a while.

"What?"

Christian hesitated. He wanted to find out if Allison already knew about Jim Marshall's being on paid leave—he hadn't told anyone else yet—but he was too tired. "The reason Marshall hasn't been around for a few days is that—"

"You put him on paid leave," Allison interrupted. "I know."

"You *do*?"

"Uh-huh. I had a drink with him. He told me. He's pissed." She put the memo down on the front of Christian's desk. "But now that I've had a chance to think about it, I probably would have done the same thing you did. I hate to admit it, but you were right. You can't have a guy like that around here. He needs help."

Christian couldn't help but wonder if she really thought that or she was just saying it because she'd just been promoted. If in the euphoria of becoming the number two person at the largest private-equity firm in the world, she was saying what she thought he wanted to hear. He shut his eyes tightly for a moment. He hated always wondering about people's motives. Maybe he needed more than just a break from the admin stuff around here, maybe he needed to get away completely for a while. After he was finished helping President Wood in Cuba, he'd take a vacation—a long one. The question was—with whom?

"I'm sure he is pissed, but, hey, I could have fired him."

"He knows that. He knows he owes you big-time. Deep down he's really just mad at himself." She waited for a few moments. "How was Quentin about it, about you making me vice chairman?"

"He thought it was a good decision. Told me he thought you were the best person for the job. Quentin likes you a lot."

"I wish you still did," she whispered.

"What?"

Allison looked away for a few seconds. "I miss you," she murmured. "So much."

He felt bad, he hadn't told her anything about Beth. "Look, I know we haven't had much chance to see each other lately, but—"

"I don't mean that," she broke in, standing up. "It just seems like we're not on the same page like we used to be. We used to be so close, and I don't feel like we are anymore."

He stood up, too, as she came around the side of his desk.

She didn't ask, she simply moved right up to him, put her arms around him, and pressed her body to his.

She was small like Beth. A little taller, but delicate in the same way. And her long blond hair smelled like a spring afternoon, fresh like the air that had rushed over and around him in the car on the way back to Washington from Camp David.

What was wrong with him? He had everything he wanted right here, but he wasn't pushing it, wasn't closing the deal. Maybe down deep he realized that once he committed to her, it was over: other women, doing anything he wanted whenever he wanted. Maybe he was afraid of that much commitment in his personal life. He'd been on his own so long maybe he wouldn't really know how to take care of someone else the way Allison wanted to be taken care of—*ought* to be taken care of.

She looked up at him. "What is it with you?"

Crazy. She could read his mind. "What are you talking about?"

"Your body language is all wrong. It's like I'm hugging a tree for God's sake."

"Um . . . well, I don't—"

"Is there someone else?" she demanded, stepping back from their embrace, her eyes flashing. *"Is there?"*

"*What?* I thought we said we'd tell each other if we ever—"

"Stop it!" She held her hands out toward him, then slowly let them fall to her sides. "You know what? I can't take this anymore, Chris. Wondering what's going on with us, what you're doing behind my back. Well, you've got your wish," she snapped, cutting him off again as he was about to say something. "We're business partners from now on and that's *it*. I'll be the best damn business partner you've *ever* had, and I won't try to start anything between us again." She turned and stalked to the door. "Have a nice night," she called over her shoulder, *"partner."*

This time he didn't try to stop her from walking out the door. It wouldn't have been fair. She was absolutely accurate about everything she'd said. The whole time Allison had been holding him he'd been thinking about how maybe there was someone else out there for him. Maybe even someone younger. Not Beth specifically, but someone like her.

He moaned as he collapsed into the leather chair, let his head fall back, closed his eyes, and ran his hands through his hair. He'd always thought men who'd talked about going through a "midlife" crisis were just weak. Men who hadn't measured up to the success they or others had expected. He'd always promised himself he wouldn't fall victim to it. So what was he supposed to call this?

PADILLA FOLLOWED Gustavo Cruz up the narrow staircase of the main house. The other five members of the Secret Six were waiting for him outside, ready to scatter into the jungle again if there was another alarm. All of them were fidgety, glancing around constantly. All of them except the attorney, Padilla thought.

They all looked exhausted, too, as if they'd just finished a marathon—and for all intents and purposes they had. But the attorney hadn't looked that way at all when Padilla had finally caught up with him again outside the house's main entrance, after traipsing all the way back down the lane and up the driveway. The attorney had been sweating a little, but not like the rest of them. And he was the oldest of the group by at least ten years. He should have been ready to collapse.

At the top of the stairs, Cruz turned left down a hallway, then left again into a room with two bunk beds each stacked three mattresses high. On the bottom bunk of the bed nearest the door sat a young boy.

"This is Ruby," Cruz said, closing the door after Padilla.

Padilla moved to where the four-year-old boy sat and knelt in front of him. He enjoyed treating kids because he hated seeing them sick or hurt. He was a devoted Catholic, never missed a Sunday service no matter where he was in the world, but he'd never been able to resolve the conflict of seeing small children in pain, particularly the cancer victims slowly losing their awful battles. Not really understanding what was going on—which was probably better. Cheerful and loving—never bitter—right to the end.

He'd asked many priests to explain it to him: why a child should suffer so terribly. But none of the men in robes had ever been able to give him a satisfactory answer. One that put his mind at ease and allowed him to accept that there was truly a purpose to the agony borne by such innocent human beings. It was the only conflict that gave him even the slightest doubt about his faith, the only thing that even came close to making him question the existence of the Holy Trinity. Though he'd never admitted this doubt to anyone—which of course he knew was incredibly irrational. It didn't matter what others thought—only what God knew. And God knew if his faith was solid whether Padilla said anything to anyone else or not.

"Hello, Ruby," Padilla began in a friendly voice, making certain as he always did when he spoke to children not to talk to the boy in some silly,

high-pitched voice. Even more aware of treating him respectfully because he had the serious, piercing expression of an adult beneath his dark
brows.

"Hello," the boy answered quietly.

"How are you feeling?"

"Fine."

Padilla pressed the back of his hand against the boy's forehead. It was
cool. He glanced back over his shoulder at Cruz. "This boy's temperature is normal." Padilla pressed his fingers to the sides of the boy's neck,
checking for inflammation of the glands, but they seemed normal, too.
"Gustavo, he doesn't—"

"The boy must have made a miraculous recovery, Doctor."

Padilla gazed at Cruz for a few moments, then stood up, aware of his
bones creaking. He was worn out after his run through the trees. Physi-
cally and mentally. He just wanted to get home and get to bed so he
could escape the pressure for a few hours. Hopefully, there would be no
nightmares tonight as there had been the last two. "What's going on,
Gustavo?"

"I wanted to get you alone for a few minutes," Cruz admitted.

Padilla could hear an edge creep into Cruz's voice. "Why?"

"I need to talk to you about one of the men in your group."

Padilla's antennae shot up instantly. "Which one?"

Cruz motioned for Ruby to leave. The little boy darted to the door
and disappeared, shutting it behind himself without having to be told.

"The older one," Cruz explained when Ruby was gone.

The attorney. "What about him?"

"He was going through my file cabinets." Cruz nodded toward the
window, toward the barn. "Through the files I keep on my cows."

Padilla's eyes narrowed. "How do you know?"

"I saw him through the little window in that room. He was the first
one in there, he was by himself. I was outside with the rest of you. I saw
him, I know I did." Cruz took off his TEAM CUBA baseball cap. Then
put it back on, then took it off again. He repeated this several times,
smoothing what was left of his hair each time he took the cap off.

A nervous habit, Padilla recognized.

"You know about those files, right?" Cruz asked hesitantly when he
had put the cap back on for good.

Padilla nodded slowly. Cruz was making certain that Padilla knew
they were falsified, that Padilla knew Cruz could get into a lot of trouble.

"I do. The general told me everything." Padilla put his hand on Cruz's shoulder. "Don't worry, your secret's safe with me." He was careful to say *me*. Suddenly he didn't know if he could say *us* anymore.

"**JUST A SECOND,** just a second," Marshall said loudly, coming out of the bedroom of his apartment, still shaking out the cobwebs as he pulled the robe together and tied it off around his waist. She'd called from several blocks away a little while ago, and she was already here. He'd figured it would have been at least another five minutes. He checked his watch as he reached the door: It was four thirty in the morning.

He pressed a tired eye to the peephole just to make sure. She was there—her back to him—but he recognized the long blond hair. He was tired, all right, but never too tired for this. He was kind of surprised she'd called. He'd left her there in the hotel passed out, not bothering to wake her up when he'd left to go to his apartment to get the spare key to the Everest lobby. Hadn't even bothered to leave her a note. But maybe he really was as good as she'd said over and over that night. Maybe she wasn't kidding, couldn't resist him. And damn, she'd sounded hot to trot on the phone. This was going to be fun, an unexpected pleasure. And it wasn't as if he had to get up for anything in the morning now that he'd been put on leave by that bastard Gillette.

"Come in," Marshall said smoothly, opening the door. "Guess you just can't get enough of my—" He gasped and stepped back as the man strode into the living room, gun leveled at his chest. *"What's the— What's going on here?"*

The man pulled the blond wig from his head and tossed it on a chair as three more men followed him inside. "Weren't going to tell us you'd been fired, huh?" The last man closed and locked the door.

"I wasn't fired," Marshall shot back, hearing fear in his voice, hoping they didn't. "What do you want?"

"This isn't going to end well for you, Mr. Marshall," the man said calmly, not answering Marshall's question. "But you can make it go less badly if you cooperate with me."

Marshall swallowed hard, heart pounding. His contacts had given him fifty grand in cash—and promised more. Suddenly he knew it hadn't been worth it. Knew he should have asked more questions—and demanded more cash up front, then run. "Please don't hurt me," he begged, the sides of his throat grabbing at the words. "I'll do anything."

"I'm sure you would," the man agreed, "but at this point nothing you could do would help me."

"I can still get into Everest," Marshall argued, his voice shaking. "I can still get information for you."

"Don't lie to me," the man snapped. "We know Gillette's security people spotted you on the building tapes going back in there the other night. We know they called you and told you that if you tried to come back in again, you'd be arrested for trespassing. We know the guards at the security desk in the lobby of the Everest building have your picture posted on the wall behind them. They've been warned to look out for you. You couldn't get into that building now unless you had plastic surgery."

Marshall sank to his knees, his eyes moving from man to man. The only way out of the apartment was the hall door behind them, and he didn't have a chance of getting past them. "I've got kids."

The man nodded. "I know, but there's nothing I can do." He waved to one of the other men. "Make him write it."

The man moved to where Marshall was kneeling, grabbed him by the back collar of the robe, and half-led, half-dragged him to the couch. Then he dropped a pen and paper on the coffee table. "Write," he demanded.

"Write what?" Marshall asked, his voice trembling.

"A suicide note," the man who'd been first into the apartment answered. "Blaming Gillette."

Marshall shook his head hard, fully grasping what they intended to do. He'd caught the man's quick glance at the sliding glass door that opened onto the small, thirty-seventh-floor balcony. "No, *no way.*"

The man walked deliberately to where Marshall sat. "I told you," he said, looking down, gesturing with the pistol, "this isn't going to end well for you. But if you don't do what I want, what happens between now and the end will be worse than you can imagine."

Marshall lunged for the gun. It was his only chance, and he caught the man off guard.

For a few seconds they struggled, Marshall trying to get his finger on the trigger—if only just to squeeze off a round or two as a call for help—the other man desperately trying to keep Marshall from getting his finger on it.

Just as Marshall finally slipped the tip of his index finger to the slim, curved piece of black metal, one of the other men nailed him with a powerful shot to the chin and he crumpled to his side on the couch, groaning. His face suddenly felt as if it were going to explode.

"Write," the man shouted, leaning over so their noses were almost touching, shoving the pen into Marshall's hand. *"Now!"*

"Screw you," Marshall retorted, his eyes rolling back in his head. "I won't do it." His mouth was already starting to swell, and he could feel and taste blood oozing between his teeth and over his tongue. "Do what you're going to—"

Suddenly Marshall felt himself being rolled onto his back on the sofa and pinned down. He saw one of the men coming from his bedroom holding a wire coat hanger, beginning to unwind and straighten it. He flailed wildly as the guy brought one end of the straightened hanger to his left nostril. "No, *no!*" With every ounce of effort he could muster, he turned his head to the right, away from the wire. *"I'll write whatever you want, whatever you want."* The thought of the hanger going down his nose was too much to take. "Please don't do that to me."

"Then *write.*"

Marshall sat up quickly, took the pen, and scribbled exactly what they dictated. Just a few words blaming Christian Gillette for the suicide. After that he signed his name.

Then they picked him up roughly by his wrists and ankles, dragged him across the floor out onto the balcony, and tossed him over the railing.

And that was that.

AS USUAL Delgado was smoking a Dominican cigar, calmly inhaling the smoke, tasting it, then blowing it up into the darkness and the broad leaves above them waving slightly in the breeze as they stood at the edge of the beach. Padilla liked the way the smoke smelled, loved the calm, cool aura the general exuded dressed in his camouflage fatigues, black boots, and jungle-green cap, sunglasses hanging from a top pocket of the nylon shirt. Padilla felt better—safer—now that they were together. The way he'd once felt being around his father at night after being at school all day.

"So you're worried about the attorney?" Delgado asked.

Padilla nodded, watching a wave roll up onto the beach. There was a full moon tonight and the water glittered in front of them like confetti. "Cruz claimed the attorney was going through his cattle files when the attorney didn't think anyone was looking."

Delgado chuckled softly. "Ah. I'll bet old Gustavo almost had a heart attack. He could get in a lot of trouble for that."

"He's definitely worried."

"He doesn't need to worry." Delgado tapped ash onto the sand.

Delgado had never met any of the other five members of the Secret Six, mostly because he didn't want them meeting him. They knew who he was, knew his name, but he would be able to deny everything if one of them ever accused him of being part of the conspiracy by claiming that they were all just raving lunatics. The way Padilla saw it, the only man who could possibly link everyone together now was Gustavo Cruz, and he was sure Delgado saw it that way, too. If Delgado ever got a whiff that anything was going sideways with the Incursion, Cruz wouldn't last long. Which was one reason he'd hesitated about contacting Delgado regarding the attorney. He didn't want to effectively sign Cruz's death warrant because Delgado suddenly decided to cover his tracks and cut the link. But after thinking about it for a while, Padilla felt he had no choice, not if he was truly committed to the Incursion's succeeding. As they'd all agreed up front, if sacrifices had to be made, so be it.

"Do you have that picture?" Delgado asked.

Delgado had told Padilla to secretly take pictures of all the other men early on, but had never asked for one until now. "Yes." Padilla pulled the photograph of the attorney out of his pocket. He'd snapped it one evening downtown with a telephoto lens as the attorney was coming out of the Ministry of Justice. Padilla gazed at the grizzled face of the man with the silver, slicked-back hair for a few moments, then held it out. "Here."

"Is this the only one?"

"No."

"I'll keep it then." Delgado slipped it into the pocket his sunglasses were dangling from.

"Yes, of course."

"What's his name?"

"Ernesto Martinez."

The general nodded. "I'll do some checking for you."

Padilla's shoulders sagged. "Thank you, General." He shook his head and looked out to sea again. "I feel terrible doing this. It's probably nothing. Mr. Martinez is probably very loyal and I'm overreacting."

Delgado wagged a finger at Padilla. "Don't feel terrible, you're doing the right thing. You have to be careful. *We* have to be careful." He hesitated. "You're a good man, Dr. Padilla. Go home and kiss your children, then make love to your wife. They're the most important things in the world. Never forget that."

Padilla looked over at the general through the moonlight. He'd never asked the general anything personal, mostly because one of the first things the general had ever said to him was that they could never be friends. Not because they couldn't find things in common, but because it protected them not to know anything meaningful about each other. Delgado had told him that the state's interrogators could pick up on how well you knew someone, no matter how good a liar you were. And once they did, they wouldn't stop until you told them everything.

"Are you married, General?" Padilla watched Delgado's eyes narrow, watched his expression harden. "I'm sorry, I didn't mean to—"

"I was once," Delgado answered, his gaze turning distant. "She was beautiful, the love of my life. We had four children." He swallowed hard. "They all died two years ago in a plane crash. I still remember the last time I kissed Maria. I'll never kiss another woman."

Padilla glanced down at the sand under his feet and pushed it around with the toe of his shoe. He'd never imagined that the general could be a sentimental man in any way. Which, of course, he realized now was silly. Delgado had to be *extremely* sentimental to be willing to risk everything for a free Cuba. The general probably had a damn good life, as senior as he was. He could have most anything he wanted, but he'd chosen to risk it all for 11 million people he didn't even know.

Sometimes life worked in mysterious ways, Padilla thought to himself. If Delgado's wife and children hadn't died, he probably wouldn't be willing to take such a huge risk, fearing the retribution they might suffer. But now the general was a lone wolf, with only himself to worry about.

"Now that I think about it," the general spoke up, emotions trickling through his voice, "why don't you get me the pictures of the other four men, too? Much better to be too careful than not careful enough."

Padilla considered the request for a second. For some reason he didn't want to do that. "I don't have any reason to think the others might be doing anything wrong. I mean, I really don't think Ernesto's done anything wrong, either, but I—"

"Get me the pictures," the general instructed. "We'll meet tomorrow right here, same time." He hesitated and touched his cap. "Until then, Doctor."

Padilla watched the general disappear into the darkness. It was the second time in a few hours that he'd felt a deep, overwhelming terror. It hadn't been *what* the general had said, it had been *how* he'd said it.

14

TYPICALLY, Lloyd Dorsey didn't get behind the wheel. Typically, Bixby drove the Caprice Classic while the senator read reports and belted out directives over one of three cell phones to his aides back at the Russell Office Building—a stone's throw from the Capitol. Having three cell phones wasn't about making sure Dorsey had coverage wherever he went. It was about each woman he was having an affair with being identified by a separate number so he was certain not to mix them up when they called—he had a name taped to the back of each phone and made sure to check that name before answering any ring. If they felt scorned in any way, they might go to a reporter, which could be disastrous. He'd almost had to deal with exactly that situation once a few years ago. But he'd managed to squirm out of the tight spot by giving the reporter an exclusive on a pending piece of controversial anti-immigration legislation he was going to sponsor—which he hated doing. Hated ever giving anyone an exclusive about anything in his life. In return, the reporter had told the woman she didn't have anything anyone would be interested in.

The cell phones weren't in his name, they were in Bixby's wife's name. So any reporters snooping around on their own wouldn't find out how many different cell bills he had and ask him an embarrassing question out of the blue at a press conference. God, he hated reporters, always had. Even the good ones, even the one who'd helped him out of that tight spot. Life on the Hill would be so much better without them. He laughed at the irony. Maybe there were a few good things about Communism after all.

Dorsey switched lanes without flicking on his turn signal and almost ran into another car in his blind spot. "Damn it," he muttered, swerving away from the sharp sound of a horn. He was definitely out of practice.

Over the last two months it seemed as if he'd driven himself more miles than he had the previous ten years put together. All because the men he was working with didn't want to take any chances of being discovered. Dorsey had tried to convince them early on that Bixby was unquestionably loyal and would never try to expose them. That Bixby would stay in the car the entire time they were meeting and never try to see their faces, even if his bladder was bursting and they'd forbidden him to pee in the flower garden or anywhere else on the grounds, *for Christ's sake*. But they'd shaken their heads and sternly forbidden Dorsey to let anyone else accompany him.

Forty-five minutes ago he'd crossed the Chesapeake Bay Bridge headed east—away from Washington—and reached Maryland's Eastern Shore just as the sun was caressing the horizon in the rearview mirror. Now he was cruising slowly through the darkened streets of Centreville, a three-hundred-year-old fishing village of a few thousand people built on the headwaters of the Corsica River. He was close.

A half mile on the other side of town he made a left onto a narrow, bumpy road, then drove exactly two miles down the lonely, tree-lined lane as the caller had directed him to this morning. Drove until he found a private drive marked by a little yellow sign that read GOLDEN RETRIEVER CROSSING where he turned left again. A few minutes later he pulled up in front of a huge brick colonial.

He climbed out of the car—stiff from the ride—reached into the back for his cane, then limped up the unlit slate path between the boxwoods. Pretty shrubs, but he hated the way they smelled. Like urine, he'd always thought. His grandparents had lived outside Philadelphia on a big spread on the Main Line that had lots of boxwoods, and he'd remembered hiding from his dad in between them during a game of hide-and-seek when he was a boy. Always hated that ammonia smell. Like hundreds of cats had marked in there.

Dorsey didn't need to knock. The big wooden door swung open toward the inside before he reached it. An older man he recognized ushered him into the foyer, then, after closing and dead-bolting the front door twice, led him through the dimly lit, rambling mansion to a den in the back.

"Sit down." The man gestured at a captain's chair positioned in front of a large window that looked into the next room—not the outside.

Dorsey sat down in the wooden chair slowly, fascinated.

"It's one-way glass," the man explained, sitting down beside Dorsey in another chair. "They can't see us."

Dorsey nodded without taking his eyes off what was happening on the other side of the glass. Two men sat facing each other. One of the men was older, like the man who'd greeted him at the door, and wore preppy clothes—a button-down, blue oxford shirt, khaki pants, and Docksiders. Also a man Dorsey recognized from before—an associate of the man sitting beside him.

The man sitting in the opposite chair had ramrod-straight posture, a crew cut, and was younger—late thirties, Dorsey guessed. A U.S. naval officer—decked out in his dress whites, cap resting in his lap. As he looked closer, Dorsey saw that the man must have had a bad case of acne as a teenager. There were deep pockmarks on his cheek, scars that had never healed.

The man sitting beside Dorsey reached for a control panel on the wall and flipped a switch. Now they could hear the conversation in the other room.

"Give me the update," the older man was saying.

The naval officer glanced at the glass.

Instinctively, Dorsey looked away, not wanting to catch the man's eye. Which was silly, he knew. The officer couldn't see him. It was like when people were on a speakerphone and they still talked softly to other people in the room even after they'd turned on the mute button.

"The audience must be ready," the officer said loudly, still looking at the glass.

"There's no need to worry about that. It's just a mirror. There's no one watching us, we're the only ones in the house."

"Uh-huh. Sure."

Dorsey noticed a guilty grimace crease the officer's face.

"Come on," the older man urged. "I'm not paying you five hundred thousand dollars for your silence."

"Five hundred grand's probably nothing for you. I should get more."

It was interesting, Dorsey thought to himself, watching the exchange. The naval officer clearly didn't want to be here, didn't want to be giving away whatever his secrets were. You could almost see the sadness etched into the lines around his mouth and eyes. But the money was too tempting. Everybody had his price for everything.

"The update. *Please.*"

The officer took a long breath, then nodded, accepting his deal with the devil. "They're almost ready to go. The U.S. civilian will be meeting with—"

"Christian Gillette," the older man broke in. "That's the U.S. civilian, correct?"

Suddenly Dorsey realized who the naval officer was. He was the deep throat inside the Pentagon, in the basement of D-ring. The man who knew about President Wood's assassination order—and probably much more.

"Yes," the officer confirmed, "Christian Gillette."

"No chance that Mr. Gillette isn't the real one? No chance he's a diversion?"

"No chance. The people in charge of this thing did set up a couple of diversions, just in case the people in Cuba figured out what was going on. The diversions include a couple of other civilians and two senior government officials. But Gillette's the real McCoy."

"Who were the government officials?"

The older man was looking for credibility, Dorsey knew. It didn't really matter who the government officials were, he was checking the story out. He'd probably try to confirm what the officer said through another source. It was what these kind of guys did.

"The undersecretary of the treasury and some Federal Reserve guy. I think it was the president of the Atlanta Fed."

The man sitting beside Dorsey reached for a pad and pencil and jotted down a few notes.

"Where does it go from here?" the older man asked. "What's the schedule?"

"Gillette will be meeting with one of the Secret Six very soon. They'll meet—"

"Wait, wait," the older man interrupted. "Secret Six?"

The naval officer nodded. "That's the name of the civilian group inside Cuba that will take on senior positions after the military has killed the Castro remnants. If Gillette approves of them," he added. "There's two backup civilian teams inside Cuba, but if Gillette gives the go-ahead on these people, they'll be it."

"Do you know who the Secret Six are?"

The naval officer looked around warily, as if he wasn't certain how far to go with this. "Look, I—"

"Unless you want me to make you take the polygraph, you will answer me."

"All right, all right. Yeah, I know."

Dorsey glanced over at the man beside him. "What was that all about?"

"The officer gets half a million dollars for five interviews," the man explained. "A hundred thousand per. This is his fourth one. Our agreement with him is that we can stop and give him a polygraph test anytime we want during the interviews. If he fails it, we don't pay him. And he knows we'll out him as a spy." The man smiled thinly. "It's a perfect game of chicken. It works because he knows we need him, too. The likelihood of us finding anyone else with this kind of information who'd be willing to help us is very small. We've told him we're working with someone else inside the Pentagon, with someone else on the team, but he knows all of those people and he could probably tell from our answers that we were bluffing." His smile grew wider. "Of course, he needs the money more than we need the information. That's what tips the balance of power. We figured all that out before we decided who to approach."

It was the first time Dorsey had ever seen the man come close to smiling. He was obviously pleased with himself.

"Come on," the interrogator in the next room urged. "Tell me who they are."

"There's a prominent doctor," the naval officer began, looking at the ceiling as though he were trying hard to remember, counting with his fingers. "A very senior attorney from the Ministry of Justice, the deputy minister of foreign investment and economic development, the number three or four guy at the Central Bank of Cuba." He hesitated for a few moments, looking at the hand he was counting on and the four extended fingers. "Um, the deputy minister of agriculture, I believe . . . and somebody in the Ministry of Science and Technology."

Again Dorsey was aware of the man beside him scribbling on the pad. He could hear the pencil tip scraping on the page. He hated that sound, always had. It made his skin crawl.

"Why the doctor?"

"He can travel easily. Just tells the Cuban intelligence people he wants to see another surgery and is real open about where he'll be."

The older man nodded several times as if he were irritated at himself, as if he should have figured that one out on his own. "Ah, got it."

"They still watch him when he's out of country, but not very carefully." The naval officer chuckled derisively. "The Cuban intel guys in the U.S. aren't very good at high-level surveillance, or hiding who they are. They're really nothing but buffoons. They've got no high-tech equipment to speak of, just old Soviet stuff. So we can get the doctor out of his hotel anytime we want without them knowing. Anyway, that's who Gillette's going to meet with first."

"When?"

"It hasn't been decided yet, but it'll be soon."

"How soon? Like in the next forty-eight hours?" the older man asked, a worried expression coming to his face.

The officer held up his hands. "No, no. Gillette hasn't even had his ops briefing yet. They're bringing him down to Maryland for that tomorrow. I'd say the meeting will be in the next few days. But remember, the doctor's got to get out of Cuba without raising any suspicions, too. He can't just say, 'I've gotta go tomorrow.' "

"What's the doctor's name?"

"Don't make me do that," the officer begged. "He's a good man. He hasn't done anything—"

"The doctor's name."

The officer scratched his temple. "Nelson Padilla."

"Where will they meet?"

"Hasn't been determined yet, but probably a major city. Someplace the doctor can say he's going to witness an operation. Boston, New York maybe."

"Miami?"

The officer hesitated. "Maybe."

The older man leaned forward and pointed, his eyes narrowing. "Are you telling me everything here?"

"Of course."

"Because our information from another source says it's Miami. *Definitely* Miami."

"I, I don't know that, but I'll find out. I'll tell you as soon as I know anything for certain." The officer shut his eyes tightly.

As if he knew he was going to regret this, Dorsey thought.

"It probably will be Miami," the officer admitted. "It's ninety-nine percent. Kind of has to be, you know? At least someplace close to that."

The older man inside the room leaned forward in his chair, excited. "Good, good. Of course, we know what happens after that meeting between Gillette and the doctor. We just have to be damn sure we know where the meeting with the doctor will be held *as soon as possible*. You got that, *son*?"

"I do, I do. But it'll be tough. Hell, those of us in the D-ring crew may not ever know for sure, at least not until it's in progress. That's going to be handled by—"

"Dex Kelly?" the older man interrupted.

The officer nodded. "The president wasn't stupid. He gave you guys lots of room, gave you your assassination order, but he set up a couple of barriers. Us and Kelly. Us to make certain nobody got the assassination order, Kelly to keep you guys in the dark about at least a few things up until the last minute."

The older man spat. "Fucking Kelly. Traitor. Stupid, too. I'm not worried about him screwing us," he said, more to himself than the officer. "I'm worried about him screwing the whole thing up. He doesn't know how to keep Gillette safe. The whole thing could blow apart if somebody else gets to Gillette first."

"You mean the Cubans?"

"*Of course I mean the damn Cubans,*" the interrogator roared. "They've got people on the inside in Washington. We've known that for forty years. Not deep, but deep enough. Shit, they don't have to be very deep with a guy like Dex Kelly running this thing for the White House." The older man glanced up. "How's Zapata doing? General Delgado. You guys still sure he's in?"

"Absolutely."

"Will the troops follow him?"

It was the naval officer's turn to lean back in his chair. He smiled. "Well, now, that's the million-dollar question, isn't it?" His smile faded. "Look, it seems like Delgado's *the* man inside the FAR. As best the CIA and the DIA can tell, the Ochoa thing is still big for those guys and Delgado's played his cards well. There've been other situations like Ochoa's, too. Other senior FAR officers who have been hauled away in the middle of the night by the D-VI and never heard from again, and that's got the military brass down there convinced they've got to act. The incidents haven't been publicized. Even the Cuban contingent in South Florida doesn't know the extent of it all. Apparently, the D-VI is run by El Jefe's son-in-law, and supposedly he's more paranoid than anybody. And getting worse every day. But it's convinced Delgado and the men beneath him that they have to act."

"God help Delgado if the D-VI suspects anything."

The officer pointed at the older man. "*That's* what everybody's freaking out about. Delgado's the key. If the D-VI suspects anything and throws him in jail or kills him, the whole thing falls apart. He's the linch-pin. And, of course, there are all kinds of rumors suddenly running around D-ring that there's a rat somewhere in the Secret Six."

"When did those rumors start?"

"The CIA's circling up with Delgado at some dairy ranch outside Havana tonight. At the last meeting he told them there might be a prob-lem."

"*Damn!*"

"Yeah, exactly. We're so close, but, like I said, if Delgado goes down, the whole thing disintegrates."

"The doctor's a key, too."

"Yeah, he is," the officer agreed. "He won't have much of a role after everything goes ballistic, but right now he's very important."

Dorsey winced. If the Cuba thing didn't happen, they wouldn't have anything to hang President Wood with. If none of the senior Cuban of-ficials were assassinated by U.S. Special Forces during the coup, they wouldn't be able to bring the president up on impeachment charges. The law was clear. There had to be proof of an assassination, and there had to be credible evidence that the president had ordered it. If they had both pieces, they had an airtight case. It was a law the last Democratic administration before Wood's had engineered. They were going to kill the liberals with their own sword. It was perfect irony, Dorsey thought to himself.

"Do you have a copy of the order?" the older man asked.

Almost timidly, Dorsey observed. As if he were afraid of the intense disappointment the wrong answer would bring.

The officer smiled proudly, reached into his pocket, pulled out sev-eral pieces of folded paper, and handed them over. "Yep." He inhaled deeply. "I almost got nailed in the copy room with the file, too. It was touch and go for a few seconds."

Dorsey watched the older man unfold the piece of paper, watched it shake in his hand as if it were blowing in the wind as he read. It was as if he'd discovered the Ark of the Covenant, it was so important. Suddenly they had half of what they needed. Now they had to get Christian Gillette to Cuba so he could give the president the green light. Then it was just a matter of a videotape.

"**YOU OKAY?**"

Allison looked up. She'd been putting a deal file away in her desk—as usual she and Sherry were working late. It was almost nine thirty and she was meeting Christian at the Plaza hotel at ten for a drink in the Oak Bar. She couldn't wait. He'd come into her office this morning and asked her on the date, even told her he missed her. She'd been tempted to play hard to get, but she'd been too excited. It seemed as if he really wanted to have time alone with her. He'd made a point of telling her it would be just the two of them.

"What do mean?"

"You seem a little on edge," Sherry answered.

Allison slid the drawer shut. "I guess I'm still trying to come to grips with Jim's suicide." Christian had told her about it and been very up-front about the note the police had found in Marshall's apartment blaming him for the death leap. He'd been subdued, obviously feeling responsible. "It's horrible."

"Yeah. I heard Jim wrote a note blaming Christian."

"How did you hear that?"

"Things get around."

Allison slipped the desk key into the drawer lock and turned. The key was strung to a long cord hanging from her neck. Her elevator swipe card was hanging from the cord, too.

"Is that a new card?" Sherry asked, pointing toward Allison's neck. The swipe cards were bright white when they were first issued, but they faded over time. "Looks like it was just washed or something. You leave it in your clothes and run it through the washing machine or something?"

"No, you're right, it's new."

"You lose your old one?"

"Yup," Allison answered curtly. "But I'm keeping this one around my neck so I shouldn't have that problem again."

Sherry twirled her hair while she watched Allison pack her briefcase. "You want to get a drink?"

"Can't. I'm meeting Christian in a few minutes." She liked telling Sherry that. It was wrong to feel that way, but ever since Sherry had lied to her about Christian asking her if she wanted a ride home, there'd been this unacknowledged tension between them. Allison hadn't confronted Sherry with Christian's story, but she could tell Sherry sensed that she and Christian had spoken about it. "Maybe tomorrow night."

"Yeah, maybe. Hey, has Christian told you about his new flame?"

Allison had been about to stand up, but she sank back into the chair. "Huh?" She tried to make it seem as if the comment hadn't floored her, but she knew she'd given away her emotions right away. Sherry had a triumphant look on her face. Clearly she'd seen the reaction.

"He's seeing this girl who's like half his age."

Allison's heart began to pound. Was Sherry lying again, or was this real information? She didn't want to ask, but she had to. "How do you know?"

"I was going home one night last week, and I saw them coming out of an Italian restaurant on the Upper West Side. Let me tell you, this girl is *gorgeous*." Sherry rolled her eyes. "And *young*. Like maybe still in college."

Allison stood up, promising herself she wouldn't ask Christian about it tonight. Which was going to be tough, especially after a drink or two. "Thanks for the good news."

"Sorry," Sherry said, standing up, too, heading for the door, "I didn't mean to upset you. I figured you'd want to know."

Sherry was right about that. But the info could have been delivered a little more tactfully.

"Oh, by the way," Sherry called from the doorway, "congratulations on being named vice chairman of Everest. That's great."

Alison watched her leave, then glanced down at the new swipe card hanging from her neck. So strange. She and Sherry had been good friends a couple of days ago, now suddenly it seemed as if they were intense rivals. As if somehow Sherry thought Christian might be interested in her. Allison picked up her purse and headed for the door. A few minutes ago, she wouldn't have thought Christian could ever be interested in a girl as young as Sherry. Now she wasn't sure. Maybe Sherry was just making all that up about Christian and a young girl coming out of that Italian restaurant on the Upper West Side. But then Christian had helped that guy start the place. How would Sherry know that? Allison moaned as she headed toward the Everest lobby. She needed a drink. A stiff one.

"**YOU KNOW WHAT** I find amazing?" Dorsey asked, gazing through the one-way glass into the now empty room. The naval officer was gone and both of the older men were sitting with him. "The Democrats are going to shoot themselves in the foot with their own gun."

"How's that?" asked the man who'd been in the room with the officer.

"They were the ones who put through the legislation prohibiting a president from ordering or approving, even *knowing about,* assassinations of foreign citizens," Dorsey explained. "Civilians at any time and military people if war hasn't been officially declared. It was a footnote in that big immigration bill a while back. I was fighting like mad *not* to have it in there, but no one would listen to me. Now we're going to nail Wood with it."

"It's an impeachable offense under the Constitution at this point," confirmed the man who'd been in the room with Dorsey. "There's nothing Wood will be able to do once we've got the evidence."

"But will a *copy* of the order be enough to prove his involvement?" Dorsey asked, nodding at the folded piece of paper in the man's shirt pocket.

"It'll be plenty enough for the House and the Senate to call for an investigation. The Republicans will scream bloody murder when the signature is confirmed as Wood's. They'll demand an investigation. Not you, of course. You'll stay out of everything, let the younger Turks on our side of the aisle do the dirty work. When they question the witnesses from the Pentagon, that'll put the finishing touches on it. The vice president will take over after the impeachment vote, but we all know he doesn't have a chance against you. You'll win the next election in a landslide."

"I don't understand why President Wood would do that," Dorsey said, shaking his head. "I don't understand why he'd sign that thing. He can't be that ignorant. His advisers must have told him what he was doing, what he could be getting himself into." He caught the two older men looking at each other. "What? What is it?"

"Several of his senior military advisers told him they had to have the assassination order if they were going to win in Cuba," one of the men explained. "If they were really going to get the job done with no chance of the Communist people coming back into power. Men who are loyal to us told President Wood that. They told him they couldn't move the project forward without it, but they also told him there was an out. They told him that the definition of *civilian* was gray. That if anything ever came out, they'd swear that the Cubans on the list were really military people, regime members, FAR regulars masquerading as civilian ministers. And they swore there wouldn't be any evidence of U.S. Special Forces being involved in any assassinations. Which, *of course,* there will be. Plenty of tapes clearly showing our guys carrying out the president's assassination order. Our forces summarily executing people on this list," he said, holding up one of the pieces of paper. "Rangers and SEALs doing what their president has told them to do." He smiled. "Really at our direction, of course."

"The president's been trying to get closer to the Pentagon ever since he got into office," the other man added. "The military was clear with him right up front. A couple of the Joint Chiefs told him in private they weren't happy about him being in the Oval Office based on his inner-city campaign speeches. The crap about how he'd make sure no social program ever took a backseat to a weapon. They told him in no uncertain terms a few days after the inauguration they were worried about him trying to make cuts in the defense budget and moving those savings over to social programs. Wood took all that to heart. He wanted to be close to the military. He understood that no matter what country you're talking about, even the United States, ultimately you need the full backing of the military." The man smiled evilly. "He took direction from what happened to Jack and Bobby Kennedy. They gave the Pentagon the finger and look where they ended up." He laughed coldly. "Oh, yeah, Wood was ripe for this. Besides, he thinks he's doing the right thing by liberating Cuba. Not only for the Cuban people, but also the U.S. He's worried about China putting missiles on the ground."

"He *is* doing the right thing," Dorsey murmured. "China is a threat."

"Maybe, but this is how politics is played, Senator. You know that as well as anyone."

Dorsey did know that. All too well.

"Let's talk about Victoria Graham," the other one spoke up.

"What about her?" Dorsey asked, suddenly suspicious.

"Does she have someone watching Christian Gillette? You weren't sure she had followed through the last time we spoke."

"She says she does."

"Who is it?"

Dorsey shrugged. "I don't know," he admitted, watching the intense irritation zip across both men's faces. They needed as many moles as possible, especially with Dex Kelly buffering everything over at the White House. "I really don't. She wouldn't tell me. But you guys are getting your information on him. You have that other person watching him." He raised one eyebrow. "Well, you *did* have him watching Christian."

"It doesn't matter what or who we have," one of the men said. "We need to know who Victoria Graham is working with and you need to find that out for us."

Dorsey glared at them. "You want Gillette so badly?"

They glared back for a few moments. Finally, the one who had interviewed the naval officer spoke up. "Christian Gillette has a lot to answer for. A *hell* of a lot."

Dorsey nodded, his harsh expression weakening. He could understand why they hated the guy. They'd spent their careers protecting the United States, taking huge personal risks and earning a lot less than they would have in the private sector as senior executives for one of the big defense companies. They were supposed to have earned all that lost opportunity back with the nanotechnology deal, supposed to have gotten penny warrants before the IPO. After they'd lifted the technology out of the government and hid it in a private company. But Gillette had gotten in the way, totally derailed that huge potential payback by figuring out what was going on. *And* they blamed him for the death of their friend Sam Hewitt, the former CEO of U.S. Oil.

"Let me get this all straight," Dorsey said respectfully. He'd never asked for a full accounting before tonight, but if he was going to commit to this fully, he wanted to know everything. "The guys in D-ring at the Pentagon are the planners, right?"

The two men glanced at each other, then folded their arms across their chests.

Not promising, Dorsey thought. But he gave them a minute to soften up.

"That's right," the one who had been interrogating the officer finally confirmed. "You heard the man in there," he said, gesturing toward the glass. "The president's been careful on this, as he should be after signing an assassination order. He set up D-ring with his own people. They're the planners, and they're insulated from us."

The older men shared a triumphant laugh.

"At least, they're supposed to be insulated from us," the one who'd been speaking continued, holding up a copy of the assassination order. "They coordinated with intel on the ground in Cuba and with the people who met with Dr. Padilla when he came to the States." He rolled his eyes. "And the president put Dex Kelly in charge over at the White House. Kelly has authority to change any part of the plan right up until the meeting with Padilla in Miami is done. Then *we* take over. Then it's our show. Then we coordinate with the Rangers and the SEALs. That's when it'll get fun."

Dorsey's eyes narrowed. "You guys aren't really retired."

They shared another loud laugh.

"Gee, Lloyd," the man who'd sat next to him during the interrogation said. "Guess that's why you're going to be the next president. You're sharp as a fucking tack, aren't you?"

"Hey," Dorsey snapped angrily, "I don't need to—"

"Easy, Senator, easy," the other one said smoothly. "Officially, we are retired. Unofficially, we're as active as we ever were at the Company." He smiled again. "This arrangement just makes it a little easier to set things up. The only problem is, it makes things harder to control, too." He pointed at Dorsey. "Which means you're exactly right. We need as many moles as possible. As many people as possible helping us get Gillette to Miami. Telling us what he's doing all the time, watching him to make sure the Cubans or anyone else aren't planning something. Once we take over," he said calmly, holding up the assassination order, "everything's jake. But we have to make absolutely certain it gets to that point. We have to take any step necessary. Because if we don't, if somehow things get fucked up, everything's lost. Including you becoming president."

Dorsey set his jaw firmly. He'd call Victoria tonight when he got home and promise her anything to get the information from her— whom she had working on Gillette. Even tell her that he'd asked his wife for a divorce. This was a chance to realize his greatest dream. Nothing was going to stop him.

· · ·

CHRISTIAN HAD ALWAYS LIKED the 21 Club. It was cozy, like being in someone's living room with its big upholstered chairs and long, thick drapes dangling next to the windows. And people gave you your space here, no matter who you were. It was nice that way.

He was sitting at a small table in front of one of the tall windows. It was pouring rain and windy outside—a late-May deluge brought on by a cold front roaring in from the west. Which was probably why Allison was fifteen minutes late. People were hurrying along the sidewalk, hunched down beneath umbrellas, bundled up in trench coats. It had gotten chilly today when the cold front reached the city.

He turned away from the window and sipped his orange juice, watching people talk—mostly business types—at the crowded, dark wood bar in front of the far wall. There'd probably been a lot of megadeals put together at that bar over the years, he realized. Mapped out in principle on paper napkins after a six-pack of Scotches or martinis. He was becoming so much more attuned to history as he was getting older. He could almost see the Manhattan deal-making titans of the past and present—Rohatyn, Gleacher, Peterson, Wasserstein, Trump, Kravis, and Schwarzman—standing at that bar bartering billions.

He glanced down and took a deep breath. God, he felt awful about Jim Marshall. He'd never seen it coming, never even considered the possibility that the man might commit suicide. It was just that the idea was so foreign to him—a human being taking his own life. How could things get that desperate? But Marshall had done it, and now Christian was feeling wave after wave of guilt crash onto his shores.

"Hi, there."

Christian looked up. "Hi, Ally." He stood up as she propped her wet umbrella against the wall. "Let me get that." He helped her off with her raincoat and draped it over the back of the third chair around the table. "Bad night, huh?"

"Terrible," she agreed, sitting down after Christian pulled the chair out for her. "But the rain's supposed to be gone by tomorrow morning. Tomorrow's supposed to be beautiful." She waved to a waiter. "Grey Goose martini, straight up, please."

"Working late?" Christian asked, settling back into his chair.

"Yup."

"With Sherry?"

"Yup."

Allison still seemed uptight, still not herself. It was as if they just couldn't get past this wall that had suddenly risen up between them. And it seemed to be getting higher and wider all the time. "You okay?"

"I'm fine. Still pretty shook up about Jim's suicide. I keep thinking about him taking that leap off the balcony, actually being so unhappy he could do that."

"Me, too." Christian's eyes dropped to the tabletop. "It's awful," he said, his voice barely audible over the background music and the dull hum of conversation. "I feel sick about it. I misjudged him, I thought he was stronger."

"Yeah, well . . ."

"I know you were close to him, I know you cared about him."

"I felt bad for him," Allison said. "He was going through a lot."

Christian glanced up, still wondering exactly how close she'd been to Jim Marshall. But her expression wasn't giving him any answers, and, even though he wanted to, he couldn't ask her if they'd ever been intimate.

They were quiet until the server delivered Allison's martini.

Christian waited for her to take a sip, then spoke up. "You know, people are—"

"What's your—"

They'd started talking at almost the same instant. Christian motioned for her to keep going.

"No, no," she said. "You go ahead."

"I was just going to say that I think people are excited about you becoming vice chairman." Most of the e-mails he'd gotten about her promotion had been very positive. But a couple of the big investors—older men—had questioned the decision. They'd asked in their replies to the announcement if a woman in her early thirties was really ready to run Everest Capital when Christian wasn't around. He'd replied that she was *absolutely* ready, italics and all. "A lot of people at Everest have come up to me and told me they think it's great. I didn't know if I would before I made the announcement, but now I kind of like having an official successor."

"What about the big investors?" she asked. "I've heard from a lot of people, too, which is nice. But a couple of the bigger investors haven't called or e-mailed. Other than Victoria Graham."

"It's all good." He didn't want to tell her about the doubt, didn't want to do anything to dampen the mood. It was the first time they'd been alone like this in a long while, and he suddenly realized how much he'd missed it. How much he'd missed her.

"Are you telling me the truth?"

Christian took a swallow of orange juice. "There will always be doubters, Ally. People doubted me when I first took over Everest Capital, when Bill Donovan was murdered. You just have to prove them wrong." He laughed. "And damn, it's not like I'm going anywhere anytime soon. So I wish we could get off this." But he saw that she still needed encouragement. "Look, all that matters is that *I* think you'll do a great job if, for whatever reason, I'm not around."

"Thanks." She fiddled with the paper napkin beneath her martini glass for a few moments, folding each corner over before looking up. "Hey, what's your favorite movie?"

Christian put his head back and laughed. "You've been hanging around Victoria Graham too much lately."

"I'm serious, what is it?"

"I'm not at liberty to say."

"Come on, Chris."

Ms. Graham asked him that question every time he saw her, but he'd never come clean. It was a game between them at this point. "What did you tell her yours was?"

"If you're not going—"

"Maybe I will if you tell me."

"*Out of Africa.*"

"That one with Robert Redford and Meryl Streep?"

She nodded. "Now you tell me yours."

He grinned. "Well, I . . ." His voice faded.

"See, *that's* the trouble," she snapped. "I give but you don't give *back.*"

"Come on, Ally, I don't—"

"I was thinking maybe your favorite movie would have something to do with a man going through his midlife crisis."

Christian's eyes snapped to hers. "What's that supposed to mean?"

"Oh, I don't know, maybe I've heard about you seeing a woman half your age."

Christian caught his breath. "Okay, I've had a couple of dinners with someone." There was no reason to deny it. Obviously, she knew. He'd find out who the informant was later. "She's a friend."

Allison glared at him for a few seconds, then stood up and grabbed her coat. "I've gotta go. I'll see you tomorrow at the office."

Christian didn't even watch her walk away this time. He closed his eyes and rubbed them. Actually, she wouldn't be seeing him at the office tomorrow. Early in the morning he was headed down to Maryland to meet with Dex Kelly—and to see Beth.

ALANZO GOMEZ had no intention of keeping the business of Los Secretos Seis a secret. He had worked many years to become a first vice president of the Central Bank of Cuba. *Too* many years to get where he was to blow it on some silly idea that Cuba could be free of the Party. As everyone knew, that was an utter impossibility. And, if everything worked out as it looked like it would, he would be president of the bank soon. The current president had only one year left before retirement, and it was clear that Gomez was his successor. Everyone said so. As far as he saw it, he had every incentive to make certain Los Secretos Seis *didn't* stay a secret. And it wasn't that he was worried that they might actually succeed, it was that he figured he could curry favor from the highest of ranks by exposing the conspiracy.

Gomez unlocked the door of his modest villa and moved inside quietly, his wife and two beautiful teenage daughters upstairs asleep. He'd been working late tonight on a top-secret project—a loan from China. The Chinese government had approached the regime a few months ago with a proposal, a good proposal for a $20 billion ten-year loan Cuba badly needed—though only a few people inside the government really knew *how* badly the island needed the money. Basically, the infrastructure was falling apart because glue and duct tape could get you only so far. But glue and duct tape were all they'd had for decades without Big Brother—without the Soviet Union. Now they wanted Big Brother back, even if it wasn't the same one.

China's proposal had seemed perfect on the surface, when they were secretly negotiating the major points verbally around the table in a glistening conference room full of antiques and fine art at the last meeting in Paris. But, as always, the devil was in the details. There were several clauses buried deep in the first draft of the three-hundred-page document that Cuba couldn't abide by—no matter how badly they needed the money. At least, that was what he had been told initially. The clauses included the pledge of all assets held in foreign banks; the pledge of certain Cuban land, actually requiring the government to subrogate its sovereign rights to China; and allowing China to influence domestic policy if the Central Bank of Cuba ever fell behind on payments or broke a major covenant.

Gomez had managed to negotiate away all but the two nastiest provisions: China's ability to construct and maintain two huge military bases on the island—one land-based, the other naval—and their ability to secretly install offensive nuclear missiles around the island as well as man the sites without any Cuban monitoring. It wasn't that they would do that immediately, they claimed, but they wanted permission right up front in the loan agreement. He'd tried as hard as he could to have those provisions removed, but to no avail. The Chinese had agreed to take out each of the other clauses—albeit grudgingly—but not the last two. Gomez had recognized early on that the first few clauses had been put in there as throwaways against the military base and nuclear missile provisions, but he'd hoped against hope he could be successful. Hoped he'd be able to get all of them out. He hadn't been. And he'd found out when he'd gone back to the regime, hat in hand with his failure, that they weren't as intransigent on the last two points as he'd originally been told they were. Money talked, bullshit walked. That was true in *every* society, especially when it was $20 billion.

Of course, it wasn't that the Party cared about the United States—that wasn't why they'd fought the last points so doggedly. In fact they *loathed* the United States, of course. Almost irrationally in Gomez's view because, unlike Cuba, the people at the top of the U.S. government were constantly changing. There were constant opportunities to make inroads there. But the men at the top in Cuba never tried. So the mandate from the top to fight the nastiest clauses had nothing to do with some latent compassion for the United States. It had to do with the fact that the regime truly believed the United States would fire their own weapons at Cuba if she allowed the Chinese to set up bases on her island. Just as they had believed it in the early 1960s when it was the Russians.

Gomez moved through the living room and out onto the patio, which overlooked a small ravine. He eased into a lawn chair and looked up at the stars. The villa was nice by Cuban standards. However, it was only something a middle-class family in America would live in—and they'd own it.

But for Gomez, life was absolute on one hand and relative on the other, and he was more concerned with the relative at this point. Maybe the house was modest by U.S. standards, but it was wonderful for here. And if he became president of the Central Bank of Cuba, it would become even nicer. And if he broke the news about the conspiracy, well, he might even become a hero.

He set his jaw firmly, comfortable now with his decision. He'd go to the Secret Six meeting tomorrow night and listen and nod as he always did. Maybe go to one more after that. Then he'd give them all away.

15

"I DON'T GO IN THERE unless *he* goes in there," Christian said, making the ultimatum crystal clear to Dex Kelly, gesturing at Quentin, who was standing beside him outside the briefing room. "If you need to talk to your boss about this, let me know, because that might take a while. We're happy to come back." He assumed Kelly was reporting directly to President Wood, and contacting the president might take some time. "I made no bones about this when we met in Lower Manhattan. This shouldn't be a surprise to you."

Over the years, Christian had learned how to effectively convey to the other side that there was no room for negotiation on a certain point. You did it with your voice—a calm and firm tone, combined with a hint of sincerity, even submissiveness, as though you were reaching out to the other party at the same time you were telling them to pound salt. With your eyes—never taking yours from his or hers. And with your body language—head bowed slightly while you leaned ever so subtly toward the door. Conflicting signals everywhere so you completely confused them. And you did it only once in any session because otherwise you lost your credibility—he'd learned that the hard way on a huge deal right after he'd taken over Everest. He'd tried it twice in ten minutes and the deal had crumbled an hour later, everyone so pissed off at him there was no chance of resurrection. Fortunately, this was going to be a short negotiation. He didn't have to worry about picking his spot.

Kelly glanced at Quentin, then back at Christian. "Wait here," he said gruffly, stepping inside the briefing room and closing the door in their faces.

Christian motioned at the door and grinned. "Pleasant guy, huh?"

"He sure isn't going to win the Miss Congeniality part of the pageant," Quentin agreed. He pushed out his lower lip, as though he were thinking hard. "Maybe the swimsuit part, though."

Christian grimaced. "Yuck."

Quentin chuckled. "Not a pretty image, huh?"

"Pretty *awful*. That'll stick with me all day."

Quentin looked around. "I hope this wasn't a wasted trip, but I'm not letting you get involved in something like this without me."

"That's why you're here, my man, that's why you're here."

They'd left New York City at five o'clock this morning in a rented Chrysler sedan. No planes, no limousines, and no fancy cars like Quentin's Beamer—per Kelly's order. They'd driven down the Jersey Turnpike to I-95, then along a few local roads to a nondescript, four-story office building on the outskirts of Crofton, Maryland—which was halfway between Washington, D.C. and Annapolis, Maryland. Driven down a steep ramp on one side of the building to a closed basement garage door, which had opened after they'd been sitting in front of it for about thirty seconds. Then they'd been directed to move ahead to a gate inside the building. As soon as they stopped at it, the garage door had rattled down behind them and they'd been ordered out of the car and frisked by five guards, shotguns drawn, then made to walk through a metal detector. Then led to an elevator by three of the guards, then to this point. Kelly had waved the guards off when he'd emerged from the briefing room after one of the guards had knocked loudly on the door.

"You see Allison last night?"

"Yeah." Christian wondered why Quentin had waited until now to ask about Ally. He'd been anticipating that question all the way down from New York.

"How did it go?"

"Not very well. Somehow she knew about Beth."

Quentin raised both eyebrows. "How?"

"I don't know, I didn't get a chance to ask. I—"

The door opened suddenly and a man in a suit and tie waved them in. He was much younger than Kelly. Early thirties, Christian judged. "This way." He pointed at Quentin. "You, too."

The room inside was bare-bones: gray walls with no art, a plain table, a few plastic chairs, and a television set on a rolling stand in one corner. Besides Kelly, two other men were in the room. The one who'd just let them in and another man who looked about the same age, also dressed in a suit and tie.

Kelly pointed to one of the seats. "That's your seat, Christian." A folder was lying in front of it on the table. "You sit beside him," Kelly said to Quentin. There was no folder in front of Quentin's chair.

"This is Quentin Stiles," Christian explained to the two younger men. "He's my head of security at—"

"At Everest Capital," the one who had let them in interrupted. "We know. We saw him when we were up in New York." He nodded at Kelly. "When you met with Mr. Kelly in Lower Manhattan. Mr. Stiles drove you downtown, then kept an eye on you while you were meeting with Mr. Kelly on the street."

Christian and Quentin exchanged a quick glance. Maybe these guys were better than they had thought.

"Open the file, Mr. Gillette," Kelly ordered brusquely. "We've been testing you. You should have expected that."

Christian opened the folder. On top of the paper pile was a headshot of a man.

"That's Dr. Nelson Padilla," Kelly explained. "As you read in the first file we gave you, he's the head of a small group operating inside of Cuba called the Secret Six."

"I do remember that," Christian said, "and what each man does. From what I remember, they'll be leading the civilian effort in coordination with a senior army officer who'll lead the military side. The officer wasn't named in that first file."

"His code name's Zapata, but you won't find out his real name until your trip into Cuba. You'll meet him then." Kelly pointed at the file. "There's a lot of backup data behind that one, which you'll get when you leave here today. So you know each man in the Secret Six like you've known him all your life by the time you get to meet him. You'll get his complete curriculum vitae, psychological profile, personal financial statement detailed right down to the penny. Everything. My guys have done a great job on this."

"When are we going?" Christian asked bluntly. "When does it start?"

"Next week in Miami."

Quentin leaned forward. "It won't be in Miami."

Kelly blew a burst of hot air through his nostrils, like a bull about to charge. "What are you talking about?"

"Just what I said," Quentin answered calmly. "It won't be Miami."

"Listen, pal," Kelly snarled, pointing at Quentin, "I know about your hotshot reputation in the Rangers, at the DIA, and in the Secret Service. But let me tell you something. I've got some pretty big stripes across my arm, too. I'm not going to let you dictate what goes on here."

Quentin pointed at Christian. "My boss has asked me to keep him safe. It won't be Miami."

Kelly gritted his teeth. "Christian, I—"

"What Quentin says goes," Christian cut in quickly, "or I don't." He could see Kelly was seething, but he didn't care. He'd thought a lot about what Quentin had said. He was going to do anything he could to keep from being kidnapped or caught in Cuba by the regime. And at this point he trusted Quentin's instincts a lot more than he did Kelly's. "I'm willing to do all I can for my country, but I'm going to listen to this guy." He sat back in his chair. "It's your decision, Dex."

Kelly shifted in his chair, then let out a frustrated breath. "Where will it be?"

"I haven't decided yet." Quentin pointed across the table. "One more thing. I'll be in charge of getting Dr. Padilla where he needs to go that day."

SANCHEZ TAPPED on the keyboard quietly, accessing his temporary unlisted e-mail account. When it cleared and the in-box screen came up, he clicked the SEND/RECEIVE icon and waited, smiling thinly when the message appeared. Heavily coded, of course, but it indicated exactly what he'd been led to believe all along: Miami. It was going to happen in Miami within a week. Beautiful. He was all settled in here, didn't have to change his base of operations. Except for that one trip he needed to make, he could stay right here and enjoy some more sun and ocean. But that trip shouldn't take long. If luck was with him, he'd be able to leave tomorrow morning and be back tomorrow night. Worst-case scenario: a one-night stay-over.

Mari moaned and he clicked away from his e-mail. She was on her side on the bed, facing away from him, naked, sheet down around her knees. He gazed at her. Her curves were stunning. They'd been having sex every night since he'd told her he had her all set up for an appointment in Europe. That he'd even sent some pictures he'd snapped of her with his digital camera to the big producer he knew and claimed that the man was eager to see her. But he hadn't really set up anything. He'd been lying to her, and for a moment he felt remorse.

He hadn't felt that emotion in a long time. Maybe it was just that he was getting older. He grimaced. He and Mari had been together outside the room too much. He'd taken her to dinner a few times, regrettably, but he'd seen that she wouldn't stand for any more straight to the room and bang-bang without it. Even with the possibility of meeting a big-name movie producer, Mari had her limits. Someone could easily have been watching, seen them at dinner, and might be able to get information out of her. He'd have her for a few more nights, then cover his tracks.

He smiled as he brought up some porn on the computer, proud of himself. The remorse was gone, replaced by the intrigue of figuring out how he was going to make her disappear.

"BETH, you remember Quentin Stiles." Christian gestured back and forth between them. "Quentin, Beth."

Quentin gave the young woman a polite smile and shook her hand. "Hi."

"Christian's told me so much about you since that day we rode back into D.C. together," Beth said. "*So* much."

"Um, great. I hope it was good."

"Terrible," she replied, winking. "Says he can't figure out how he ever got mixed up with you in the first place."

She was trying hard, Christian could tell. A little *too* hard. "We're going upstairs to visit Beth's mother for a few minutes," he explained. Quentin already knew that, but it was the only thing Christian could think of to say. "Then I thought we'd all go out to dinner."

They were standing in a parking lot of the Greater Baltimore Medical Center. It was a sprawling hospital facility, located in Baltimore County about twenty miles north of downtown.

"Sure." Quentin glanced back at the car. "I've got plenty to do out here with that new project we've got. Lots of stuff to review."

"Thanks, pal. We shouldn't be more than an hour."

"Take your time."

Beth slid her arm into Christian's as they turned and headed for the huge brick building. "I like him," she murmured as they walked, moving her hand down and slipping her fingers into his, leaning against him a little as they walked. "He's very cool. I know that sounds silly, but I don't know how else to describe him. It's like he's out of a movie or something."

Her hand felt so small, and she seemed to be shaking. She was probably nervous about introducing him to her mother. "Doesn't sound silly at all, Beth. I know exactly what you mean. I tried calling him Shaft in the beginning, but he didn't like it."

"What *do* you call him? You must have a nickname for him."

"Why?"

"Because it's obvious that you two are really close. And all the guys I know who are real good friends usually have nicknames for each other."

She was right. "Yeah, I call him Q-Dog sometimes."

She scrunched up her face, as though she didn't like it. "*Q-Dog?* No way. He's more like a Silk, or a Smooth. What does he call you?"

"Chris."

"Well, that's real original," she said sarcastically.

"What should my nickname be?" They'd almost reached the main entrance.

"Grumpy," she answered as they moved through the automatic doors, punching him gently in the arm.

"*What?* Now that's not fair. Why would you—" Christian interrupted himself. She'd headed to the reception desk and started talking to an older man behind it. Telling him who they were and whom they were here to see. When they were down the short hallway and inside the elevator, he finished off the question. "Why Grumpy? That's not very nice."

"You seem pretty sensitive about it," she observed, moving close to him when the doors were shut. They were the only two in the car.

She was right, he was sensitive about it. In the past he'd heard whispers that he was too serious, that he could never seem to let loose and really enjoy himself—Ally had even said something about it a few times. But people didn't understand. A lot of times you had to sacrifice civility for efficiency. It wasn't that he was trying to be rude, but he could understand how people would interpret it that way.

"It's better than Dopey," she said, slipping her hands around his neck and pressing her body to his.

"Sounds like you have a dwarf fetish." She was gazing up at him with a faraway look in her eyes. He wanted to tell her it wasn't going to be a romantic thing, but now wasn't the time. "Don't start calling me that," he warned.

"What should I call you?"

"Chris is fine."

"I want a nickname. Something that's just ours."

He grinned and ran his fingertips slowly up the side of his neck several times. "How about Godfather?" he asked in a raspy voice. She was shaking her head hard. "No? Well, what about Cool Hand Luke? Or Dirty Harry?"

She put her hand to her mouth and burst into laughter. "Sorry. I know every guy in his forties wants to be Clint Eastwood and carry a .44 magnum, but I don't see you as a Dirty Harry." The car was slowing down. "Do you like movies?"

He did, very much. It was a great release every once in a while just to lie back on the couch in his apartment and watch one, even one he'd seen many times before. "I do." The doors opened.

"What's your favorite movie of all time?"

Christian hesitated for a moment in the car, an eerie feeling overtaking him as her words echoed in his head.

She stopped in the hallway outside the elevator and turned around quickly, her short skirt flaring high on her thighs as she twirled. She motioned for him to come on. "What's wrong?"

"Nothing."

But Christian couldn't stop thinking about what she'd just asked him, couldn't stop thinking about that day he and Quentin had been coming back from Camp David. Or that she always avoided answering questions about herself. Quentin had been able to get a little bit more on her from his friends in Washington. She was from a small town in Missouri and had gone to the University of Nebraska. Quentin had finally gotten both pieces of information after a bunch of calls. Other than those two things, they still didn't know much about her.

"You okay?" She moved back into the car and took his hand.

"Fine." He smiled and squeezed her hand.

"Was that a bad question somehow? About your favorite movie?"

"Of course not, I've just never really thought about it before. Kind of took me by surprise, that's all."

"Oh."

He noticed a strange look come to her face. As if she couldn't understand how in the world that question could evoke such a strong reaction. "Come on." He pulled her out of the elevator and back into the hallway. "Where are we going?"

She pointed to the left. "This way."

Christian had always hated hospitals and the sterility that pervaded them. The smell of alcohol and bad food, the bare walls, the uniforms. They seemed more like prisons than places of comfort. It seemed to him that administrators ought to take more time to make patients feel at home, especially on floors like this one where people had basically come to die. He glanced at an elderly man who was shuffling the other way, one hand sliding along the wall for support. The man was wearing a plaid bathrobe and shabby slippers. His thin gray hair was tousled, as though he hadn't combed it in weeks, his eyes were sunken, and he had that awful ashen hue to his skin.

When they were past him, Christian looked over at Beth. He could see tears already building on her lower lids, and her bottom lip starting to quiver. Suddenly he felt awful about his doubts of a few moments ago.

It was so quiet on this floor, he thought to himself, looking away so as not to embarrass her. Not even the faint sound of television sets coming from rooms because most of the doors were closed. People on this wing wanted seclusion, wanted to suffer in privacy. Like wild animals going off on their own to die. Deep into the forest, or to a cave.

"Hoosiers," he murmured.

She looked up, wiping a tear from one eye. "What did you say?"

"Hoosiers. That's my favorite movie of all time." He'd never told anyone that, not even Quentin. Never told anyone how deeply the film affected him every time he watched it.

It was based on the true story of a tiny, rural high school in Indiana with a total enrollment of just sixty kids winning the 1954 state basketball championship against incredible odds. Against an inner-city high school with thousands of kids. An even greater story because it couldn't happen anymore. In the fifties, every high school in the state competed in the same tournament. These days, there were separate tournaments for different-sized schools. It always inspired Christian to watch people pull together to achieve something great by caring about and trusting each other so much. To achieve something they really shouldn't have achieved simply because they were more committed to the goal than the more talented people. It was always emotional for him at the end of the movie—as the team huddled in the locker room just before they went out on the court for the championship game—to hear the coach tell his players he loved them. So Christian never watched it with anyone, always alone, so no one would see his emotion. Which was why he'd never told anyone that it was his favorite movie. He never wanted to watch it with anyone.

Beth stopped outside a door in the middle of the long corridor, slipped her hands to his face, rose up on her toes, and tried to kiss him on the lips.

But he moved forward too fast, pressed cheeks, and gave her a hug.

"Thanks for coming with me," she said, giving him a strange look. As if she couldn't understand why he wouldn't want to kiss her. "That walk from the elevator was so much easier for me than it's ever been before. It's wonderful having you here. It means a lot."

For a moment Christian thought of his father, thought about how many times he'd wished he could have had one more conversation with him. How one moment he'd felt secure knowing his father was in the world, how the next he'd felt so insecure because he wasn't. He could feel the emotions welling up, remembering that moment he'd found out about the crash so many years ago. Still seemed as if it were yesterday. "Thanks for asking," he said, his voice raspy. Her lips would have felt so good on his, but he couldn't do it. "I just want to help any way I can. Is this it?" he asked, pointing at the door.

"Yeah."

"You ready?"

She nodded hesitantly.

Christian opened the door and moved into the room first, but held up only a step inside. This time the sterility of the surroundings overwhelmed him.

Beth's mother lay on her back on the narrow bed, eyes closed, bone-colored covers pulled up to her chest. She had that same pasty tone to her skin the old man shuffling down the hallway had, tinged with a hint of faded yellow. Her cheeks were hollow, lips dry and pale, hair completely gray and pulled away from her face. She looked sixty, but he could tell from her features she was probably at least ten years younger—the disease making her seem so much older. He gazed at her face for a few moments. She was asleep, but her expression wasn't peaceful. He could still see the pain the cancer riddling her body caused. It was the same expression he'd seen on his sister's face as she slept in that Los Angeles hospital a few years ago, battling lung cancer. Nikki had fought long and hard, but ultimately it had killed her.

The rest of the small room reminded him of the room he'd met with Dex Kelly in this morning down in Crofton. Stark and uninviting. The floor tiles were gray, as were the walls, ceiling, and drapes. Even the barely touched food on the tray beside the bed looked bland.

He turned, brushed past Beth, and headed down the corridor back toward the elevators.

"Chris," she called. "Christian!"

ANTONIO BARRADO guided the Boston Whaler along the shallow, narrow canal—thirty feet across at most—bordered by an endless wall of eight-foot-high reeds. Dodging alligators as he roared ahead at thirty knots—their noses and tails visible, sometimes directly in his path. He had only a half hour of light left, and he didn't want to have to find his way back to the camp in the darkness—he didn't like it out here at all by himself now that he'd had the other guys with him for a while—and he didn't want to have to use lights. You never knew who was watching.

He strained to see through the last dim rays of the sun, looking for that break in the reeds on the left—the last turn on the way to the camp. It was only six or seven feet wide, barely enough to get the boat through, and he'd already missed it a couple of times on the way out here. He'd thought about putting up some sort of indicator—a handkerchief tied to a reed, maybe—to make finding the break easier. But he was worried someone might figure out why it was there and come looking.

Barrado powered down, easing the throttle back with his right hand, keeping his eyes peeled for the break—and for gators in front of him. Two days ago he'd seen a thirteen-footer near the camp and shot it—not wanting it to steal into one of the crude huts they were using while they were asleep, looking for an easy meal. He wasn't certain he'd killed it, despite hitting it squarely in the back of the head from close range with a nine-millimeter hollow point. It had thrashed about on the surface wildly for a few seconds, then gone down. He'd heard stories about these things coming after tormentors, and it had stared at him as he'd approached in the boat—not afraid. He winced. Being dragged to the bottom of the canal and rolled by a thirteen-foot alligator would be a horrible way to go.

A moment too late he spotted the break in the reeds.

He swung the Whaler back around and carefully guided the bow through the opening, scanning the reeds for snakes that might drop into the boat. On the other side of the break, this canal opened back up to twenty feet. Not as wide as the other one—and it was even shallower— but that was all right. There were no more turns to make. He felt better now. He'd be sure to run into the camp as long as he hugged the right bank.

He smiled. Only a few more days out here before everything went into motion. Two of them would head into Miami early next week and stay at one of the nice hotels where they'd make final preparations. The other two would stay here to guard the camp, and to prepare.

Barrado's eyes narrowed as he came around a bend—the camp was only a few hundred yards away now. He thought he'd seen that monster gator again, but it was almost dark and whatever it was had sunk beneath the surface before he could tell for sure.

"**NOW THAT'S BETTER,**" Christian said, satisfied. "Don't you think?"

Beth's mother, Kathleen, glanced around the room—now decorated with flowers and plants from the shop downstairs—in awe. He'd even bought a game of backgammon and a big jigsaw puzzle at the gift shop, as well as a few magazines—to go with the ones on the floor beside her bed.

"It's very nice," she said weakly. "Thank you so much."

"Now you can see why I adore this guy," Beth said, coming up behind Christian and putting her arms around him.

Christian checked the magazines on the floor beside the bed. All business rags. He recognized himself on the covers of two. Beth hadn't been kidding. Her mother really had read all about him.

"I certainly can." Kathleen motioned for him to come close, took his hands when he got to the side of the bed. "Thank you very much. It feels so much more like home now."

"So where is home for you?" Christian asked politely, hoping his agenda wasn't obvious.

"Well, I live—" She covered her mouth and began to cough hard.

"You all right, Mom?"

Christian backed off as Beth moved in front of him and grasped Kathleen's fingers. He'd spoken to the doctor on his way back up. Kathleen was in bad shape, but she was hanging in there. There was no telling exactly how long this would go on. Which almost seemed sad, Christian thought. She looked awful. Almost looked as if she'd rather be out of her misery.

ALLISON GAZED WARILY at the cages of snakes and lizards. It seemed as if they were closer this time, as if the office weren't as big as she remembered. Maybe it was because everything in her life seemed to be closing in around her.

"Still not used to them, are you?" Victoria Graham asked from behind her office desk.

"No."

"What's wrong, dear?"

Allison glanced out the window into the darkness twenty stories above Fifth Avenue. She couldn't decide what was bothering her—at least, what was bothering her *the most*. The fact that Christian had been gone all day and hadn't told her where he was going. The fact that she'd acted like a child last night, storming out of the 21 Club. The fact that Sherry had told her as she was leaving Everest to come over here tonight that Christian had gone to Baltimore to see the young woman he was apparently dating. The fact that Sherry seemed to know so much about Christian's schedule lately. Or was it what she was doing for Victoria Graham that bothered her most?

"I saw that Christian sent out the official announcement about you being promoted to vice chairman," Graham said happily when Allison didn't respond. "I got it the other day. That was a good thing."

"I guess," Allison said.

"Don't you want to talk about it, dear?"

"What's *your* favorite movie?" Allison did want to talk about Christian seeing a woman who was so much younger than he was, wanted to get Ms. Graham's opinion about it. Just talk about it with *someone*. But she didn't want to seem weak, either. "I told you mine, now you tell me yours."

Graham put her head back and laughed. "I told you it was a great question. It's got you thinking, hasn't it?"

Allison nodded. Thinking about how Christian wouldn't tell her what his favorite movie was, but had probably already told this new woman. Who was gorgeous, according to Sherry. This morning, she'd asked Sherry to describe the girl. Tried not to, tried to keep from asking, but ultimately she couldn't help herself. She *had* to know. Short, dark hair, a beautiful figure, awesome legs. Christian had always claimed he was partial to long blond hair.

"My favorite movie is *Sabrina,* and not the newer version with Harrison Ford. The older one with Audrey Hepburn and Humphrey Bogart. I guess I'm just a sucker for a good love story."

Me, too, Allison thought. "Are you sure what we're doing is right?" she asked bluntly. She'd taken Ms. Graham at her word for everything, assumed that she wouldn't lie. Hoped she hadn't done all that because Ms. Graham had engineered the vice chairmanship for her and that was clouding her judgment.

Graham leaned forward, her expression turning grave. "Absolutely. We've been over and over this. You know it's the only way."

"But I don't know if—"

"It won't be much longer, dear, but we must stay the course."

MELISSA WAVED as Christian and Quentin drove off. She was standing beside her car in the parking lot of the restaurant where the three of them had gone to dinner. An Italian place in Towson, a town outside Baltimore near the hospital. She and Christian had said good-night in front of the restaurant while Quentin had gone to get their car—just a polite kiss on her cheek and a warm embrace. She'd found herself wanting so much more, but how fair was that? She'd basically been hired to spy on him, to make certain they knew his every move. They'd been clear yesterday, too, very clear. If she screwed this up somehow, she wouldn't just be sacrificing her paycheck.

She walked across the small area to the car they'd provided her—a Ford Taurus—searching the shadows for any sign of them. But she saw nothing. They wouldn't be watching her now, wouldn't want to take any chance that Christian might see them watching.

She removed the car keys from her purse, unlocked the car, then stopped and banged the roof. She'd been so stupid, asking him what his favorite movie was. She'd seen in his eyes right away that he thought it was a strange question. She'd seen in his eyes that he was connecting the dots. He hadn't given any indication at the hospital or later at the restaurant that he had connected anything, but you never knew with Christian. He was as cool as they came.

Melissa felt tears coming to her eyes, real ones this time. Not those crocodile drops she'd shed before. Christian had been so sweet to that poor woman they'd found to play her mother—who really was sick. He'd bought her all those flowers and everything else, made her feel so good. Like the Lionhearted should have done for her mother eight years ago on her deathbed. But, of course, he hadn't, he'd ignored both of them. He wasn't a man like Christian Gillette who noticed and cared for those around him. Her father was selfish, completely into himself. Of course, that was 50 percent of who she was so maybe she needed to worry. Maybe that's why she was willing to screw up Christian's life in exchange for a few dollars. She swallowed hard. Maybe even *take* his life. They hadn't told her yet exactly what this was all about, but if they were threatening her life, it had to be just as serious for him.

She took a deep breath, thinking about how she'd actually suggested the hospital idea, suggested the whole thing about a dying mother. As a way to really reel Christian in, as a way to dig that barbed hook into his mouth as deeply as it would go. They'd looked at her as if she were crazy when she'd come up with it, as if they couldn't believe she'd have the emotional strength to pull it off. After all, she'd gone through exactly the same thing eight years ago. But she'd told them she was an actress, an *Oscar-winning* actress, and that she could pull anything off. Still, they'd shaken their heads. Maybe they were right after all. Maybe it wasn't just acting, maybe she really was that cold.

"I hate you, Beth Garrison," she muttered angrily, unlocking the car door and throwing it open. "I hate you, you bitch."

16

TONIGHT THE SECRET SIX were meeting by the beach where Padilla typically met alone with General Delgado. Padilla had waited until just a few minutes before five this afternoon to drape the paper napkins over the bushes in the park with that single spot of superadhesive glue he always used—which made them stay in place even if a breeze blew in off the ocean. He was always careful to take the napkins off the bushes early the next morning, before he went to the hospital, so the prisoner crews that infrequently sauntered through the park occasionally picking up trash wouldn't get suspicious and alert their guards. He'd been worried that not everyone would see the signals on the bushes, but they had. All six of them now stood in the darkness beneath the swaying palms that lined the beach like a row of sentinels. The banker, Alanzo Gomez, had been the last to arrive.

"What was so urgent that we *had* to meet tonight?" the attorney demanded.

"It's going live," Padilla answered directly, his voice strained. "This is it."

More and more Padilla worried about what he'd gotten himself—and his family—into. More and more the romanticism of being part of the Incursion had been replaced by the reality—and a horrible dread. He'd hardly slept in three days—it was as if he were doing his first few weeks of residence again. Every time he closed his eyes his mind conjured up awful images of what might happen if the attorney—or Delgado—turned out to be a spy for the Party and the conspiracy was uncovered. Or if the Incursion didn't work because the United States didn't deliver on its promise of support—as it hadn't at the Bay of Pigs—or not enough of the FAR rank and file turned their allegiance and followed Delgado. He shuddered, thinking about his wife being tortured to death in a prison cell, about his children being slowly and systematically dismembered—fingers and toes first, then arms and legs—over several hours until they bled to death. He'd heard rumors that those were the consequences for the families of men convicted of treason against the state. Suddenly, he was hearing a lot of things like that. Maybe it was just because he was listening more, or maybe somebody was trying to tell him something.

"It's all actually starting to happen," he whispered.

"When will you meet with Christian Gillette?" the banker asked.

"In two days."

"Where?"

Padilla glanced at the banker through the night. Now *he* was asking a lot of questions. Padilla's shoulders slumped slightly. He hated this, suspecting everyone of turning on him. God, maybe even his wife would turn on him to save the children. "Miami. In a hotel there, I think."

"After that it's here in Cuba, right?" the banker asked. "With all of us and the general. That's the next meeting, yes?"

Padilla glanced at the attorney. He was stroking his chin, looking at the ground as if deep in thought. "Yes. We'll meet at the Cruz ranch that night, then it will be only a day or two later that the Incursion begins." Padilla gestured at them. "Do you all have your codes?" He was referring to the codes they would need to relay to the U.S. military if they called the emergency numbers on their satellite phones. If they needed to get out quickly because the Incursion was failing. He suddenly realized that those numbers probably wouldn't be much good at that point. But it was something to hang on to psychologically—which they all needed at this point. At least, five of them did.

They all nodded somberly.

Padilla turned and looked out to sea, at the breakers rolling up onto the beach. The white foam roiling the waves was visible in the moonlight. He'd never been more scared in his life.

. . .

DORSEY WAS MEETING WITH the two older men again. Like before, he was meeting with them in their mansion on the Maryland Eastern Shore. Like before, he'd been forced to drive himself over here, concocting another story for Bixby—who he could tell was suspicious at this point. But the two older men had warned him against relaying to *anyone* what was going on. Dorsey half-suspected that Bixby had followed him—or had him followed—tonight. He appreciated Bixby very much, but the man was a paranoid son of a bitch. Of course, now that Dorsey thought about it, maybe that was one reason he was so good at being chief of staff. Because he *was* paranoid.

"We thought you were close to Victoria Graham," the man who'd interviewed the naval officer last time said in a challenging tone. They were all sitting in the mansion's tastefully decorated living room in the dim light cast by a single banker's lamp sitting on an antique table in a far corner.

"I *am* close to her," Dorsey shot back defensively, noticing for the first time that the house had a musty smell to it. As if it wasn't used much.

"Then why in God's name isn't she telling you who she has keeping an eye on Gillette?" the other one barked. "That's what you asked her to do, didn't you? What we told *you* to tell her to do."

"Yes," Dorsey said quietly. "You did. I understand why you're—"

"And she did tell you she's got someone close to him, right?"

"She did," he confirmed. "Someone *very* close to him."

"But she won't tell you who it is."

Dorsey rubbed his forehead. He was starting to feel one of those migraines he'd been getting more and more often. He'd asked Victoria three times to tell him who the person was, and each time she'd given him a different excuse. "Look, she told me the second Gillette moves, she'll call me. Like she's already done. She's been right so far, hasn't she? About him going to Washington, then to Baltimore. That all checked out, didn't it?"

"We want the name," one of the men said fiercely, chin out.

"All right, all right," Dorsey answered quickly. "I'll get it out of her, I promise." But he wasn't so sure he'd be able to. For some reason, Victoria was holding out. No amount of coaxing seemed to be working.

"Well, you better do it fast."

"Why? What's wrong?"

The man who'd interviewed the officer jabbed a thumb over his shoulder toward the back of the house, toward the room with the one-way glass. "We spoke to our guy here an hour ago. It's happening. The thing's going down in the next forty-eight hours."

Dorsey shook his head and held up his hands. "Why are you two so worried about having someone close to Gillette if you've got that guy in your hip pocket? Telling you everything that's going on? I don't understand."

"We can't be sure he's giving us the right information."

"Hasn't he been right so far?"

"So far," the second man agreed, "but now we're getting down to the end. He might be a plant, or the higher-ups might be using him to throw us off track. We haven't been able to triangulate."

"Frankly we're *very* worried about that," the other man added. "About not being able to get an independent confirm. You never know, you just never know. When *we* were in charge of missions like this, at this point in the operation we had everybody watching everybody else. A guy like the one we're working with wouldn't have been able to pick his nose without somebody seeing it and reporting back. Unless, of course, we were using him to plant disinformation." He let out a heavy breath. "We can't figure it out."

Dorsey nodded again, more to himself than the other two this time. He knew this was how spooks got near the end of a mission. They worried about disinformation and plants and what was real and what wasn't—and for good reason. Dorsey's years on the Armed Services Committee had taught him that. At this level you couldn't take anything for granted. When you did, that's when you got burned. Even when it was something that seemed innocuous.

"*You've got to find out who it is.*"

"*I hear you.* I hear you." Dorsey eased back into his chair and scratched his head. "This is just Gillette meeting with the one man, correct? The doctor? Padilla?"

"Yes."

"Then what's the problem?" Dorsey knew the men hated Gillette for screwing up the nanotech plan a couple of their buddies were going to get rich from. And for the death of Sam Hewitt—an establishment legend who they'd been close to and who had helped them with more than a few of their missions through U.S. Oil, the huge company he ran. But it seemed as if they'd have plenty of chances for revenge later, plenty of time to take Gillette down after the Cuba thing was done. "I mean, I know you hate Gillette," Dorsey spoke up. "But are you worried you won't have another chance to kill him or something?"

The man who'd been sitting with Dorsey watching the interview with the officer last time folded his arms over his chest and smiled cynically as if the senator were crazy. "*Kill him?* Why would we want to kill him?"

Dorsey swallowed hard, suddenly feeling as if he were groping in the dark. "I just thought because of—"

"We need him *alive,* for the love of Pete. At least for now."

"That's the whole problem," the other one chimed in. "We're worried that someone might get him before he gets to Cuba. That *somebody else* might kill him. Christ, if that happens, we're all screwed." He jabbed a bony finger at Dorsey. "If that happens, you can forget about being president because then we won't have anything to hang Jesse Wood with. We need the coup to happen, we need the SEALs and the Rangers to go in there and assassinate these people on the list, and we need video of it. Then we'll have Wood right where we want him. The coup doesn't go down, we've got nothing." The man paused. "But rest assured, Gillette won't be coming back from Cuba." He exchanged a knowing glance with the other man. "In all the confusion, somehow he'll be lost."

"You mean—"

"I mean the Rangers will take care of Gillette, too. Christ, do I have to spell out *everything* for you?"

Gillette had to realize how dangerous the mission was going to be, but he couldn't have any idea that the real danger came from inside his own government, not the Cubans. "Who are you worried about?" Dorsey asked. "Who's the 'someone else' going after Gillette?"

The two older men glanced at each other again.

"We don't know," one of them admitted. "It's just white noise coming through the speakers at this point. You never know about these things, but our source is credible. That's the problem, that's why we're worried. It's someone we've gotten good information from before, on other matters. A person we used when we ran the Company."

"We've got to protect Gillette," the other one said strongly, "at least for the next two days. At all costs. But it's going to be damn hard to protect him if we don't know where he is."

"You know he's going to Miami," Dorsey pointed out. "Granted,

Miami's a big city, but if you know that's where he's going, that makes your job a little easier, doesn't it?"

"Sure. If we could really count on him going to Miami."

"I thought it was all set." It was Dorsey's turn to point back toward the room with the one-way glass. "I heard that naval officer say it myself."

"Actually, he said he was—"

"Just find out what's going on with Victoria Graham," the other man interrupted. He hesitated for a few moments. "Have you ever heard of a woman named Allison Wallace?"

Dorsey nodded. "Of course. She works at Everest with Gillette. She's from one of the wealthiest families in the Midwest. Victoria talks about her a lot. Likes her. Says she's very capable."

"Any chance she could be involved in this thing? Could she be the one Victoria Graham is using?"

CHRISTIAN AND BETH were back at the Italian restaurant in Manhattan, halfway through their entrées. Beth had come up this afternoon from Washington on the spur of the moment. A call at three this afternoon to him at his office out of the blue to tell him she had to see him, that she was going crazy thinking about him. He'd tried to tell her he had an important dinner with the CEO of one of Everest's biggest portfolio companies, but she'd told him she was already on the train before he could explain.

Instead of saying he was sorry and there was nothing he could do, he'd canceled dinner with the CEO. Putting it off for a week even though the guy had come all the way in from St. Louis just for the dinner and was sitting in the lobby of the St. Regis cooling his heels. Christian had arranged for the guy to fly back to St. Louis immediately— apologizing profusely—by giving him a lift out of New York on the Everest G4, which was hangared at La Guardia.

He'd actually met Beth at Penn Station—they'd agreed on the phone that, as usual, she'd catch a cab and come straight to the restaurant. But he'd surprised her instead, picking her up and twirling her around when she ran to him as he stood beneath the schedule board in the middle of the station. And he hadn't felt the least bit self-conscious about it—even with three of Quentin's men watching. Now that everything was going into motion, Quentin was stepping up the bodyguard count. This morning Christian had picked up a coded e-mail from JRCook that the final order covering the first meeting would come soon.

"This veal tastes so good," Beth said, sliding her hand to Christian's. "I love this place. It's like *our* place." She looked around at the decorations, mementos from the town in Italy where the owner had been born. "We should come here all the time."

He realized she was staring longingly into his eyes and he glanced away. His intention tonight had been to explain to her all about Nikki, about how Beth reminded him of his dead sister, and how he wanted to keep seeing her and helping her. But that it wasn't going to be a romantic thing for him. Which would be hard to do now. He groaned softly to himself. He wished all this romance stuff came to him as naturally as the deal business did.

Beth leaned close to him and ran her hand up his arm. "Chris, I want to make love to you tonight."

PADILLA HAD GONE to his car after the meeting of the Secret Six had broken up, gotten in, and driven three miles. When he was certain none of the other five would see him, he'd turned around and headed back to the beach.

"How did it go?" General Delgado asked.

"Fine."

"Everyone at the meeting?"

"Yes."

"The attorney?"

"Yes."

"Good. Good." Delgado took a satisfied puff off his cigar and smiled.

As if he'd been here before, Padilla thought to himself. Not the physical place but the psychological place. As if he understood Padilla's conflicted state of mind exactly because he'd experienced it many times. "Why are you smiling?" Padilla asked, irritated that Delgado could be so cool at a time like this.

"It will be all right, Doctor," the general said soothingly, "it will be all right."

Padilla swallowed hard. Delgado understood exactly the terror he was feeling. "How do you know, General? How do you *know* it will be all right?"

Delgado removed the cigar from his mouth and handed it to Padilla. "You're a religious man, aren't you, Doctor? You have faith, don't you?"

Padilla took a long drag off the cigar, noticing that this was a different brand of Dominican than the one the general usually lit up. He held the smoke in for a few seconds, then let it out with a long, smooth exhale. Only one puff, but he was already starting to feel the effects, already starting to feel light-headed. Perhaps that was why the general was smoking this brand. It was stronger. Perhaps, despite the man-of-steel exterior, the general was feeling his own anxieties. "I am, but how would you—"

"An educated guess, Doctor. Don't overthink things at this point, my friend."

Padilla handed the cigar back to the general. "What does being religious have to do with anything?"

"With religion, you must put your faith in God. Whichever god you pray to. With the Incursion, you must put your faith in me."

Delgado was amazing. It almost made Padilla cry to be in the presence of such greatness. As a doctor he could save lives, but Delgado had the power to reshape them. Delgado was about to change the course of Cuba's history on the strength of his own personality, on his own inner strength, making many lives so much better. If the Incursion was successful, Delgado would be a god in Cuba.

Of course, if it failed, he'd be nothing but a footnote, another execution, the subject of another website put together by someone in Miami.

The things that made Delgado amazing were his willingness to take the ultimate risk—and his supreme self-confidence. That he believed so strongly in himself he was willing to bet his life on being able to influence *forty thousand* men. If he was wrong and couldn't, unlike the Secret Six he'd have no chance to escape. He'd be taken into custody immediately.

"Did you find out anything about the attorney?" Padilla asked.

"I did." Delgado reached into his pocket. "And tomorrow the name of your secret group will be wrong because there will be only five of you."

Padilla nodded dejectedly. It was almost as if the attorney had known he was a dead man. Padilla could see it in his eyes tonight.

The general took one of Padilla's soft, small hands in his large, leathery one. "Here." He pressed the cow's ID tag into the doctor's palm. The cow Padilla had hit that night in front of Gustavo Cruz's ranch.

"Give this to Christian Gillette when you meet with him. If Mr. Gillette gives it back to me when I meet him here, I will know we have support from the United States." The general smiled. "Enjoy yourself in Naples. You're doing a great thing."

Padilla glanced down at the small piece of metal with the number etched into it, then up into Delgado's eyes as he thought about what he'd just heard. "Naples?"

ALLISON STOOD across Columbus Avenue from the restaurant, staring through the glass at Christian and the young woman. It was exactly as Sherry Demille had said—she hadn't been lying. The girl Christian was seeing was young and so beautiful.

Allison tried to swallow, but it was hard. The lump in her throat seemed to be the size of an orange. She'd followed Christian this afternoon when he'd left the office. Followed him to Penn Station, then followed *them* here and watched them eat dinner. It was all exactly as Sherry had said. It made her want to cry.

AS HE DROVE, Alanzo Gomez hummed along with the music drifting from the tape deck. He'd bought the deck in Paris in an odds-and-ends shop on rue de Morgan, when he was there last negotiating the huge loan from China. Brought it back with him—along with several tapes of classical music—hidden in one of his bags. Simply flashed his Central Bank identification card to the people at customs, and he was whisked through with no problems, quickly recognized as a senior member of the Party.

A *loyal* member, he thought to himself proudly as he drove along listening to *Aida*. First thing tomorrow he would approach his superior—the president of the Central Bank—and lay out for him what was going on with the Secret Six. And thereby cement his position as the next president of the bank. Cuba would stay safe. He would be a national hero, the other five would be executed.

Gomez slowed down as he came around a turn and saw the roadblock in his high beams—two FAR jeeps facing each other perpendicular to oncoming traffic and four soldiers, three of whom were armed with rifles. The fourth held up both his white-gloved hands and walked a few steps ahead. Gomez's eyes narrowed as he dimmed his lights and came to a stop. These kinds of things weren't unusual—but they weren't common, either. It was probably just where he was coming from that was making him nervous, he thought to himself as he rolled down the window of the Studebaker.

"Good evening, sir," the lieutenant said politely but firmly. "I need to see your identification."

"Of course." Gomez pulled out his wallet. He'd been thinking of showing the man his Central Bank ID, showing how senior he was, then thought better of it. No need to show the officer any more than he'd asked for. That might cause suspicion. "Here you are."

The officer took the faded, folded piece of paper. "Thank you. I'll be back. Please turn off the car."

Gomez winced. This didn't feel right. He watched the officer warily as the man strode stiffly back to one of the jeeps and climbed inside. "Damn it." He peered at the jeep. The problem was, if he spilled his guts during a military interrogation, it would look as if he were trying to protect himself. It would look much more suspicious than if he walked calmly and confidently into the office of the president of the Central Bank of Cuba and laid out in a coherent fashion exactly what was going on and who was involved. He felt the sweat beginning to seep from his palms. "Shit."

But just as the nerves were starting to get to him, the officer hopped out of the jeep and headed toward him in the same slow, stiff stride, smiling as he handed the identification back and waved to the driver on the right to back the jeep up.

"Thank you, Señor Gomez. Have a good night."

Gomez restarted the car. "Thank *you*, Officer. And thank you for your service to Cuba."

BETH STOOD next to Christian on the balcony of his two-story Fifth Avenue apartment overlooking Central Park. "It's beautiful," she murmured, gazing up into the clear night. "I never thought you'd be able to see stars out over New York City. I thought the lights here would be too bright."

"It is nice," he agreed.

She leaned against him. "Have one glass of champagne with me. Please, Chris," she begged. "One glass won't hurt."

"Finish that one and we'll see." There was no way he was having champagne. He'd brought her up here to tell her everything because he couldn't bring himself to do it at dinner, but he was still finding it difficult. She kept looking at him in that way.

She tilted the glass, took three gulps, and the champagne was gone. "Okay, finished."

"Yeah, well, I—"

Beth's cell phone rang loudly from inside the apartment. "Sorry, but I'm worried about my mom," she said, heading back through the open sliding-glass door. "I'll be just a minute."

"Take your time." He watched her go, trying to figure out how to do this.

SANCHEZ CREPT QUIETLY down the tile floor, the smell of formaldehyde heavy in the long hallway. It smelled like death to him, which was fine. He didn't mind death. Death was why he was here. Death had been his career.

He reached the room number he'd been given, glanced up and down the corridor, and moved inside. He cringed as the door squeaked slightly, but there was no reason to worry. No one else was in the hallway at this late hour, and the woman was fast asleep. According to his information, she was dying but she didn't want to wait. The pain was excruciating. Victoria Graham had explained it all to him in Miami.

Sanchez moved to the bedside, making certain the woman wasn't plugged into any monitors that would alert a nurse in a station somewhere that she was flatlining. He placed the small bag down on a table beside the bed, next to a half-finished jigsaw puzzle, opened it, and pulled out two lengths of cord. Gently securing her wrists to the retractable metal railings on either side of the bed—she never showed any signs of waking up. Maybe she was already dead, he thought to himself, pressing two fingers to one of her wrists. That would save him the trouble. But she wasn't dead, there was still a pulse—still strong, too.

He pulled out a rag and a needle already filled with the solution from the bag and with no hesitation pried open her mouth and jammed the rag far down her throat, covering her mouth with one of his hands. Her eyes flew wide open instantly and she began to scream—but her cries for help were muffled by the rag. She fought furiously, straining against the ropes binding her wrists to the bed, kicking wildly, which Sanchez found fascinating. Supposedly she wanted to die, but the body's natural instinct to live was so strong. At the moment of truth, what your mind wanted had nothing to do with it. At the moment of truth, it was all about millions of years of survival instinct completely taking over.

Sanchez had secured her right wrist—the one closest to him—firmly and made certain her arm was extremely extended. She could barely move it. He slid the needle into her forearm deftly with his right hand— left still pressed firmly to her mouth—and injected the solution. She fought for another thirty seconds. Then her fight subsided, her eyes rolled back in her head, and her body went limp.

He pulled the needle from her arm, untied her wrists, stowed his gear in the bag, and headed out. When the nurses made rounds, they would find that the woman had died of heart failure. There would be no evidence of murder whatsoever.

Now it was back to Miami and Mari, he thought to himself as he pushed through the door that led to the stairway he'd climbed a few minutes ago to get up here. One more night of her glorious body, then the end of her life, too. Then it would be time for Christian Gillette.

ALLISON HAD GONE BACK to the office to print out the pictures she'd taken of Christian and the girl sitting at dinner in the restaurant. It was late, almost eleven, but she couldn't wait.

She taken the shots with a digital camera from across Columbus Avenue. Managed to do it without Quentin's guys noticing because they were all inside. She felt guilty about spying on Christian like that, but it was for his own good, for his own protection. She was simply carrying out Ms. Graham's orders, as self-serving as that sounded.

Allison held up one of the prints. Taken through the glass at the front of the restaurant without even using a telephoto lens and the quality wasn't too bad. A little grainy, but still, you could tell who they were. She shook her head. Today's technology was truly amazing. Tomorrow's would be out of sight.

Allison stared at the young woman in the picture for a few seconds. She was leaning in toward Christian, her hand on his. She was beautiful, Allison had to admit. And it certainly looked from the body language as if she was sincerely into him. It was just that with all Victoria Graham had told her, Allison was suspicious of everything at this point. It wasn't that a younger woman couldn't be attracted to Christian, she could easily see that. It was just that it had happened *now.* It seemed so coincidental.

She shut her eyes tightly, then put the print down and glanced at the file lying on the right side of her desk. She'd found it this afternoon before heading out to follow Christian. It was a file from the Dead Deal room. A room of cabinets full of folders with information about transactions Everest Capital had turned down as long as fifteen years ago. Investment opportunities the firm had looked at, but had, for whatever reason, elected not to pursue—all arranged by industry. Christian kept the files so that when someone at Everest looked at another deal in the industry, they already had a significant amount of research on hand in the file as well as the reasons they'd decided not to invest in that specific company. He was all about efficiency, she thought to herself with a smile. God, she loved that man. Even if he loved someone else.

The file had to do with an insurance company based in Ohio. Allison glanced at the cover memo on top one more time—she'd already scanned it this afternoon before bugging out quickly when she found out from Debbie that Chris was leaving the office. Apparently, Victoria Graham had tried to persuade Christian to use Everest to buy the Ohio company a couple of years ago. Obviously, he'd refused. And it didn't actually say so, but as she read between Christian's lines on the page, it implied that something not quite aboveboard was going on with Graham's proposal. Christian was much too savvy to ever write anything down in a file that could be used against anyone later, but it looked to Allison as if he were concerned about Ms. Graham's motives. Allison got at least ten e-mails a day from Christian and she'd gotten used to his writing. She'd gotten used to reading the words—then understanding what he really meant. She could feel his voice in the words on the page and there was suspicion.

She let her head fall slowly to the desk. What in the world was really going on?

SO CLOSE. A couple of more lonely miles and he'd be home, Alanzo Gomez thought to himself happily. Just down the big hill, a right at the dead end at the bottom, a left, then another right, and he could swing into his driveway, walk inside, and climb into his nice, cozy bed beside his plump, little wife with the secure feeling that tomorrow morning he'd wake up, go to the office, and save Cuba. The roadblock had strengthened his resolve to do it now, not to wait another day. It was too big a risk to wait any longer because perceptions were everything on this island. Being *re*active could mean prison, even death. Being *pro*active could mean being a hero.

He could just picture the Central Bank president's face when he broke the news tomorrow morning. The man would try to grab the glory—as all high-level bureaucrats in Cuba regularly did—but Gomez had a plan for that. He'd tell his boss just enough to get the saliva dripping, but no more. Not enough for the man to be able to walk into the Party office across the street and grab anything by himself. Just a little taste so the man would *have* to take him along on that walk across the street.

Gomez eased off the accelerator as he approached the top of the hill. It was steep, very steep, and long—at least a quarter of a mile. At the bottom of it was his lovely neighborhood and the house he would live in until he died. Unless the hero thing really took off and the Party urged him to move because a man of his stature needed to live in a bigger, fancier home. He would do whatever they told him to do. Mother Cuba forever, he thought to himself, making a tight fist with one hand.

Gomez put his foot on the brake when he reached the crest of the hill and pressed. The Studebaker slowed slightly, but the reaction didn't feel normal to him, didn't feel as if the brake pads grabbed the way they usually did. He pressed the pedal harder. It went straight to the floor with a bang—but didn't come back.

"*Oh, Jesus!*" His eyes shot to the speedometer—forty-five and increasing quickly because the steepest part of the hill was at the top. Within seconds he was at sixty. "My God," he whined pitifully, zigzagging on the two-lane road in an attempt to stop, careening ahead, tires screeching. The trees on both sides of the road flashed past—suddenly two big blurs now out of the corner of each eye as the speedometer's needle blew past seventy. "*Help me! Someone help me!*" he screamed, stomping on the brake pedal with his foot, trying to get it to come off the floor. Instinctively, he yanked on the emergency brake—nothing there, either. "*Stop, stop, stop!*" he shouted, pounding on the steering wheel. He should have pulled into the trees as soon as he realized the brakes were gone, he realized now. Taken his chances then on some bad injuries—but not death. But it was much too late for that—the needle was on eighty and the cement wall at the bottom was rushing up to meet him. *"Oh, Geeeooood!"*

As the car raced toward the wall, Gomez jerked the steering wheel to the left, trying to turn onto the level street, but the forward momentum flipped the car over. It rolled twice before slamming into the wall at eighty-five.

THE TWO FAR JEEPS pulled up to the crash, and the officer who had taken Gomez's identification at the roadblock hopped out. While he had been keeping Gomez occupied, another man had slipped beneath the car from behind and cut the brake line—in such a way that Gomez could drive a few miles, but when he really needed to stop, the brakes would fail.

The officer leaned down and looked into the front seat. Gomez was a bloody mess, obviously dead. There was no need for any follow-up. He stepped back into the jeep and nodded to the driver. A car was coming and they couldn't be seen here.

IT WAS AFTER MIDNIGHT and Christian was headed to his study to check e-mails. Beth was asleep on his couch. She'd fallen asleep there, cuddled up next to him while they were watching *Hoosiers*. One minute he was explaining something about the movie, a rule of basketball, the next she was breathing heavily, eyes closed.

Guess it wasn't going to be *her* favorite movie, he thought, chuckling as he sat down and clicked to his e-mail. Well, you couldn't expect a twenty-two-year-old woman to care much about high school basketball in the 1950s.

Christian clicked into his received-messages folder, still thinking about Jim Marshall—God, that thing was haunting him. His eyes opened wide as the list of new e-mails popped up. There it was. A message from JRCook. His eyes skimmed across the screen. It was going down tomorrow. Everything was going live. He reached for the phone to call Quentin.

"Chris."

Christian spun around in the chair and dropped the phone, taken completely by surprise by the voice from behind him. It was Beth, and through the dim light he could see she was crying. Tears soaked her cheeks, and her mascara was smudged all around her eyes. He got up and moved to her, subtly shoving the code card into his pocket. "What's wrong?" he asked, wrapping his arms around her. She melted into him.

"Chris, I just got a call from the hospital in Baltimore. My mom died tonight." She burst into a loud sob. "And I wasn't there for her."

17

CHRISTIAN EMERGED from the entrance to his apartment building on Fifth Avenue with three bodyguards as Quentin pulled up in his silver 760. It was only six o'clock in the morning, so traffic was still light. They'd had no problem spotting Quentin coming from up the block.

As he moved across the sidewalk toward the BMW, Christian searched for signs of anger on Quentin's face, but, as usual, there was nothing. No hint that Quentin was in any way surprised or pissed off about Beth coming toward the car, too. Christian opened the back door of the spacious car for Beth as Quentin rose up out of the driver's seat and gestured back toward the entrance. When Beth was in the car and Christian had shut the door, he followed Quentin back across the sidewalk to the bottom of the steps in front of the building.

"What's going on?" Quentin asked calmly, glancing at the car as he took a bite of a granola bar.

Christian spread his arms, watching one of the bodyguards load bags into the car's trunk. "Going on? What do you mean?"

"Chris, we don't have time for—"

"Okay, okay." For some reason, every once in a while Christian enjoyed trying to get a rise out of Quentin, liked trying to penetrate that cool veneer. He hadn't been able to often over the past few years, but when he had, it had been fun. And right now, he needed a tension breaker. "Sorry I didn't call you. She lost her mother last night. She's a basket case."

Quentin's eyes narrowed. "So, what are you saying?"

Down deep, beneath the steel exterior, Quentin was a compassionate man. Christian knew he felt sorry for Beth, but his first reaction had been to stay focused on the matter at hand. He was the consummate professional. "I'm saying I can't let her be alone right now. She wouldn't be able to handle it. She doesn't have anyone else to lean on."

"You can't be serious. I've planned every detail of this trip right down to the letter. I can't have another variable like this one suddenly thrown on top of everything else. Not if you expect me to make this go off like we want it to. You coming back alive, I mean."

"I think you're overblowing this just a tad," Christian said, holding his thumb and forefinger up barely apart. "I don't think this is the trip to worry about. Now, when we're about to go into Cuba, we'll both do some worrying." He noticed Quentin look past him up Fifth Avenue.

"Hopefully, we're dropping her off in Washington," Quentin said, taking another bite of the breakfast bar.

Christian shook his head.

"She's going with us to Florida? Is that the bottom line?"

"Yup." For the first time in a long time Christian thought he saw a flash of anger cross his best friend's face.

"No talking you out of it?"

"No."

"You realize that we really know next to *nothing* about this woman. Only where she's from and where she went to college."

"I know about her," Christian said firmly. "I know she's a good person. I also know this is a pain in the ass. But I'm not going to let someone else down."

"Someone *else?*"

Christian looked down at a cigarette butt wedged into a crack of the sidewalk. "Yeah."

"You mean Jim Marshall?" Quentin put his hand on Christian's shoulder. "You can't blame yourself for what he did. My God, you were going to pay for him to go to a rehab clinic out of your own pocket."

"Yeah, but I didn't get him there." Christian gritted his teeth. "I was too busy being tough on him. I'm not going to be tough on her, too."

Quentin glanced at Beth, who was sitting beside one of the bodyguards in the back of the BMW. "Just for the record, I think this is a very bad idea."

"I know." Christian's expression brightened. "I also know you'll get me through it."

Quentin popped the last bite of granola bar into his mouth. "Speaking of which, if you take a quick look up Fifth Avenue while we're walking to the car, you'll see a blue sedan at the curb about fifty yards away. That sedan's been following me ever since I left my garage to come pick you up."

SHERRY DEMILLE sat in Christian's office at Everest, typing password after password into his computer—the two older men from Maryland had sent her a long list of possibilities last night by e-mail and ordered her to try them, ordered her to look for anything that might be relevant on his computer, in his desk, on his credenza. But none of the passwords were working and she was getting more and more frustrated. Not only that the passwords weren't working, but at what she'd let herself get wrapped up in. For letting Jim Marshall have his way with her at the hotel just so she could get closer to him. Then finding out he'd been fired anyway because the two men no longer had any use for him. She was certain Marshall's drop from the balcony of his apartment building hadn't been suicide, which was the only reason she'd broken into Christian's office this morning when the two men had told her to. She didn't want to end up like Marshall. Nothing but a stew of flesh and bones on a sidewalk. The men had been beside themselves last night on the phone, almost panic-stricken.

"What are you doing?"

Sherry's gaze snapped from the screen to the doorway. Allison was standing there, eyes ablaze.

Sherry rose deliberately from Christian's chair and walked slowly to where Allison was standing, not taking her eyes off Allison's. Then bolted past her toward the lobby.

QUENTIN PULLED the silver 760 into a freight warehouse in Newark, New Jersey. As soon as they were inside, the huge door that had been raised to let them in descended again. Quentin steered the BMW to the right and eased to a stop beside an identical 760—except that this one's windows were tinted.

"Everybody out," he ordered, climbing from the car, careful not to bang his door into the maroon-colored minivan to the left.

Christian, Beth, and the bodyguard who had ridden in the back with Beth climbed out.

Within fifteen minutes, Quentin's 760 had been outfitted with window tinting and new license tags. Now there was no way to see into the car, and no way to identify it from the silver 760 they'd pulled up next to.

ALLISON GLANCED WARILY at the cages and aquariums lining the walls as she moved hurriedly into Victoria Graham's office. At least the alligator wasn't here anymore.

"What is it, dear?" Graham asked. "Why did you need to see me so badly?"

Allison moved to the desk and dropped the photos she'd taken last night onto Graham's desk. "You told me to tell you as soon as I thought there was something weird going on."

Graham picked up one of the pictures. "Christian in a restaurant with a pretty girl." She looked up. "What's so strange about that?"

"The girl's half his age."

Graham put the photograph down. "Men go through these things when they're in their forties. It's sad, but they do. Even a man like Christian."

"She just showed up," Allison said, sitting in the chair in front of the desk. "Don't you think that's odd?"

The older woman raised both eyebrows and smiled grimly. "I do think it's odd, but not because of the timing."

"But—"

"He'll get over it, dear," Graham interrupted. "I promise."

Allison knew what Graham was thinking. That this was all just about petty jealousy. But it wasn't. She was really worried about Christian. "An hour ago I caught a woman named Sherry Demille trying to get into Christian's computer at Everest." Graham's eyes raced to hers. This time her reaction wasn't so measured. "Sherry's an associate with the firm. She'd gotten into his office." Using that key on top of the molding obviously. A mistake to trust anyone, she thought to herself. As Christian always preached.

Graham leaned forward. "What did she say?"

"I didn't have a chance to ask her anything. She ran. I chased her through the emergency exit in the lobby and down the stairs, but she got away. I even phoned the security desk in the main lobby and told them to stop her, but they never saw her come into the lobby. Maybe she went out through the freight entrance."

"Do you think she got into his computer?"

Allison shook her head. Suddenly Victoria Graham wasn't so calm. "No. I checked after I called security and the computer was still requiring a password for access." She saw Graham's shoulders sag slightly.

"Good."

"What's going on, Ms. Graham? Do you think what Sherry did is related to what we're doing?"

Graham shook her head. "I don't know, I just don't know."

Allison rose from the chair and placed a folder down in front of her. It was the folder she'd found in the Dead Deal room related to that Ohio insurance company Christian had decided not to pursue. "Does it have anything to do with this?" she asked, pointing at the file.

ANTONIO BARRADO had just dropped down from the camp's dock into the Boston Whaler when he heard one of his men yelling wildly for help from behind the shack to the far right. A desperate scream with a tone so eerie it sent a shiver up his spine. He scrambled back up onto the rickety planks and raced toward the shouting, aware that the other men in camp were sprinting from the left, where they'd been clearing brush and laying down the load of wood he'd brought last night. Which was where he had been headed when the yelling had started. To get another load.

Barrado reached the scene first and could barely believe what he saw. He'd heard about this—about people letting their pets go free in the Everglades—but never thought *this* could be possible. He whipped the .44 magnum from his holster just as the other men made it to where he was standing, leaned down, pressed the barrel to the massive snake's head so the bullet wouldn't hit his man, and fired. Blowing the head completely apart, severing the rest of the snake, which was tightly coiled around the man's body, from the jaw—the hundreds of backward-tilting, razor-sharp teeth so deeply impaled in the man's thigh that the jaw stayed right where it was.

Instead of going limp, the dead snake's coils constricted even more tightly, then started to writhe wildly. It took several minutes to completely separate the snake from the man. When they finally had him free, they measured the python. Twenty-two feet—even without the head.

Barrado gazed at the tape measure, barely able to believe what he'd seen. Thank God this part of it was almost over.

THE MAROON MINIVAN moved quickly out onto the tarmac of the small, central New Jersey airport toward the waiting Gulfstream. The vehicle moved directly to the bottom of the lowered stairs, where it stopped abruptly. Christian, Quentin, Beth, and the three bodyguards hopped out and hurried up the stairs into the jet. Now they were headed to Naples, Florida—a two-hour drive directly across the state from Miami.

VICTORIA GRAHAM gazed at the photographs Allison had taken. Allison was just doing what she'd been told to do. To be aware of things that seemed strange, not normal. It was a good thing, too. Not because of the photographs but because Allison had told her about Sherry Demille. They were already trying to find Sherry, but that was going to be difficult, she knew. Sherry was probably already dead. At the least, running for her life.

Graham leaned back in her desk chair and shut her eyes. Christian ought to be on his way to Miami by now. And if it wasn't Miami, she'd know where it was soon enough. That was the whole reason that Melissa Hart—aka Beth Garrison—was with him.

PART
THREE

18

"**CHRISTIAN,** *please* don't let her come with us today."

They were just passing over Tampa on the way down to Naples. Twenty minutes to touchdown and Beth had gone to the restroom in the back of the jet to freshen up. Quentin was taking advantage of this small time window—he hadn't been able to speak to Christian alone since they'd boarded in New Jersey—to make his case. Beth had curled up next to Christian on the sofa as the plane was taxiing toward the runway and hadn't moved for two and a half hours. Christian hadn't gotten anything done, either, just spent the entire flight caressing her head and hair, consoling her. Quentin couldn't remember the last time he'd seen his boss go this long without pulling out a file on one of Everest's portfolio companies, firing up his laptop, or at least doing one of his beloved crossword puzzles. This was crazy.

Maybe Christian really did feel something for this girl—which somehow rubbed Quentin the wrong way. Maybe it was jealousy—which was hard for him to admit. Maybe it was that he didn't like seeing Christian so distracted—which wasn't good for Everest. He knew the jealousy thing was unfair and the Everest thing was unfounded. Christian hadn't really had time in years to have a meaningful relationship with a woman, and Quentin knew his boss would never let anything get in the way of his responsibility to the Everest investors. But damn it, there was a job to do, and Quentin knew what he was saying was right.

"The pilot's an old friend," Quentin continued. "He'll drop us off, refuel, then take Beth anywhere she wants to go. I've already talked to him about it."

"I can't do that," Christian said firmly. "You saw her on the way down here. She's devastated. She's been crying since we boarded, since last night when she got the news, really. She hasn't stopped."

"I've got to be able to protect you," Quentin argued gently. "Having her around makes that much tougher."

"I can't let her down, pal. I can't turn my back on her and send her home right now. Besides, do you really think she could be working for somebody?"

Quentin could feel the plane descending. They were getting close. He didn't have much time. "Anything's possible at this point." He took a deep breath, trying to erase the aggravation from his expression. "How about this? What if I send one of my guys back with her? And you promised that as soon as this thing's done, you'll come right to her. That could be as early as tonight, couldn't it?"

"And it could be a week," Christian shot back. "I can't do that to her. *How many times do I have to say it?*"

"She's bad news, Chris."

"How do you know?"

"I don't, I just feel it."

"That's bullshit."

"Why are you defending her so hard?"

"Why do you dislike her so much?"

"I don't dislike her," Quentin muttered. I hate her, he thought to himself, glancing toward the rear of the plane. One of his men was sitting halfway toward the restrooms and looking at them over his magazine with a strange expression. As soon as they made eye contact, the guy looked back down at the magazine. It didn't do any good for the troops to see them arguing. Quentin couldn't remember the last time they had. Not like this anyway. "It's just that—"

"Look, I'm not saying she should be anywhere near the meeting," Christian interrupted. "She'll stay in her room while we're at that."

Out of the corner of his eye, Quentin noticed Beth emerging from the restroom. "I've got some feelers out, people I know. About Beth. If I find out something incriminating about—"

"Then I'll send her away, I promise. *Immediately.* But you've had those feelers out for a while," Christian reminded him, "and nothing's turned up."

"I know," Quentin admitted grudgingly. "Is it all right if I at least take her cell phone while we're here?"

Christian smiled. "Sure, but I don't think that's going to—"

"Right," Quentin agreed as Beth stepped between them and retook her spot next to Christian on the sofa. "But I've got to feel like I'm doing *something*."

IN VERY SOUTH FLORIDA, Interstate 75 runs straight to—or away from—the sun, depending on the time of day. One of the few places in the United States where an odd-numbered interstate runs east-west for an extended distance. Here it connects Naples on the west coast with Fort Lauderdale on the east. It's a lonely stretch of highway that cuts through the northern portion of the Everglades and the Big Cypress National Preserve for eighty miles. In that eighty-mile stretch there are only two exits that pierce the tall chain-link fences that rise on either side of the highway to protect travelers from the wildlife living in the massive swamp. Even at eighty miles an hour—the average speed on the road— you can see gators basking in the canals on the other side of the fences at dawn and dusk. Which is why it's known as Alligator Alley.

Antonio Barrado stood on the State Road 29 overpass. There was only one other overpass for fifty miles to the east and none for thirty miles to the west. There was nothing out here as far as you could see except the interstate, a few vehicles, cypress trees, and swamp. And nothing in the swamp but gators, snakes, panthers, deer, and wild boar. An amazing place and one he was glad to be leaving soon. He'd come up SR 29 from the south this morning, from Everglades City, which was the last speck of civilization before you got into the truly remote areas of the Everglades just above the Keys—where his camp was. He would have taken SR 41 over to Miami—it was an older road that paralleled I-75 about twenty-five miles to the south, closer to the camp—but Hurricane William had destroyed long sections of 41 last fall and a lot of the road still wasn't open.

Barrado was parked on the overpass because his cell phone reception was best up here—he could almost see the microwave tower in the distance, to the east. He was completely prepared, ready to head toward

Miami to carry out his mission—but he wanted final confirmation of the location first. A few days ago his contacts had started hedging on the spot, and it was pissing him off. Two of his men were in the SUV with him, ready to carry out their duty as well. The one who'd been bitten by the python was back at camp, tending to the nasty bite in his thigh, and making certain anyone who happened to come around didn't stay too long. Other than that, everything had gone off without a hitch, everything was ready.

However, at the last minute, there seemed to be a problem.

When the cell phone rang, Barrado answered on the first ring. "Hello," he barked angrily. "*What?* What do you mean you still aren't sure? What am I supposed to do now?" he demanded, eyeing the thunderheads already building high in the sky past the cell tower. Rolling in from the east the way they did almost every day in the summer. "Yeah, yeah." Hurry up and wait. He hated it. *"Bastards,"* he hissed, ending the connection and turning up the air-conditioning inside the SUV.

"What's up, boss?" the man in the passenger seat asked after Barrado tossed the cell phone on the dashboard in disgust.

"Nothing," he answered angrily. "A whole lot of nothing."

"**WHERE ARE YOU GOING?**"

Beth stopped and stared at Quentin. They'd just made it inside the terminal at the Naples airport. "To the ladies' room. Is that okay with you? It was kind of a long flight."

"You just went to the bathroom," he said, glancing over his shoulder at Christian, who was headed toward the men's room. "On the plane, right before we landed."

"Do I need to be graphic? It's that time of—"

"All right, all right. But let me have your cell phone."

"Are you kidding?"

"Never been more serious."

She stalked toward him, until they were close. "Do you have a problem with me?"

"Nope. I'm just being careful."

Beth dug through her purse and pulled out the small phone. "Here," she said loudly, sticking her chin out as she pressed it into his hand. "Please take it. *Now* can I go to the bathroom, Daddy?"

She sure wasn't crying at this point. As soon as Christian had walked away, the tears had dried up. "Uh-huh." Quentin wanted to search that purse himself, but that might set off World War III: Christian had told him not to do exactly that. And she could always go to a landline if she was working with someone. "Hurry up," he called loudly as she walked away. "Don't be long."

PADILLA STEPPED into the cab outside the Miami International Airport. It was an orange minivan with RICK'S AIRPORT TAXI SERVICE written on both sides in black script. Phone number printed beneath the script in block letters. Taxi number on the top: 3742.

Delgado had given him that number at their meeting late, late last night. A second meeting that had taken place *after* Alanzo Gomez had been killed. After the banker had slammed into the cement wall doing eighty-five miles an hour, ripping his car and himself into shreds. Delgado hadn't told Padilla anything about the assassination at their first meeting of the evening. He'd played it cool, close to the vest at that time.

Padilla was saddened by the news, shocked that Gomez would be the one to roll over on them—not the attorney. But Delgado had assured Padilla that they had irrefutable evidence of Gomez planning to tell his superiors everything. A diary detailing every meeting of the Secret Six with entries indicating exactly whom Gomez was going to tell first—the president of the Central Bank.

"Where to?" the cabdriver asked.

"Hotel Renaissance. Fourth floor." The code from Delgado. No need to tell a driver what floor you were going to.

"You can count on me," the driver said, pulling into the heavy traffic of the crowded airport. "I'm your man."

Just what he was supposed to say.

As they headed out of the airport onto I-95, the cabdriver eased beside a huge tractor-trailer just as another one pulled in behind the cab, momentarily cutting off any view anyone on the highway could have of anyone inside the taxi.

"Now," the driver called loudly.

Padilla ducked down, then dropped to the floor just as another man crawled over the arm of the seat and took his spot. From the floor,

Padilla glanced up and could barely believe his eyes. The man now sitting in the seat was as perfect a double as possible. It was as though they'd found his long-lost identical twin.

BETH MOVED QUICKLY into one of the stalls in the ladies' room, closing the door and jamming the latch shut. It didn't go through the slot right away and she took a second try at it, pushing at it hard. Finally it locked and she breathed a sigh of relief. Her heart was pounding, and she could feel the perspiration soaking her clothes—cold against her skin in the air-conditioning. She'd been certain Quentin was going to rummage through her purse and find it.

She sat down, placed her purse on her lap, and pulled it out. A small cylindrical case that looked exactly like lipstick—but a quarter the normal size, the size of a 9 mm bullet. It was a transponder, which would lead them right to her as soon as she turned it on. They'd been afraid that Quentin might take her cell phone—actually hadn't wanted her to use it anyway because the call numbers would show up later on a bill somewhere and they didn't want that. Didn't want anyone to be able to see that Beth had made any calls after landing wherever it was she was going.

Beth held the device up, pulled off the cap, then switched the blue button into the ON position as they'd shown her how to do. Now it was sending out a strong homing signal, and they'd be able to track her as soon as they picked up the transmission. She just had to keep it with her wherever she went.

She exhaled heavily again, replaced the cap, and put the transponder back into her purse. She'd made her choice—as awful as it was.

DORSEY SLAMMED the phone down. The two older men had been shouting at him for several minutes, berating him for still not having any information. As one of the most senior senators in Washington, he wasn't used to being so brazenly dressed down. But they were clearing the way for him to be the president of the United States, so he'd managed to keep his temper.

Victoria still hadn't returned his phone calls of last night and this morning—had basically ignored him. And the men on the other end of the phone were certain Christian Gillette was on the move. They'd tailed him to a freight warehouse in Newark, New Jersey, early this morning—then lost him. They'd described to Dorsey how two identical 760s had emerged from the warehouse twenty minutes after the one they were certain Gillette was riding in had disappeared inside. Emerged at exactly the same moment from different entrances. Because they'd been careful and had a helicopter up in the air, they'd been able to follow both cars—one with the chopper and one with the car they'd followed him with from Manhattan. But after a couple of hours, they'd realized that Gillette wasn't in either. That he'd slipped away.

What was really causing them heart failure was that it had become clear Quentin Stiles must have suspected something. Why else would he be so careful? Why else would he have switched vehicles at the warehouse? And if he suspected something, there must be a *reason* for him to suspect something. Which meant that their suspicions could be true. That someone else was coming after Gillette.

Dorsey picked up the phone and dialed Victoria one more time. But it rang and rang until the voice-mail greeting finally answered.

SANCHEZ WAS DOING 110 miles an hour, tearing across Alligator Alley toward Naples. They'd picked up the signal from the homing device an hour ago, and he was on his way, closing in on the target.

He was keeping himself amused during the long straightaways by thinking about how the woman he'd met with in Miami had given him strict instructions that no one else was to be killed during this mission. He laughed out loud. She was so naïve. She was supposed to be some big financial executive or something, probably savvy in her world. But she was out of her league in this one. He wouldn't have taken the job if he'd been aware of all the limitations at the beginning—but now he was glad he had because he'd quickly figured out the right way to play it. The woman was paying him a million bucks—which wasn't too bad. But he had no intention of sticking to his promise to her of not killing anyone—or of just making a million.

Sanchez backed off quickly to seventy-five when the radar detector started to ping. It sure wouldn't be good to be pulled over by the South Florida cops going 110—especially with Mari's body in the trunk. The movie producer would have liked her a lot, he thought to himself. She was pretty—much prettier than the other woman he'd sent before—and she had a nice personality. She might actually have made something of herself in the movies or on television. But he couldn't risk Mari living another day. She knew too much. So he'd killed her this morning. He'd dispose of the body later—probably out here somewhere on the way back to Miami.

Sanchez nodded subtly at the trooper car as he flashed past—not that the guy could see him do it, but it was always a good idea to salute your enemy before going into battle. A mile later he cranked the car back up to 110.

"**I'M LEAVING,**" Christian said, walking over to Beth and hugging her. "Will you be okay?"

She let out a little sob. "I'll be fine." She pressed her head to his chest and squeezed tightly.

God, he felt awful for her. She'd been shattered by her mother's death. And she wouldn't even be able to start putting it behind her until after the small funeral next week. He'd move any meeting he had, he was going to be with her for that.

"I shouldn't be long. I'm thinking Quentin and I will be a couple of hours at most. You should go down to the pool and relax, get some sun." They were staying at the Ritz Carlton, which was right on the beach a couple of miles north of Fifth Avenue South—Naples's main drag. They were in separate rooms, though she'd made it clear this morning that it would be okay with her if they stayed together. He'd politely declined. Her room was down the hall. "It's a beautiful day," he said, gesturing toward the window. "If you forgot your bathing suit, get one down in the lobby. Put it on my room."

"Thanks," she said, pulling back and wiping tears from her eyelids.

He kissed her forehead gently and broke the embrace. "I'll see you in a little while."

"Wait, wait," she said, running past him to where his briefcase sat in a chair by the door. "I have something for you," she said, holding up an envelope so he could see it. "I want you to know how much I appreciate you doing all of this for me." She turned her back to him and blocked his view of the briefcase for a moment. She slipped the envelope past the zipper, into one of the open pockets. Then subtly dropped the homing device into another pocket. "Make sure you aren't around anyone else when you open the envelope," she said, zipping both pockets shut. Then she picked up the briefcase and brought it to him.

"Why not?"

She smiled slyly as he took it from her. "Oh, there's a picture of me in there I'd rather you see when you're alone." Her smile grew wider. "If you know what I mean."

CHRISTIAN STOOD UP as the other man entered the suite. He was short—only about five-seven—and slight—no more than 150 pounds. He had small, round wire-rim glasses, a thin mustache, wavy black hair, and a gentle but competent look in his eye. Christian noticed right away how he was constantly rubbing his hands together, too, as though he were washing them. Maybe surgeons washed their hands so often it was a natural habit to pick up.

"Dr. Padilla?"

Padilla smiled as they shook hands. "Yes," he said, looking up at Christian. "I hope you are Christian Gillette, yes? If you are not, I think I am in trouble."

"I am Christian Gillette," he said, laughing. He guided the other man toward a chair beside the one he'd been sitting in. "Please make yourself comfortable. Would you like something to drink, Doctor?"

"No, thank you." He tapped his watch as he sat down. "I'm supposed to be observing an operation at five o'clock this afternoon back in Miami. It's a new open-heart procedure we haven't seen in Cuba yet. I need to keep this short so I'm not late. Obviously, I . . . *we*, I mean, *we* don't want the people who check up on me to get suspicious."

Padilla's English was quite good. Choppy in places but a hundred times better than Christian's Spanish. "Everything go all right with the trip over here?"

Padilla laughed. "Very well. The man they have as my double? Well, he looks more like me than me. If my mother were alive, I don't think she could tell who was who. He has all of my markings, right down to the moles. It is amazing."

Christian nodded to Quentin, who was standing in one corner. The guy was a master. He'd created the double with just a grainy picture from that file Kelly had given Christian at Camp David. "Good." He felt that he already knew Padilla well. He'd spent a lot of time studying the detailed background files Dex Kelly had provided him on each of the Secret Six. "I want to tell you how impressed I am with what you men have done. It takes a lot of courage. President Wood believes very strongly in you. I'm looking forward to meeting the other five as well."

"Thank you."

Christian thought he noticed a cloud cross the other man's face for a moment, but then it was gone. "Well, I have lots of questions. We should get started so you can get back in time."

"Please," Padilla said, opening his arms wide, "ask me all your questions."

For the next hour Christian did exactly that, rapid-fire. At times it was frustrating because Padilla couldn't provide the level of detail he was looking for when it came to how certain of the ministries were run, or how the black markets were set up, whether the men of the Six really understood the dynamics there. But he had expected that. After all, Padilla was a doctor. A man who saved lives. Not a man involved with capital markets, production levels, and currency reserves.

At the end of the hour, Christian leaned forward, smiled, and patted Padilla on his knee. "Thank you, my friend. This has been very helpful." The most important thing Christian had learned during the hour was that he trusted this man—completely. You could never be 100 percent sure, but Padilla certainly seemed like a man who was deeply committed to a democratic Cuba—and to the rebellion that would make the island free. Nervous, even scared—as he should be—and apologetic when he realized by the look in Christian's eye that he probably wasn't giving Christian all the information he wanted. But Dex Kelly had been confident about this man. Now Christian saw why.

"We'll help you," Christian assured the doctor. There was one more element to all of this—that clandestine trip into Cuba to meet with the rest of the Six as well as the general—but Christian was confident all that would check out. That he would recommend these men to President Wood. "I'm looking forward to meeting the rest of your associates."

Padilla smiled widely, revealing two rows of bright white teeth. "Thank you, Mr. Gillette," he said gratefully, reaching into his suit pocket. "Take this," he said, handing Christian the cow's identification tag Delgado had given him. "You need to bring it with you to Cuba. You need to give it to the general when you meet him. It is the signal that you are real. You must show it to him. He's very careful."

THE MEETING with Padilla had been held at the Naples Beach Hotel and Golf Club. Like the Ritz, the club was located right on the ocean. But it was much closer to town. It consisted of a hotel by the beach—an older wooden structure that was just two stories tall—a pool area, and a bar that overlooked the white sand beach and the smooth Gulf waters beyond. And, on the other side of the first hotel, on the east side, another hotel with a golf course and tennis facility close by.

Christian and Quentin headed down the outdoor stairs from the second floor of the hotel near the beach, one of Quentin's men in front of them, the other two behind. As they reached the ground level, the bar and the pool were to their left, and in front of them was a wide, beautifully manicured grassy area where the club hosted wedding receptions and parties. The tall palm trees surrounding the area swayed in the light breeze and provided nice shade for the walkway that bordered the grassy area.

Christian looked up through the wide leaves at the clear blue sky and took a deep breath of the fresh sea air. "God, it's nice down here, Quentin." He glanced over as they walked. Quentin was checking messages on his cell phone. "Maybe we should move the office," Christian kidded. "What do you think?"

Quentin held up one finger and stopped walking. "Just a—" He interrupted himself, pressing his palm over the other ear, the one he didn't have the cell phone up to.

Christian stopped, too, watching Quentin's face intently. His expression had turned so serious. "What is it, pal?"

Quentin pulled the phone from his ear and stashed it in his pocket. "Remember the day we first met Beth? In Maryland?"

"Of course. Why?"

"You told me there was a state police chopper, right?"

"Yeah," Christian answered. "Flew right over us. The guy who was chasing Beth and me was aiming his gun at us right by the river. Scared the hell out of the guy, scared him off basically. Back into the woods."

"You called 911 while you and she were running through the woods, right?"

"Yeah. You told me you did, too. So what?"

Quentin tapped the pocket he'd shoved his cell phone into. "I got a message from a buddy of mine at the Secret Service. He's got a friend who's a Maryland state trooper out in Frederick. It's a town close to where we were that day. The trooper did some digging and found out that the call that got the chopper in the air wasn't either of the ones we made. It came from someone else a few minutes before we called."

Christian swallowed hard. "Who made it?"

"He doesn't know yet, hasn't been able to trace the number." Quentin hesitated. "There's something else."

Christian was starting to get a bad feeling. That once again he'd been a fool not to follow Quentin's advice. "I hate to even ask. What?"

"My buddy also asked the state police if there was a tree down on that road that went by Grayson's Market the day we were there. Remember? That's why we went back to the store to get a drink, because it was going to be a few minutes before we could get through?"

"I remember."

"No record of it, and typically the police would have been the ones to get the 911 call about something blocking the road, right? They would have been the ones to dispatch the guys to get the downed tree out of there. And there would have been a trooper on-site directing traffic."

Christian's eyes narrowed. "What does all that mean?" he asked, knowing exactly what it meant.

Quentin glanced around, then grabbed Christian's shoulder and began tugging him toward the parking lot that was across the quiet street that separated the two hotel facilities. "It means that Beth Garrison is a setup," he said loudly as they jogged. "If that's even her real name. It means that whole thing at the store was arranged so that you'd meet her in a situation you'd remember, under stressful circumstances so you two would have a bond. It's classic stuff." Quentin snapped his fingers and held up, pulling Christian to a sharp stop. "Did Beth give you anything before you left the Ritz today?"

Christian hesitated. "Yeah, an envelope."

"Where is it? Back at the hotel?"

Christian shook his head and slid the briefcase strap down his shoulder. "It's in here."

"Let me see it."

She'd warned him about letting anyone else see what was inside the envelope. "Quentin, I can't—"

"Let me see it!" Quentin roared.

Christian unzipped the briefcase pockets and rooted around for a moment. "Here," he said, holding the envelope out.

Quentin grabbed it and ripped it open, pulling out a provocative photo of Beth. On the back of the photo was a short note, telling Christian how much she loved him. "Damn it." He handed the photograph back. "Sorry." He put his hands on his hips, frustrated. "Let me see your briefcase," he snapped.

Christian handed it to him. "Here." He'd never seen Quentin like this.

Quentin grabbed the briefcase and knelt down. Suddenly he pulled out what looked like lipstick. "Something you're not telling me?"

"What the . . . ?"

Quentin stood and held the small case up, inspecting it. "It's a damn homing device," he said, turning it off by depressing the top.

Christian grabbed it and stared at it for a few moments in disbelief. Beth had been faking everything, and he'd bought it all. Unbelievable.

"Come on!" Quentin yelled, pulling Christian along again. "Let's get the hell out of here."

The five men sprinted toward the parking lot, toward the rental car they'd driven down from the Ritz. Christian hopped into the back, a bodyguard on either side, while Quentin and the other bodyguard clambered into the front.

The last thing Christian remembered was a loud pop and the car suddenly filling with a foul-smelling gas. Then his eyes rolled back and everything went black.

19

VICTORIA GRAHAM sat in her office, watching the baby boa stalk a small gray mouse she'd picked up at a pet store on her way into Manhattan this morning. The life-and-death struggle fascinated her—it always had. The way it played out every second of every day somewhere in the world. Survival for one—the end for another. And, though it was terrible to admit, she liked having a hand in the outcome. From facilitating the mouse's death to preventing Christian's.

Steven Sanchez was a seedy character, but it was far better for Christian to be in his hands than to go to Cuba and be murdered. She knew the men backing Dorsey would kill Christian if he actually made it to Cuba—she'd seen it in Dorsey's eyes when she'd asked the question: What's going to happen to Christian? But she'd really known it way before then. When she'd found that file in Dorsey's desk in the Georgetown house. Back in the fall of last year when she'd been snooping around looking for something to convince her Dorsey was serious about divorcing his wife. Instead she'd stumbled onto a manila folder in a desk drawer with a lot of handwritten notes Dorsey had taken.

They hated Christian for what he'd done to their cronies and them—exposing the nanotech scam and interfering in their plot to derail Jesse Wood's election. Which had ultimately resulted in the deaths of a couple of their close pals—Samuel Hewitt and Stewart Massey. So they'd decided to use Christian, then kill him. A double score in their eyes. Perfect revenge.

Jesse Wood was president of the United States, but that didn't mean he controlled what went on at the CIA or the Pentagon, Graham knew. In fact, it was the other way around. The old-boy military machine controlled Wood. They'd been able to manipulate Wood into signing the assassination order for Cuba because he desperately needed their support—and the damage was done. They'd told Wood and his advisers they had to have the assassination order to carry out the Cuba offensive, and Wood's administration had bought it—apparently. Christian was a chess piece in all of that—and wouldn't survive the game.

So, through an acquaintance, Graham had arranged for Steven Sanchez to kidnap Christian, then demand a huge ransom—$25 million. Which would, of course, never be paid. Sanchez already had half his money—five hundred grand. He'd get the other half in a couple of weeks. She was expecting the bogus ransom note tonight. There'd be nothing in it related to Cuba, just some babble about the perpetrators being allied with an Iraqi terrorist group. It would have to be viewed by Wood and his administration as just terrible luck. An act of aggression within the United States' borders that they'd want to keep silent. No one would ever interpret it as in any way related to Cuba—which was all that mattered.

The negotiation with Sanchez would take weeks, and the president would be forced to delay the initiative because, without Christian, he'd have no way to assess the capabilities of the Cuban civilians who were supposed to take over the government after the Communists were ousted. Ultimately, the president would have to choose someone else as his emissary when the phantom negotiations broke down. At that point, when Wood chose another emissary, Christian would be safe. Sanchez would let Christian go a few days later, get the second half of his money, then disappear forever. And the establishment would get Wood.

Christian had saved her career—her life really—by turning down the Ohio insurance company deal. And by standing up for her in her darkest hour. The fact of the matter was that two of her MuPenn board members had uncovered what she was trying to do independent of Christian—*not* because Christian had told them. A senior executive at the target—at the Ohio insurance company—had figured out that Victoria was trying to execute an end run around the state regulators—then called the MuPenn board members and told them. Christian had met with the two board members at their request—without even telling Victoria—and convinced them she was acting on the up-and-up and that the senior executive at the target company had concocted the lies about Victoria because he was worried that if she got the company, he would be fired. Christian had put his reputation on the line for her, and she'd never forget it.

She'd been mad as hell at first when she thought Christian had screwed her. Then promised herself she'd never let him down when she realized the truth. She'd played along with Dorsey these past few months, because what else *could* she do? If he had known where her loyalties truly lay, it would have ruined everything between them. Wouldn't have done Christian any good, either. Might just have gotten him killed faster.

The easiest thing to do when she'd found out what the establishment boys had in mind for Christian would have been to tell him. The problem was, she still wanted Lloyd Dorsey—despite what he was helping do to Christian. She loved Lloyd and she wanted to be with him. He'd made it clear he was going to leave his wife soon—he'd shown her a draft of a letter he intended to send to Dallas asking for a separation—and she didn't want to screw up her chance at ultimate happiness. But she couldn't give Lloyd information on Christian, and she couldn't tell Christian what was going on because Lloyd might ultimately find out she was the snitch. Then she'd have no chance with him.

What she needed was someone to get close to Christian, and Melissa had been the perfect candidate. She was young and beautiful, in dire need of money, and one great actress. An Oscar winner. Who could be better for the job?

Graham had gone to great lengths to create another life for Melissa. A fake background for Beth Garrison that Quentin Stiles would have a difficult time piercing. It had taken some doing, but she had friends in that small Missouri town and at the University of Nebraska—through the insurance world—and she'd made it happen. Even made certain the woman who had played Beth's mother had known the background. According to Melissa, Christian had started asking the woman questions at the hospital once, but she'd sidestepped the whole thing beautifully by going into a coughing spell so he hadn't had the chance to dig into details.

Christian and Melissa's "chance" meeting in the forest east of Camp David had gone perfectly. The men had chased them to the edge of the

Potomac River, then the chopper had come roaring in just in the nick of time. They'd had a harrowing experience together, which was a perfect way to begin a passionate relationship. Christian had been the knight in shining armor, Melissa—Beth to Christian—the damsel in distress. He'd fallen for it so fast, and she'd played it so well. Graham shook her head. Melissa had suggested the whole dying-mother routine herself, even after being bedside when her own mother had died. Amazing. Well, it just went to prove that the Hollywood types were a little off.

It had all fallen into place so neatly, and now it was all actually happening. Graham had gotten word five minutes ago that Sanchez had Gillette in the trunk of his car and was heading back toward Miami from Naples.

AS CHRISTIAN STARTED to regain consciousness, he figured he was in an oven: It was pitch-black and 150 degrees in here. Loud, too, and it smelled like rubber. There was something soft beside him. It felt like another person. Maybe it was Quentin.

When his mind was clear, he realized he was actually in the trunk of a car. A car going fast, judging from how loud the noise of the wheels was. He moaned loudly when he tried to move. His head was killing him—from whatever gas had exploded in their faces right after they'd shut the doors of the rental car—and the arm he'd been lying on for however long he'd been inside here was asleep. He tried to scratch an itch on his nose, but his hands were tightly tied behind his back.

"Quentin," he hissed. "Quentin." No response. He started to call again, then he remembered. The transponder.

Slowly he moved both hands to the right side of his body and was able to slip two fingers into his front pocket. He could feel the intense pressure ratchet up on the ligaments in his left shoulder as he stretched, but he was able to shift slightly in the trunk to give himself more flexibility, to allow his fingers a little more play. Still he couldn't feel it. Maybe whoever was driving had found it and gotten rid of it. Maybe the person had known it was there because he or she was the one who'd been tracking him—with Beth's help.

"Damn her," he muttered, pushing one more time as deeply as he could into his pocket. There it was. His fingers curled around it, and he managed to pull it close to the top of his pocket. But he had to make sure it didn't fall out. He'd never find it if that happened.

Then he felt the car begin to slow down. He kept trying to pull the top of the transponder up, time after time, so he could engage it, but it was almost impossible to do with just two fingers. It was maddening. Then the car suddenly slowed down, and it rolled him forward. His head hit something sharp—probably the trunk hinge. He almost yelped, but managed to muffle his cry. He nearly had the damn top up, almost to the point where he could flip the tiny switch. Jesus, *come on.* The car screeched to a sharp stop, banging his head against metal again. He shook it off and kept trying. Just a little more. *Just a little more.*

Then he heard the car door open.

SANCHEZ HOPPED out of the car, supremely satisfied with himself. It had been so easy to outwit Gillette's security team, to break into the rental car. And the canisters of chloroform had worked perfectly. Five unconscious men seconds after he'd set off the tiny charges remotely. He'd hauled Gillette across the passed-out bodyguard and out of the backseat, thrown him into the trunk of his car beside Mari's body, and tied his hands behind his back. Then calmly driven out of Naples and back to Alligator Alley. Now it was time to get rid of Mari's body.

He'd pulled off into a deserted, trash-strewn rest area. There were no amenities here, it was just a place to stop if you were tired. But it was bordered on one side by something important to him: a canal.

Sanchez glanced around, making certain no cars were coming. He popped the trunk—glad to see that Gillette was still passed out—picked up the heavy cinder block with the rope attached, and lugged it to the fence by the side of the canal. Then he jogged back to the trunk, picked up the woman's body, laid her down next to the cinder block, and tied it around her waist. Giving a grunt, he hoisted the block over the waist-high fence and let it land with a thud. He did the same with the body, then reached down and gave the block a strong push. The block rolled and, after an odd moment of stillness, the body followed it over the bank and into the water. She disappeared beneath the surface. A couple of days with the gators and there'd be no trace of her, not even bones. Problem solved.

Now it was time to send the communication to Victoria Graham that would blow her mind.

■ ■ ■

MELISSA HART trotted through the impressive lobby of the Naples Ritz Carlton, past a huge arrangement of fresh flowers, and out the front door into the warm Florida sunshine. She just wanted to get out of here as fast as possible. She'd even left her bag up in the room. There was no need for it anymore. Besides, she didn't want to keep anything that reminded her of Beth Garrison.

An attractive young man dressed in blue shorts, a beige golf shirt, and tennis shoes smiled at her. "Can I help you?" he asked. "Do you have a car with us?"

She shook her head. "I need a cab."

"Where you going?"

"The airport in Fort Myers." The Fort Myers airport was the big, regional airport—about thirty miles north of here. The Naples airport was more for general aviation and corporate jets. She hadn't even decided where she was going yet, but she already couldn't wait to get there. "Quickly. *Please*."

"Sure."

She watched the young man jog out from under the porte cochere and down the driveway, waving toward a small parking lot at the bottom of the gently sloping hill. A minute later a cab pulled to a quick stop in front of her. "Thank you," she said, handing the young man two ones. She could tell he wasn't happy about how small the tip was, but too bad. He was lucky to be getting anything at all. She'd never see him again. "Fort Myers airport," she said to the driver.

"Got it."

At the bottom of the hill that led down from the hotel, the driver turned right.

Melissa had been checking in her purse to see how much cash she had, happy to have made it out of the Ritz. At this point, Christian, Quentin, and the bodyguards had probably been incapacitated—that was the plan. But she'd been worried that somehow it wasn't going to be that easy. Quentin had been suspicious of her—that was obvious— and he was careful. She didn't know much about him, but she knew that.

"Excuse me," she said, looking up. "Aren't you going the wrong way?"

"Wrong way?" the driver asked. "What do you mean?"

"When we came into the hotel this morning, we came from that direction," she explained, pointing back over her shoulder. "From Vanderbilt." He was slowing down behind a black sedan parked by the side of the road. "*Hey,* what are you—"

Suddenly she realized she was in trouble—that the cabbie wasn't taking her to the airport, never intended to—and she lunged for the door, even as the taxi was still moving. She tumbled onto the grass and scrambled to her feet—right into the arms of a tall African American man.

"*Lemme go!*" she screamed, beating him around the face. "*Lemme go!*"

Then someone grabbed her wrists and brought them firmly behind her back, locking them in place with handcuffs. Before she knew it, she was in the back of the black sedan and it was speeding away. Getting her out of the Ritz without raising any suspicions had been choreographed perfectly, she realized, and she'd fallen right into their trap—whoever *they* were.

SANCHEZ HAD RENTED the small house several months ago in anticipation of his huge score, in anticipation of everything that was finally coming together. The run-down three-bedroom ranch was in a poor section of Miami. A crack house was on one side, a single mother with eight children on the other, and a burned-out shell of a house across the street. A neighborhood of trashy yards, gangs, and kids dressed in rags playing in the street. Perfect for what he needed.

He had an errand to run—needed to send that e-mail to Victoria Graham—and Gillette was back there in a closet of one of the unfurnished bedrooms, tied up tightly. There was no way he could escape. Sanchez had tied up lots of people in his time, and no one had ever managed to get out of his knots. Besides, Gillette still hadn't recovered from the chloroform—which was beautiful. Sanchez hoped the bastard didn't wake up for another couple of days.

He swung into the parking lot of the Cyber Café. The place was only five miles from the nasty ranch house where Gillette was tied up in the closet, but this was a much better neighborhood. An upscale shopping area full of high-end stores. Amazing how closely huge wealth and poverty coexisted in Miami.

Sanchez locked the old Cadillac with a turn of his key in the door, moved casually into the café, ordered a latte and thirty minutes of Internet time, then headed for an open table in a corner in the back. It was late afternoon and the place wasn't crowded. He sat down, took a sip of the latte, then accessed his newest untraceable e-mail account and began tapping out the message. Just three lines, short and sweet. A demand for $50 million. But not the fake letter he had agreed to send. This one was real and the woman would quickly realize *how* real.

He chuckled as he hit the SEND button. He'd figured out that this was the chance for a big score only a few minutes after the mission had been proposed to him. Realized that he could make enough money on this one job to retire forever. It was beautiful. What was so beautiful about it was that Victoria Graham had never seen it coming.

Sanchez spent the rest of the twenty-seven minutes of Internet time he'd purchased looking at porn. He was surprised that the computer would actually let him do it, but, hey, this was Miami.

VICTORIA GRAHAM let her head sink into her hands after she read the e-mail from Sanchez for the third time. He'd called himself Emilio in the e-mail, but she knew exactly who he was with his talk of the "Nepal Package"—obviously a reference to Everest Capital and Christian. He wanted $50 million and he wanted it right away. This wasn't the fake demand they'd carefully scripted out, this was real. She'd completely misjudged the situation—and Sanchez. God, how could she have let herself be taken in like this?

She reached for the phone. She needed to talk to Lloyd. He was the only one she could think of to turn to at this point. She'd have to lay it all out for him, beg his forgiveness. The people Lloyd knew were the only ones who could save Christian now. And they *wanted* to save him, *needed* to save him—at least at this point. As with anything in life, you could count on people with incentive. They had an incredible incentive—and they were good.

She let her head sink all the way to the desk. She'd tried to have it all. Tried to save Christian, have her relationship with Lloyd, and screw President Wood's health-care initiative. She'd gotten greedy, taken it too far. Now she might not get any of it. She shut her eyes. She should have known better.

"WHAT HAPPENED?" Quentin's face was two inches from Beth's. She was trying to turn her head, but he had a firm grasp on her chin, and two of the men he'd sent down here a couple of days ago to scout the area were holding her still. She wasn't going anywhere. "Tell me," he hissed. They'd taken her into a grove of trees beside a deserted field. She was whimpering, clearly scared for her life. Well, she ought to be. *"Tell me!"* he roared.

BARRADO WAS RACING through the streets of Miami in the SUV with his two men, headed toward an address he knew was in a nasty neighborhood. The men back in Maryland had found out where Gillette might be. A transponder that had been planted on him in Naples was still sending out a signal. It was weak, but they'd pinpointed it to the house ahead thanks to an urgent call from Senator Dorsey. There was no way to tell if it was really leading them to Gillette, but it was worth a try. It was the only lead they had.

"ALLISON," Quentin barked into the phone. "It's me." Thank God he'd been able to reach her so quickly on her cell phone. "Christian's been kidnapped."

And thank God that Beth Garrison—or, he now knew, Melissa Hart—had broken so fast and told him all about Victoria Graham paying her to get close to Christian. Told him that Graham was behind it all, and that Melissa had planted the transponder on Christian before he'd gone to meet with Padilla.

"You've got to find Victoria Graham right now," he said loudly, interrupting Allison's cry from the other end of the line. Quickly he explained why. "She's the key for us at this point, Ally."

SANCHEZ KNELT DOWN beside Christian and pulled his head up by his hair—he was still tied up. Gagged now, but no longer blindfolded. "You're going to make me a lot of money, you rich prick." He laughed loudly and the harsh sound echoed in the empty house. "I should have told her I wanted more than fifty million. You could easily afford that, according to *Forbes,* anyway. But you see, I'm not a pig. I just want my fair share."

He let Christian's head fall heavily to the wooden floor, then stood up. As he turned to leave the room, he came face-to-face with the long, shiny shafts of three double-barreled shotguns. Suddenly he realized he hadn't flown far enough below the radar on this one. Not even close.

The single shell Barrado fired completely disintegrated Sanchez's heart, blowing his body violently backward against the closet wall.

QUENTIN'S CELL PHONE finally rang. He and his men had been standing outside the Ritz for what seemed like an eternity.

"Hello."

"I got everything out of Victoria Graham," Allison said quickly. "She set the whole thing up. That young girl Christian's been seeing, the kidnapping, everything. I should have known, damn it, *I should have known*."

"Calm down, Ally." She was talking a mile a minute, sounded as if she was on the verge of tears. "What do you mean *you should have known*?"

"Graham told me a few weeks ago that Christian was going on a trip, a very secret trip involving national security, and that he'd be away for a while. She'd found out somehow, not from Christian, and she told me she was very worried about him. I didn't know then how she found out. I asked her but she wouldn't tell me. *Now* I know. That's why I was made vice chairman, Quentin, because Christian was going to be away. Turns out he was going to be away because she was the one kidnapping him. She was trying to help him, trying to save his life, but it backfired on her. At least, that's what she claims. Apparently the guy she used to kidnap Christian turned the tables on her. She'd told me to keep an eye on Christian when she told me about the trip, but not to say anything to him. And I didn't because I trusted her. But I should have said something to Christian, or you. It's all my fault. If I had just let you know."

"It's not your fault," Quentin said firmly. "How did Graham find out about Christian's trip?"

"Senator Dorsey. She's involved with him or something. She found out last fall about this thing in Cuba." Allison hesitated. "Do you know about that?"

"Yeah," he admitted, "I do."

"Well, I bet you don't know this. They're going to kill Christian while he's down there."

Quentin's eyes narrowed. "*Kill* him?"

"Yeah. After he meets with some people who are working with the military to take down the Commun—"

"Why would they kill Christian? What's the deal?"

"I don't know. Graham wouldn't tell me. You should have seen her, though. She was a mess. Sobbing, not making any sense. I couldn't believe it. All she told me was that they were going to kill him while he was in Cuba, but she wouldn't tell me why. I think she's worried about herself at this point."

Probably ought to be, Quentin realized. "Why didn't Graham just tell Christian when she found out what was going on?"

"She couldn't let Dorsey know she was the one tipping off Christian. But after the guy turned the tables on her, she called Dorsey right away. She called Dorsey before I got to her."

That didn't make any sense. "But if she knows the people carrying out the Cuba thing are going to kill Christian, and Dorsey's involved with them, why in the hell would she call Dorsey?"

"She thought those people were the only ones who could rescue Christian from this guy who kidnapped him," Allison explained. "She said she didn't know what else to do."

"Where is Christian?"

"Miami. Apparently he set off some transponder or something and they tracked it."

Quentin shook his head. Christian was one cool customer. "How long ago did she call Dorsey?" he asked, afraid of the answer.

"It's been a couple of hours."

Quentin motioned for his men to relax. At this point Christian was back with the spooks—or dead. There was no point racing to Miami. They'd be way too late. "I guess he's on his way to Cuba then." If the spooks had him, that was where Christian was definitely headed. And Quentin wanted Allison to hear him be optimistic. "I'd try to get down there myself, call a few of my buddies in the Rangers and see if there's a way to parachute in or something. Problem is, I wouldn't have any idea where to go when I got there." Dr. Padilla would know, but he was observing the operation with his Cuban handlers. There would probably be no way of getting to Padilla without alerting the regime at this point, either. "Ally." Nothing but silence from the other end of the phone. *"Ally?"*

"What if I could tell you where to go?" she finally asked.

"How could you do that?"

"Stay where you are," she said excitedly. "I'll call you back as soon as I can."

. . .

CHRISTIAN HOPPED UP onto the spindly pier of the camp, followed by Barrado. He'd never been so happy to see anyone in his life. After they'd killed the guy who'd kidnapped him, they'd untied him and told him who they were. Told him they were taking him straight down into the Everglades. That from there he'd be choppered out to a navy ship waiting for him in the Gulf of Mexico. On the ship he'd board another chopper, then be dropped into Cuba early in the morning along with his protection squad of Rangers. Time was of the essence now, they'd told him as they'd hurried him out of the ranch house to the SUV. Told him that he needed to meet with the rest of the Six as quickly as possible to give President Wood the word—thumbs-up or -down. If it was up, everything would explode. By this time tomorrow, the old regime might no longer control Cuba.

Christian knew right away these guys were real. They had details about the mission that convinced him. And Barrado had asked for the transponder as soon as he was untied, smashing it with his boot on the floor beside the kidnapper's body when Christian handed it over. Christian had wanted to hug the man—but he hadn't.

He wanted to call Quentin, too, but they wouldn't let him. Barrado had said that he didn't want to chance someone picking up the transmission, but they'd been in downtown Miami—and it wasn't as if they were staying or that he would have been stupid enough to say anything that would have given away their location. You could trace a cell phone to a specific antenna—he knew that—but they were on the move. By the time anyone could have figured out what antenna he was in contact with, they'd be long gone from that cell. But he hadn't argued, too glad to be safe.

"Come with me, Christian," Barrado said, waving. "I want you to take a look at this snake we killed this morning. It'll blow your mind."

"**HI, ALLY,**" Quentin said quickly. It had been a couple of hours. "I was getting worried."

"It took me a while to get back in touch with Ms. Graham."

"What did you find out?"

"The government guys got Christian back. Graham called Dorsey. He confirmed that Christian's safe."

"Thank God."

"Yeah, safe for now. Dorsey wouldn't tell her anything else."

"Of course he wouldn't. Frankly I'm surprised he'd even tell her that." Quentin glanced out at the ocean. They'd been sitting on the beach. There'd been nothing else to do. "I didn't think Dorsey was going to tell Graham where Christian was meeting with people in Cuba," he said glumly. He'd assumed that was what Allison was going to try. "I thought that was a long shot, Ally."

"I didn't need to ask her that. I already know. I just wanted to make sure Christian was safe before you went to Cuba."

Quentin sat up in the chair. "What? How do you know where the meeting is?"

"When Graham told me to watch Christian, I took her seriously. I snuck into his office one night, and I found a file," she explained triumphantly.

Something clicked in Quentin's brain. The file Dex Kelly had given Christian at Camp David.

"He almost caught me that night," Allison explained. "I'd made a copy of it, and I was putting it back in his desk when he showed up. I had to hide in his closet until he left. I read it when I got home. I figured it had to do with what Graham had told me, about the trip he was supposedly taking. It made me believe she really knew what she was talking about. But I never showed it to her, and I never told her I'd found it."

Good girl, Quentin thought to himself. "It has the location, doesn't it? Where he's supposed to be meeting with the Six?"

"It does." She hesitated. "You really think you can get down there?"

CHRISTIAN KNELT in the high grass and cattails as the helicopter settled down through the darkness onto the lit, makeshift pad the men had constructed close to the camp. The aircraft couldn't actually set down—the ground was too soft and it would have sunk into the mire—so it hovered a few inches off the area they'd cleared of brush.

"Let's go!" Barrado yelled above the *thud-thud-thud* of the whirling rotor and the scream of the engine, grabbing Christian's arm.

Christian rose up and jogged forward through the hurricane and the mud, bent over at the waist, helped along by Barrado. As he made it alongside the chopper, arms reached out to pull him and Barrado inside. Moments later they were up in the air, speeding through the night toward a ship in the Gulf.

20

THE MARINE TRANSPORT HELICOPTER sped along at low altitude through the darkness, skimming just above the calm ocean. It was two in the morning, the weather was clear, and they were close. Christian could see a few faded lights well off to the east—the very outskirts of Havana. Around him in the troop area were eight men. Eight Army Rangers in full combat gear, right down to the green, black, and brown camouflage paint on their grim faces. Brandishing what looked like nasty weapons. He'd never felt so exhilarated in his life.

One of the men—the lieutenant in charge of the mission—tapped Christian on the shoulder, then handed him a helmet, pushing it roughly against his stomach.

"Put it on!"

Christian nodded. The guy was only a foot away, but he could barely hear him it was so loud. They'd given him fatigues and boots back on board ship—the suit and leather loafers he'd worn to meet Padilla in Naples weren't going to cut it in the jungle.

"Three minutes!" the lieutenant yelled as the helicopter climbed quickly above tree level, then raced over the breakers rolling up onto the beach. "We'll be near the ground for less than five seconds. You gotta jump as soon as I tell you."

Once again Christian nodded.

"We start taking any fire, you stick right with me!"

Christian touched the grip of the Beretta 9 mm they'd given him after he'd climbed into the chopper, as it was lifting off the deck of the ship. The gun was in the holster on his belt. "Don't worry, I will." The lieutenant hadn't needed to tell him that. If they started taking fire, as far as Christian was concerned, the lieutenant was going to have a Siamese twin.

He felt the chopper slowing, then it settled down into a clearing. Moments later it was only a few feet above the grass and the lieutenant was in his face shouting at him, *"Move, move, move."* Suddenly they were on the ground, tearing for the tree line, and just that quickly the deafening sound of the helicopter was gone, replaced by the peeping of frogs in the trees.

"Count off," the lieutenant hissed when they'd reached cover.

Christian heard each number in rapid succession. Then they were moving again, hustling through the jungle. He was glad he wasn't carrying all the equipment each of the Rangers was—fifty pounds for this mission. Even without that extra weight it was all he could do to keep up. They were good. Strange to feel this now because they were in hostile territory, but he felt remarkably safe. As if these men could take on an entire Cuban brigade and probably hold their own.

When they'd gone half a mile, the lieutenant signaled for the squad to halt. During the last few minutes, they'd climbed a ridge, and now they could see back to the clearing where they'd landed. Well, the two men with night-vision binoculars could. Christian watched as each man trained his field glasses on the spot.

"We want to see if any unfriendlies show up so we know whether or not they saw us coming in," the lieutenant explained. "We'll be here for an hour. Unless the unfriendlies show up," he added ominously.

QUENTIN CLIMBED INTO the cargo area of the helicopter, then turned to shake hands with his old friend Jack Haley, now a colonel in the Rangers. "You're the man, Jack!" he shouted over the roar of the rotor. Haley had informed him belowdecks that Christian had taken off from this same deck only two hours ago. "Thanks again."

"No problem, pal. Godspeed."

The chopper lifted off and Quentin gave Haley a quick wave. Then the ship quickly grew smaller and smaller as they gained altitude. It was just him, the pilot, and one other man in the helicopter. ETA to the clearing where Christian and the squad had landed was forty-two minutes. Quentin hadn't needed Allison's directions after all. The Rangers had been only too happy to get him to Christian, happy to help an alumnus. It was nice to have old friends, he thought to himself, turning away from the open door. Loyal friends.

"Sorry, sir!"

Quentin glanced up into the haunted eyes of the young man who had been ordered to accompany him to Christian. "What the—" Suddenly he felt an awful, searing pain as the bullet tore through his chest, followed quickly by the sense of being pushed out of the aircraft and falling through the darkness. Then he hit the water. He saw the lights of the chopper turn and head back toward the ship, then he sank beneath the surface.

AFTER WAITING AN HOUR on the ridge to make sure no one showed, they'd hiked through the woods another hour toward the rendezvous point—what Christian understood was a cattle ranch. Now they were just inside a tree line, watching the ranch's main house. It was four o'clock in the morning and it didn't look as if anyone was awake. The house was pitch-black—no lights at all. It didn't look as if anyone was even *here.*

The lieutenant jabbed in the air toward two of his men, then jabbed toward the barn that was fifty yards from the house, off to the left. The men he'd signaled to nodded and threw off their packs, then took off across the open ground in the moonlight, quickly disappearing around a corner of the barn. Less than four minutes later they were back, talking in hushed voices to the lieutenant. After a few moments he moved to where Christian was.

"Everything's ready. They're going to take you in," he whispered, gesturing toward the men who had just raced to the barn and back. "But there's one hiccup," he growled. "Seems like there always is, damn it."

"What's the problem?" Christian asked.

"There's only five of them in the room in the barn. Supposed to be six, right?"

Christian nodded.

"Well, the men waiting for you wouldn't tell my guys what happened," the lieutenant explained. "Wouldn't say what happened to the sixth guy. Said they wanted to tell you first. Sounds suspicious." He hesitated. "You still want to go in? I can get you out of here if you want. We got choppers up in the air off the coast round the clock at this point."

They'd come this far. There was no turning back. "Is the doctor in there?"

The lieutenant waved to the two men who had gone in. They were beside Christian and him almost instantly. "Ask them," the lieutenant ordered.

"Is the doctor in there?"

"Yes, sir. Dr. Padilla. He's waiting for you."

Christian glanced at the lieutenant. "Let's do it."

"All right." The lieutenant waved to the others. "Give 'em cover, boys," he hissed to the rest of the squad.

Moments later the three of them raced across the yard toward the barn, then around the corner and inside. The strong scent of manure hit Christian's nostrils as they moved down a straw-covered corridor between a long row of stalls filled with black-and-white cows.

"There, sir," one of the Rangers said, pointing with his weapon.

Christian knocked on the door. Two hard raps.

"Come in."

Christian recognized Padilla's voice and burst through the door. The five men were sitting around a makeshift table—the room was lit by a single candle, and a blanket was over the lone window near the ceiling. Christian didn't know why—it was instinct more than anything—but he strode right to Padilla, the only one standing, and hugged the man strongly. The return hug was even tighter, impressive for a man of such small physical stature.

"My friend," Padilla said softly, pulling back. "You've come to free my country."

Christian saw mist well up in the doctor's eyes. As if a tsunami of relief had just washed over him. As if he hadn't been confident that Christian would actually show up, even when the two Rangers had burst into the room a few minutes ago. As if the only thing that would make him believe that it was real was the sight of Christian in front of him. "I told you I would."

"A man's word is one thing," Padilla murmured. "His actions are quite another. Now I see that you are a man of action."

"It's going to be all right, Doctor," Christian said soothingly. "I promise." He glanced around. The other four men were staring at him expectantly. "We will support you," he said to them firmly. "This won't be like 1961." They nodded respectfully, understanding the terrible risk he was taking. "The banker's not here." He'd studied the files diligently. He recognized right away which one was missing. "Why?"

"He was a spy," Padilla explained. "But he never got a chance to tell his story."

Christian gestured at the two Rangers. "Secure the entrances. I'll be out in a while."

When they were gone, Christian began the questioning. All the things he needed to ask to test the men. An hour later he realized they were even more competent than he'd hoped. An hour wasn't much time to decide the fate of a country, but oftentimes the most crucial decisions had to be made on the fly. And this one felt good.

"Thank you for your time," he said politely. "Thank you for the risks you've taken."

"What's the verdict?" the attorney asked.

Christian liked that. A bottom-line guy. Blunt, no bullshit. "I'm going to tell President Wood that he should support you. He's told me he'll follow my recommendation."

"Even without the banker?"

Christian smiled. "That's going to be my job anyway."

Padilla moved to Christian's side. "Thank you, my friend," he said, shaking Christian's hand warmly. "Now there's one more person you must meet."

Christian understood. The general. Zapata. He shook each man's hand in turn, then followed Padilla out of the room and back down the corridor between the stalls.

Just before they reached the door to the outside, Padilla turned left into a small room. Christian smelled the cigar even before he saw the general. When they were inside the room, Padilla shut the door and Christian noticed a figure move out from behind a stack of hay bales. The only light in the room came from the tip of the cigar, but it was enough.

"Señor Gillette," the general said, shaking Christian's hand. "I am Jorge Delgado."

Christian had never felt a firmer grip. "Señor Delgado. It's an honor." As soon as they finished shaking hands, Christian reached up with both hands and pulled the chain from around his neck. He handed it to Delgado. "I believe you needed to see this."

Delgado chuckled as he held up the cow's identification tag dangling from the end of the chain. Held it up in the glow of the cigar tip. "You are a good man, Christian Gillette. A very good man." He closed his fingers tightly around the tag, then stared intently into Christian's eyes. "Now it all starts."

"IT'S GOT TO be quick, sir," the lieutenant said, holding the satellite phone out for Christian.

"I understand." Christian took the phone. "Mr. President?"

"Yes, Christian," the president confirmed, his voice deadly serious. "What's the verdict?"

"I support them," Christian said, recognizing Wood's voice at the other end of the line.

"You sure?"

"*Absolutely* sure."

MELISSA HART raced to the first ATM she could find in the Los Angeles airport. The money should be there. She'd held up her end of the bargain. Victoria Graham better have held up hers.

Melissa slipped the card into the slot and nervously punched in the code—one she hadn't used in a while—waiting breathlessly for it to take. When it did, she selected the CHECK BALANCE option, still holding her breath. As the number came up, her shoulders sagged. Fourteen dollars and twelve cents. She'd been screwed. All that risk and she'd been screwed. She felt the tears beginning to flow. No choice now but to go back to her father and beg for forgiveness.

As she trudged through the terminal she glanced at a television monitor. On the screen were stark images of chaos in the streets of a city she didn't recognize. She squinted to read the words rolling across the bottom of the screen. It was Havana. A coup was breaking out in Cuba.

FROM HIGH ATOP a ridge Christian watched the Incursion's initial stage play out. Plumes of smoke rose from different sections of the city, and the sounds of gunshots peppered the early morning.

"Good early reports," the lieutenant spoke up after signing off from his radio. "Delgado's basically already in charge of the city. There are pockets of resistance, but ninety percent of his troops supported him.

The troops on the east side of the island are putting up a pretty good fight, but Delgado's command thinks they'll have everything there secured by tonight."

"That is good," Christian murmured. He hadn't looked over at the lieutenant while the man was speaking, just kept his eyes focused on the city, on the history playing out before his eyes. It was awe-inspiring, making everything else he'd ever done in his life seem trivial. If he'd said no to President Wood, none of this would be happening. But he'd said yes. Slowly, Christian became aware that it was just the lieutenant and him now. The other men of the squad had moved off, down the hill a ways out of sight. "What now?" he asked. "When do we go down there? I want to get started right away."

"You won't be going down there, sir."

Christian glanced over at the lieutenant. "What the—" The Ranger was standing, a pistol in his hand.

"Sorry, sir. You won't even be going home."

THE PRESIDENT of Cuba's Central Bank hurried to his car. His wife and children were still asleep upstairs. The hell with them. They'd slow him down and whoever was behind the coup wasn't going to care about them. It was him they'd want. He cursed himself as he reached for the door handle. He should have figured something was up when Alanzo Gomez hadn't shown up for work.

As he settled in behind the wheel, three men rose up in front of the car and unloaded the clips of their small machine guns into his body, blowing out the windshield and the back window. He was dead instantly, his head almost severed from his body by the withering fire.

Down the street two other men recorded the entire sequence from inside a van.

CHRISTIAN SWALLOWED HARD, staring down the steel barrel of the pistol. He was ten feet from the lieutenant. No chance at all to rush him.

Then the extraordinary happened. Dr. Padilla appeared from behind a tree in back of the lieutenant and rushed him. Padilla had stayed with Christian all morning, but Christian had thought he was down the hill with the rest of the squad. Just as the lieutenant brought the pistol up to fire, Padilla hit the officer from behind, knocking him forward violently, but not the gun from his fingers.

Christian raced toward the two men sprawled on the ground and grabbed the lieutenant's wrist, trying to get the gun. They struggled wildly, but the lieutenant was able to fire twice before Christian hit him with a crushing blow to the chin, knocking him out cleanly. He rose up on his knees, straddling the man for a few seconds, breathing hard. Then he looked over at Padilla. The doctor lay on his back, a red stain on his white shirt. It was growing bigger by the second, spreading out across his chest.

"Oh, no." Christian grabbed the lieutenant's gun and crawled quickly to where Padilla lay dying. "I gotta get you out of here."

Padilla shook his head weakly. "No chance for me," he gasped, touching his chest. "Save yourself. Go to my house in Havana. The address is in my wallet, on my identification." He grimaced, pain overcoming him. "She'll help you get out, help you find the general. You can trust him."

Christian could hear the rest of the squad climbing the hill, alerted by the sound of the two shots. "I've got to try to save—"

"Go," Padilla urged, teeth gritted. *"Now."*

Reluctantly, Christian took Padilla's wallet, turned and sprinted off, obeying the dying man's final wish.

EPILOGUE

December

CHRISTIAN WATCHED from a side door. Watched Allison work her magic up in front of the packed ballroom. He couldn't have picked a better vice chairman.

It had been seven months since he'd somehow made his way to Nelson Padilla's house outside Havana and found refuge. It had taken him almost twenty hours to get down out of the mountains and through the smoking neighborhoods until he found the address the dying doctor had given him. Dodging burning houses, listening for gunfire so he could avoid it, dashing behind anything he could find to hide him many times. Several times he'd been certain he was going to be taken into custody by U.S. troops roaring past in jeeps. Which would probably have been as bad as—maybe worse than—being detained by FAR loyalists who were hiding out in the hills or pockets of neighborhoods.

It had taken him several minutes in the foyer of Padilla's house to convince his wife what was going on—fortunately she spoke English—but the doctor had given him enough details before he'd died to make the story stick. Then Christian had to tell her about her husband. It had been awful, and he'd held her for a long time after breaking the news.

Christian hadn't gotten to the bottom of what was really going on—

why the Rangers had turned on him and Padilla in the mountains overlooking Havana—until a Senate investigation into President Wood's alleged civilian assassination orders had been uncovered and reported by *The New York Times*. He'd been stonewalled up to that point—the same way he had been stonewalled trying to find out what had happened to Quentin.

Then, when the story broke, it had all made sense. The establishment boys—the same crew who had been involved with the nanotech conspiracy a few years ago—had ganged up on Wood and Christian. Hanging the assassination order on Wood and killing Christian in Cuba was a neat way for them to kill two birds with one stone. A slick way for them to get Wood out of the White House and Christian off the face of the earth. To get him back for the money he'd cost them and their perception that he had been responsible for the death of their pal Sam Hewitt. But, in the end, it hadn't worked. Wood was still firmly in control of the White House and Christian was still very much alive.

But Victoria Graham was out of her job at MuPenn and Melissa Hart—a.k.a. Beth Garrison—had destroyed her father's political chances when Jesse Wood found out what had happened. Fortunately, the end result was a positive for both of them. Graham had retired to her Florida home and Melissa was spending time with her father. He'd gotten past his anger at Melissa—they were actually talking every few weeks—and he was glad that nothing criminal had been levied at Graham. She'd always been a friend, and after all, she'd really just been trying to help him.

Christian hung his head for a moment. His best friend was gone. Quentin had been killed on his way to Cuba, had given his life to try to help Christian. And the bastards hadn't even seen fit to give the man a rightful burial.

They'd killed a good man in Nelson Padilla, too. A doctor, a husband, a father—and a hero. At least General Delgado had seen to it that Padilla would never be forgotten. A statue of him had already been erected in downtown Havana.

Christian looked up and smiled, watching Allison giving her speech to the Everest Capital investors from a raised podium at the front of the room. He'd invited all one hundred of the Everest limited partners, along with husbands and wives, to the Ritz Carlton in Naples, Florida, for the firm's annual meeting and a long weekend—footing the entire bill himself. He usually held the meeting in New York, but it had been a bitterly cold December in the city. Besides, somehow the Ritz in Naples seemed more appropriate this year.

The crowd was finishing dessert as Allison began to get into details of Everest's strong financial results for the year, making use of slides projected onto a large screen behind her to make points. Christian usually did this presentation, but he'd called her a couple of hours ago to tell her he'd been delayed coming down from New York and that she'd have to do it. He hadn't been delayed—he'd actually called her on his cell phone from his room upstairs—but he'd wanted her to do it. He grinned as he watched her. She was doing a great job, as he knew she would.

When she was almost finished, he moved out from the doorway. She didn't see him until he was almost to the podium. When she did finally spot him, he grinned widely, seeing the surprise on her face. Probably at what he was wearing: a casual linen shirt opened two buttons at the top, khakis, and Docksiders. Everyone else from Everest who was here was wearing business attire—suits or nice dresses.

"Hey there," he said softly so his words wouldn't be caught by the microphone. "Nice to see you."

She grinned back. "Hey, Mr. Casual. Nice to see you, too."

"Let me say a few words, all right?"

"Of course. It's your show."

She backed off a few steps as he took the podium to thunderous applause. These people were keenly aware of how much money Christian had made them over the years.

He held his hand up, politely asking for quiet. "Thank you very much and good evening, ladies and gentlemen," he began as the clapping finally faded. "Thanks for coming this weekend. I want you all to have a wonderful time." He grinned. "One thing, as all of this is on me, I wish you'd try to remember to use your cell phones at all times. Those room calls can add up." There was a loud round of laughter. "Seriously," he said, again holding his hand up for quiet, "I want to thank our vice chairman, Allison Wallace, for pinch-hitting. I caught the last few minutes of her act up here, and she did great. Just like I knew she would." He gestured toward her, and once again the ballroom was filled with the sound of long applause. "I think she's pretty special," he added as the clapping subsided. "I think you all should, too."

Christian hesitated, taking a long, lingering look around, nodding to familiar faces in the crowd. "Maybe some of you are wondering why I'm dressed so casually. Well, it isn't because I was late and didn't have a chance to change." He hesitated again, aware that the ballroom had gone completely silent. As if the people sitting at the tables in front of him were suddenly aware that he was about to say something extremely important. "I'm stepping down." A murmur raced through the crowd. "I've had enough," he said, raising his voice above the buzz. "There are things I want to do while I'm still relatively young that I can't do as chairman of Everest Capital. There just isn't time. And your firm will be in great hands with Allison Wallace." He glanced over at her. She was openmouthed, in shock. "That's it," he said with a smile, suddenly feeling completely liberated. He beckoned to her, then pointed to the podium. "It's all yours, Madam Chairman."

With that, he moved off the podium and back toward the side door he'd come through a few minutes ago. Not even giving people time to clap or try to shake his hand. He hated good-byes.

He headed quickly out the back of the hotel, through a deserted courtyard, and down a wooden walkway across the dunes to the beach. The sun was just setting over the Gulf, a perfect ball of orange flames a centimeter above the glassy water. "How beautiful is that?" he murmured, moving down the stairs to the sand, kicking off his shoes, and starting off toward the water.

"Hey!"

Christian turned sharply. Allison was standing at the top of the stairs. He took off his sunglasses slowly. "What do you want?" he demanded, then broke into a wide smile. "Don't you have a big investment firm to run now?"

"What was that all about?"

He moved back across the sand toward the stairs as she descended to the bottom step, until they were close. "Just what I said in front of everyone inside," he said softly. "I've had enough, Ally. I'm tired of it. I've done everything I wanted to do. I want to accomplish some other things while I still can."

"What about me?" she demanded, her voice strained.

"You'll be fine. I've been watching you over the past seven months. You're ready to take over."

"And that's it? That's all the explanation I get?"

"That's all the explanation you need. You're one of the most powerful people in the financial world now. I think that's pretty good."

"I'm not talking about Everest or the financial world," she called as he turned away and started toward the ocean again. "I'm talking about you and—"

"By the way," he interrupted, turning back to her. "Something oc-curs to me."

She hesitated, searching the sparkle in his eyes. "What?"

"We don't work together anymore."

Her eyes narrowed and her expression became serious, not under-standing. Then she got it and she smiled. "Hey, that's right, we don't."

It had been nice to see that smile. So sincere. A display of emotion he knew he could trust. Now that he was out of business, he was looking forward to spending time only with people he knew he could trust. It would be quite a change, but quite a welcome one, too. "Call me tonight after you've finished your Everest duties."

"Where will you be?"

Christian grinned and pointed down at the sand. "Right here, honey. Right here."

ABOUT THE AUTHOR

STEPHEN FREY is a managing director at a private equity firm. He previously worked in mergers and acquisitions at JPMorgan and as a vice president of corporate finance at an international bank in Manhattan. Frey is the bestselling author of *The Successor, The Protégé, The Chairman, Shadow Account, Silent Partner, The Day Trader, Trust Fund, The Insider, The Legacy, The Inner Sanctum, The Vulture Fund,* and *The Takeover.* He lives in Florida.

ABOUT THE TYPE

This book was set in Galliard, a typeface designed by Matthew Carter for the Merganthaler Linotype Company in 1978. Galliard is based on the sixteenth-century typefaces of Robert Granjon.

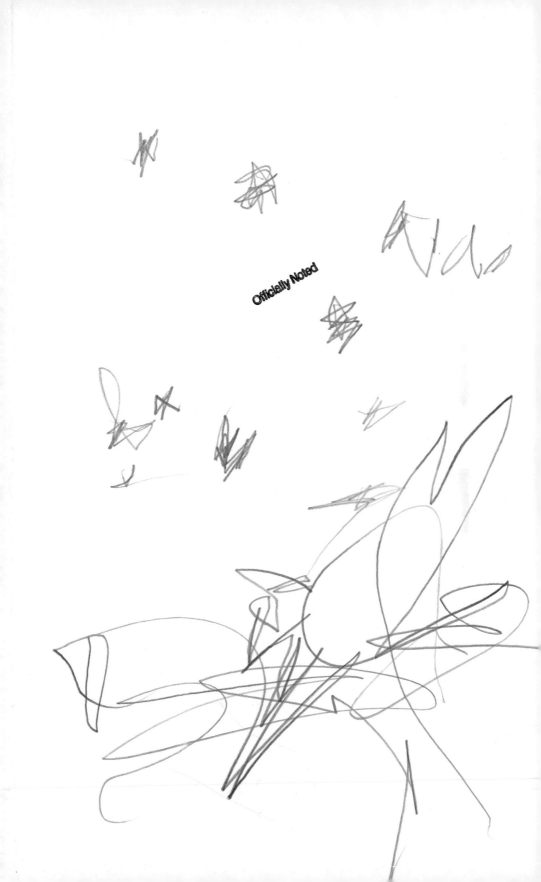